ALSO BY SAV R. MILLER

MONSTERS & MUSES

Promises and Pomegranates
(includes the novella "Sweet Sin")
Vipers and Virtuosos
Oaths and Omissions
Arrows and Apologies
Souls and Sorrows
Liars and Liaisons

PROMISES
&
POMEGRANATES

PROMISES & POMEGRANATES

SAV R. MILLER

sourcebooks
casablanca

Published by Sourcebooks Casablanca, an imprint of Sourcebooks
P.O. Box 4410, Naperville, Illinois 60567-4410
(630) 961-3900
sourcebooks.com

Originally self-published in 2021 by Sav R. Miller.

Cataloging-in-Publication Data is on file with the Library of Congress.

Printed and bound in the United States of America.
PAH 10 9 8 7 6 5 4 3 2 1

For my thirteen-year-old self. Your obsession with Greek mythology, bad guys, and romance novels will eventually bring you here. I'm proud of you.

And for those who prefer the violent, broody villains. May you find your Kallum Anderson.

Your fate is mortal: what you ask for isn't.

—OVID

We must bring our own light to the darkness.

—CHARLES BUKOWKSI

---⁎---

Dear Reader,

Although I have written six books (roughly) since the
original publication of this one, Promises & Pomegranates
continues to shine in the depths of my heart
and soul. It has been a gateway between
myself and thousands of readers, and I will never
be able to adequately express my joy and gratitude.
This book changed my life.
At its core, it is a Hades and Persephone-inspired
romance that is full of drama, lust, self-
acceptance, family, violence, blood, and love.
There is so much love (and lots of sex, hehe).
Kal and Elena's journey is certainly not an
easy one, nor is it for everyone. But it
is a story I enjoyed writing immensely.
This version is chock-full of fun stuff, and
I hope you enjoy it as well.

xoxo,
SaraR.M

---⁎---

CONTENT NOTE

Kal and Elena's story is a dark contemporary romance based *loosely* on the framework and characters of the myth of Hades and Persephone.

Please be aware that it is not fantasy, historical romance, or a literal retelling.

This book is a dark romance, meaning it contains things like graphic violence, explicit sexual scenes, and other mature situations that may not be suitable for all readers. For a more detailed list of content warnings, visit savrmiller.com

While *Promises and Pomegranates* is a standalone, reading the prequel may enhance your reading experience. You can find "Sweet Sin" at the end of this book.

Look for the footnotes scattered throughout to see what the author was thinking as she wrote *Promises and Pomegranates*.

PLAYLIST

"POMEGRANATE SEEDS" — JULIAN MOON

"LOVE RACE" — MACHINE GUN KELLY FEATURING KELLIN QUINN

"FOREVER YOURS" — GRAYSCALE

"SHE'S A GOD" — NECK DEEP

"GODDESS" — JAIRA BURNS

"GOSSIP" — SLEEPING WITH SIRENS

"MASSACRE" — KIM PETRAS

"DEVIL I KNOW" — ALLIE X

KAL

AS A CHILD, I GOT USED TO SILENCE.[1]

The kind found in sleepy hospital rooms, hidden between the dull, intermittent beeping of an electric monitor and the steady drip of an IV bag.

With each interruption, nurses entering to draw blood or family members coming to offer false moral support, my body craved the void.

I fell in love with the innate stillness of it—the calm it provides, the secrets you can wedge into its depths.

Learned to seek it out in times of chaos, a force to ground myself in.

Eventually, it became a necessity.

The most difficult addiction to curb.

An *obsession*.

A...condition.

My peers in college and later my colleagues dubbed it a psychological disorder. Said my brain had wired itself to short-circuit

---

1 I rewrote the start of this book many, many times, but this line was the one thing I never changed.

under certain stimuli—sometimes simply the existence of stimuli at all.[2]

I felt it made me weak.

Dysfunctional.

Thus, I craved an outlet. Somewhere I could go and not lose myself in the noise. Where the violence coded into my DNA could be satisfied and the parts of me aching for death and destruction would be sated.

Working for Rafael Ricci, the don of Boston's—at one time—premier crime family, was never supposed to be a permanent thing. He'd plucked me from the streets and promised me a life of luxury, if only I could get my hands a little dirty.

But like all other things, it snowballed out of control.

I learned I quite enjoy the taste of brutality on my tongue.

Love the way it blossoms like a flower springing from the earth, igniting a compulsion like no other.

A desperation only relieved by the feel of another's heart pulsing beneath my fingerprints—the flutter delicate and innately *human*, petrified and struck stupid in my wake.

A desire quelled only by bloodied hands and bodies mangled by them—*my* hands, the very pair sworn to an oath of healing.

I let the darkest wants live inside me, manifesting through my obligation to an organization I joined before I knew what I was doing, allowing myself a pass because of the decency of my day job.

It was supposed to be enough.

Moral licensing I didn't think twice about, until the lines bled too fully for me to distinguish between them.

Until Elena.

The most forbidden of fruits.

---

2 Kal's peers were the type to diagnose after one psych class, but in this case, they called his misophonia.

Persephone to my Hades, as some used to call me. Springtime in a world rife with death and destruction.

A woman I scorned until I found myself blinded by a new obsession.

Until I tasted her—the dewy essence of her supple skin, the tang of her arousal glistening on her own fingertips, the salt of her tears as I shattered the last vestiges of her innocence.

Whether she knows it or not, she gave herself to me that night.

Surrendered her soul under the guise of *choice*.

And though I left the way Death usually does—silently, before dawn—it was never my intention not to return and collect.[3]

---

3 For context, see "Sweet Sin" and the end of this book.

CHAPTER 1

KAL

SLURP.

Slurp.

Slurp.

Gritting my teeth until my jaw aches, I glare at my boss while he sips from a mug of steaming tea, watching the video playing on his computer.

The sound of his lips sucking in liquid grates on my nerves, a dull knife sawing at the frayed edges. By the time he pushes the piece of paper in my direction, sets his mug down, and removes his glasses, I've imagined all the ways I could kill him.

An overdose of insulin would be the easiest, cleanest route—especially since he keeps his meter and pens in the top right drawer of his desk, unprotected.

Though I suppose most men in our world wouldn't take the time to research hit methodology; they want quick fixes and dumped bodies, and they don't care if their crimes can be traced, because they bankroll the local police anyway.

All they care about is maintaining their power.

Their *edge*.

And an overdose isn't satisfying.

Not in the same way as cutting into someone's chest cavity, breaking and peeling back their rib cage, and severing their beating heart while the life bleeds from their eyes.[4]

There's something magical in the act of holding another's life in your hands. A kind of symmetry found in nature, where you're given the opportunity to bring beasts to grisly fates or heal them instead.

They're completely at your mercy.

Power the likes of Rafael Ricci can't even begin to imagine—which is why he has me.

Finally, scrubbing a hand over his clean-shaven jaw, Rafe removes the glasses from his nose and sits back in his leather chair, looking up at me. His dark eyes are blank as they study me, not giving even a hint as to what's happening behind them.

Crossing one leg over my knee, I grip the joint with a gloved hand, waiting. After almost twenty years working together, I'm sure he realizes I'm not a fever you can sweat out.

If he wants to sit in silence until one of us cracks, I'll play.

It's only his daughter's life on the line.

Snapping his fingers, Rafe gestures for the two beefy guards in the room to leave, the fat gold ring on his thumb glinting in the overhead lighting. He reaches into his desk drawer, pulling out a decanter with the Ricci crest and two crystal tumblers.

Without speaking, he pours the alcohol into the glasses, shoving one in my direction before bringing the other to his mouth and taking a generous swig. Some dribbles down onto the collar of his white dress shirt, but he doesn't seem to notice.

I palm mine, holding it above my knee, but don't drink.

---

4 My search history while writing this book definitely put me on a list.

Sighing, he cocks an eyebrow. "It's rude to refuse hospitality from your boss."

"Not when my boss knows I didn't come here for happy hour."

Downing the rest, he slams the tumbler back on the wooden desk, wiping his mouth with the back of one cuffed sleeve.

"What *did* you come here for, Anderson? So far, you haven't actually said."

"The video speaks for itself, no?"

"I see you fucking my oldest daughter in *my* house, even though she's been engaged to someone since her conception."

My blood boils at the thought of another man's hands on her soft, supple flesh, his lips on hers, his DNA where mine first ventured. Curling my hand around the glass, I squeeze until my fingers go numb, tempering my reaction.

Knowing I can't afford to lose control.

"Well, we all know fidelity isn't exactly a Ricci strong suit."[5]

His jaw ticks, but he doesn't take the bait. Perhaps because he isn't sure whose affair I'm referring to—his or his wife's. Or perhaps because it doesn't really matter, since rebutting my claim won't make it any less true.

"Elena is not like the rest of us," he says, glancing at the framed picture of her on the corner of his desk. In it, she wears her high school cap and gown and lies in a field of flowers, with the Fontbonne Academy in the foreground.

The picture of scholastic success, although she likely knew even then that her dreams of higher education and a career would be short-lived.

Hard to pursue personal interests when your livelihood depends on whether you adhere to certain duties.

---

5 Not even Kal is safe from the sassy man apocalypse.

Though that didn't stop her from pursuing me.

Shrugging, I lean forward and set my tumbler on the wood surface, reaching into my trench coat pocket for the letter tucked inside. Pulling it out, I smooth it down over my pant leg and hold it up for him to see.

"Doesn't matter if she's worse. This is a letter I received at the home I rent across town," I say. "Not mailed or taped to the free clinic I used to work at. It was slipped directly through the mail slot in the front door of the home, meaning—"

"Whoever delivered it wanted to send a message." Rafe rubs at his chin with the heel of his hand, scanning the page. "You don't have to fucking explain to me how blackmail works, Kal."

Slapping the letter down, I slide it in his direction. "Great. So then I also don't need to explain that if they're not afraid of approaching *me*, they certainly won't hesitate to accost Elena."

"I like to think my name holds a lot more weight in Boston than yours," he says.

"It doesn't."

His face reddens, irritation spiking with every new word that falls from my lips.

"At one time, sure. But then you got sloppy, and now your main source of power comes from *alliances*."

"Watch it, Anderson." Wagging his finger in my direction, he sits forward, the metaphoric hackles on the back of his neck rising with his anger. "You're treading a very thin line between the truth and disrespect here, son."

Internally recoiling at the nickname, I shrug again, unbothered by his intimidation tactics.

You can't conquer what doesn't fear you, and with us, it's always been the other way around.

"The *point* is," I continue, ignoring him. "The author of the letter lays out very clearly what they want and how they'll proceed if they don't get it. You ready for your entire operation to be outed?"

"Please. The feds won't come sniffing around unless the local police give them a reason to, and we won't have any problems with them. They tend to cooperate."

"I'm not talking about cops. But since the other *families* you do business with have supposedly been on a strict no-drug rule since the eighties, I doubt they'll love hearing about what you're doing in Maine with the Montaltos."

Rafe's tan skin flushes slightly as he swallows, and he glances at the computer screen again. "I can't give them Elena."

Rapping my knuckles against his desk, I nod. "Your funeral."

Pushing to my feet, I smooth my hands down the front of my suit and button my black trench coat. I snatch the flash drive from where it's stuck in the side of the monitor, slip it in my pocket, and turn on my heels to leave.

Disappointed, but not surprised. There are few things the former king of Boston's underworld cares about other than his image. Apparently, his daughter's safety also comes up short, which makes my stomach twist as I reach the door.

I'd been hoping to make this easy, and my entire plan, my *freedom*, banked on his desire to protect his family. Now I need to reevaluate my next step.

I've just pushed open the door and stepped over the threshold when Rafe clears his throat behind me, making me pause. I don't look back, waiting to see if it was an intentional sound, my palm flush with the intricate oak in front of me.

"What…" He trails off, and I turn my head to the side, my eyes focusing on the wall where a massive replica of Michelangelo's *David* sits, combining Rafe's religion with the one thing he despises most: art.

That's what planted the rebellious gene in his daughter.

Drove her to me.

"Don't waste my time, Ricci," I warn, growing impatient with the silence following his half sentence. I'm way out of line, but I know he won't do anything about it.

How do you control Death when it knows your every weakness?

Blowing out a breath, he tries again. "You could protect her."

Blinking, my gut churning like a tropical storm, I take a step back and pull the door shut, turning slowly to face him again. I glance at the picture on his desk, feeling myself get lost in her cappuccino gaze for a moment before nodding.

"I could."

He taps his finger against his chin, then drops both hands to his desk, twisting his thumb ring as he contemplates. "What will we do about Mateo? He won't give her up without a fight."

Satisfaction settles in my bone marrow, making me lightheaded. Giddy almost.[6] My plan is coming along nicely.

"I'll take care of him."

Rafe's eyes narrow, studying me once again, and he sucks on his teeth. The suckling sound is a shock to my system, a trigger I'm not expecting, and anxiety floods my blood before I have a chance to control it.

The response is immediate, growing in urgency as he continues using his tongue to clean his veneers. My shoulders tighten, my muscles growing taut as the violent *need* to end the sound washes over me, blurring my vision.

And for a moment, I see him slumped in his chair with a bullet wound ripping away the flesh and bone in his forehead. I see myself covered in his blood as I carve the cartilage and skin from his ears, harvesting them like a farmer bringing in vegetables.

---

6 Kal being giddy makes me giddy. Even if it is because he's imagining murder.

His voice pulls me from the episode, and I resurface, blinking away the intrusive thought as my body tries to readjust to reality.

"I know you don't do things for me for free," Rafe says. "What do you want?"

Inhaling deeply, soaking in the aroma of stale cigars and expensive liquor, I smother the grin threatening at my lips. My heart rate kicks up, relief taking the place of violence.

My mind travels to the poem I once left for Elena, a promise and threat rolled into one.

I just hadn't known it at the time.

Dis, almost in a moment, saw her, prized her, took her: so swift as this, is love.

The Rape of Proserpine.[7]

Not love, but something far more sinister and deadly in this case.

I think about the picture burning a hole through my wallet— brown eyes just like mine, the long black French braids. An ache flares in my chest at the thought of her, reaffirming my decision as I'm reminded of the *who* behind it.

If I want a single shot at a relationship with my long-lost sister, this is the only way.

Meeting Rafe's gaze, I raise my eyebrows. "Elena's soul."

---

7   This is the Romanized version of the myth from *Metamorphoses* by Ovid. I drew from mostly Greek sources like Homer and Hesiod for the construction of this story, but the Ovid version is more popular and thus what these two would be more familiar with.

CHAPTER 2

ELENA

MOST OF THE GIRLS I KNEW GROWING UP FANTASIZED ABOUT their dream weddings.

My younger sister Ariana dreamed of soft pastels and virginal white, despite being anything but. Years of ballet meant she knew the exact song and dance she'd bring our papà out for, and she'd look incredible doing it.

Even Stella—the youngest and smartest Ricci daughter—had the menu scribbled down on a piece of paper, using it as a bookmark for her textbooks.

I planned my funeral.

Up until today, my vision of a marble casket and bouquets of dahlias and lilies felt like little more than a pipe dream. A delusion I'd concocted to help alleviate the dull reality facing me.

Now, though, as I stare at my reflection in the mirror while my mother tries to yank my dress shut, I realize maybe the two events are synonymous.

My marriage to Boston's favorite volatile playboy, Mateo de Luca, marking the end of life as I know it.

"*Dio mio!* Suck it *in*, Elena," Mamma snaps, anchoring her elbow to my hip as she pulls. "You just got fitted for this gown two weeks ago. How is it possible you've gained this much weight already?"

Heat floods my cheeks at her question, shame slicing through my skin like the dull edge of a blade. "It's only a couple of pounds," I say, trying to obey anyway by inhaling as deep as I can.

"Probably just stress or water," my aunt Anotella says from where she's perched on the edge of the bed, gnawing at a chocolate-covered strawberry from the lunch platter we had delivered. "Or all that time she spends with her nose buried in a book."

"Or she's giving up. Kids these days don't go through honeymoon phases anymore." Nonna, my paternal grandmother, reenters the room just in time, a bright blue gift box in hand.

"Explain, Frankie."

Nonna shrugs. "Back in my day, a woman waited at least a few *years* before letting herself go. Now, they treat keeping in shape like an option and then wonder why half the country ends up divorced."

Humming, Mamma gives a final tug, stealing the breath from my lungs. Stepping back, she brushes a strand of dark hair from her face, huffing with finality. "There. Good thing we went with the lace ties and not a zipper."

Face flushing, I glance down at myself in the sleeved gown—the smooth, *flat* expanse of my stomach, the excessive cleavage that I know is hidden beneath the conservative dress because Ariana insisted I wear it.

"This is the first time Mateo's seeing you naked," she said, beaming at me from the lingerie section of the bridal shop. "Make him eat his heart out."

In truth, the only person I'm interested in inspiring something like jealousy within most likely won't even show up for the ceremony.

Not that he'd see what's underneath the dress anyway. *Not again.*

Crossing my arms over my breasts, I spin away from my reflection, embarrassment making my stomach cramp. Perspiration slicks down my spine and along my hairline, and I busy myself with checking the seating chart, making sure every guest is accounted for.

Nonna walks over, licking the pad of her thumb and rubbing it across my cheekbone. "Anotella, get your makeup bag. We're going to need to keep it nearby if she keeps sweating it off."

My aunt hurries from the room, bringing the main hall of the de Luca estate into view for the briefest moment. Catering staff bustles by as the door swings back into place, the scent of lobster and marinara sauce heavy in the air, making my stomach growl.

I haven't eaten since dinner yesterday, and now that my weight seems to be a topic of concern, I'm sure that if I try sneaking a bite in before the ceremony, Mamma will likely have my head.

God forbid there be a hair out of place on my wedding day unless it's by her own hand.

Image has always been the most important thing to my family though, especially in recent years with the shrinkage of organized crime. It still exists, but it's with limited involvement—behind screens, hidden in the shadows. Papà and his men, along with the other *families* around the country, have to be more skillful about the way they conduct business.

"*Control the narrative,*" Papà always says. "*That way, you control the story.*"

If people don't think you're a violent criminal organization, then they have no reason to report you.

It's why I'm being married off to the heir of Boston's premier media firms, despite the fact that the only feelings I hold for my future husband are those of disdain.

Not that my feelings matter of course.

Not in this world.[8]

All that matters to *la famiglia* is that I keep my head down and abide by my duties. Help them maintain their power in the most archaic fashion.

Sighing, Mamma places her hands on her hips, scanning me from head to toe with narrowed eyes. Out of the three Ricci daughters, I'm the only one who favors the beautiful former debutante Carmen—we share the same long dark hair and golden eyes, while my sisters fare lighter, like Papà.

I know the similarities in us affect how she views me. That she finds little insignificant things to critique because it's too late to fix them in herself.

I wish that knowledge made it easier to stand up to her perusal, but…it doesn't.

"All right, ladies. Let's get a move on. We need to be at the church in half an hour," Nonna says, moving to the side of the room where the lunch tray sits. She plucks an olive from the silver platter and plops it into her mouth, staining her fingertips with bright pink lipstick.

"*Ugh*," a voice moans from the hall. Ariana's slender form appears in the doorway suddenly, the burnt orange evening gown she has on hugging her ballerina's body.

Jealousy tears through my chest at the sight of her, long and lithe and beautiful, while I stand here in my wedding dress feeling like an ugly duckling. I swallow it down, trying to dispel my mother's comments from where they repeat in my brain.

---

8 A recurring theme in this series is the freedom of choice and autonomy, especially with the female leads. I wanted to create a world where they are able to obtain the freedom women are so often denied, and Elena, I think, was the perfect character for the introduction of this motif. She bridges a lot of common problems from being the oldest daughter in a highly traditional, and dysfunctional, family, warring between duty and self-sacrifice.

"Not again," Mamma mutters, tucking a stray piece of hair behind my ear.

Nonna rolls her eyes. "Ariana, can you do *anything* other than complain?"[9]

"No." My sister blinks, her doe eyes widening as she looks at me. "Jesus, E. You look gorgeous."

I smile gratefully at her, guilt gnawing at my insides. From what exactly, I'm not sure. "I feel like a porcelain doll."

"You'll get over it," Mamma says, waving dismissively.

Scoffing, my sister crosses her arms over her chest. "Why do we have to go so *early*? The guests won't even arrive for another two hours."

"Because, *nipotina*, we're on setup duty. Like I trust anyone in this town to get my first granddaughter's wedding *just* right." Nonna winks, walking over to my sister and slipping her hand around her waist, tugging her from the room.

"You're about finished, *carina*. We have your something borrowed, something blue…" Pursing her lips, my mother looks around the room, eyes landing on the gift box Nonna was carrying earlier.

She walks over, slips the top off, and pulls out a tiara with a veil attachment. I turn around as she comes back, watching her steps in the mirror. Her fingers brush my temple as she slides the band into my hair, securing it with pins she pulls from her pocket.

Arranging the veil so it falls over my shoulders, past the length of my hair, she lets out a satisfied squeal and wraps her arms around my shoulders.

"Perfection," she says, squeezing me. "Mateo isn't going to know what hit him when he sees you at the altar."

---

9 Ariana is a character I relate to deeply.

Apprehension fills my gut like cement, solidifying until I ache from the weight of indecision.

"Was it like this for you?" I ask softly, knowing our looks aren't where our similarities end.

"What do you mean?"

I chew on the inside of my cheek, hesitating. "Did it feel like you were being led to your death?"

Her gaze falls to her fingers splayed across my collarbone, covered in various rings. She tilts her head, deep in thought, eyes unfocused as she seems to check out momentarily.

"You'll find ways to make peace with it," she says finally, kissing my forehead. When she releases me, she offers a smile, but it feels forced and wobbly, so fragile, it could break in an instant, its shattered pieces scattering along the floor in ruins.

Clearing her throat, she clasps her hands together and takes a step back. "There you go, *figlia mia*. You're ready to be someone's bride."

I glance at the reflection, seeing a hostage trapped in an elegant white gown, but nod anyway. "Should we leave now?"

Mamma nods. "I think we—"

"Miss Ricci!"

A member of the waitstaff bursts into the bedroom, her cherub cheeks flushed and almost as bright as her hair. She bends, gripping her knees as she tries to catch her breath, holding a hand up to keep us in place.

"Mr. de Luca requests your presence."

I clench my teeth, annoyance prickling against my skin. "He can't see me before the wedding. It's bad luck."

Plus, I don't want to spend any more time with him than absolutely necessary.

"Please, miss. He's not feeling well and says you're the only one he'll speak to."

Sighing, I look at Mamma, who shrugs. "We make our own luck anyway, right?" Kissing me on both cheeks, she slings her purse over her shoulder, heading for the door. "Take care of it, and meet us at the church as soon as possible!"

I stare at the staff member's name tag—*Marcelline*, it says, printed in big block letters—silently for a few beats, wondering if this is another of Mateo's ruses to goad me into a fight or something worse. Still, I don't want him causing a scene and delaying the inevitable, so I follow this woman down the hall to Mateo's bedroom.

Once inside, I pause, noting that it looks as much like a guest room as the one I've just left; with no hint of memorabilia or personal effects cluttering the walls or dresser, it's almost as if this room belongs to a ghost.

Or, I realize as I find Mateo sitting on the edge of the bed, someone on their way to becoming one.

"What the fuck?" I hiss, hurrying to his side.

He clutches his stomach, hunching over to hurl violently into a plastic wastebasket.

"Jesus, Mateo, what happened?"

Sucking in a breath that sounds like it gets caught in his throat, he glances up at me through glassy eyes, panic lacing his brown irises. A deep crimson flush crawls up his exposed skin, and his hand lashes out awkwardly, grasping at nothing as another wave of vomit barrels out of him.

"I heard food poisoning," comes a voice from somewhere behind me. "Doesn't present like it though."[10]

One I recognize better than my own.

It caresses my skin, its heat ghosting across the back of my neck, telling me the owner is close.

---

10 This line gives me chills every time.

"What do *you* think, little one?"

A sheen of sweat beads along Mateo's brown hairline, and the basket falls from his grip to the floor, toppling onto its side as he collapses in a convulsive fit.

My stomach churns, bile teasing the back of my throat as the voice materializes at my side, the physical manifestation of the phantom I've tried to rid myself of over the last few weeks.

I don't speak, fear gripping my entire being in its claws, squeezing until I'm completely helpless to watch my fiancé writhe on his bed, seizing and drooling with no interference.

Even though the man at my side is a *doctor*.

His presence tells me that right here, right now, he's my father's fixer.

That this was a hit.

As Mateo's body goes slack, his life force bleeding from his body within minutes, I watch Kal Anderson from my peripheral, trying to reconcile this being with the man I once cared for.

The man who took my virginity eight weeks ago and left me before the sun was up, scarred in more ways than one.

Tousled inky-black hair sweeps back over his head, like he's spent his time combing through it. His jaw is sharp enough to cut glass, covered in a thin layer of stubble and framing Adonis-style bone structure, while his dark eyes are more reminiscent of the evil he's rumored to be.

He towers over me, taller than anyone else I've ever known, the black material of his expensive suit perfectly fitted to every muscle and curve of his lean, sturdy body.

His gloved hand lifts, pointing a cell phone in my direction, and I realize what he's doing.

Why I was called up here.

"Let's chat."

CHAPTER 3

KAL

MY DICK STIFFENS BEHIND MY SLACKS AS ELENA LICKS HER PLUMP lips, her soft eyes glued to the corpse in front of us. I try to focus and fix my sight on anything else, but I can't stop remembering how it felt to have them wrapped around me, sucking like her life depended on it.

"You're back," she whispers.

She blinks, over and over, as if she can't quite believe what she's seeing.

"Is he…?"

"Dead?" I ask, hitting the record button on my phone to stop the video. Shoving it into my coat pocket, I nod, finally breaking away from her mouth to note Mateo's sightless gaze. "Quite, I assure you."

Silent for several beats, I can see the gentle rise and fall of her chest, breasts straining against the white lace material of her dress. She's more covered up than I've ever seen her, the dress little more than a sheath that clings to her like a second skin, but somehow she's never looked more sinful.

Perhaps it's the context: her, in a wedding gown, standing over her fiancé's dead body. Yet her only real reaction was to *me*, as if his death bears no consequence to her.

Bending down, she presses two fingers to Mateo's jugular, and my shoulders tense, the thought of her DNA anywhere near him making me nervous. Not because I care if she's implicated—it won't matter in a few hours anyway—but because I simply don't want her touching him.

The tiara ensnared in her hair shifts as she moves, and mascara is smudged beneath her eyelids, making her look sullen and defeated, though I know her to be anything but.

I didn't see or speak to her except in passing over the years, but I kept watch over her after she turned eighteen, fulfilling a favor owed to her father before allowing my depravity to take hold, giving in when she asked me to ruin her.

Therefore, I know everything there is to know about the woman before me: her favorite poems—Shelley's "The Masque of Anarchy" and Browning's "My Last Duchess"—as well as what she prefers for breakfast—whole wheat toast with peanut butter and fresh fruit—and that she loves learning.

If she'd had her way, she'd be studying literature and not just how to teach it.

I know about the little pomegranate tattooed beneath her breast and have traced the line work myself with the tip of my tongue. She even tastes like the fruit, explosive and utterly bewitching, the kind of succulence you want to sink your teeth into.

And fuck, did I.

Her blood is just as sweet.

I know she's drawn to darkness, having watched her bask in the low hum of the stars as moonlight spilled across her pale skin more times than I care to admit.

As I study her now in her state of disarray, I know she's not upset about the death of her fiancé.

It's a mirage, as much as their marriage would have been. A sham for the press, making her father look good while destroying the tattered remains of the soul I broke weeks ago.

Elena sniffles, and for a moment, I think she's about to burst into tears. I lean on the balls of my feet, ready to sweep her away from the scene before she becomes hysterical, but then she glides her hands down the front of Mateo's chest, slipping one beneath the flap of his tuxedo jacket.

And I realize, as she peels that piece back, revealing the blood-soaked dress shirt beneath, that she wasn't sniffling—she was *smelling* him.

A shock of arousal jolts down my spine, hitting me like a bolt of lightning, singeing my bones. Perhaps she's not all prey after all.

Perhaps my little Persephone is actually fit for her fate.

She stares at the wound, the curved handle of my knife still protruding from the area, and gives the smallest shake of her head. "Insurance."

"What?"

Replacing the jacket over the area, she gives a little shrug. "Insurance, right? The stab wound? In case whatever else you did to him didn't work."

My mouth parts to refute her claim, the need to distance myself from the crime second nature at this point, but I don't. There's no reason if she already knows this was my doing.

Part of me—the sick, disturbed part I stuff down into the recesses of my brain—*wants* her to know anyway.

Wants her to see what I'm capable of and what happens to those who defy me.

Mateo's decision to go through with this wedding, even when I told him to find a way out of it weeks ago, was the ultimate act. And since I couldn't let him ruin my entire plan and keep her from me, I needed to remove him from the equation.

I'm not typically so crass and careless with my hits; I like to spend my time learning a person's nuances, what makes them tick, what keeps them up at night. But his existence became a threat, so he needed to be eliminated.

My only regret is not allowing her to be part of the initial poisoning.

Letting out a long breath, Elena tilts her chin up, turning to face me. Unlike most people I meet, Elena's never had a problem with eye contact. She matches my gaze head-on, like she knows it's exactly what I want and can't help but give it to me.

I can only hope she's as pliant in a few moments.

She stares up at me like she sees beneath the cold, rotten exterior to the molten interior. I shift forward, my body an object caught in her magnetic field, losing myself in her warmth.

Golden irises glisten like melted luxury, and my hand lifts of its own accord, reaching for the ends of her chocolate-colored hair.

"Why?" she asks, the single syllable devoid of even a fraction of emotion.

It gives me pause, my fingers brushing against her as they fall back to my side. "Why not?"

"That's a very selfish way to look at it."

My eyebrows arch in surprise. "Whatever gave you the impression I was anything but?"

She scoffs, folding her arms over her chest, tucking her hands beneath her armpits. "Wishful thinking, I guess."

Behind us, the door to Mateo's bedroom opens slowly, my employee's strawberry-blond head poking in. Marcelline glances around with her wide blue eyes, then slips inside with a duffel bag thrown over her shoulder, closing the door shut as she walks over.

Elena's gaze latches on to my housekeeper's form as she hands me the bag, blazing with unrestrained rage, even though Marcelline won't look past my clavicle. She watches Marcelline's pale fingers brush mine, anger radiating off her supple body in waves, deliciously intoxicating.

Jealousy isn't a quality I typically look for in a woman, but the existence of it within the spring goddess before me is like fresh soil, ready for me to dig in and plant my roots.

It's the foundation for corruption, that green emotion, and I plan to use it to build us from its rubble.

"Marcelline," I say slowly as my housekeeper backs away.

She pauses, furrowing her brows, likely wondering if I'm about to give her another task beyond her pay grade. I make a mental note to offer her a bonus and vacation, knowing I've already involved her too much.

But loyalty, I've learned, is a small price to pay for some people.

It's how I got into this mess in the first place.

Unzipping the bag, I reach inside and begin pulling out cleanup equipment, setting up at Mateo's bedside. I pull the knife from his chest first, extracting it slowly so as not to spatter the blood still hemorrhaging from him. It empties in a last pump, spilling from the wound onto the marble floor, and I curse myself for not putting a plastic tarp down beforehand.

With a handkerchief, I clean the blade, then gesture toward Elena flippantly. "Have you met my future wife?" I ask Marcelline, reveling in the sharp silence that follows.[11]

It's the kind I go out of my way to create, that cuts through the air like a whip.

Bending down, I wipe up the blood with a hospital-grade cleaning solution and disposable towels, then toss them into the wastebasket. With one finger, I flip Mateo's eyelids closed, then pull his comforter up to his chin, tucking it in at his sides.

---

11 Have I mentioned the sass?

If you didn't know any better, and with the smell of the cleaning solution overpowering the stench in the room, you'd never realize he's dead.

"I'm sorry." Elena's the first to recover from my assertion. "Your *what?*"

As if on cue, the bedroom door opens once again, Rafael entering with a bald priest in tow. He holds a Bible close to his chest and beams at Elena when he sees her, sweeping his gaze over her dress.

I glance at Marcelline. "Any chance we have something else she can wear?"

Frowning, she shakes her head. "No, sir."

Sighing, I drag a hand through my hair and push to my feet, discarding my leather gloves. I don't necessarily want Elena wearing a dress meant for someone else, but I suppose there isn't much choice.[12]

Shirking off my coat, I toss it onto the bed beside Mateo's body, smoothing over the lapels of my suit jacket. The father speaks in Italian, the smile on his ruddy face indicating he has no idea what's going on.

Probably thinks this is the ceremony he was hired to officiate in the first place.

Elena eyes her father, then the religious one beside him, before her wary eyes land on me. They narrow into little slits, her nostrils flaring, as if she's trying to force my combustion.

"What's going on?" she asks, hands curling into fists at her sides.

No one answers immediately, presumably waiting for my explanation. Seeming to sense that I'm about to move, Elena flinches the second my feet start in her direction, launching herself toward the door. I lunge for her at the same time, anticipating her attempt to escape, catching her around the waist with both arms.

---

12 I mean, he could've married her properly, but that wouldn't have been as exciting.

Slamming her back into me, the gentle swell of her ass pressing obscenely against my cock, I wrangle us around so we're directly in front of the priest, whose eyes are now wide and confused.

He hisses something to Rafael, who shakes his head and offers soft, soothing tones back. I dip my lips to Elena's ear as she struggles against my hold, apparently unaware that it's her fighting spirit that drew me to her in the first place.

The more she tries to get away, rubbing her ass against me, the harder I get.

"*Careful*, little one."

Shifting forward, I slip one of my hands down over the expanse of her belly, pushing down with my fingertips. She sucks in a little breath, undoubtedly feeling the evidence of my reaction, and freezes immediately.

Our audience does nothing to suppress the arousal traveling south; if anything, it seems to heighten it, knowing she's completely at my mercy. One wrong move, and I'll humiliate her in front of her father, more than I already have.

Gesturing to the priest with my free hand, I keep her anchored to me with the other.

"What the fuck are you doing?" she hisses, jerking her shoulder against my chin. "I am *not* marrying you."

"I'm afraid you don't have a choice."

"Papà," she breathes, glancing at him pleadingly. "You see what he did to Mateo, right? Why are you not stopping this?"

"Even if he wanted to, I assure you, there's nothing he could do." Shooting the priest a dirty look, I snap my fingers, telling him to get on with it.

"My father is the most powerful man in the city," Elena says, speaking over the priest as he begins his speech.

I snort. "No, he isn't."

Rafe stiffens, but I ignore it. That can't be news to him anyway.

"We're gathered here today to celebrate one of life's greatest moments, the joining of two hearts in the presence of God. Here, in this...*chamber*, we witness the union of one Dr. Kallum Anderson and Miss Elena Ricci together in marriage."

A pause. The priest hesitates.

"Oh my *God*," Elena gasps, beginning to struggle again. "What the *fuck*? Stop it! Let *go* of me!"

Clamping one hand down over her mouth, I nod at the priest. "Continue, please."

He licks his dry lips, then raises his Bible again, pressing on. "If anyone present has just cause as to why this couple should not be united, speak now or forever hold your peace."

Elena's shrieks reverberate off my skull, the vibrations from her throat rippling through my forearm. I tighten my grip on her mouth, moving so my index finger slightly blocks her nostrils; she screams and screams, the sounds muffled and broken, until she realizes she's not regaining oxygen.

Breaking off on a strangled cry, she halts, face reddening. I cock an eyebrow, craning my head to look into her eyes. They're feral, flames dancing in the golden rings, and part of me wants to feel bad for forcing her into this.

From her world into mine, knowing she really doesn't deserve it.

But she's in danger, and my plan can't happen any other way, so in truth, neither of us have a choice here really.

"Kallum, do you vow to trust and honor Elena? To laugh and cry, love her faithfully through sickness and in health, and whatever may come, 'til death do you part?" the priest asks woodenly.

"I do," I say, something pinching in my chest as I say it, the lie bitter on the back of my tongue. He repeats the same vow for her, and she shakes her head, tears welling in her eyes, mouth still covered. "When I remove my hand, I want you to say it. Say you do."

Her eyes harden, the tears soaking up.

"I'm *helping* you. Say you do," I murmur, just low enough for her to hear, "or I start picking off the people you love, one by one. Mateo was just the start, little one. Next is your father if you don't do what I say."

She whimpers, the sound making my dick stiffen even more, and huffs a single breath. Slowly, I slide my hand to her chin, ready to pounce if she screams again.

But she seems to think better of it, instead focusing on my eyes, refusing to look away.

"Why?" she whispers, and I think about her asking the same about Mateo, how she didn't seem to judge, just wanted to know my reasoning. As if every action, even the most despicable ones, can be explained away if you try hard enough.

I hook my thumb under her chin, tilting her head up, admission on the tip of my tongue. My secrets beg to be split wide-open, to bleed out on the floor for her, but I know I can't risk it.

Not yet anyway. Not before she's mine.

So instead, I shake my head, offering her a little grin. "Why not?"

CHAPTER 4

ELENA

I HAD A TEACHER WHEN I WAS YOUNGER WHO SWORE THAT OUR mindsets had infinite power over our lives. She lived and breathed the notion that time was little more than a social construct and that people have the ability to create their own realities.

She'd say humans are made up of energy, and that energy has a certain magnetism to it that attracts both what we fear and what we desire, and it was up to us to reflect the kind of life we wanted to the universe so it would be able to deliver.[13]

Incidentally, not a great look for a Catholic school teacher.

Still, standing at the threshold of forever, staring into the soulless eyes of the man who's haunted my dreams for the last eight weeks, I can't help wondering if what Sister Margaret said was true.

In the weeks after Kal left me alone in my bedroom on my twentieth birthday, I must have dreamed a dozen times that he'd come back to steal me away from Mateo, though it never continued beyond that.

Is it possible my nightmares morphed into real life?

I glance at Papà, who seems to look everywhere but at me as the

---

13 This section was one thousand percent inspired by my best friend. Shout-out to Emily.

priest goes on his spiel about love, quoting Corinthians as if it isn't obvious this union is a farce. For Christ's sake, Kal still has one arm wrapped around my waist, one hand collaring my throat, yet we're all acting like this is normal.

Like he didn't just threaten my family if I didn't acquiesce.

Betrayal burns the back of my throat, liquid fire scorching a path down my sternum, and I strain against his hold once more. Ignoring the hard length pressing between my ass cheeks and the way it makes my thighs clench, I try to wiggle a hand free.

He tightens his grip, crushing my hip bone, and I wince. Moving my hand back, I brace the meat of my thumb along his leg, digging my nails into his thigh until my fingertips go numb.

The only evidence that he even registers my attack comes when he forces me to bend slightly, shoving his pelvis tighter into my backside. He's so hard, I can make out the entirety of his erection, hot and heady as it moves into the crack of my ass, the layers of clothing between us no match for it.

His hand momentarily leaves my throat, eliciting a strange, empty sensation in his wake. He wrenches my fingers from his leg and pushes my hand to my side before gripping just below my jaw, tilting my head slightly upward.

"Do that again," he breathes into my ear, a slight strain lacing his voice. "And I'll fuck you in front of everyone."

I scoff, my voice just as soft, just as strangled. "You wouldn't."

There has to be a line somewhere. One that not even Kal Anderson will cross, and something tells me fucking your boss's daughter—a Mafia don, no less—while he watches might be the ultimate form of disrespect.

"I *would*, and you'd love every filthy second of it."

Okay then.

He pushes my chin up more, capturing me with his eyes; they're so dark, endlessly devoid of color, it's like staring into two black holes and trying to maintain solid footing. "I'm not your enemy, little one."

"You're not my friend either."

A muscle thumps beneath his left eye, and his gaze drops to my lips. "No," he agrees, sliding his hand so his thumb brushes over my mouth, plucking my bottom lip like a guitar string. "I'm your husband."[14]

Before I have a chance to protest—not that there's anything that I can say anyway, since I *did* finish my vows—his hand glides around my head, tangling in my hair, and he crashes his mouth to mine.

I'm so startled by the assault that I don't react at first. Kal isn't a kisser. Even the night he took my virginity, debased me in what I thought was every way possible, his lips never once touched mine.

Sure, they slid across every inch of my skin, caressed my most sensitive flesh, and spoke affirmations to my soul, but he hadn't *kissed* me.

Now that he is, I don't quite know what to make of it.

The kiss is gentle, almost sweet, as he eases me into the language of it, guiding my movements before I can fully relax and take part. His fist tugs on my roots, angling me for better access as he coaxes and teases, and my hands reach up to his chest.

I push, reflexively trying to extract myself, and then he's shifting, smothering, *consuming* me with his heat, deepening the kiss.[15] My breath catches in my throat as his tongue pushes past my lips, entwining with my own.

It laves the back of my teeth, the roof of my mouth, its tip leaving me tingling.

The arm around my waist crushes me to him, fitting our hips together, and the last remnants of my resolve crumble as I melt into it.

Into *him.*

---

14 A "your husband" moment never misses. This is science.

15 My absolute favorite scenes to write are first kisses. I love the culmination of tension and lust and how they finally collide. *swoon*

Our teeth clatter and scrape, the dull sound of a primal coupling creating a low heat in my belly. Tiny kaleidoscopes of bright, neon colors burst behind my eyelids as we wrestle for dominance, our mouths fighting a war my mind doesn't quite understand.

It's almost painful, *this* kiss. Painful in the way being with Kal has so far proven to be—a sharp, sudden ache that feels like being torn open and ripped apart, but your body *craves* the sensation.

Like you need it to survive.

A low, guttural moan emanates from his throat, making a home in my bones. The warmth in my belly spreads like a wildfire, burning everything in its wake, until I'm practically climbing his lean form, trying to get him to make the sound again.

Someone claps at our side, snapping me from the moment; my eyes pop open, seeking our audience. The priest smiles, chanting something in Italian that I can't translate, while Papà looks on and Marcelline studies her white sneakers.

Self-consciousness flares in my chest as I come down, trying to disentangle myself from Kal's limbs. He resists, pressing one last searing kiss against my mouth before finally releasing me so suddenly, my knees buckle.

I reach out, grasping his sleeve to steady myself, sucking in a deep breath. My lips feel swollen and raw, and I smooth a finger over them, trying to commit the evidence to memory, since it's the last kiss I plan on ever having with him.[16]

"*Rings,*" the priest says, gesturing toward our hands. "You're skipping steps, Mr. Anderson."

"Kind of like you skipped courting, proposing, or generally asking for my consent in any of this," I mutter, watching as Kal reaches into his suit pocket, pulling out a burlap pouch.

---

16 Yeah, okay. Sure, Elena.

"Would you have said yes?"

I blink, frowning. "What?"

"If I'd *asked*." He pulls one ring out, a simple black band, and shoves it onto his own finger, then reaches for mine. "Would you have said yes?"

"I..."

In truth, I want to say yes. That my infatuation with this known killer would've led me to do anything he asked of me. But Mamma drilled into my head at a young age that such an admission was practically a death wish, so instead, I shake my head.

"No."

Yanking the ring from Mateo off, he tosses it to the ground, replacing it with a solitaire diamond.

His jaw ticks. "No?"

Pulling back, I fold my hands over my arms. "*No*, Kallum, I wouldn't have. I was engaged—"

"Didn't stop you from begging me to fuck you."

"That was different. It was a—"

"We ask these blessings for them in the name of the Father, the Son, and the Holy Spirit," the priest interrupts, moving forward and gripping our shoulders. "By the power vested in me, I now pronounce you husband and wife." He hesitates, sunken eyes darting between us. "Er...well, I suppose you can kiss her again, but if you're going to, I request enough time to leave the room beforehand."

Kal holds up his hand, shaking his head. "No need, Father. We're leaving."

Marcelline ushers the priest from the room, slamming the door shut as she exits. Kal cringes as it clicks loudly into place, then swallows, walking back over to the bed. He bends, collecting his things, no longer paying me any attention.

"Um?" I arch my eyebrows. "Do I get a say in *anything*? I still don't even know what's going on." Turning to Papà, I hook a thumb at Kal. "Why didn't you stop this? Hasn't he just ruined your contract with Bollente Media?"

"No, you did that when you decided to sleep with the man." Papà's face hardens, disappointment melting his features. "And because you weren't discreet about it, someone has video evidence that they're using to try and blackmail *la famiglia*."

My throat constricts, the blood rushing to my face as I process his words. "Someone was watching us?"

Disgust pulls at Papà's mouth, his lips curling in a sneer. "Someone is *always* watching, *figlia mia*. And now, we're all paying for your fuckup."

Glancing over his shoulder at Mateo's corpse, he shakes his head.

"Can't we...tell the Elders or something? Surely, there's another way."

"The entity blackmailing us has a very specific set of rules that are to be followed, or they take us down. And since we have no leads and no idea who they are, they quite literally have us by the balls." Papà cocks his head. "Besides, if we tell the Elders, they'll have you killed anyway."

Kal's words from before ring in my mind. *"I'm helping you."*

I swallow as tears prick behind my eyes, trying to will them away, even as my world spins completely on its axis.

"I thought picking you for this contract was the smart decision. Spent my whole life trying to keep you out of trouble, sure that if I could just get you married, everything else would work out on its own." Papà sighs, giving me a once-over. "I thought I could count on you, Elena."

Sadness curls around my spine like ivy, wrapping so tight it feels like it might snap in half. My hands lift of their own accord, reaching for him, to provide comfort or apologies—maybe both.

Anything to erase the despair from his gaze before it burrows so deep within my soul, I can't ever clean it out.

"Papà, I'm—"

"Here." Kal shoves a piece of paper in my hands, cutting me off. I glance down, my stomach knotting even more.

THE COMMONWEALTH OF MASSACHUSETTS CERTIFICATE OF MARRIAGE

Somehow, it didn't feel *real* until now.

My hands shake, the certificate slipping from them as anxiety floods my chest, clogging my arteries. "I can't sign that."

Heaving a low sigh, Kal catches the paper and drags me over to the bed, positioning the page on top of Mateo's chest. He pushes a pen between my fingers, then curls his own around them, guiding my signature.

Resentment burns furiously inside me as I watch him effortlessly forge my name as if he's done it a thousand times.

I avoid looking at Mateo's lifeless form, my stomach on the verge of rejecting yesterday's dinner as it is. When Kal lets go, I swing away from him, smothering a sob with my palm.

If I'd known sleeping with Kal was going to result in this, in the complete stripping away of any semblance of freedom I've ever had, I never would've done it.

Right?

When you spend your life resigned to a certain fate, making yourself comfortable with the inevitable, even an ounce of change can feel like the end of the world.

And while it's true I didn't want to marry Mateo any more than I want to be married to Kal, at least I knew what to expect with him. We'd been friends, after all, once upon a time. Back before he sought out power and violence and decided to wield it against me when he didn't get what he wanted.

But I could have handled that.

Spent the last several years navigating around it, using it to my advantage, meeting his fists with my own bruised knuckles. It was *manageable*.

This thing with Kal, though, hasn't been charted out. I've never seen him with another woman, though presumably, there have been many in his thirty-two years.

I can't even reconcile why he was okay with any of this, considering the last time I saw him, he fucked me raw and left before the sun was up.

Only a poem, scribbled on a scrap piece of paper, and a black rose remained, making me wonder for a long time if I'd dreamed the entire encounter in the first place.

> *Touch has a memory.*
> *O say, love, say,*
> *What can I do to kill it and be free?*

If anything, his parting words, though borrowed from Keats, indicated he wanted nothing more to do with me. Yet here he is, having just forced my hand, acting as though there was no other choice in the matter.

As Papà leaves to go find my mother, I watch as Kal continues packing up, a sinking feeling weighing in my gut as I remember what else he said to me all those weeks ago.

"I'm not like the boys from your little private schools. I'll ruin you and not think twice about it."

"So ruin me," I'd said, so confident in my ability to withstand it.

Now, I can't stop wondering what the hell I've gotten myself into.

CHAPTER 5

KAL

"WELL, THIS IS AN INTERESTING TURN OF EVENTS."

Crossing my leg over the opposite knee, I adjust the second hand on my watch so it ticks in time with the grandfather clock across the foyer. I'm fully aware of the younger Ricci daughters leering from the top of the staircase, observing me as though I'm some sort of zoo animal, but it's hard to pay attention to anything other than the offbeat ticking.

Typically, I go out of my way to avoid social interaction, especially with the likes of teenagers, but this wasn't something I could very well avoid.

I don't put it past Elena to run. She feels trapped, like a broken bird caught in her gilded cage, eyeing the lock on her door without fail in case there's ever a chance to bolt.

Since I can't very well risk that, I had to return to the Riccis' Louisburg Square home with her, ensuring her wings stay clipped.

At least for now.

The whole ride over, she kept toying with the new ring on her finger, stealing glances at me from the corner of her eye as though she didn't think I could feel the weight of her gaze.

That's part of my problem when it comes to the little goddess; I'm hyperfocused on every move she makes, my body so used to studying her from behind a screen that the openness of our interactions now feels somewhat alarming.

Of course, that doesn't explain why her perusal immediately makes my dick hard, but that's another issue entirely.

One I'm not willing to entertain right now, especially after the severity of the kiss we shared.

I have to bide my time if I want all of this to pan out correctly.

"You know, girls," I say, meeting their stares, sliding my watch from my wrist, "a picture lasts much longer."

The youngest, Stella, ducks her head when I look up, playing with the end of a pigtail. Her brown eyes widen behind the square frames of her glasses, and she nudges her older sister with her elbow, grunting as if trying to get her to move.

Ariana, next in age and beauty to Elena, snorts, folding her forearms on the banister and leaning over. She doesn't break eye contact or bow her spine, a malicious grin spreading across her face, igniting in her dark irises.

"Too bad vampires don't photograph."

"Clever." I brush some dirt off my pants. "Sure you want to antagonize your new brother-in-law, especially if he is a vampire?"

She shrugs, moving past Stella to glide down the stairs. Her movements are lithe and gazelle-like, ballet bleeding into even her mundane activities.

Pausing on the bottom step, she squints at me, wrapping an arm around the railing. "What happened to Mateo?"

"I don't know what you mean."

"I *mean*," she says, glaring, "why are we not in a church right now, watching him marry Elena? Why have you been here half an hour, and he hasn't even shown up to fight for her?"

The fine hairs on the back of my neck stiffen, my nerves reacting even though there's no reason to. "I'm sure he knows better."

She snorts again, crossing her arms over her chest, the rust-hued dress she's in flushing the color from her face. Hair pulled into a sleek bun, lips lined with a bright red gloss, I can't help noticing the differences in the sisters.

It's very clear to me that Ariana's elegance isn't something she has to work at; it comes naturally, like breathing or sleeping, and I can't help wondering who she inherited the poise from.

Certainly not her mother.

At least not the Carmen I used to know.

Elena's finesse, on the other hand, seems to require a conscious effort. Her interest in the arts and finer things is something she's had to force until it became part of her personality, like some sort of Pavlovian response to the life she's shackled to.

There's a thinly veiled darkness resting beneath her carefully coiffed exterior, one that often results in bruised knuckles and bloody lips.

She suppresses it, buries it deep to make her family happy and fulfill her duties, but it's there, just begging to be unleashed.

Part of me is curious to know what that would take.

"Is my sister in some kind of trouble?" Ariana asks, still apparently intent on getting to the bottom of this union. And here I'd had the younger one pegged as the inquisitor.

Stella moves to the end of the banister, hesitating on the top step. "*Ari*," she whisper-shouts, gesturing for her sister to rejoin her. "Leave him alone."

Her dark eyes shift down to me, brushing my gaze for a millisecond before quickly sweeping away. She blushes furiously, and I smother a chuckle, not sure why I find her discomfort so amusing.

Maybe it reminds me of someone.

Sighing, I shift on the bench, adjusting the flap of my suit jacket. The tick of my watch falls behind the grandfather clock again like a heart arrhythmia, and I clench my jaw against the sound, trying not to focus on it.

"I just think something weird is going on," Ariana says. "Can you see Elena marrying…*him*?"

"I don't know," Stella grumbles. "I couldn't really see her wanting to marry Mateo either."

"Yeah, but that at least made sense. They'd been together forever."

"*Were* they though? I mean, he was definitely into her, but it always seemed like she was just going through the motions." Stella pauses, seeming to reflect on something. "I think this makes more sense than Mateo."

Ariana makes a weird noise in the back of her throat. "But he *loved* her—"

"*Enough*, ladies."

My voice is low, the strain from their bickering and the barely audible ticking stretching my nerves until they're almost ready to snap. Curling my fingers over the edge of the wooden bench, I can feel the old material splinter beneath my grip, anger a red-hot tidal wave crashing along my insides.[17]

"I appreciate your concern, because I know it comes from a good place," I say, focusing on breathing evenly. "But do not *ever* speak of my wife and her former fiancé, unless it's to say what a good pair we make in comparison. I don't want his name associated with hers ever again."

Ariana's mouth falls open, her tongue darting across her lips, and I can see she wants to spite me. There's a fire in her eyes, defiance threaded through her slender form, and I can tell it won't take much to ignite it.

---

17 As someone who lives with misophonia, writing Kal's triggers was somehow both a
   struggle and very cathartic for me.

Maybe she's more like her sister than I realized.

My phone buzzes in my pocket, drawing my attention; I take it out and scan the screen, exhaling slowly when I read the name that pops up. Pushing to my feet, I nod at the sisters, aware that my threat is open-ended if I leave without another word.

That's not a hit my reputation can take right now.

So instead of trying to convince them of the point more, I take the Rolex, drop it to the floor, and let my irritation spike from the ticking; like any other trigger, the sound builds until it's like a waterfall rushing between my ears, drowning out every other noise around me.

Episodes like this are suffocating, all-consuming in the rage they provoke. It vibrates along my spine, knotting in my chest until it peaks, exploding like a volcanic eruption. Usually, I avoid the violent outbursts my thoughts conjure, but now, I draw the gun from my waist and aim it right at the watch face.

A bullet pops free from the chamber, embedding bits of glass, shrapnel, and leather into the floor where it ripples from the impact.

Somehow, like a phantom limb, the ticking remains.

Chest heaving, electricity zinging through my veins, I stare at the hole and replay the gunshot over and over in my head, my shoulders tense and heavy.

I don't—*can't*—move until the ticking stops.

Finally, the silence floating in the air around us permeates my hazed brain, and I feel like I can breathe again. I see the girls wince from the corner of my eye and clear my throat, returning the pistol to its spot on my hip.

When I breeze from the room, hitting accept on the incoming call, temporary relief floods through me as my body struggles to go back to normal.

My associate's utter bewilderment at the prospect of me getting married starts to give me a complex the longer he drones on about how he "bloody can't believe it."

Standing in the hall outside Elena's childhood bedroom, I pace back and forth with my phone pressed to my ear, regretting having given Jonas Wolfe my cell number.

"These are some pretty extreme measures you're going to here, Anderson," he says, his British accent thickening the more he talks. "Are you sure she's worth it?"

"Only one way to find out."

He hums, and I hear the distinct zip of a body bag being sealed shut, disappointment settling in my gut. Normally, I'd take care of the cleanup myself, but since I had to chaperone my new wife, there was no time.

Still, I'd hoped to be the last person Mateo's physical form saw on this planet before he's tossed to the bottom of the Charles.

"Have you made contact with your target then? Let her know what's going on?"

Voices rise behind Elena's closed door, and I pause, my gaze flickering toward it. *Who is in there right now?*

I haven't seen anyone come or go, and I've been keeping watch for the last ten minutes. After leaving the foyer downstairs, I'd set up shop here, ready to bust in the second it seemed like maybe she was trying to flee.

Until now, it's been silent, and I don't like the way the sudden intrusion tightens the tendons in my neck.

Slinking toward the door, I answer Jonas with a brief "no," aware that if I don't, he'll start badgering me again.

When we met a decade ago on Aplana Island, the place my mother used to drag me when she had the money to spare, the only thing I'd known about him was that he wasn't allowed near Primrose Manor, where the island's owning family lives.

I had no clue what I was getting into when I bailed him from jail and hired him to come work for me, but it's one of the only lasting relationships I have, so I put up with him despite his incessant chatter.

"So you're really not thinking any of this through," he says.

"Everything has to happen a certain way, Wolfe," I snap, keeping my voice hushed so as not to draw attention to my presence to whoever is inside the room. "I can't simply drop her into the thick of things and expect her to be okay with it."

"But...*marriage*? When you left for Boston, you never mentioned that."

"Plans change. It's the easiest and quickest way of getting me what I want."

Money. Power.

Family.

Jonas sighs. "Okay, okay. I'm sure you know what you're doing." A pause, hesitancy pulsing through the line. "You don't think she'll be a problem?"

My hand finds the doorknob, twisting slowly, my heart racing as I begin pushing open the door. As my eyes adjust to the scene in front of me, laughter bubbles up in my chest, teasing the back of my throat.

Though the humor in it is missing, replaced with betrayal so hot, it knocks the breath from me.

Hanging up and pocketing my phone before giving Jonas an answer, I step inside, gritting my teeth when my gaze connects with that of Elena's mother.

Even being in the same room as her makes my lungs feel like they've caught fire and I'm trying to breathe through the singed rubble.[18]

---

18 It's very important to me that I note he does not mean this in a hot way.

Carmen's eyebrows knit together when she sees me, the tan skin around them remaining perfectly still.

"What the hell have you done, Kallum?" she hisses, making my hands ache as they curl around empty air. "Why is my daughter not marrying Mateo de Luca right now?"

"Elena chose to marry me instead."

"You fucked her, didn't you?" Carmen's lips curl back. "You *knew* that if you screwed her, you'd screw us over too. You've just been waiting for your opportunity."

"She chose to marry me of her own free will."

"Oh, and I'm sure Mateo was just all too happy to step aside."

With her, it's always been about the reaction. She knows what buttons of mine to push and how hard to push them until I pounce.

Once upon a time, it was almost a game we played; she'd dig beneath my skin with her quips and harsh words, her jealousy and spite, and like a fucking lamb, I'd follow her right to the slaughter.

I smirk, not bothering to answer as I sweep the room, noting the half-cocked balcony door just behind her.

The layout of this room is seared into my memory, its white walls much more familiar to me than those of my actual home, the books on the built-in shelves ones I've mentioned over the years.

Their presence gives me pause; there's no way Elena wouldn't pack at least *The Romantics*, yet I see volumes of poetry sitting where they have forever, untouched and left behind.

My gut tightens, my gaze swinging back to Carmen's. She glares at me, putting her hands on her wide hips.

"Where is she?" I ask, forcing my tone to remain level even as my body itches to propel forward and shove her into the wall.

She shrugs. "Seemed rather eager to let me help her escape. Kind of odd for a newlywed, don't you think?"

"I don't know, Carmen," I say, moving toward the balcony as

a shadow dances behind its doors. Never stopped you from trying, did it?"

Her mouth falls shut, and she moves with me, trying to block my exit. My skin prickles when she brings her hands to my chest, disgust swirling inside my gut, making my vision blur.

"I won't let you corrupt my daughter," she says, tears welling up in her big brown eyes.

At one point, her pain may have worked on me, back when I was young and naive enough to think Carmen Ricci was capable of caring for someone other than herself. I can even feel myself wavering as the tears spill over, slicking down her cheeks. The effects of her manipulation linger even now, regressive in nature despite the time that's passed.

But then she speaks again, breaking the illusion.

"Don't use her to get back at me."

Biting down on the inside of my cheek until that sweet, coppery taste floods my senses, I let out a low chuckle, bending so my lips brush her ear. She shivers, and it makes me nauseous.

"I'm not going to corrupt her," I say, taking Carmen's hands in mine, curling my fingers around hers. "I'm going to *ruin* her, and every time she bleeds for me, I'm going to think about how she likes everything you didn't."

Snapping my hand forward, I hear the distinct crack of bone splintering, and she lets out a high-pitched wail as I shove her away. She cradles her broken fingers to her chest, a harsh sob racking her body, but I ignore it the way she once ignored my pain.

I don't plan on touching Elena yet.

But Carmen doesn't know that. Right now, she thinks the marriage is legitimate in more than just the legal way, and that's what I need her to believe.

Revenge is an afterthought for the most part when it comes to my next steps, but I won't ever pass up the chance to see Carmen suffer.

Throwing open the balcony doors, I find Elena still dressed in her gown from earlier, a little pink backpack thrown over one shoulder, one book held to her chest.

Her hair is a mess, makeup smudged beneath her golden eyes, and she leans against the railing with a bored expression on her face, not even fazed by her mother's cries.

When she sees me, she sighs. "Took you long enough."

Like she isn't surprised I came after her.

Even more, when I produce the syringe from my pants pocket and uncap the needle, she tilts her head and pushes her hair aside, as if inviting me to take her.

The needle plunges into her skin smoothly, and I lean down, laving my tongue over the site, unable to help myself. She goes limp after a moment, and I scoop her over my shoulder, taking the book from her hand and trying to ignore the title.

Ovid's *Metamorphoses*.

As I leave Carmen in a blubbering mess on the floor and carry Elena's unconscious form to the car waiting outside, I recall Jonas's question.

I don't *think* Elena will be a problem. She already is one.

CHAPTER 6

ELENA

THE FIRST THING I NOTICE WHEN I COME TO IS HOW DRY MY mouth feels. My tongue sticks flat against the roof of it, practically becoming one with the ridges, and I can taste the mint bubbly water I had on the ride to my parents' house on my taste buds.

The second thing I notice is the unfamiliar room; it's cramped yet luxurious, with polished paneled walls and an electric stone fireplace across from the bed I'm tucked in. A dull ache flares at the base of my neck, where collarbone meets shoulder, and I sit up, stretching my arms above my head, working through the kink.

The *third* thing I notice, when the silk sheet falls away from my chest and bares my nipples to the chilled air, is that I'm topless.

Slipping my hand beneath the white sheets, I glide down between my thighs, sucking in a sharp breath.

Not topless.

Naked.[19]

Clenching my thighs together, I cover my breasts with my palms, glancing around the room for my clothes. The backpack

---

19 As we all are at some point during the day.

I had on at the house sits unzipped on a dresser beside the bed, empty.

There's a single, circular window in the wall beside my head, and I reach out, pushing the shade up to look out, confirming what the dread in my bones already knew.

I'm on a plane.

My stomach leaps into my throat, blocking the air from my dry mouth. I struggle to inhale, an image of plummeting through the sky playing on repeat as I stare into the white clouds, marring my view of the earth below.

Gathering the sheet around me, I slide out of the bed, standing still for a moment while my body gets its bearings. My knees wobble, my entire being rebelling against our airborne state but also powerless against it.

Using the mattress as an anchor, I shuffle to the dresser and pull open the drawers, hoping to find *something* of mine inside.

But they're all empty.

Why would he tell me to pack, just to take my things away?

Frustration spills into my bloodstream, bringing heat to my cheeks as I spin in a circle, trying to figure out what to do now. One peek into the bathroom shows an immaculate granite shower stall, toilet, and a compact sink in the corner, but again no clothes.

Well, not *my* clothes anyway.

A single pair of black boxers and a black T-shirt hang on the shower door, the plexiglass wet with condensation. My belly cramps at the thought of Kal stripping bare and showering mere feet from my sleeping form.

He never fully undressed during our one night together, as if still trying to keep some of his mystery intact. It always made me wonder what he thought he was hiding.

I'd been flayed wide-open, *literally*, while he'd remained as tightly wound as ever, making my body bend for his in ways I hadn't known it would.

Flushing at the memory, I move so the inside of one thigh rubs against the other, sensitive, mangled flesh grating against smooth skin.

I should've run the second he drew the blade against me, but the slight pain it caused was erased by the immediate feel of his tongue trailing after, keeping me from bleeding onto my bedsheets.

All my life, I chased bruised cheeks and bloody knuckles, created brokenness beneath my fingertips by picking fights with others, because I thought it would make my Papà happy. That he'd see me as more than his little Mafia princess and maybe let me live the life I wanted.

Until last Christmas, I didn't realize the pleasure that could blossom from having someone else do the breaking *for* you.

Swallowing around the lump of desire wedged in my throat, I move to turn away from the bathroom, immediately colliding with a familiarly rigid chest.

My heart thumps wildly against the ribs caging it in, keeping it from bursting free.

"Kallum," I breathe, my eyes finding his even though I know I shouldn't dare look. Not after everything he's pulled. Yet, like a moth to a flame, I chase his heat.

His eyes darken, the mahogany color eclipsed with lust, flickering over me as his hand brings the meat of a Granny Smith apple to his lips.

When he bites down, juices sparking in various directions, I feel the crunch in my core. It echoes in my ears, my gaze falling as he pulls the apple away to chew, his mouth moist as it moves.[20]

A pulse vibrates between my legs, the dangerous expression on his face making me dizzy.

---

20 I'm fairly certain this scene was inspired by a particularly juicy apple I had one day. You're welcome.

His throat bobs as he swallows, taking a step closer even though we're already flush with each other. Blood rushes between my ears, temporarily stalling the parts of my brain that process logic and reason, making me forget every single reason I have for being wary.

"Fuck," he says, his voice little more than a husky whisper, "my name sounds damn good on your tongue, little one."

"Wh-where are my clothes?" I stutter, amazed at my ability to form that coherent sentence, when all I can think about is his lips on mine.

"Unpacked and hanging in the hall closet. I didn't think you'd be up before we landed."

He takes another step, pushing me back over the threshold to the bathroom.

"My dress?"

A muscle ticks in his jaw, making a dimple appear in his left cheek. "Incinerated. Took care of that before we left the airport."

My mouth parts, shocked. "You *burned* my wedding dress?"

"I didn't appreciate you marrying me in the gown you'd intended to be on Mateo's bedroom floor tonight."

I frown. "To be fair, I *wasn't* planning on sleeping with Mateo. Ever, if I could get away with it."

He takes another step, backing me into the sink. I put one arm behind me to keep from falling, holding tight to my bedsheet, and he leans in to place his hand on the counter beside my hip.

"No?" he asks, warm breath ghosting over my face. "So you *didn't* wear that skimpy lingerie for him? Didn't shave your sweet little pussy just in case your new husband wanted a taste?"

Licking my lips as he fists the knot holding my sheet closed, I shake my head. My breathing scatters as he shifts even closer, so close I'm not even sure we're two separate beings any longer.

Chest tight, I glance up at him through hooded lashes, trying to keep my breathing even, dipping my toe in the pool of attraction trickling between us. "Maybe I wanted the dress to be on *your* floor tonight."

Kal's irises darken even further, a breath hitching in his throat. "Were you going to think of me when he fucked you?"

Not waiting for an answer, he tugs at the satin, uncurling my fingers with his free hand as he takes another bite of the apple. The obscene slurping sound as he pulls the fruit away sends a violent shiver down my spine, and I clench my thighs together as moisture pools at the apex, warming me from the inside.

With one sweep of his hand, the sheet falls away from my body, catching at my waist where I'm pinned against the sink. Kal lets out a shaky exhale as he chews, raking his hungry gaze down the length of my body.

"As sinful as I remember," he mutters, setting the apple on the counter behind me, then reaching out with sticky fingers to brush the pomegranate tattoo beneath my breast—the one I got because I wanted nothing more than to be his Persephone.

His touch is icy, devoid of the warmth his eyes hold, yet it scorches me anyway.

What is wrong with me?

Just a few hours ago, this man blackmailed me into marrying him. Threatened the lives of everyone I love, just so I would become a willing pawn in some weird little game I don't even understand yet.

I'm not sure I buy his story about being blackmailed himself either. A man dubbed Doctor Death by everyone he comes into contact with is not one who so easily bends to the will of others, so his immediate default to accepting the terms of his tormentor set off red flags in my mind.

But since I also have no other leads to go on and know he doesn't make idle threats, I'd had no choice.

That doesn't mean I have to enjoy our little arrangement, though, yet the longer he stares, the faster my resolve liquefies.

My hand grips the counter until it aches, the effort to keep myself from touching him back overwhelming.

His thumb glides over my tattoo, making me shake like a leaf, and he smirks, moving downward. It curves over my hip, grazing along my pubic bone, before dipping farther to caress my clit.

A small gasp falls from my lips, and his smirk widens, the lines at the corner of his mouth deepening.

"You didn't shave for him, but I don't recall you being bare for me," he says, the timbre of his voice rumbling against my chest. "So who have you been fucking in my absence?"

Tracing along my seam, he creates a repetitive sweeping motion, each time rubbing my clit on the descent. My throat constricts until it *hurts*, and I frantically suck in air, trying to keep myself from exploding.

One little touch from this man, and I'm already there.

"N-no one," I answer between staccato breaths, swallowing the moan burning at the base of my esophagus.

He parts me, making a *tsk*ing sound with his tongue. "For your sake, that better be true."

"It is, I swear." *There's never been anyone else.* My mouth opens to ask him the same, but nothing comes out, my mind blanking as it gets lost in the pleasure.

"Good," he murmurs, that one word flooding my gut with liquid fire, making my pussy clench wantonly. "Just because we won't be consummating this marriage tonight doesn't mean you can try with anyone else."

I blink, the haze of arousal around me popping. "What?"[21]

---

21 It was so funny to write how angry she was with him for leaving her and then forcing her hand, juxtaposed with how badly she wanted him. The disappointment here is palpable.

"When we arrive at our destination, I'll have to leave for a bit to take care of things. And the plans I have for you, little one…" His eyes rove over me in a slow stroke, making me shiver. "Unfortunately for right now, no matter how badly your pussy wants me, my cock won't be filling it."

Arching a dark eyebrow, he revamps his efforts between my thighs, parting them to make room for his entire hand. Two fingers rim my entrance, prodding gently as if testing the waters; he grins darkly when he feels the wetness there, then plunges in to the knuckle.

"My fingers, on the other hand…"

The sudden intrusion compresses the air from my lungs, and when he moves forward, grinding the heel of his hand on my clit while pumping in and out in a smooth rhythm, curling his fingers against my inner walls, I come undone almost immediately.

He grunts as I spasm around him, smoothing a hand down over the top of my head. "What a good little wife."

My lips fall open on a moan, and he takes the apple from the counter, shoving it between my teeth. Bending down, he locks eyes with me as he keeps finger fucking, taking a bite from the opposite side of the fruit.

A gurgling sound catches at the back of my throat as our noses brush, my pussy clamping down around him as lightning licks up my spine, creating little fires in its wake.

Pulling back, Kal takes the apple with him. I bite a piece off, chewing and savoring the sweet tang on my taste buds, knowing he gave me a taste because he knew it wouldn't be enough.

My core throbs with the aftershocks of my orgasm, and when he withdraws, he spits the apple into a nearby trash can and brings his fingers to his lips, sucking off *my* juices.

Grinning like the predator who's just caught his prey, he steps back so he's standing in the bedroom, then gestures over his shoulder at the door.

Until now, I hadn't realized it was open, and when I peek down the short hall, heat swarms my cheeks.

The redheaded employee stands at the end of the hall with her back to us, making drinks at a minibar.

"Make sure you get dressed before you join us," Kal says, tossing me a wink.

Mortification washes over me and I reach down, yanking the sheet back up so it covers me.

"We land in fifteen."

CHAPTER 7

KAL

ELENA DOESN'T LEAVE THE BEDROOM UNTIL THE SECOND WE land. I sit in the cabin with my legs crossed, nursing the scotch Marcelline handed me, waiting for her to enter and give me a piece of her mind, but the moment never comes.

A dull twinge radiates in my gut, thorns spiraling outward and clawing at the organ beating inside my chest. Something adjacent to guilt, brushing the corner of the feeling without letting it fully set in.

I haven't felt bad about my actions in years, due in part to the fact that I engage in a lot of charity work at free clinics in order to absolve myself.

Not that it helps me sleep any better at night, but at least it keeps my mother from rolling over in her grave.

Yet now, considering the way I dragged Elena into my mess and the way I'm leaving her half-satisfied, shame worms its way into my brain, cloaking me in its vile shadows.

Downing the rest of my drink, I focus on the burn of the alcohol as it glides down my throat, dwarfing the sensation before it has time to grow roots.

The bedroom door slides open as soon as the pilot tells us we've reached Aplana International, and Elena slinks out, wearing black leggings and a thin white blouse.

Her leggings cover the *K* carved into the inside of her thigh, and my cock twitches at the memory of putting it there.

How she *preened* as the blade drew against her sensitive flesh, back bowing, pussy cresting around another orgasm. The way her blood tasted as it dripped down her pale skin and how I lapped at its coppery essence like a man dying of thirst.

And I was.

Dying to drink her, to consume the young virgin the way she had me since the night she asked me to be her first.

I figured that night that it would be the only one we had. I hadn't realized at the time that our quarters would eventually be so... *intimate.*

I've already broken my own unspoken rule to take things slow by driving my fingers into her tight, needy heat, helpless against the way she looked at me while I ate that fucking apple.

I bit into the soft fruit with more gravitas than necessary, trying to convey what I'd instead love to do with her pussy.

Feast on it, conquer it, *ruin it.*

She looked like she would die if I didn't.[22]

It'd taken all my willpower not to drop my slacks, rip my dick from behind the zipper, and thrust into her right then, but these things have to be timed correctly in order to work.

Consummation has to wait.

Marcelline comes over and pops the jet door open, exiting without a word, probably desperate to get back to her regular duties.

Slumping down in the leather seat across from me, Elena leans her head back, staring up at the spotless wood paneling on the ceiling.

---

22 This line and the one before it slay me. Swoon.

I flip idly through the *Better Homes & Gardens* magazine in my lap, waiting for her to say something.

Pinching her eyes shut, she sighs. "You own a private jet."

Glancing at the dated yet lavish interior of the lounge area, I nod. "I do."

She snorts, shaking her head. "Figures."

I bought the jet—a vintage 1987 McDonnell Douglas MD-87—at an auction a few years back, but since I rarely visit the island, I haven't had much of a chance to use it.

Mostly, it sits in the private hangar I rent while I take public transportation from one jobsite to the next. Other than short flights from the usual crew and tune-ups, this is the plane's first actual voyage.

Seems fitting, I suppose, using it as a way to transition my old life into the new.

Cocking an eyebrow, I fold my magazine shut and set it on the conference table between us. "Do you have a problem with private jets, Elena?"

"Aside from the fact that they're toxic to the environment? Not particularly. I just wouldn't expect someone like you to own one."

"What, pray tell, is that supposed to mean?"

One golden eye pops open, sizing me up slowly before snapping shut again. "Seems like something that would put you on the map, and isn't that what all of my father's men typically try to avoid?"

"I'm not some sort of vagabond. I *do* have material possessions. A house, even, as I've said before."

"Does anyone else know about it?"

My eyebrows knit together above the bridge of my nose as I study her still form. There's something off-kilter about her, something broken and timid that wasn't there just moments ago. Her hands clutch the armrests, knuckles bleaching as she tightens her grip, carefully drawing in deep, shuddering breaths.

I recognize fear without even having to witness it. The pheromones released when a person feels threatened are minimal, but when you spend enough time studying them, noticing the slight change in scent and behavior becomes second nature.

It's musty and damp. Soaked in sweat, it bleeds from our pores, affecting the chemical makeup of our brains. Makes us do and say crazy, unpredictable things.

And right now, Elena is afraid.

"Elena," I say slowly, carefully pronouncing each syllable. "Are you all right?"

She remains perfectly still. "I don't like planes."

"You don't?"

Shaking her head, she lets out a breathy laugh. "I know Riccis are supposed to be fearless. At least that's how Papà tried to raise us, why he put us in self-defense classes when my sisters and I were kids. You should've seen the way his eyes lit up the first time I put those skills to use."

I think of the bruised knuckles and bloody lips she seemed to sport each time I saw her in passing over the years, how the broken flesh seemed a permanent fixture. For such a warm, intelligent girl, her apparent appetite for violence never made much sense.

Though I suppose, when you grow up in a world rife with it, you'll do anything for a modicum of attention.

"Anyway," she continues. "There's nothing my fists can do to protect me from free-falling out of the sky, so I usually try to avoid air travel."

I'm sure it helps that Rafael rarely lets his family leave Boston.

"You know, statistically speaking, you're far more likely to die in a fiery automobile accident than you are in a plane crash."

"Tell that to Buddy Holly, JFK Jr., and Ritchie Valens."

"To be fair, two of those were the same crash." I point a finger in her direction. "So that's not really an honest comparison. And you're far too young to have been traumatized by them anyway."

Elena hums quietly, sitting up and peeling her eyes open. They sweep over me as if cataloging every visible inch of flawed flesh she can. Tilting her head to one side, she purses her lips.

"You killed Mateo," she says slowly.

"Had to. He posed several problems for me, and there was a good chance he was involved in the security breach at your home."

"Is that what you base your line of work on?" Her eyebrows rise. "A *chance*?"

Inhaling deeply, I fold my hands over my lap and pin her with a dark look. "No, little one. In fact, every single decision I've made in my adult life has been carefully coordinated after exhaustive consideration. I don't take risks unless I'm sure of the outcome."

"And this marriage is, what? A royal flush?"

Instead of answering immediately, I lean back in my seat and reach into the sideboard to my right, riffling around until I feel the aged spine of a book I once kept on my person at all times.

I used to write down verses from the book and then tear them from my journal, leaving them on her balcony the few times a year I visited Boston.

Of course, I hadn't known it was *her* balcony; I'd thought it was her mother's, and back then, I didn't understand how evil Carmen was. It hadn't fully registered what she'd done to me, so I was still stuck in a cycle of confusion. It wasn't until Elena was eighteen and approached me at a cocktail fundraiser that I learned *she'd* been the one collecting the notes and sometimes leaving her own in return.

That night, she asked me to take her. To give her the gift of choice, the same way I'd given her hope to withstand her father's world.

She said she'd recognized my handwriting and wanted to make our connection more concrete.

I'd refused, misquoting *Paradise Lost,* and spent the next month trying to erase the image of a young Elena Ricci sprawled out like a feast beneath me.

She was of age and willing, and frankly I'd barely noticed her presence before then, but she was also the child of the two people who'd irrevocably changed my life.

Then Rafael asked me to watch her, and poetry became the only way I could communicate with her.

The only way I wanted to.

Pulling the tattered book out now, I flip to a dog-eared page, my finger immediately finding the line, even though I know most of William Blake's poems by heart.

"'Til the villain left the paths of ease to walk in perilous paths, and drive the just man into barren climes.'"

I hold her electric stare when I recite the line, and she frowns. "'The Marriage of Heaven and Hell.'"

"The marriage of *opposites.* Good and evil. Theoretically speaking, we aren't a sure thing," I say, snapping the book closed and sliding it across the table in her direction. "But given the situation, we don't have room to fail. I'm imprisoned in this union as much as you are. Therefore, for better or for worse, your sentence is a permanent one, *wife.*"

She grunts, tapping her fingers on her knee, seemingly lost in thought. "What are the chances of you killing me too?"

"Zero."

One eyebrow arches. "You sound awfully certain for someone who just killed my fiancé and whisked me away from my family. How do I know you're not about to take me out to the middle of nowhere and murder me?"

Her tone prods at some barely hidden annoyance bubbling inside of me, and I bristle, reaching up to undo the top button on my suit jacket. She tracks the movement with blazing eyes, that sharp little tongue darting out to wet her bottom lip.

My dick pulses greedily behind my zipper, *aching* to be set free. I reach down, keeping my gaze locked with hers, and palm my erection, the heat of it scorching the base of my hand as I shift in my seat.

I shouldn't toy with her—I'm barely staving off the temptation as it is. But for some unknown fucking reason, I just can't help myself.

"You're of no use to me dead, little one," I say, squeezing slightly—not enough to make much of a difference but enough that I feel a bead of precum ooze from the tip, soaking into the fabric of my boxers.

"But you're not going to sleep with me?"

Horny little bitch. I watch as she flushes, nibbling on her bottom lip, and wonder if *I* know what I've gotten myself into here. "Not yet."

"Then…what's the point? What are you waiting for?" she asks, squirming in her seat. Pressing her thighs together, she wiggles around, likely trying to ward off the need swirling between her legs. "Are you not…interested in me that way anymore?"

Pink stains her cheekbones, embarrassment flushing a path down her neck, making her look innocent and fragile.

It's not that I'm not interested, it's that I'm too interested.

Once we start, I know we won't be able to stop.

"Don't worry, my little Persephone," I say, releasing myself and sucking in a deep breath before getting to my feet. "You'll get fucked. Just not immediately."

My cock doesn't deflate until she averts her stare, her blush darkening.

Brushing my hands over the front of my suit, I extend one out to her, waiting patiently for her to take it. If she really does hate airplanes, I can't imagine disembarking will be particularly easy; it's a wonder she made it out of the bedroom at all, since the shift in altitude fucks with even the most experienced flyer.

She looks at my hand, then back up at me.

I tower over her when she's standing at full height, my frame larger than average, but looming over her while she's eye level with my cock sends an entirely new sensation pounding through me, heightening the lust I'm trying to ignore.

"I didn't want to marry you," she says, her voice soft and unlike I've ever heard it before.[23]

A lump forms in my throat, making it difficult to breathe. Such a familiar fucking sentiment. "So you keep saying."

"What do you expect me to do here?" she asks, pushing up out of her seat. She wobbles, off balance for a half second, before gathering herself and crossing her arms over her chest.

I'm hit with the tangy, sweet pomegranate scent of her shampoo, and I'm half tempted to draw her into my arms and show her what I *should* expect of her as my new wife.

All the ways I'd worship her tight, perfect body if given the chance. How I'd drag her to the depths of hell but convince her she'd gone to heaven, using my tongue to write wordless poetry on her sensitive, swollen flesh.

All the ways I'd treat her right, if I *could.*

If there wasn't too much for me to lose.

If I thought I could actually love her and not just use her as a pawn in my twisted games.

Instead, I settle for what's safe, because right now, that's more important.

"We can discuss logistics later," I say, turning to the side and

---

23 Reader, Elena is a dirty little liar.

gesturing toward the exit, hoping she doesn't notice the way my nostrils flare just at her proximity.

She gets too close, and suddenly I feel like I've ingested the sweetest, deadliest poison.

"First, I want to show you something."

CHAPTER 8

ELENA

'ARE YOU NOT INTERESTED IN ME THAT WAY ANYMORE?'

Sinking my nails into the meat of my thighs, I mentally berate myself for letting the question slip from my lips.

My mind was too hazy, partly from the orgasm I'd had less than a half hour before and partly because the cabin was starting to feel like a coffin, and suddenly the question barreled off my tongue and hurled itself in his direction.

As if sleeping with Kal Anderson is the single most important thing in the universe.

True, I've thought of very little else in the weeks since he tore through my virginity, but still. Given the absolute chaos of the last twenty-four hours, the complete upheaval of life as I once knew it, sex should be the *last* thing I'm worried about.

I should be glad he doesn't want that from me. It should make me feel strong, like he's letting me keep the only bargaining chip I've ever had.

Yet as I glance at him from my end of the black sedan we were ushered into after disembarking from the jet, that familiar ache spreads from my pussy outward, flowing through my veins like it belongs there.

And all I feel is unwanted.

He's practically glued to his door, his suit jacket folded on the seat between us. The sleeves of his black button-down are flipped up to mid-forearm, revealing corded muscles and more bronzed skin than I've ever seen from him.

Scrolling through his phone with the pad of one thumb, he strokes at the underside of his stubbly jaw with the other. The screen shifts so quickly, it's hard for me to imagine he's even processing any of the information.

Pursing my lips, I bend down and feel around in my backpack for my phone, coming up empty. I turn my head, brushing my hair out of my face, my mouth falling open to ask where he put it.

"A liability," he says before I've even uttered a word and without sparing me a glance. "When we're home, I'll get you set up with a new device."

Home. Smoothing my hands over the soft material of my leggings, I look out the tinted window as the green-blue terrain of wherever we landed whips past. The ocean stretches out just beyond the treetop horizon, although I'm unsure if that means we're still on the mainland.

"Where exactly *is* home?" I ask.

"Aplana Island, though natives just call it Aplana. It's just outside the Boston Harbor Islands."

"Never heard of it," I say, my finger pressing a button that inches the window down.

It whirs as it descends, the sound puncturing the silence around us, stirring a calmness in my gut I haven't felt since I walked into Mateo's bedroom. Up and down, I repeat the motion, mesmerizing myself with it.[24]

---

24 I find this is a very subtle characterization of one of Elena's core traits, which is a curiosity/fascinated spirit that sometimes gets her into trouble.

From the corner of my eye, I see Kal shift in his seat, crossing and uncrossing his legs as if he can't quite get comfortable. His left hand comes down to grip just above his knee, squeezing until the veins strain against his skin, his throat bobbing repeatedly as he swallows over and over.

I wonder if he's having second thoughts about all of this— marrying me, fucking me, stealing me from Boston. Is it possible the bad doctor didn't quite know what he was getting himself into when he stepped in as my knight in not-so-shiny armor?

Before I have a chance to ask if it's too late for an annulment, Kal's hand lashes out, covering mine just as salty air blasts my face; he pries my finger away, returning the window to its original closed position, labored breaths tearing from his chest.

Tipping my chin up, I note the tightness around his eyes and the shrinkage of his pupils. He looks savage, like a monster come to life in dire need of his pound of flesh, and it steals the oxygen from my lungs for the briefest of seconds.

Not because I'm afraid though.

Because I *like* it.

The chaos in his eyes sucks me in like an undercurrent, pulling me deeper into his dangerous waters.

For a moment, I'd rather drown in them than resurface.[25]

A lump materializes in my throat, and I swallow over it. My heart skitters inside my chest, that cinnamon and whiskey scent I spent weeks trying to forget assaulting me as he looms over my body. His gaze skirts along the edges of my face, madness lighting his features and keeping him distant.

Gripping the doorframe, he blows out a long, low breath, his chest rising sharply with the action. Blinking rapidly, he seems to snap

---

25 See what I mean? Chaos.

back into his normal state of being, dark brown eyes meeting mine as the pupils correct themselves.

"Are you okay?" I ask, my voice barely audible, unsure of what's just happened and not wanting to set him off again.

"Fine. Just…don't roll your window down."

As he wrenches himself away from me, sliding back into his seat like a piece of metal drawn to a magnet, I frown. "What, is someone worse than you going to grab me or something?"

Tugging at the collar of his dress shirt, Kal gives me a stern look. One I feel straight to my core.

"There are *many* things out there worse than me, little one. And it's not a matter of *if* they come for you but when." His voice is flat, unwavering, whatever episode he had seconds ago completely forgotten as his mask of composition morphs back into place. "I didn't marry you so you could fuck around and get yourself killed, so when I tell you to do something, I expect you to listen. Don't make me regret trying to protect you."

"You've also said you're using me," I point out, crossing my ankles as the driver slows to a stop. "That I'm no good to you if I'm dead. So which is it? Did you marry me to save me or to wield me like a weapon?"

Our vehicle shifts into park, jarring us slightly forward as it shuts off. A moment later, Kal's door swings open, a uniformed, gray-haired man standing just outside, a stoic expression on his aged face. Reaching over, Kal unbuckles my seat belt, then slips from the car, leaving me without an answer.

Rolling my eyes, I follow in his direction. Heat from the sun grazes my skin as I step out, pulling my backpack along with me. We're parked at the end of a curved driveway, and I'm too busy gawking at the massive wrought iron gate to notice Kal's fingers wrapping around my forearm, yanking me back when I try to go through it.

"You're not a *weapon*," he says, his touch burning me from the inside out. "You're a pawn. That ring on your finger makes you *my pawn*. Don't forget that."

Resentment notches against my sternum, defiance rearing its head like an angry welt bubbling against my skin. "Or *what*, Kallum? What else are you planning on doing to me? Gonna lock me up in your house and throw away the key?"

His nostrils flare, eyes lingering on mine like he can't help himself, but then he's moving forward and dragging me along behind him.

The gate opens automatically, revealing a perfectly manicured lawn bordered by tall privacy hedges, the far end of which overlooks the ocean. A massive house with gray siding, a wraparound porch, and three brick chimneys sits at the center of the lot, the only freestanding structure visible once we step inside.

"Jesus," I breathe, staring up at the building with wide eyes. "Is this where you *live*?"

"Technically, yes. Though I admit I don't spend much time here."

"Hm. Pretty spacious for one person."

"The Asphodel used to be a hotel. I purchased it some years ago and renovated it into a residential property."

The Asphodel. How strangely fitting.

I can't help wondering if he senses the irony of his home being named after part of the Greek underworld.

Kal glances at me as we stop at the front door, a tendril of black hair falling over his forehead as he tips his chin down. My fingers twitch, the urge to brush the lock away making my body vibrate as I rebel against it, grateful for the restraint he has on me.

Wanting my new husband shouldn't stir such a profound disgust within my bones—under normal circumstances, it'd be expected. Warranted.

Yet as he stares at me in silence for several beats, I'm reminded once again that none of this is normal. Least of all my reaction to being forced into a marriage at the threat of harm to my loved ones.

I should've been more disturbed as I watched my fiancé's life leave his body.

I should've put up more of a fight when his murderer asked for—no, *took*—my hand.

Should've scraped and kicked my way out of it, the way Papà taught me.

The way I know Kal would have if the situation were reversed.

Clearing my throat, I tear my eyes from his, and he drops my arm the second our stare breaks. Reaching into his pants pocket for a set of keys, he pulls one free and pushes it into the brass doorknob, turning until we hear the lock unlatch.

A little thrill shoots through me as his hand finds my lower back, his icy skin somehow blazing through the material of my shirt, making my insides all gooey. I repress the sensation, trying to focus on the open entryway we walk into.

Imperial staircases separate the two floors, an arched doorway splitting the two and leading down a long hallway. The floors are a deep cherrywood, polished to the point I can see my reflection in them, while the furniture all looks as though it was ordered straight from a Pottery Barn catalog.

An elegant crystal chandelier hangs from the ceiling, and the cream-colored walls are sparse, punctuated only by occasional gold-framed hotel-grade art.

Down the hall, I see a white kitchen with marble countertops and the seascape through a bay window above the sink, separated by a stretch of lawn and more privacy hedges.

With his palm still trained on my back, Kal guides me to the left side of the staircase, motioning for me to take the steps up. Gripping the rail so tight it makes my knuckles ache, I walk a few paces ahead of him, trying to ignore the way his touch intoxicates me.

Honestly, Elena, get it together.

We round the top of the stairs and his hand leaves me, wrapping around my shoulder and turning me to the left. Passing a dozen closed doors on either side of the hall, we finally stop in front of the last one, and he removes himself from me entirely.

"This is...our room," he says, pushing the door open with a sweep of his hand.

"Ours?"

Unlike the rest of the house, the master looks distinctly *Kallum*— still no personal effects in sight, all-black furniture strategically placed in different spots around the room, and long drapes above the windows blocking out any chance of the sun poking through.

"Yes. Did you think I'd make up a room special for you?"[26]

Shrugging, I press my palms into my thighs, rolling back on my heels. "I don't know how fake marriages work. I guess I just assumed our living arrangements would be separate."

The creases around his eyes deepen, a glare rippling between his brows. He takes a step forward, a harsh glint liquefying his irises, and I move back until my ass hits a dresser, trapping me in place.

"This isn't the first time you've suggested our union is less than legitimate," he grumbles, stopping when the toes of our shoes touch, keeping his body a hair's distance away from mine. "What the fuck do you think is going on here?"

I swallow, my nostrils flaring as I choke on the way his scent envelops me. "I don't *know*. You haven't told me anything."

"Let's get one thing straight, little one." His hand grabs my ass, squeezing harshly before sliding up my side and around to my neck.

---

26 Anyone else questioning Kal's bedside manner?

Wrapping his fingers in a collar around my throat, he presses in at the sides, expelling the air from my lungs as he leans in and drags his nose along mine. "We're *married*. Husband and wife before the good Lord himself. It's as legitimate as yours to Mateo would have been, except maybe even more so since we know each other so *intimately*."

Rising up on my tiptoes, I try to gain purchase and relief as the lack of oxygen burns the back of my throat. Desire stirs low in my belly at the rough feel of his hands on me, and even though fear is a close accompaniment, that's what I find myself focusing on.

"Do you remember how I felt inside you?" Kal asks, shifting so he can push my jaw up and capture it between his teeth. Biting down, he latches on to my skin, the flash of pain sending a jolt of red-hot lust down my spine. "The way I split you apart with my cock and made you beg me to hurt you?"

Releasing my jaw, he skims down the slope of my neck, sinking his teeth into the base. I draw in a sharp gasp, a burst of red clouding my vision as my flesh breaks for him.

"Do *you*?" I grit out, rotating my hips in a slow grind against him, goose bumps popping up along my arms as I become acutely aware of his arousal.

"It's the subject of my every goddamn nightmare," he hisses, shoving his erection into my stomach, swirling his tongue over the sensitive spot he's just made on my neck.

His free hand finds my left breast, plucking at the nipple with ghostlike strokes, making my back arch as pleasure courses through my veins.

"Every time I close my eyes, I see you. Spread out and bleeding beneath me, your sweet little pussy *weeping*, just waiting to get fucked." He pinches my nipple, grunting when I let out a soft moan.

I stare at the recessed lights in the tray ceiling, trying to ground myself as they distort my sight, but Kal's touch demands my attention.

Straightening, he abandons my breast to trail his fingers over the bite mark on my neck, a heavy look of satisfaction hooding his gaze.

"Would that prove to you that this marriage is real?" he asks, his thumb smoothing back and forth over my mangled flesh. "If I took you again? Was the first taste of ruin not enough for you? Do you still crave my darkness, little one?"

Lust clogs my throat even as he releases me, moving backward. My hand comes up, rubbing over the now raw area, and he just chuckles to himself, adjusting the collar of his shirt.

Shame scalds my cheeks, both at the fact that I'm little more than putty to this man and that he seems to know it too.

Whatever resistance I might have thought myself capable of when it comes to my new husband disappears the second he touches me, and it causes a cramp to flare up in my stomach like a bad omen, warning me of what's to come.

Clearing his throat, he moves back through the doorway, gripping the knob with the same fingers that just held my windpipe beneath them.

"Supper is at eight. I'll have Marcelline bring you a new phone, and you're free to explore the property." He hesitates for the briefest moment, and I wonder what he's thinking.

If he wants me as badly as I want him or if this is all a game to him. A means to an end, just like I was to Mateo.

I know he's said he was blackmailed into the marriage, same as me, but I can't shake the feeling that there's something else going on either.

My gaze flickers to the large windows across the room, sizing up the likelihood of them being accessible. I wonder how far of a fall it is from this floor, if I could make it out of this marriage before it destroys me.

Mamma's voice rings in my ears, screaming at me to get out while

I can. Her shoving things into my suitcases, trying to push me over my balcony herself when she learned who I'd married instead of Mateo.

I knew then that there simply wasn't time, but that didn't stop her from trying. Didn't stop her from planting the idea in my head.

"If you run," Kal says, somehow reading my thoughts, a cold note to his tone that contrasts deeply with the man who just had his hands all over me, "I will find you. And you will regret it."

With that, he pulls the door shut, leaving me to sag against the dresser and collect myself in this strange, new place.

CHAPTER 9

KAL

"YOU TREAT ALL YOUR HOUSE GUESTS LIKE PROSTITUTES OR JUST the ones you need something from?"

As my hand drops away from the doorknob, I turn around and see Jonas leaning against the wall at the opposite end of the hall.

His dark brown hair has grown since I last saw him in person, the ends curling around his earlobes and brushing his bearded jaw. Bright, violet eyes stare back at mine, disapproval lining the extraordinary irises.

Wearing a black leather jacket with his bar's logo—a fire-breathing Minotaur driving a chariot—and dark jeans ripped at the knee, he looks completely out of place against the backdrop of modern, unused decor littering my home.

When my mother and I visited Aplana, we stayed at the Asphodel Inn on the southern, more isolated border; the stretch of beach behind the hotel was rockier and lacked a proper marina, so tourists tended to avoid it altogether.

Each year, my mother pinched and saved every extra cent she earned from a daycare job in Boston and by walking from our crummy apartment in Hyde Park, forgoing dinner after ensuring I had enough to eat, and making our own clothes on an electric sewing machine she'd found in an alleyway when I was an infant.

In all honesty, I'd probably have preferred a meal that didn't consist of beans just *once* growing up over a weekend vacation in the dead of winter—the only time she could ever seem to get off work—but it was important to Deidre Anderson that her only son experience *some* life outside of Boston.

Outside the poverty my sperm donor had thrust us into that her eventual cancer would exacerbate.

The first time I returned to the island years after my mother's death, Jonas Wolfe was something of a household name; some of Aplana's few year-round residents, his parents moved from London when he was a child, and he grew up on the north end of the island where businesses flourished and everyone seemed to flock.

One summer, a talent scout recruited him for their modeling agency, catapulting him to fame before he was even a teenager.

Given that Aplana is primarily known for its crab export and wild mint, Jonas's discovery gave the island an advantage over those included in the Harbor's National Recreation Area, and for a long time, they did whatever they could to lure people to the very place where *America's Next Heartthrob* lived.

Until his twenty-first birthday, when he was arrested and charged with attempting to assassinate the owner of the island, Tom Primrose. After a brief stint in jail, during which he confessed to having ties to some secret organization, the residents of Aplana mostly shunned him. A restraining order was taken out by Tom himself that didn't allow him within spitting distance of the Primrose mansion.

I recognized a lot of myself in him when news broke about his arrest, so I hired a lawyer, got his sentence reduced, and was there to greet him as soon as he was released.

During his incarceration, I acquired ownership of the Flaming

Chariot, his dive bar that clearly operated as a front for whatever gang or society he was loyal to, then offered a partnership in exchange for his services.

He'd only failed at the attempt because of a leak, it turned out.

Among the criminal underground on the East Coast, Jonas Wolfe was evidently known for quick, traceless hits, and I made sure to make myself indispensable to him. Even back then, I knew one day my time with the Riccis would come to an end. I just hadn't realized how soon it would be.

As with Elena, Jonas plays a huge part in the success of my plans, though I wasn't expecting him to show up at my home unannounced. His presence now notches unease against my spine, curling over each vertebra like a boa constrictor, squeezing until my vision blanches.

Leaning against the bedroom door, I stuff my hands in my pockets, forcing a casual stance. "You looking to find out?"

He chuckles. "Seems like an odd way to treat your wife is all. Are you *trying* to make her hate you?"

Yes. Her hatred would be so much easier to deal with than the liquid heat blazing in her gaze every time she fucking looks at me. It'd probably also help if I wasn't so keen to shove her against a wall every chance I seem to get.

"She'll be fine."

"Windows still painted shut in there?" he asks.

I shrug, pushing off the door and starting down the left staircase to my office at the back right corner of the house. We pass Marcelline dusting the top of the refrigerator in the kitchen, and she averts her gaze immediately, probably still traumatized by the things I made her an accomplice to.

Jonas follows, hot on my heels, and still his presence unsettles me.

"Did you come here to talk about the logistics of my house or because you have something to give me?"

"Bloody greedy, aren't we?" He shakes his head, moving past me to the bar behind my desk, pulling out two tumblers and ingredients for a cocktail.

I settle in behind my desk, pulling up the house's security feed and finding the one set up in the master bedroom instantly. As I click into her camera, a wave of déjà vu washes over me, reminding me of the last time I saw her like this from behind the same screen.

On the camera hidden in her room, I noticed her sporting a few new bruises. Ones I knew her fiancé had caused, and though at the time I vowed not to touch her again, I lost my fucking mind and showed up to demand she tell me what happened anyway.

We fucked instead. Sometimes it feels we rarely have a real conversation without things getting heated, not that either of us seems to mind.

My dick jerks to life inside my slacks, and I rub a palm over my zipper, watching now as she perches on the edge of the king-size bed and runs a hand over the black upholstered headboard.

God, I want more than anything to march back upstairs, flip her over on the mattress, tie her to the bedposts, and reenact our time together at Christmas.

This time, I'd stay. When she awoke in the morning, bloody and raw from my cock and fingers and knife, I'd work her over until she was pleading for another ride. Begging for me to cause her pain all over again.[27]

And then I fucking would.

"Blimey," Jonas says, rounding the desk with two dark pink drinks, strategically keeping his eyes trained above my head. "If you need a moment alone with her, just say the word and I'll take my information and skedaddle."

---

27 Isn't he so romantic?

Rolling my eyes, I shift so my lap is situated better beneath the desk, taking the tumbler he extends to me. The drink is refreshing and tangy as I tip it to my lips, sipping slowly, waiting for him to continue.

He gulps his vodka cranberry down in five swift swallows, dragging the back of his hand over his mouth when he's finished. "Right then. On to why I'm here. We've been trying to trace the identity of the person who sent you that sex tape for three days now. We're no closer than we were seventy-two hours ago, and Ivers says there's no end in sight. Whoever uploaded it onto that flash drive didn't want to be found."

"Ivers International is supposed to be the best fucking security firm around, but you're telling me they can't find a simple origin file or computer?"

"They're running the drive through the wringer—Boyd Kelly's words, not mine—but evidently it's quite the process. He just wanted to inform you that he'd need an extension."

Clasping my hands together, I exhale, irritation making my skin itch. "Fine. But if I have to step fucking foot in King's Trace myself, there will not *be* an Ivers International when I leave. Make sure he gets the message."[28]

Jonas raises his eyebrows, his purple eyes piqued with curiosity. "Isn't that your protégé's family company?"

True, Kieran Ivers took over for me when I scaled back on my work for the Riccis' remote operations in Maine; the hermit took to *fixing* the way I took to Elena—as easily as inhaling a single breath and releasing it back into the air.

Though he's hardly my *protégé*. I taught him everything I know because I knew he could do it and I needed him to step in, not because I was looking to become a mentor.

---

28 Characters who get introductions like this probably have their own book.

Just another cog in my machine.

I wave Jonas off, gesturing for him to go on as I take another sip of my drink. He pulls out a small notepad from the inside of his jacket, flipping to a middle page.

He hesitates, then sighs. "Violet is still rejecting your payments."

My jaw ticks, but I nod still. "To be expected. I didn't think she'd really warm up to the idea until she met Elena anyway."

Jonas scowls. "Does the Mafia princess have a particularly persuasive tongue?"

His question sends a wave of desire through me, and I smirk. "Not one she'll be able to use on my sister, no. I thought maybe if Violet saw me as part of a familial unit rather than as some random drifter trying to get to know her and pay her debts, she'd be more receptive to the idea."

"Right." He taps his thumb on the side of the notepad, pursing his lips. "About the whole...*familial unit* thing."

Setting my drink down, I pin him with a look. "If this is about me marrying her again, you need to let it go. What's done is done, and I'm not going to be reversing it. She needs my protection from whoever is trying to blackmail the Riccis, and I need—"

"A wife," he finishes, setting his notepad down on the desk. I just stare, confusion jumbling my thoughts, and he shrugs. "I know what the terms of your trust are. Your lawyer talks a lot when he's drunk."

I make a mental note in the back of my mind to find Miles Parker the next time I'm in Boston and slit his throat.

Especially since it's all a ruse.

Jonas's gaze shifts to the computer, where Elena reclines on the bed in her room, stretching her arms out above her head. The movement makes her tank top ride up, exposing the smooth expanse of her taut stomach, making me pulse between my legs.

I grip the edge of the desk, trying to get a fucking handle on the visceral way my body reacts to her.

"Anyway, it's not that." Jonas pulls his phone from his jeans pocket, unlocking the screen and holding it up for me to see.

My name is entered in the search engine's box, a dozen news articles trending, some with live updates listed below my scarce bio from when I was a resident. Annoyance ratchets down my spine as I scan the headlines, my hand already reaching for my own phone, dialing Rafe's number before I can suck in another breath.

Disgraced Doctor Kidnaps American-Italian Socialite; Original Media Mogul Fiancé Missing in the Aftermath.

Rage bubbles up inside me, red-hot as it licks a path up my sternum, spreading like hot lava through my chest. When my call is declined, crimson splashes across my eyesight, the dial tone making my body vibrate with violence, and I slam the phone down so hard on my desk that the screen shatters.

Shoving back, I push to my feet, smoothing my hands down the front of my suit and sucking in deep, shallow breaths as I try to maintain my self-control.

All he had to do was keep his fucking word, just this one time. I should've known better—the only thing Rafael is really known for these days is being a snake and biting when backed into a corner.

Just days ago, I uprooted his life, taking his most prized possession right out from under him, and while my plan had been to navigate my next steps carefully and intelligently, this little ploy changes things.

If Rafe wants a war, I'll bring the fucking battle to his feet.

Walking over to the wardrobe in the back corner of my office, I yank the door open and pull out a fresh pair of black leather gloves. Sliding them over my hands, reveling in the familiar stretch of the material against my skin, I admire the sleek look, knowing that soon they'll be painted red.

And despite the noisy, intrusive thoughts playing on repeat in my head as I leave the Asphodel with Jonas, my nervous system has never been more at ease.

CHAPTER 10

ELENA

"THIS IS DEFINITELY WHERE HE TORTURES PEOPLE."

The small shack stares silently back at me, the green vines twisting and growing through the stone siding seeming to mock me as I converse with myself. It's the only other building on the property, sitting far off to the side like the separation makes it somehow less conspicuous.

"You're not fooling anyone, Kal," I murmur, narrowing my eyes at the metal bars framing the opaque window and the boards nailed to the front door, barring entry.

What else could the building *possibly* be used for?[29]

"Are you talking to yourself?" Marcelline calls from the window in the kitchen, close enough that she doesn't have to scream.

"Yes, Marcelline, I am. You won't give me a guided tour so I'm making it up as I go along."

In truth, I've already scouted out the Asphodel three times since the day Kal left me in our room. I hadn't planned on another round across the acreage, but since the internet here is spotty at best and I'm

---

29 She has a point.

not fully interested in continuing the program I'm currently enrolled in at Boston U, I figured why not.

Marcelline, despite being a permanent fixture in the renovated hotel, refuses to participate.

She did, however, assist me in unpacking the belongings Kal had shipped to the island, though seeing the sets of lingerie I'd gotten at my bridal shower made her face flame the color of her hair.

Exhaling, I turn with my hands on my hips, surveying the rest of the yard: the concrete wall bordering the property and hedges left untrimmed, probably to deter peeping Toms; the stone patio with sparse furniture, a rusty charcoal grill, and a hot tub in need of a good cleaning; the partial garden across from the kitchen windows that seems to function as a bed of weeds only.

Just over the fence sits a stretch of beach, blue water kissing the distant horizon, making me more than a little homesick. Reaching into my pocket, I take out the phone Marcelline set up for me, pulling up one of the few contacts available.

My sister Ariana answers on the fourth ring, her face lighting up the screen as she shifts it into a video call. She has on an avocado face mask, and the sight causes a pang to slash across my heart—face masks and pedicures were our Friday night *thing* growing up, and not being there now to indulge in it with her is more than a little unnerving.

It's not been long since I last saw her, yet it feels like eons of time exist between us.

"There's my favorite newlywed," Ariana singsongs, barely moving her lips so the mask doesn't crack. "How's the world's very first *Mrs. Kal Anderson?*"

"Slowly spiraling into insanity," I say, casting another glance at the outbuilding.

"Oh, Jesus, what did you see?"

I frown. "What did I see?"

"Come on. You've been with Doctor Death for a week now. Tell me all about his little shop of horrors."

Making my way back to the house, I slide open the glass patio door, stepping inside the kitchen. Marcelline is gone, so I flip the camera around, showcasing the room with its black marble countertops and stainless steel appliances.

A formal dining room sits through a doorway on the left, and a sunken family room with a huge stone fireplace and a white sectional with gold sides brackets the other exit from the kitchen.

There are no paintings or photos adorning the cream-colored walls. No dust dirtying the baby grand in the oval sitting room off the foyer or the bookshelves in the library down the hall. No real evidence that anyone other than Marcelline existed here before I moved in, and I can't help wondering why Kal owns such a large place if he doesn't *live* in it.

When he is here, he locks himself in his office, not even coming out to join me for dinner. I've eaten every meal at the dining table in complete silence, staring at the window overlooking the luscious side yard, dreaming of all the ways I might one day escape.

"Yikes, it's even creepier than I expected." I switch the camera back, and Ariana raises her perfectly arched brows. "Where's all his *stuff*? I didn't even see a TV!"

Taking a seat at the rectangular island, I prop the phone against a fruit bowl and twist the diamond ring on my finger, shrugging. "I know. There's one mounted in the bedroom, but it isn't hooked up to a cable box or even the internet."

"So weird. Does he not have hobbies?"

"I don't know."

"You don't know?" She pauses, furrowing her brows. The orange flecks in her hazel eyes shimmer as she shifts the phone, moving out of the direct sunlight on her balcony and heading back into her room.

"That feels like an important piece of information to know about your husband."

Chewing on my lip, I reach up and run the pad of my thumb over the bite mark Kal left on me the other day, concealer catching in the ridges of my fingerprint.

"He likes poetry," I offer, knowing where the conversation is headed.

She clicks her tongue. "So do you. Pick something less boring. Something we don't already know."

"Hobbies aren't something that have really come up is all."

Her eyes narrow into slits. "Elena. Tell me you knew more about Kal than just the size of his dick before you married him."

I sputter, dropping my hand from my neck. "*What?*"

"Come on. We all know about what happened at Christmas. Papà told us about your *affare illecito*. So very grown up and out of character for his little people pleaser."

I bristle at the condescension dripping from her words. "I am *not* a people pleaser."

"You so totally are. Not that any of us blame you. We all chose whatever defense mechanisms worked best against Papà. Yours happened to be the path of least resistance."

Scoffing, I reach for a plum, plucking it from the bowl and biting into its purple flesh. "Well, Papà wasn't pleased with how my wedding day turned out, that's for sure."

"Oh *God*," she groans, tipping her head back. "He really did steal you away from Mateo, just like Mamma said. What does he have on you, and how can I help extract you from his clutches?"

"Jesus, Ari," I say, sweat beading along my hairline and slicking down my back. "You make him sound like some sort of supervillain."

"He *is* one! Don't act like you've suddenly forgotten all the rumors about him or the gossip we used to hear from Mamma and her sisters."

Not husband material, I remembered one zia insisting, though I never quite understood why. How could a man with the face, body, and mind of a Greek god not be worthy of marriage?

I suppose if that Greek god were the one reigning over the Underworld, the way Kal seems to reign over everyone he comes into contact with.

But even Hades took a wife.

Emphasis on *took.*[30]

Swallowing the bite of plum, I glance around the house again, its absolute emptiness echoing around me like a vast cavern, neglected by man. It sometimes feels like the temperature drops at night, as if his ghosts come out to play when we're supposed to be sleeping.

Maybe this is what they meant.

Men in the world of the Mafia are all plagued by their demons. I can't help wondering what *exactly* Kal's might be and if I'm here to act as a buffer between them.

"You know," I say slowly, taking another bite of fruit. "I remember you mentioning wanting to hook up with Kal at the Christmas party."

She makes a face. "And? Fucking someone and marrying them are two different things, E. You'd know that if you'd been with more than one person." Pausing, her eyes glaze over for a moment, as if she loses herself in thought, then refocus in the next second. "Is that what happened? Did he seduce you and get you addicted to his cock?"

"*Ariana.*"

"What? It was your first time, presuming what Papà said about

---

30 My favorite lines, I think, from the whole book. For me, this really solidifies the similarities between the myth and Kal and Elena's situation, and it fell into place so naturally as I was writing it.

you and Mateo waiting was accurate. It makes sense you'd feel an unnatural, soul-deep connection to him."

I chew on the plum silently, considering this. It would make sense, but it'd also suggest my motives behind accepting his forced proposal were actually less altruistic than I'd thought, and I don't want to think about the fact that I'd probably have thrown my family to the wolves if only the dark-haired, sharp-jawed sociopath asked.

So instead of doubling down on the realization, I shove it to the recesses of my brain and backpedal. "Wait. You said he *stole* me, just like Mamma said. What did you mean by that?"

"He hasn't told you yet? Papà and Mamma slipped a tip to Bollente and a few other national news stations downtown, saying Kal slit Mateo's throat and kidnapped you from your very own balcony. They're offering a *gigantic* reward for any information on your whereabouts."

I watch as she sets the phone down, dusting her eyelids with a soft gold shadow. My makeup bag sits upstairs in my packed suitcase, probably wasting away at this point—though where's the sense in doing myself up for a man's haphazard attention the few hours he's actually home?

Maybe Nonna was right, and my generation really does give up early on in marriage.

Puzzlement twists my face up. "They *know* where I'm at. And even if they didn't, I'm video chatting with you right now. How hard would it be to trace my location?"

"Harder than you think, apparently. Why else would Papà go to the trouble of drawing attention to himself?"

An uneasy feeling settles low in my belly, anchoring me to my fears. Something doesn't feel quite right here.

I hang up with Ariana, assuring her that I'm fine and don't need to be rescued just as the front door swings open, banging into the wall with such force the sink window rattles.

A few silent beats pass, and I half expect Kal to come in, even though seeking me out doesn't seem to be part of his afternoon routine.

If I'd known being married to him was going to be this lonely...

"You'd what, Elena?" I mutter to myself, tapping my nails on the counter. The diamond on my finger sparkles under the pendant lighting, fracturing the shadows reflecting off of it. "He didn't give you a choice. No one ever does."

When another five minutes tick by, it becomes obvious he isn't looking for me.

I slide off the barstool, toss my plum seed in the garbage, and go find him instead.

Tiptoeing down the hall, I try my best not to step on any creaking floorboards as I reach his office, tucked in a corner at the very end. Light spills out from beneath the door, and I turn the knob gently, pushing it open with the tip of my index finger.

He's wearing navy scrubs, leaning over a huge wooden desk, one palm flattened on the surface to support his weight, the other curled around a crystal tumbler. His black hair hangs in wet strands, dripping onto his desk and soaking the neck of his shirt, as if he's just stepped out of the shower.

My throat tightens just at the sight of his backside, the way the muscles in his biceps groan against the confines of his skin as if begging to break free.

God, what this man must look like naked.

A flash of red catches my eye as he shifts; it's dull, spattered across the front of his pant legs, but it's there, taunting me.

Reminding me that I know very little about the man I share a life with and that it should terrify me.

Or be looking for a way to escape.

"Leave, Elena." His voice is a low rumble I feel inside my chest, commanding and sharp as it slices right through me. "I'm not in the mood for company."

I should probably listen and find something else to do. *Anything* other than indulge the desire pooling in my core.

"Your wife is hardly company," I say, pinching my thigh with two fingers in order to keep my voice from wavering. "And I'm bored."

He sets the tumbler down, raising his head without turning to look at me. "Bored?"

"Yeah," I say, shifting my weight from one foot to the other. "You dropped me in this strange place and then have ignored me ever since."

Swallowing over the mix of desire and nerves solidifying in my throat, I take a step inside the office, toying with the fabric of my robe. It's rose pink and satin, matching the pajama set I have on beneath, and as I move closer, the silky material glides against my skin, cooling me where his presence sets me aflame.

"I know the concept of entertainment might be foreign to you," I say. "But *I* need *something* to keep my attention. And all the books upstairs are ones I can recite by heart."

"Shouldn't you be studying?"

"Well…I withdrew from my courses."

His head snaps to the side, eyebrows knitting together. "Why would you do that?"

"I don't know. It seemed…pointless. I'm not interested in teaching, and I can't imagine trying to balance a career in education while being your prisoner."

Turning slowly so he's facing me, Kal stares down at me in silence, his dark gaze flickering back and forth between my eyes as if trying to figure me out.

Good luck.

"You're not my prisoner," he murmurs, something heavy settling in the air between us, making my bones seem dense and rendering me immobile. Electricity pulses in my blood, carrying it to the rest of my body as my heart falters, skipping a beat when he moves forward.

"Oh," I breathe, my brain unable to form another word.

"But if you don't turn around and leave right now, I'll make you feel like one."

CHAPTER 11

KAL

ELENA'S EYES FLARE TO LIFE, FIRES BLAZING IN HER GOLDEN IRISES as she drags her impertinent little tongue over her plump lips.

"I can handle it," she practically purrs, arousal coating her words as they stroke across my skin.

The flimsy pink outfit she has on does nothing to hide the fact that she's turned on, her nipples sharp as they strain against the satin fabric. A deep, scalding flush inches up her throat, highlighting the mark I left at its base even though she tried to cover it with makeup.

I wasn't being dramatic when I said I wasn't in the mood for company. In fact, before she walked in, I was mere seconds away from reentering the soundproofed outbuilding and continuing on with the job I started.

Leo "Knees" Morelli's blood still stains my scrubs, my need to get a message across to Elena's father the only goal I've had in mind for the last few days.

Unable to get through to the Riccis in Boston and unwilling to leave Elena at the Asphodel alone, in case there's some sort of plot to steal her away from me, I've been something of a sitting duck since finding out about the stories making headlines.

Waiting, watching, biding my time.

Keeping myself locked away from my wife, trying to keep my anger toward her father completely separate from our little arrangement.

Then Blue, one of Jonas's employees at the Flaming Chariot, noticed an out-of-towner who seemed to pop up out of nowhere. No family or friends and no interest in doing tourist activities. He'd walk into the bar, take a seat in a back corner booth and drink beer all day, then disappear at night without a trace.

He walked with a limp, Blue reported back to Jonas, and had a very distinct zigzag scar running from the top of his kneecap to the back of his heel. No one would've noticed it if not for the fight he got in during his second night in town, where he pinned a waiter down for spilling wine on his table.

I *know* that scar. Dragged the dermaplane tool that created it through his thin flesh myself.

Knees is a Ricci cousin, though a shitty one at that. Years ago, he got caught cooking the books at one of Ricci's illegal gambling operations, and rather than send him to the bottom of the Charles like the Elders wanted, Rafe had me put the fear of *la famiglia* into him, then excommunicated him from town.

Last I knew, they weren't on speaking terms, although his presence in Aplana proves otherwise. I don't know what exactly Rafe sent him to do, couldn't get him to admit anything, but it's not happening now.

Jonas should be delivering his head to the post office on the north end of the island soon.

Taking a small step toward me, Elena reaches out, brushing her fingernails against my scrub top.

I haven't practiced medicine in *months*, but the scrubs were the only other thing in the basement when I arrived earlier, and I hadn't wanted to run upstairs and risk Jonas laying into Knees before I could.

Curling her fingers under the hem, she pulls herself closer, leaving just enough space between us that I can feel the slightest whisper of her breath against the base of my throat.

"I'm not sure this is a good idea," I say, swallowing as she tips her chin up, hooding her sweet gaze with her thick lashes.

I'm already thinking of all the ways I might take her, make her regret ever meeting or propositioning me in the first place.

Things I swore to myself I wouldn't even consider until she was here enough time for me to get her settled, yet here I am, succumbing to the hysteria in her eyes.

She shakes her head, dark hair swishing back and forth over her slender shoulders. "I *know* it's not."

Without another word or even time for another conscious thought, she fists my shirt and yanks me flush against her. Pushing up on her toes, she fuses her mouth to mine, taking charge before I can put a stop to it.[31]

This is only the second time we've kissed, yet somehow it feels as if it's our millionth and first all at once.

Fuck, if she doesn't taste as wicked as she did before, the slight tang from a fruity snack lingering like a film of temptation. It mixes with the scent of her pomegranate shampoo, and suddenly I don't want to ever eat another fruit as long as I live.

If Elena is even half as divine as the fruit in the Garden of Eden, I absolutely understand Eve's surrender.[32]

---

31 Considering there is a foot's worth of height difference between them, this is quite the feat on Elena's part.

32 I use a lot of biblical and Romantic language, especially with these two, because that's the connection I feel they have. Their romance felt more like a divine intervention in their lives than anything else.

Maybe she *is* just bored, and maybe I'm skipping valuable steps in my plan, but fuck if I'm considering any of that when her mouth devours mine.

A growl passes between our lips, though I'm not sure whose chest it tears from. My dick swells as I wrap my arms around her waist, fitting myself into the pliant curves of her body, and turn, shoving her back against the desk.

Grunting when her ass smacks against the wood surface, she slides her hands up my chest and locks them around my neck, using her fingers to maneuver my head the way she wants.

Sucking and nipping, she creates a storm, lashing her tongue against mine, mapping out the interior of my mouth like it's an uncharted island.

One of my hands drops to her right ass cheek, fingers digging into the meaty flesh, while the other reaches up to tug down the lace neckline of her camisole. The pale, rounded flesh of her breast pops free, baring one dusty pink peak, and I roll my thumb over it, relishing in the shiver my touch elicits.

Arching into me, she groans, the guttural sound making our lips vibrate.

"Do that again," she whispers into my mouth, flicking her tongue over the inside of my upper lip.

My dick jerks at her sultry tone, so far removed from the tentative virgin I practically maimed weeks ago. I don't know what's changed, if maybe she lied about not being with anyone else, but as I knot my fist in the hair at the base of her neck, forcing her back to bow and present her perky tits, I realize I don't fucking care.

At this particular moment in time, she could tell me she'd made her way through the entire city of Boston, and I'd still have this *need* to sink inside of her.

To make her forget there was ever anyone else before me.

Pulling back, I look into her wide eyes, hazy with lust. "Once we do this…"

She scrapes my neck with her nails, sending a jolt of white-hot electricity down my spine, right to my balls. "Once we do this?"

"I'm not going to be able to stop."

"Who's asking you to?"[33]

Wrapping my lips around her nipple, I suck on the puckered peak, dropping my free hand to the top of her thigh. I skim beneath the edge of her shorts, searching for my brand in her skin, moaning around her the second I come into contact with the mark.

A whimper escapes the corner of her lips as I sweep over the scar, traveling farther up her leg. Yanking the material of her shorts to one side, I brush my knuckles over her sopping core, cursing under my breath when I meet unmarred flesh.

"I haven't worn panties since we got here," she hisses, cutting off on a moan as I circle her clit with my thumb, pressing until she bucks into the motion.

"No?" I ask, raising up to capture her mouth once again, taking charge as her muscles become more pliant. "Has my slutty little wife been walking around every day, hoping to get fucked?"

"God, *yes*—"

A harsh, insistent knock raps at the front door, echoing down the hall just as I shove a finger into her warm, deliciously wet pussy. Her hands fall from my neck, clawing at my biceps, alarm flooding her features even as her inner walls spasm around me.

I freeze, stroking forward slightly, listening for my housekeeper's footsteps.

---

33 When I created Kal's character, I knew that whoever I paired him with would need to be as formidable as him in every aspect of his life. He needed someone who could stand toe-to-toe with him, and Elena is truly perfect in that regard. She doesn't let him hide from his desires, which I love about her.

Silence.

"Marcelline?" I call out, turning my head to look over my shoulder, as if that might give me some sort of insight as to her whereabouts.

"Um," Elena squeaks, shoving my shoulders. "Can you *not* say another woman's name while your finger is inside me?"

I look down at her, cocking an eyebrow. "Jealous?"

Her eyes narrow. "Not at all. Oh, *Mateo*, that feels so fucking good. Don't—"

Slipping my index finger from her pussy with lightning speed, I tug her head back and stuff it inside her mouth, interrupting her. "I can't kill him twice, Elena. Sure that's a road you wanna go down?"

The knocking starts again, growing in volume, and she hollows out her cheeks, swirling her tongue over my digit. My cock leaks a bead of precum as the memory of her slurping at my length resurfaces; she smiles around the intrusion, finally releasing me with a pop when she's finished.

"I know you like to keep a clean workspace," she says. "*Tools* and everything."

My mouth parts to say something, but the knocking doesn't cease, the dull pounding grating on my nerves like nails raking over a chalkboard.

Flexing my fingers in her hair as that familiar irritation takes root in my gut, growing like a weed to the cognitive part of my brain, I inhale sharply and let her go at the same time.

She blinks, her left breast still hanging out of her shirt, rubbed red and raw from my lips and scruff. "You're not going to answer that, are you?"

"I don't get a lot of visitors. I kind of think I have to, no?"

"Right, but...we were in the middle of something. Can't you *visit* with them some other time?"

Normally, I'd say fuck it and ignore the knocking, but add in the betrayal from her parents and my elimination of a low-ranking Ricci *soldata*—but *soldata*, nonetheless—and I'm inclined to believe anyone visiting my house is here with ill intent.

No one but Jonas and Marcelline know this place belongs to me. Even the phone I had set up for Elena pings her location at the north end of the island, some special feature the guys at Ivers International equipped it with.

Reaching out, I pinch her chin, forcing her to stare up at me. "Go upstairs, strip yourself bare, and climb into bed. Wait for me there, and I'll make this visit short."

Her lips curve up at the corners, and she nods. I smirk, flicking my fingers against her.

As she slips from the office, I admire her ass sashaying away from me, then quickly discard my scrubs in the biohazard bin hidden in the closet, pulling on a pair of flannel pajamas.[34]

Pulling my pistol out from where it's strapped beneath my desk, I tuck it into the waistband of my pants, draping the tail of my shirt over it. Scrubbing a hand through my hair, I take several deep breaths, trying to make my dick deflate before walking to the front door.

When I peer out the peephole, I don't see anyone. Palming my gun with one hand, I slowly ease open the door with the other, mentally scouring the porch for signs of an intruder.

Instead, all I'm met with is an envelope taped above the mounted mailbox.

Tearing it off the wall, I quickly slip back inside and rebolt the door, leaning against it as I tear the envelope open. My stomach drops to my ass as I finger the contents, returning to my office to resituate my pistol.

And even though my gut already knows, I pull the flash drive out

---

34 There's something really endearing about (and kind of hilarious) about this image.

anyway and shove it into the USB port in my laptop, pushing play when the media window pops open.

I'm met with grainy footage of a private moment between Elena and I, from *minutes* before the knocking began.

I glance around my office, apprehension licking a path up my sternum, making it hard to gather a normal breath as I search for signs of a hidden camera.

CHAPTER 12

ELENA

THE LONGER I LIE NAKED IN KAL'S BED, STARING UP AT THE CEILING with my arms crossed over my chest, the more embarrassed I feel about mauling him downstairs.

Not long ago, I watched him murder my fiancé and then force me into marrying him. Apparently, after the initial shock and anger wears off during times of stress, my brain takes a back seat and lets my vagina do the driving.

Or maybe it's just the effect Kal has on me. Maybe an entire lifetime of obsessing over him when he never even looked at me twice has brought me to this point, and now I'm free to explore it, regardless of how fucked up the situation is.

I exhale slowly, plucking gently at my nipples, trying to recreate the feeling of Kal doing the same. Goose bumps spread like a rash over my forearms, heat creeping over my chest as his words from before echo in my mind.

"Has my slutty little wife been walking around every day, hoping to get fucked?"

Not consciously, no. Or at least not with the *express* intention of Kal finding me sans underwear and taking advantage of the easy access. But with no one else around and my parents' rules about modesty and purity no longer a factor, ditching the panties just seemed like the next logical course of action.

Another nail in the coffin of allowing the Ricci lifestyle to dictate how I live mine.

Maybe that's why I dove headfirst into unknown waters, approaching Kal despite him being covered in blood and the almost feral look in his eyes.

When presented with the opportunity for choice, I seem to err on the side of reckless abandon. That much was obvious when I asked Kal to take my virginity in the first place, and it's even more evident now.

Sure, he threatened the lives of the people I love. Blackmailed me into this union. Yanked me from the only life I've known and plopped me down in a foreign place, alone and confused.

But he was a skilled lover, and my body is beginning to remember his talent.[35]

The muscles in my stomach tense up as I slide my hand past my breast, gliding through the slick heat he left behind.

"Whoever said Kal Anderson isn't husband material clearly never felt his hand between their thighs," I mutter, biting back a moan at the memory.

"Is that so?"

Even though I'm expecting him, the sudden intrusion of Kal's deep voice startles me; my arm snaps to my breasts while my hand covers my pussy, acting on autopilot.

Lifting my head, I see him standing across the room in black pajamas, leaning against the doorframe with a strange look on his handsome face.

---

35 Elena is all of us when we see a dark, broody, villainous character, honestly.

It's not quite arousal, not quite irritation. Somehow, his features seem frozen in a place between the two, his dark gaze unwavering in its hunger and his mouth firm in its rage.

He rakes his eyes over me, lingering on my flushed skin, reaching up to stroke his bottom lip with the back of his thumb. "Don't let me interrupt. You were saying?"

"I was just talking to myself."

"Do you hear a lot of gossip about me?"

"Not a *lot*," I say, heat searing my cheeks. "Just stuff my mom and her sisters sometimes say."

"Ah, yes. Carmen and her big fucking mouth."

The animosity in his tone catches me off guard; I know he and my parents have a relationship that predates his time as a Ricci Inc. employee, but it was always my understanding that he was like family to the two of them. The distant, mysterious extended relative who only came to town when he absolutely had to and made a stink about it every time, but family nonetheless.

Kal blows out a breath as if trying to collect himself. "Well. What else?"

Blinking, I frown. "What do you mean?"

"What else do they say about me?" His eyebrows raise, practically grazing his hairline, and he holds his palms out to the sides as if in offering. "Did they turn you against me? Give you the gritty details of all the evil I've done?"

My tongue feels too thick for my mouth. "Papà always avoided specifics."

"But you still heard rumors, right? You can't exist in this fucking world without the mills working overtime, especially when you make it clear you just want to be left alone."

Bracing my heels on the mattress, I push into a sitting position, trying to feel slightly less vulnerable as he glares at me. My clothes are draped over the chaise at the foot of the bed, so I grasp at the cotton sheets, moving to duck beneath them.

"What are you doing?" he asks.

I pause, my fingers gripping the bedspread until my knuckles cramp. "This feels like a conversation I shouldn't be naked for."

"Put your fingers back on your pussy and show me what you think of the shit they say about your husband." Licking his lips, Kal moves forward to kneel on the bed with one leg. His arm lashes out, grabbing my wrist and uncurling each individual finger from the sheet.

"I don't even *know* my husband," I snap, trying to twist out of his grip. The arousal I was feeling minutes ago evaporates as his agitation manifests in his sharp tone, and in its place is the need to fight.

Baring my teeth, I rear my free hand back, sending it sailing through the air at his face.

Stupid, really. Kal catches my hand before it even makes contact; he wrenches the one holding the sheet behind my back, then brings my other hand up to his lips.

"You know more than you let on," he replies, taking my index and middle fingers and separating them from the rest. Sucking on the two digits, he laves his tongue over them without breaking eye contact, and it sends a renewed ripple of awareness through me, making my toes curl of their own accord.

Betraying body syndrome, Mamma once called it. When you're powerless to carnality, despite your mind knowing better. She'd been trying to comfort me before my wedding to Mateo, saying that as long as he *made it good for me*, my body would learn to enjoy it.

The mind, she mused, was a different battlefield entirely but one she swore could eventually be conquered, citing her own success in the matter.

Problem was I already knew what it felt like to *want* your lover, and there was no chance Mateo would have ever compared.

Even now, as I try to brush off my body's reaction as biology, I know her reasoning isn't entirely true. My body isn't betraying me at all; I just wish it were.

It'd certainly make all of this easier.

Wrapping my fingers in his fist, he brings my hand back to the apex of my thighs, ghosting them over my seam. My hips jerk into the motion, and he smirks, nostrils flaring.

"So?" he taunts, raising an eyebrow, forcing my fingers to swirl gently around my clit. My breath catches, and he leans into it, bending so we're eye level. "What else do you know about me, little one?"

My head grows heavy in this position, pain lancing through the muscles in my neck; I let it fall back as the pleasure singing in my veins intensifies, making my legs shake.

"You're thirty-two with a Halloween birthday. You like reading poetry and memoirs, though you don't write at all. You got your medical degree from Tufts and did your residency at Johns Hopkins."

He makes a sound, but I can't tell if he's impressed or bored by my recitation of his sparse Wikipedia page. Outside of it, I don't actually know that much about him, except that he's a danger I've never been able to resist.

"Did you know that before you met me in my office downstairs, I'd just finished killing a man?" Kal whispers, his hot breath skimming my face.

I can barely focus on his words, though, too lost in the sensation of him guiding my fingers, creating magic between my thighs.

"That's why there was blood on my clothes. I know you noticed; saw the flash of distress in those tantalizing eyes of yours, then watched your concern drain when you decided you cared more about getting off than what I do in my spare time."

Releasing the arm twisted behind my back, he palms my shoulder, shoving me so I'm flush with the mattress. He still puppeteers my fingers, switching the motion to a counterclockwise rotation that has me drawing my lip between my teeth to keep from crying out.

"You've never cared what people thought of me, have you?" he asks. "Didn't care about the souls I've stolen or the lives ended at my bare hands."

I feel his fingers drift over the scar on my thigh, then back up, circling my entrance. The tip of one breaches me just slightly, eliciting a soft gasp from my chest.

My stomach churns, something feral burgeoning inside me as the truth in his words soaks into my skin, furthering my chase for release.

I don't care about the lives he's ended. That's always been my problem.

"Someone is watching us," he says, setting off red flags in my mind. My eyes widen, searching for him, but in the same second, he plunges three fingers inside of me, stealing the words from my tongue.

I moan as he curls them against my inner walls, teasing and massaging as he distracts me.

"I have a feeling it might be your father. I'm just not entirely sure why."

My hand starts to pull away as his words penetrate my hazy brain, but he smacks the inside of my thigh, and I jolt from having the sensitive flesh there brutalized.

"I didn't tell you to stop." He starts to move his fingers quicker, shallow thrusts that have me canting my hips up, silently pleading for more. "If he wants to watch, we're going to give him a show."

The notion should give me pause or make me recoil in horror, but it doesn't. An invisible fire ignites in my core, spreading like a fever throughout my body, settling in my bones.

"I fear your parents—your mother, in particular—think they can rescue you from me. So in case they've planted that little seed in your mind, let me uproot it entirely, once and for all."

My orgasm crests as he picks up his speed, and I furiously rub my clit in an effort to keep up with his pace, the dueling sensations causing my vision to blur.

"You're going nowhere, my little Persephone. I didn't bring you back to my island just so you could leave, and I'm certainly not relieving you of your sentence. You'll serve it at my goddamn side as the queen of my little Underworld, and all your family will ever be able to do is *watch.*"

I gasp as he finishes his sentence, the image of my parents watching Kal fuck me deliciously forbidden and intoxicating for some reason. An ultimate act of defiance, I suppose.

Arching my back, my release shatters through me, breaking me into a million jagged little pieces. It pulses so thick and fully through me that I choke on it, my sticky hand falling to my side as my clit throbs violently with aftershocks.

"You're *divine* when you come, little one."

Kal withdraws from me, wiping his fingers on my scar, then reaches up to smooth his thumb over my cheekbone. The expression on his face makes my stomach knot up, the gentleness with which he touches me now at odds with how he has every time before.

"Who was at the door?" I ask, coherent thought finally making its way through my brain, the memory of what interrupted us before crashing the post-orgasm glow. "And what do you mean, you think Papà is watching us?"

"Don't worry about that." Straightening, Kal slips off the bed, clearing his throat. "Get some rest, Elena."

And then he disappears from the room.

CHAPTER 13

KAL

"WHAT *IS* THIS PLACE?"

I glance down at my wife, a twinge of nausea tickling my esophagus.

Maybe it's because I was scarcely around her as she grew up, spending my time with either of her parents while they kept their children hidden, but it's never occurred to me just how sheltered she was until now. A twenty-year-old should know what a bar is, even if she's never been in one.

Most twenty-year-olds in the city *have* been in one.

Part of me should feel bad that I'm ruining the girl's life before she's even had a chance to experience it, but the other, darker part of me recalls how mine was stripped away by her parents, and that erases the guilt.

I was far younger than she.

"A bar," I answer, gesturing at the stretch of counter to our left. One of Jonas's men, Vincent, sits on a stool behind it, picking his teeth with a plastic fork.

She makes a face at him, then glances around. "How did I get in? I'm not twenty-one yet."

"You're with me, and the same rules that apply for the general public haven't applied to me in years."

Placing my hand on her lower back, I try not to admire the soft cotton feel of the red, long-sleeved dress she has on. The neckline plunges between her cleavage, knotting below her breasts, and I want more than anything to untie it and feast on her right here, right now.

In the days since the flash drive showed up on my porch, we've settled into a sort of routine; I've been working overtime trying to find the culprit—to no fucking avail—and she spends hers ordering shit with my credit card and trying to figure out how to use it.

The first day, it was fishing. She ordered a neon pink pole and matching tackle box and was up and out of bed at four in the morning, prepared to put her research to the test.

She was back inside within an hour, huffing about how no one told her fishing was so *boring*.[36]

Another day was stargazing, though she passed out before the best constellations appeared.

I only know because I haven't slept since her arrival, sitting in the living room armchair each night with a bottle of scotch, trying to get up the nerve to join her in bed.

But there's a reason she hasn't seen me naked yet, same as why I can't let myself be that vulnerable next to her. The cartography of my body, though lean and sculpted through years of rigorous exercise, is marred with many blemishes.

Evidence of my evil deeds tattooed permanently into my skin.

All of that has nothing to do with why I haven't fucked her yet though. There really isn't a concrete reason behind that fact, just the reality.

---

36 Elena's sheltered-ness is obviously a huge point of this chapter, but I think it kind of comes through how bad it was even just here—she doesn't have many interests/hobbies because her parents didn't let her have them, so now she's just trying everything.

When I fuck her, I want to do it right, and I don't want to risk losing a hard-on because I'm too busy thinking about the people coming after us or how my plan is unraveling before I've even executed it.

Our first time was hasty. A stolen moment before she was to be married off to Mateo.

I want more than that. More than *just* her body.

Hence our arrival at the Flaming Chariot. With its rickety wooden floors and the boards nailed into the windows, blocking all sunlight, I'm surprised my little wife doesn't turn and make a run for it.

This certainly isn't a place she'd frequent of her own volition.

Yet the second my hand touches her, she almost melts into the motion, allowing me to guide her across the room. My shoulders tense as we walk, irritation bleeding down my spine as heads turn and eyes rake over her curves, as if on display for them.

They must not recognize me in this light.

We settle into a booth at the back—the same one Knees Morelli sat in two weeks ago. Gwen, a waitress with spiky blond hair and a nose piercing, comes over to take our order, and Elena tentatively plucks a paper menu from the napkin dispenser, pursing her lips as she scans it.

"I don't eat a lot of seafood," Elena says, turning the menu over in her hands. She glances up at Gwen. "What would you recommend?"

"Nothing solid," Gwen drones, tapping her pen on the end of her notepad.

"Gwen," I mutter, resting my arm along the back of the booth where Elena sits. "Customer service manners, remember?"

She rolls her eyes, shifting her weight to the other foot. "I'm trying to save her from definite food poisoning. Vincent's manning the kitchen today, and *Jonas* won't even eat his cooking." Glancing at Elena, she widens her brown eyes. "Jonas eats *anything*. Just not if Vincent's touched it."

Sighing, I rub the spot between my brows with a knuckle, trying to dispel the ache I get each time I step foot in this establishment. If it didn't have such a cultlike following on Aplana, there's no way I'd allow it to continue on in the shape it's in, but my mother always told me not to break things if they didn't need fixing.

So it stays, in all its shitty glory.

"Why is Vincent behind the bar if he's also supposed to be in the kitchen?" I ask.

Gwen shrugs. "We're short-staffed. The new girl called in sick, so Blue's been helping make drinks."

The new girl called in? Fuck. "And who's at the door, if Blue's in here?"

"Um…" Gwen shifts, casting a quick look around the room as if searching for the six-foot, two-hundred-thirty pounds of muscle I hired to keep an eye on our patrons. Of course, having come in through the front, I already know the answer. "No one?"

Inhaling deeply, I try to tamp down the rage bubbling like a piping cauldron inside my gut. It burns, threatening violence. Gwen takes a step back from the table as if she can sense an impending explosion.

"I'd like to try the shellfish lasagna. Stick as close to my Italian roots as I can get, you know?" Elena says suddenly, sliding the menu across the table. "And I'd love a Diet Coke."

Gwen studies Elena, raising an eyebrow. She doesn't touch the menu, then swings her gaze back to me, as if waiting for approval.

Elena stiffens, her shoulders brushing my arm. "I don't need Kallum's permission to order food."

The waitress's eyes flash with a dull amusement at the use of my full name. "I'm just not sure you know how bad of a cook Vinny is—"

"I'll be the judge of that." Elena turns her chin up, scooting toward me in the booth until our thighs touch. Her warmth is like a live wire to my groin, the sweet scent of her shampoo intoxicating.

I'm not even sure if she's aware of her migration, and I'm about to retreat to give her space when her hand comes down over mine on the table, the diamond on her ring finger glittering in the bar light. Snorting softly, Gwen nods, swiping the menu and jotting something down on her notepad as she turns away.

As soon as her form disappears through the kitchen door, Elena snatches her hand back, shoving it beneath her thigh as she moves away. "How do you know that girl?"

"I'm her boss. Well, by proxy. Technically, my associate Jonas is her boss, but he works for me, and I own half the bar, so…"

"You own a bar?" She glances around, tucking her dark hair behind her ear. "*This* bar?"

I smirk, scooting to my left, eating up the distance between us again, because for whatever reason, her absence leaves me feeling bereft.

"You didn't think my work for your father was my only source of income, did you? How do you think I afford my home? My jet? My solitude?"

She frowns. "I guess I thought Papà paid well."

I laugh, but it's short and hollow. "Rafael doesn't pay nearly enough."

"Is that why you do clinic work too?" she asks. "To offset the poor salary?"

"No, that work is typically unpaid."

"You volunteer at hospitals?"

My jaw works from side to side. I'm unsure how much I should divulge about my past to her. I don't want her to start piecing together how I came to know her parents. "I grew up very poor, so I suppose in some ways, the volunteer work is how I give back. Health care in this country is outrageously expensive, and free clinics are notoriously understaffed and overworked, so it's just me trying to help a bit."

"It's so weird to think of someone who's friends with my greedy parents doing nice stuff for others." She lifts her gaze to mine. "In between the criminal activity, I mean."

"Well, I wouldn't call myself a friend of your parents." I lean in, sliding my index finger along her bottom lip. "But we both know I'm not good all the time."

Not even half the time, in reality.

Her breath spikes, eyes blazing in a way that tells me she's fully aware, and she doesn't mind.

I force myself to look away.

Pulling my phone from my pocket, I click my message app open, typing a quick one out to Jonas.

Me: Thanks for the heads-up that Violet called in today.

He replies within seconds.

Jonas: Piss off. I had no clue she wasn't going to be there. Haven't been in this week.

Dread funnels in my stomach, a storm of unease brewing. Pushing my tongue against my cheek, I pull up the text thread with my sister. The last six I've sent her have gone unanswered.

I knew luring her to the island with a bartending gig was a long shot, but it was the only way I could think to get her close enough to try talking to her again.

My last attempt had not gone well, hence the one-sided messages.

Even when I reminded her that our association would solve *all* of her financial troubles, she still made it a point to stay away.

Though we share DNA, it's clear my long-lost sister is at least somewhat aware of how to avoid the things that are bad for her.

Unlike my little wife, who's staring daggers at Gwen from across the bar.

"Careful, little one," I murmur, bending down to speak against the shell of Elena's ear. "People might get the impression that you *like* me."

Elena scoffs, placing her palms on the table. "I'm your wife. I'm *supposed* to like you. But I just think it's rude to flirt with married men."

Her comment feels like a stab wound, gliding through bone and muscle in a direct hit to my heart. I rub at the soreness in my chest, nodding to Gwen when she comes back over with a Diet Coke for Elena and a pint for me. She says the food will still be a minute and saunters off to another table, unfazed by the look my wife gives her.

"We aren't staying for food," I tell her, opening up the GPS tracker on my phone to ping Violet's location.

"But I ordered lasagna."

"I've said it before, and I'll say it again: you're of no use to me dead, Elena. Don't eat the fucking food."

Sliding away from her, I pick myself up out of the booth, catching Vinny's attention as I leave her behind and approach the bar. He flips his dark blond hair from his hazel eyes, leaning against the counter.

"'Sup, boss?"

"You see that girl in the back corner booth?"

He tilts his head to the right, looking past me. Appreciation shines in his gaze, and he nods enthusiastically. "Sure fuckin' do. Where'd you find a bombshell like that? Wouldn't mind takin' her for a ride on the LL Vincent, if you know what I mean. Certainly looks like she could use a little unwinding."[37]

My annoyance with how this entire afternoon played out ramps up, burgeoning in my throat. Lashing my arm out, I grab Vinny by the collar of his bowling shirt, looping my fingers through the gold chain around his neck.

Pulling tight, I yank so he's angled awkwardly across the bar, clawing at my hand.

"Can't…breathe," he rasps, face blooming a bright crimson color.

"Good. Remember this feeling the next time you decide to talk about my wife like she's one of your little whores."[38] Shoving back, I release him, ignoring the disappointment running through my veins at the lack of finality in my threat. "Except next time, I'll just cut your esophagus out and watch you choke on your blood. Got it?"

"*Jesus*, Kal." He rubs his throat, shooting me a glare. I don't respond, smoothing my hands down the front of my suit, and he straightens on his feet, leaning against the soda tap. "Got it. I didn't even know you got married."

"Now you do." My phone vibrates, my chest pulling tight when I see the name lighting up the screen. "Keep an eye on her. Make sure she doesn't wander and that no one looks at her too long. I'm all too aware that she's too enticing for her own good."

Vinny nods. "Aye, aye, *captain.*"

Choosing to look over his smart mouth, I head for the front door, keeping my chin straight ahead. I can feel Elena's eyes on me as I leave the bar, burning holes directly into my back, and I'm tempted to stay inside and sit with her instead.

But I have shit to do.

The sunlight is a bright contrast to the dark interior of the bar as

---

37 Imagine saying this to Dr. Kallum Anderson.

38 Because Kal is the only one allowed to talk to her like that, MKAY?

I exit, and I'm too busy trying to adjust to notice the girl standing at the curb, arms folded over her chest.

She scoffs when she sees me, mouth pressing into a firm line. "I *knew* it."

CHAPTER 14

ELENA

I'M STILL GLARING AT OUR WAITRESS WHEN KAL EXITS THE BUILD-
ing, leaving me alone inside without a single word in parting. I blink
as sunlight quickly floods the floor, momentarily allowing me to see
the ocean-themed artwork hanging on the paneled walls and the giant
talking bass mounted above the bar.

Having never been to one in Boston, I can't accurately judge,
but I'm willing to stake my life on this being a completely different
atmosphere from the nightlife there.

Maybe it's part of the small, kitschy island charm. Maybe I'm just
sour because Kal's best trick seems to be ditching me.

This had all the makings of a date, yet here I am alone. As
usual.

Gwen walks back over with a ceramic bowl in hand, setting it
down on the table in front of me. Thick steam rolls off the dish, its
vomit scent smacking me in the face. Wrinkling my nose, I push it
away, taking a sip of my drink.

Placing her hand on her hip, Gwen nods at the lasagna. "Aren't
you gonna eat what you ordered?"

Her tone gnaws at my nerves, eating away at my resolve. "I don't know. Are you going to stand there and watch?"[39]

"Probably not. I don't want to bear witness when you puke your guts up."

Rolling my eyes, I fish my phone out from my purse, checking my unread texts. There aren't many, a couple from Ariana asking my opinion on her wardrobe, one from Stella saying she misses me being a buffer between her and Ari's fashion choices, and one from Mamma saying not to panic, because she's coming for me.

Apparently, even though I've been in Aplana over a week now and have sent no distress signals home, my parents are still pushing the narrative that I'm some sort of unwilling victim in this marriage.

Ironic, considering they had no problem tying me to the same fate with another man, though I suppose my relationship with Mateo benefited them in a way mine with Kal doesn't.

Still, they never gave me a real choice. It was their way or face certain death by the hands of the Elders.

I should've picked death.

In the end, I feel like I did anyway.

Typing out a quick reply to my sisters, I leave my mother's message unanswered, stuffing my phone back into my purse and scooting from the booth.

Gwen quirks a blond brow. "Leaving without paying? Classy."

I sling my purse over my shoulder and hold it tight against my side, unwilling to let her know that even if I wanted to pay, I wouldn't have anything to do it with. Not only does my super considerate husband abandon me in town, but he also leaves me with no money or knowledge of my whereabouts.

---

39 Making friends is clearly not one of Elena's interests.

"Apparently my husband owns this place, so…put it on his tab or something."

Spinning around, I don't wait for her response as I head for the front door. My hand grazes the push bar at the same time someone's fingers curl around my elbow, yanking me backward.

My arm flails blindly, jabbing in the direction of my assailant; the back of my hand connects with his cheek, a satisfying crack echoing through the air as I smack him.

"*Jesus*," the man says, wrenching my hands behind me, pulling so I'm flush with his chest. His breath is hot in my ear, and I squirm violently as I try to get away, wondering why the other people in the bar aren't helping me.

"Stop *moving*, bitch," he grunts, shaking me a little.

"Let *go* of me and I will," I spit, strands of hair sticking to my face. Sweat beads along my hairline, fear wedging its way into my heart even though I've been in this kind of situation before.

With Mateo, I always knew how it would end, with bruises and chipped teeth. By the time he was seventeen, Mateo had had two oral surgeries and at least four veneers put in because of me fighting back.

But this is a stranger, in a foreign place, and I don't necessarily know any of his potential weaknesses. In the position I'm in, arms pinned to my back, my normal defense mechanisms are skewed at best.

Still, I manage to slip one arm free, balling that hand into a fist and swinging it over my shoulder; I hear it connect with bone, feel it split beneath the force, and my assailant drops me, clutching his nose and hissing a string of profanities.

"*Fuck*! This bitch just broke my nose!" he moans, cupping his palms over his face. His chin-length, dark blond hair falls over his eyes as he stoops over, trying to catch his breath.

"Dr. Anderson finds out you called her a bitch, and I guarantee he'll break more than just that," Gwen says from behind the bar, stopping at the tap to fill a glass.

The few other customers milling about have either managed to somehow miss the scuffle or are trained to ignore commotion, because no one even bats an eye as I distance myself from my attacker. After I have a second to collect myself, I recognize him as the man behind the bar when we first walked in, the gold chain around his neck giving him *mobster* vibes.

His boat shoes, however, do not.

"He's the one who asked me to keep an eye on her," the man grumbles, narrowing his gaze at me. "Should've known he was just setting me up. I bet he thinks Violet calling in is my fault."

Gwen rolls her eyes. "As much as you love playing the victim, Vinny, I doubt he thinks you had anything to do with Violet not showing up. That's just the way seasonal hires work. He knows that; you can't own half the island and be unaware of how business is."

Kal owns half the island?

A heaviness descends on my bones with the realization that I don't actually know this man at all.

The man I've watched and admired from afar since I was a kid, who inspired a love of poetry and nature and *life* in me despite being the embodiment of the very opposite, seems to be entirely different from the one who forced me to come here.

I'm not exactly sure how to reconcile the two.

Finally straightening, Vinny drops his hands, stretching his lips in a circular motion. He makes eye contact with me just as I turn to leave again, a strangled sound ripping from the back of his throat.

"Seriously...*woman*. You can't leave. Kal will skin me alive if I don't keep an eye on you like I promised."

I raise my eyebrows, nodding my chin at the bruise spreading up the bridge of his nose. "If you try to touch me again, I'll *wear* your skin. Kallum isn't the boss of me, nor do I need a babysitter."

"What you need is cash," Gwen mutters, sliding down the bar to tend to a customer with a big, purple sun hat.

Vinny sighs, taking a step toward me. "Please don't make this harder than it needs to be."

His hand slips into the pocket of his cargo shorts, and I have a momentary flashback to the recurrent nightmare I kept having in the weeks following my one night with Kal—how they always started out so tame, with me reading or writing in a beautiful meadow, connecting with the earth in the most primal way.

How Mateo's presence always seemed to ruin them, and they'd end with me being accosted with a chemically laced cloth until I passed out.

The image lashes against my brain so quickly, I see a quick burst of white light. Then it's shifting, molding from my imagination to something more concrete, something real.

A *memory*, not just a dream.

Kal approaching me on my balcony back home, removing a syringe from his coat pocket. Me giving in immediately, just because I didn't feel like fighting it.

What was the point, when he'd find me regardless?

For only the second time I could recall, I'd been given a choice. A shitty choice, but a choice nonetheless: marry Kal or watch him slaughter my loved ones. And after, probably me.

I knew he could do it.

Even worse, I knew he *would*.

That's the problem when you associate with men like him. The kind who ooze power, know how to wield it, and know what to do to keep it. The kind who will spit in your face, then offer a handkerchief to wipe it off, so you end up owing him something instead.

The kind with very little to lose.

I haven't had one of those nightmares since I've been on the island. Maybe that's because the nightmare manifested.

Whatever the reason, when I see Vinny pull out a similarly shaped object, uncapping it with his thumb, my instincts kick into overdrive for the first time since all of this began.

"Uh…" Gwen says, moving back down the bar toward us, eyeing the needle in Vinny's hand. "Did he tell you to *drug* her?"

Vinny scoffs. "He said to keep an eye on her. I can't very well fuckin' do that if she isn't here, now can I?"

"This is definitely not going to end well for you," she mutters, shaking her head.

But she doesn't stop him.

He pounces like a hunter zeroing in on its prey, hands vying for my neck, and I lean into the movement.

He's stocky, but it's clear the second I grab his wrists that he's only concerned with glamor muscles; he loses his grip easily, the syringe falling from his fist and clattering to the floor. He bends to get it, shoving his elbow in my face. It connects with my eye, and I stumble back from the sudden blunt force, pain lancing across my forehead.

I can already feel the bruise, blood coagulating beneath the surface of my skin.

Satisfaction rolls through me like a thick fog, settling deep in my soul as I focus on the pain, using it to propel me into action.

Raising my leg, I kick upward, aiming for his groin.

When my shin makes contact, Vinny groans long and throaty, like a man with sudden tonsil issues. He doubles over, losing the needle again, and I kick once more for good measure, then walk around as he writhes on all fours, gripping his ears with my fingernails and driving my knee into his forehead.

Putting his arms up in surrender, he ducks his head, one hand dropping to the floor. I glance up at Gwen, who's watching with a bored expression on her face, like this kind of thing happens all the time.

Given the complete disinterest of the other customers, maybe it does.

Pushing my purse strap farther up on my shoulder, I lift my foot and drop it onto Vinny's fingers, reveling in the crunch of his bones beneath my weight. He squeals like a gutted pig, his other hand stretching and twitching as if having sympathy pains.

I start to turn away, my eyes on the exit, when I feel a sharp sensation prickle on the back of my calf. Glancing down, I see Vinny's hand wrapped around the needle from before, which he drags quickly from where it's just penetrated my skin.

Panic floods my chest, and I look up at Gwen, who stares with wide eyes, mouth slightly parted.

"Vinny…" she says, an edge of worry creeping into her voice.

He rolls onto his back, tossing the needle behind the bar and grabbing his crotch. "Whatever. She had it coming."

My chest tightens as the seconds pass by, my feet apparently frozen in place as I watch Vinny go fetal on the floor. My heartbeat kicks up, pulsing so fast and loud it's all I can hear between my ears, and fear claws at my throat, making it difficult to breathe.

I turn around, unsure of what to do or how long it'll take for whatever he just injected me with to kick in.

Gwen doesn't come after me even when my feet start forward, moving me to the door. Pushing it open with shaking hands, I squint against the sunlight and ignore the cool sea air, taking a moment to let my eyes get used to the drastic atmospheric change.

Heart in my throat, I glance up and down the alleyway, realizing I've somehow exited through the wrong door. Unsure of how I got turned around, I grab the handle to get back inside, finding that it's locked behind me.

Swallowing, I shuffle down the alley, my eye throbbing with each step I take until I come to a stop back on the main street.

I don't see Kal anywhere, and the idea that I've actually been abandoned resurfaces, making my stomach cramp. Confusion solidifies in my psyche, rejection weaseling in and making me feel like an idiot.

Just because he gives you his credit card and a couple of orgasms doesn't mean he's interested in more.

Besides, I shouldn't even want more. Barely any time has passed since our forced union, so what exactly did I think was going to happen? That he'd reciprocate the level of obsession I've held for him my entire life and somehow we'd find a way to make it work despite the outside obstacles hell-bent on keeping us apart?

No, Elena. This isn't a Disney movie or some romantic poem.

Stupid, stupid girl.[40]

I've been letting my attraction defy reason, and it's been keeping me locked inside that house without even trying to escape.

Casting a glance up and down the street again, I purse my lips, considering.

Sucking in a lungful of air, I ignore the unease rippling inside of me and straighten my spine, adjusting the hem of my dress with one hand.

And then I run.

---

40 Ugh, I feel so bad for her here. I just want to give her a hug.

KAL

THE SECOND MY SISTER OPENS HER MOUTH TO SPEW VENOM, I'M hit by a wave of nostalgia that damn near knocks me off my feet.

For the slightest blip in time, I'm a kid again, standing on the sunken concrete porch of a little house in North Carolina, rain stitching my clothes to my skin. Droplets of water roll off the end of my nose as I wait, hoping that maybe this time the man who helped give me life will answer the door.

My fist curls around the scrap of paper in my trench coat pocket—my mother's goodbye. I've read it so many times at this point, I know the words by heart.

Auden's "Funeral Blues" scribbled by cancer-riddled hands, a single space above the address of a man she never spoke of.[41] A man who, thirteen years prior, met a dark-haired mystery in a nightclub, took her home, and never contacted her again after that.

It wasn't until she sought him out with evidence of their tryst together that she learned he was married.

His wife had just given birth to their first son.

---

41 All of the poetry mentioned in this book makes my heart so happy.

He didn't want me. Told my mother to take care of the problem and not to come around again.

She didn't.

Take care of me, that is.

And I spent the first decade of my life without the knowledge that I was a reject. The product of a bad decision, brought about because my mother was practically a saint, and she didn't want to punish anyone else for her mistakes.

Still, the universe didn't reward her.

Which is why I found myself on my sperm donor's doorstep, praying that thirteen years may have lessened the blow of having a child outside of his marriage. That maybe he'd be happy to have another son, like a built-in friend for the one who wasn't a bastard.

Throat tight, I wait in front of the door like I've waited four other times this week, my knuckles red from all the knocking. The downpour doesn't erase the sound from my head; in my mind, the knocking never ceases, even after I drop my hand.

I don't know what I'm expecting, in all honesty. My mother's been six feet under for less than a day, and I'm already out trying to find a figurehead to replace her.

Maybe I am as evil and selfish as my grandfather always says.

A light flickers on in the big bay window at the front of the little white house, and a second later, the door creaks open. Hope blooms in my chest like the sunflowers planted to my right, bright and wide, ready to absorb any ounce of potential nourishment I can get.

Instead, a little girl with onyx hair appears, clasping the door in her hand. She blinks at me through the storm door, big doe eyes reflecting an innocence mine never have.

Her pale, moon-shaped face turns up, a thousand-yard stare taking me in, processing silently.

Now, with that same little girl staring up at me again as an adult,

I can't help the pang that comes next as I return to the present. I ran when I saw her back then, and everything in me wants to repeat that scene, to get as far away from my sister as I can before my existence ruins her.

One of my legs shifts, as if trying to escape, but Violet notices and scurries in front of me, blocking my path. "Oh no. You're not going anywhere. You lure me to this shitty little island with a job that I just *knew* was too good to be true, the least you can do is explain yourself."

I clear my throat, glancing down at her all-black outfit, so ridiculously similar to my own that I almost laugh. Nature versus nurture, I guess.

Steeling myself against the nerves fluttering inside my chest, I stuff my hands in my pockets and shrug. "I'd say you already know the reason you're here, Violet. You won't cash any of the checks I send, and you've blocked my ability to wire transfer funds into your bank account. This was the next logical step."

Her brows arch. "Actually, the next *logical* step would be to leave me alone, like I've asked you to a hundred times."

"Take the money I'm trying to give you, and I'll leave you be."

"I don't *want* your money!" she snaps, turning a few heads of the people passing by on their way from the Dunkin' down the street. "Honestly, Kal, it's a nice gesture, but…it's not warranted."

Clenching my jaw, I exhale roughly. "You're drowning in debt, Violet. Let me help you."

"God, you don't *get* it, do you?" Shaking her head, she turns on her heel, scanning the sidewalk as if looking for eavesdroppers. As if anyone in Aplana is at all concerned with the happenings of others— that's why the island is primarily made up of tourists year-round. People come here to escape.

Or, in my case, to hide.

They definitely don't come for gossip, and the locals know better than to put their noses in my business, even if they don't know exactly *why* they shouldn't.

"Have a cup of coffee with me and explain it," I offer, nodding at Dunkin'. Such an odd franchise for this part of town, given the number of mom-and-pop shops littering the streets, but it does surprisingly well.

"I don't want to have coffee with you. I don't even want to *be* here, on this island. But I came, even though my best friend told me something sounded off. I thought, it's an island with a population of less than a hundred people. What could possibly happen?" She snorts sharply, narrowing her eyes. "Just when I was starting to forget about you."

Her words are a barb aimed directly at my heart; it sinks inside the muscle, flaring so it latches on tightly and refuses to relinquish its hold. I rub at the ache they cause, taking a step back, wondering if I should go back inside and leave her be after all.

"This is your problem, Kal. You want to force a relationship by fixing what you feel are problems. I didn't ask for your help, and I know damn sure my dad didn't either."

I bite the inside of my cheek in silent protest. *Her dad.*

Not *ours.*

I don't reply, letting the weight of her words pull them down between us, anchoring them to the space where I once stood.

Finally, she exhales, mimicking my movement backward, shielding her eyes from the sun with one hand. "Did you…did you really kidnap that girl?"

"Keeping tabs on me, sister?"

She scrunches up her nose. "You can't go anywhere back home without hearing about it. She's a Mafia princess, Kal. What are you even thinking?"

Part of me almost laughs again at the condescension seeping from her tone.

Like I'm afraid of the fucking Mafia.

"I know who she is, and I didn't *kidnap* anyone. Elena married me of her own volition. If you want the sordid details of how she pursued me, then I her, I'll give them to you as soon as you cash one of my fucking checks."

"Wasn't she supposed to marry someone else? Some news reporter or journalist?" Violet tilts her head, studying me. "You know they found his body, right?"[42]

Annoyance burns hot on the back of my tongue. "I'm not sure why that would concern me."

She presses her lips together, glancing down at the Birkenstocks on her feet. "It probably doesn't, and that's part of our problem."

Slipping my hands from my pockets, I reach up and tug at the collar of my dress shirt, shaking my head. "Actually, we don't have a problem. In fact, per your request, we don't even have a relationship." I start to head in the opposite direction down the street, pausing once to see the astonishment coloring her features.

"I've been poor, you know. Most of my life, that was my identity. It sucks, and I wouldn't wish it on anyone. Not even on the man who still to this day won't recognize me as his own."

Violet blinks, reminding me so much of the little girl on the doorstep all those years ago, staring up at me like I was a stranger.

Which I suppose I am. Even now.

"I'll tell Jonas you're no longer interested in working here," I say, moving back toward the front door of the Flaming Chariot. "See to it you're off my island by sundown."

And with that, I head back inside.

---

42 Fun fact: Violet was the first character I ever created from this world, over a year before I wrote this book. It's so funny to me to see how things play out with these two.

CHAPTER 16

ELENA

I DON'T GET VERY FAR, SINCE I'VE NOT BEEN GIVEN ANY TIME TO explore the island outside of Kal's home and therefore don't know anything about the layout.

I run until I'm blocks away from the bar, hyperaware of the wind kicking up the skirt of my dress each time my feet hit concrete. *At least I wore underwear today.*

There's a bus station at the end of a connecting street, and I duck in as soon as I reach it, trying not to feel immediately paranoid about the lack of people inside.

To be fair, it seems as though this island doesn't have a wide variety of folks anyway. I'm sure the majority of them travel by foot or car.

At least that's what I tell myself as I approach the ticket window, searching for any sign of life inside. The lights are off in the office, the computer screens black. It looks like no one's been here in weeks.

Groaning to myself, I lean my head against the counter, mentally assessing my body for signs of the drug Vinny injected me with.

It's been several minutes, and I don't feel any different, except more on edge than ever as I wait for symptoms to set in. Exhaling, I walk over to one of the plastic benches in front of the window and flop down, pulling my phone out.

My sister's name flashes across the screen, requesting a video call, and I decline, exhaustion clouding my brain. The phone vibrates again, an unsaved number I know by heart popping up, making the organ clench inside my chest like a closed fist, barring itself from further hurt.

I decline that call too, slumping on the bench and dropping my head to rest on its back.

Tapping my fingers on my bare knee, I contemplate my next move. There probably isn't very much time, considering Kal knows Aplana and I don't, and he's also likely tracking my phone. I'm only minutes from the bar, and I know the first place he'd look for me would be an apparently abandoned bus station.

Because he's smart. A predator at his very core, alert and cognizant at all times, like a lion lying low in the grass before an attack.

I could hide in a bathroom or a storage closet. Maybe try to find a door that locks or mask my scent with the soil from one of the potted plants near the exit.

But deep in my heart, I know it's useless. Kal didn't take me as his wife for no reason, so there's no chance in hell he'd ever give me up for anything less.

With a hand that feels like lead, I turn my phone over, wondering if Mamma was right to try and rescue me from this life.

At least with Mateo, I wouldn't have been a prisoner to the feelings inside me; they're volatile waves that ebb back and forth, tossing me like a ship as I try to decide between my infatuation and my fear. Lately, the former's been winning out, my sex-starved brain short-circuiting when any part of me comes into contact with my husband.

The latter, though, is the option that makes sense. I should fear him. Should be spending all of my time figuring out how to get as far from him as possible rather than melting into a needy puddle any time he's around.

Maybe if I hadn't been so openly wanton, he wouldn't have taken me to that bar, and I wouldn't have been attacked.

Maybe if he hadn't left you alone, you wouldn't have been.

My phone rings again, that same number popping up. Against my better judgment, I answer, hitting the speaker button with my pinky as the rest of my body starts to feel like it's taking on water.

"Where the fuck are you?" Kal's voice is cold, hard steel, hurled at me like a lightning bolt.

A lazy smile works over my lips. "Wouldn't you like to know?"

"I'm not in the habit of asking questions I don't want the answer to," he says darkly. "You know better than that, Elena."

I make a face at the window. "You sound like my dad."

A long, pregnant pause stretches through the line between us, heat scoring my cheeks.

"Yeah?" Kal clips. "Then get back here so I can discipline you properly. Put you over my knee, show you how I feel about you running away from me."

Tension expands in my core like an unraveled thread, tangling like a spiderweb between my thighs. Biting my lip, I try to latch on to the anger bubbling in my chest, even as warmth spreads from my pussy outward, my body melting at the image of me bent over for him.

"I didn't run away from you," I lie, swallowing over the emotion threatening the back of my throat. "You weren't anywhere around when I left. Which, by the way, thanks for ditching me *again*. And thanks for recruiting a monster to babysit me."

He sighs, and I can just imagine him pinching the bridge of his nose, trying to maintain composure. "I didn't realize Vincent was going to be a problem. I will deal with him."[43]

Tears burn my eyes, and I sniffle as I fight them off, pulling my legs to my chest. Laying my cheek on my knee, I tap the phone, checking the time. "I hate it here."

"Tell me where you're at, and I'll come get you."

"No," I say, shaking my head even though I know he can't see me. My eyelids droop, obscuring the plexiglass in front of me, and I find it easier to let them rest. "*Here*. Aplana Island. I'm lonely."

He doesn't say anything for several beats—so long that I'm pretty sure the next time he does, I'm dreaming. "Yeah," he agrees, the ice evaporating from his tone with that single syllable, making me wonder what exactly he's agreeing with.

Maybe Hades was lonely too, and he brought Persephone to his realm because he knew she'd bring the light with her.

Somewhere in the distance, a door slams shut, the sound echoing in the rafters. Voices drift in my direction like a storm cloud, rough and angry as they draw closer.

Kal curses under his breath. "Elena. Where are you?"

Fatigue rolls over me, slow and steady as it envelops my brain, making it difficult to focus. The voices drift nearer, growing angrier, and if I could pay more attention to them, I'd probably be afraid. But my mind feels like a raft lost at sea, floating slowly among the waves as they carry me away.

"Where did you go?" I ask instead. At least I *think* I ask, though it's hard to feel my mouth all of a sudden.

"I had to meet someone."

"A girl?" I can't hide the bite of jealousy; it slips out like a serpent's tail, lashing quickly.

---

43 SWOON. The way Kal just immediately is ready to kill anyone who hurts her makes me a puddle of goo.

"Yes. But not like that." A pause, then a sigh. "My sister."

"You have a sister?"

"Yes. Sort of. It's...complicated." Kal clears his throat, and I wonder what he's doing right now. If he's standing over Vinny's prone body, a gun pressed to the back of his skull, waiting to know if I'm safe before exacting his punishment. "But never mind that, little one. Tell me where you are."

"I don't know," I admit, my words coming slower. The sound behind me picks up, footsteps pounding against the cement floor, but I still don't open my eyes. "Some bus station."

"*Bus* station?" Another drawn-out pause, and then Kal curses again, something shuffling over the line. "I need you to get out of there, right now."

"Can't," I say, that warmth from before traveling through my veins, making my insides feel like jelly. "Too sleepy."

"*Elena.*" I can tell he's speaking through clenched teeth. "That drug Vincent gave you was a diluted version of a very powerful street drug, and it's probably kicking in right now. I need you to fight it and get the fuck out of there and outside where people can see you."

Laughter floats around me, shadows casting across the bench where I lie. I see them from behind my eyelids, but I'm too tired to open them and see what's going on. Maybe the staff's come back from a lunch break.

"Well, well," a voice says with an accent I can't quite place, "what have we got here, boys?"

And then everything goes dark.

CHAPTER 17

KAL

I'M NOT A MAN WHO VERY OFTEN LOSES HIS COOL.

When it comes to both my lines of work, anxiety is a luxury I've never been able to afford.

But when the line linking me to Elena crackles and goes silent, worry sinks into the core of my being, digging in and planting roots. I blink at the wall in Jonas's office, waiting longer than necessary to see if the call revives itself before I'm met with the ear rape of a dial tone.

It bleats for a full minute, causing a spasm to rip through the muscle beneath my eye, darkening my vision slightly. An itch flares beneath my skin, the sound echoing long after it falls silent, and I slowly set my phone down on Jonas's metal desk, turning around.

Vincent sits duct taped to a plastic chair, one of Jonas's dirty gym socks shoved in his mouth to block out his pathetic whimpers. I've barely even touched him, and the fucker's already pissed himself twice.

Perching on the edge of the desk, I steeple my fingers together, watching him struggle against his bindings. His fear would smell so sweet if not for the unspoken violence lighting his gaze, telling me he's not in the least bit sorry.

Which makes my decision a hell of a lot easier.

My phone vibrates a moment later, an incoming text from Jonas flashing across the screen.

Jonas: Station Thirteen, at the corner of Fifth and Poplar. En route now.

Though he hadn't been around the bar so far this week, Jonas had still been close by, overseeing an export of some craft beer he's been working on in his spare time. I'd grouped him in on the call when I dialed Elena in case he was closer and able to get to her quicker.

Cuffing the ends of my sleeves, I do my best to hide the blood coating them, admiring the addition to Elena's handiwork on Vincent; when I entered the bar, he'd been curled into a ball on the floor while Gwen tried to wrap his hand, which she remarked she thought was broken after giving me the CliffsNotes of what happened.

His fingers certainly weren't bent correctly, nor was he able to move them when prompted. When I noticed the discarded needle across the room, a detail Gwen left out of her account, I'd smiled at Vincent and stomped down on top of his already mangled hand, relishing in the garbled scream that tore from his chest.

If it wasn't broken before, it is now.

Dragging him into Jonas's office with the help of Blue, who finally came back from an extended lunch, I split my knuckles wide-open on his swollen nose, using the heel of my hand to make sure that cartilage cracked too. While I cleaned myself up and called Elena, I had Blue strap Vincent to the chair and gag him, waiting to hear from my wife before I proceeded.

Unfortunately for him, the end of that call probably isn't what Vincent was hoping for.

Blue watches from the corner of the room where he lounges on an old leather sofa, one of his hands wrapped around the neck of a beer bottle. Nicknamed for the ocean-like quality of his gaze, he keeps it trained on me, silent and waiting for more orders.

Picking my suit jacket off the coatrack by the door, I shake it free of any debris, slipping it on over my shoulders as I take in Blue's calm demeanor. He'd gotten back from his break and sprung right into action, no questions asked.

It's the kind of quality you look for in an employee. A soldier.

Without knowing much about his actual background, the squared, neat cut of his dark hair and the anchor tattoo on his tan skin, peeking out from beneath his shirtsleeve, tell me he probably has some military experience, which means he understands loyalty.

His existence here as a bouncer makes me less irritated with Jonas and his shitty hiring skills.

Slightly.

"You just gonna leave him here?" Blue asks as I head for the door, cocking a thick brow.

I pause. "Got a problem with that?"

He holds his free hand up, shaking his head. "Nope. Just making sure we're on the same page."

"I'll be back for him. Don't let him out of your sight, and don't let anyone come in while I'm gone."

I should stay for an interrogation, though the idea of not being there to retrieve Elena makes my stomach churn. I've no doubt Rafael had something to do with Vincent's attack, but I'll find out more later.

Closing the door behind me with more force than necessary, I quickly scan the bar floor, making sure all of the patrons found their way out. After I kicked Gwen's skinny ass to the curb, I announced to the few customers that we were closing early, bolting the doors so no one else could get inside.

Pushing out the back door, I lock up and walk down the alley to my waiting town car, informing the driver—drivers change so often around here, I haven't bothered to learn his name—of our destination. He guides the vehicle through the streets, practically empty this time of year, until finally turning onto Fifth and stopping in front of Station Thirteen.

It's not an active bus station, hasn't been in years. The Primroses, majority owners of the island, scaled back years ago on public transportation costs, arguing that we don't get enough tourists each summer to balance out the expense.[44]

So the few stations we had were either torn down and turned into something more profitable, or—on the south side of the island—they became hotbeds for criminal activity.

This one in particular is known for its shady operations, but Elena wouldn't know that, because I dropped her in the middle of my world and gave absolutely no explanation.

Took her from one cage and imprisoned her in another, possibly for naught, depending on what I find inside.

If they've touched a hair on her head, I'm not sure what I'll do. It's been a long time since my blood cried out for a massacre, yet as I climb out of my car and head for the glass front door, that's the exact image surfacing in my mind.

It would be all my fault too.

That knowledge is a poisoned knife to my gut, hell-bent on a quick and painful demise.

All that talk about her being of no use to me dead, yet I went and put her right in Death's path anyway.

Jonas meets me just inside the door, a plastic toothpick sticking out of the corner of his mouth. He unzips his leather jacket, falling

---

44 This is the weirdest island. I can see why they don't get many tourists, considering all the criminal activity.

into step with me as we survey the area, searching for signs of distress or struggle.

I don't see any at first. He veers off without a word to check the bathrooms, leaving me to wonder if the noises and voices I'd heard on the other end of the phone had been my imagination.

A flash of dark hair catches my eye toward the front of the lobby, and I do a double take, not recognizing the form at first glance.

Elena lies across a plastic bench, the hem of her dress pushed up her thighs, hair matted with sweat, and...

"Fucking hell," I mutter, rage burrowing into my bones, merging itself with the marrow. I stand frozen in place, my eyes roving over her unconscious form, my pulse speeding up as my anger builds.

The K carved into the inside of her thigh is visible the way her dress sits and partly reopened; blood streaks across her skin, long and drawn out like her attacker dragged his fingers over her.

Touched what fucking belongs to me.

I hear Jonas's footsteps approach as he leaves the bathrooms and hear his sharp intake of breath as he soaks in the aftermath.

"Bloody hell," he says, carding a hand through his curls. "Is that..."

Swallowing over the disgust solidifying in my throat, I nod. "Looks like it."

"How is this even possible?" he asks, his eyebrows furrowing. "You were barely off the phone with her for ten minutes, and she's accosted for the second time this afternoon?"

Violence vibrates off my body in waves, the urge to maim the men who did this to her overwhelming in its intensity; seeing her lying there, defenseless and used, elicits an entirely visceral reaction in me, setting my soul aflame.

Jonas glances at me. "Do you think they..."

Gritting my teeth, I cut him off with a quick shake of my head, unwilling to entertain that thought, although it certainly doesn't look promising. "Let's get her somewhere safe, and then I'll worry about doing a full workup."

"Shouldn't she go to a hospital—"

My head snaps in his direction, nostrils flaring with the half-voiced implication. "Do you think there's something they'll find that I can't? Something I won't be able to treat?"

"No, I just think she might need a breather. You know, in case she wakes up and all she can remember is her attack and the fact that you left her alone in a strange, frankly seedy, bar."

Moving around the bench, I note every single abrasion, cataloging them for the future. A purple welt brackets her eye, while her neck is rubbed raw, as if someone had their hands around it. Shucking off my jacket, I pull her dress over her thighs and drape it across her, tucking it around her form.

"You think this place has a security system? Camera, audio?"

Looking around, Jonas frowns. "I can't imagine they'd waste their time with that in a mostly abandoned building. You know crime isn't the same here as it is in the city. It's not...organized."

Sliding my arms beneath Elena's frame, I brace myself with my knees and lift her off the bench, ensuring the jacket covers any indecencies. Cradling her against my chest, I ignore the stench of the bodily fluids in her hair, carrying her to the front door.

My chest throbs as I walk, guilt blooming like a field of poisonous flowers inside me; one single indulgence, and I'm a goner. A slave to the aggression and pain I otherwise keep at bay.

Anyone who touched her will die.[45]

"Anderson," Jonas says as I reach the door. I cast a glance over my shoulder, seeing him standing in front of the ticket window, holding

---

45 That's my man!

up what appears to be a note card with the Ricci insignia on it. He cocks an eyebrow.

Breathing heavily, I focus on the black piece of paper, shifting Elena's weight so she isn't slumping. My mind races, trying to settle on a single course of action, while the blood in my veins comes alive with electricity, singing as it pulses through me in a frenzy.

The note card taunts me, evidence that Rafael and Carmen are still trying to push the narrative that I stole their daughter rather than negotiating her hand fair and square. I'm sure this was another ploy to play up my evil existence, whoever assaulted Elena probably taking the evidence with them in order to make me look worse.

Or they wanted to scare her away from me. Maybe both.

But how did they know she'd be here?

We're clearly being watched, and I wonder about the flash drive with footage of the inside of my house on it. If that was a part of this.

How far will the Riccis go to send a message?

My brain itches to figure it out, trying to determine whether Vincent was involved in this too or if it was a single string of luck, but then I remember the broken goddess lying in my arms.

Right now, getting Elena medical attention feels more important, so I leave the building and tuck her into the back of my car, laying her across the back seat. When Jonas follows a moment later, he slips me the card before heading off in another direction.

CHAPTER 18

ELENA

WHEN I WAS A KID, MY MOTHER TRIED TO TREAT ONE OF MY BLACK eyes with a warm compress, swearing that the heat would cause the blood to separate and expand and that I'd be able to go to school the next day without feeling embarrassed about getting into *another* fight.

It didn't work; instead, the heat made my skin swell, blurring my vision in that eye for two whole days. I wore a patch to school, shame flaring in my cheeks as the other girls whispered and pointed, like black eyes in a private, Catholic all-girls school weren't a common occurrence.

All of us had more pent-up rage than our tiny bodies could handle, a result of the life we'd been born into that had us repress everything, and it often manifested at recess in the form of flying fists and discarded boots.

My parents never asked what happened when I came home with a new cut or bruise, but there was always a little glint in Papà's eyes that filled my chest with a gooey warmth. One that silently said he was proud of me for fighting, even if he didn't know the circumstances.

It didn't matter, because as a Ricci, fighting is in my blood. It's expected.

Necessary, even.

So when I pry my eyes open and am met by the harsh, disgruntled glare of my husband, I'm momentarily taken aback. Mainly because I don't know why he's glaring at me.[46]

Blinking the sleep from my eyes, I look around the room, recognizing the black furniture and drapes covering the windows of our bedroom. If not for the dim glow of the bedside lamp, we'd be entrenched in complete darkness.

"Hi," I croak, the one word like fire scraping up my esophagus.

"Drink," Kal deadpans, holding out a Styrofoam cup with a straw. So straight and to the point, completely devoid of any emotion as he meets my gaze.

Not even a hint of relief.

Talk about bad bedside manners. I always heard that Dr. Anderson was efficient yet ice cold when dealing with patients, but until now, I've never seen it in action.

It's…powerful, his tone leaving no room for argument. A stark contrast from the calm yet passionate man I've come to know, though I suppose there's very little room for passion in a medical setting.

I take the drink, sipping gingerly, trying to keep my cool even as the liquid sears the inside of my raw throat.

Closing my lips around the straw, I study him as his gaze drops to my chin. He's wearing the suit I last saw him in, though it's now rumpled and sporting various degrees of stains, and his hair is completely disheveled, sticking up at odd angles as though he's been continually running his hands through it.

I wonder if he feels bad about leaving me.

Probably not, I muse silently, switching focus to the aches decorating my body.

---

46 Angry, caring Doctor Death has entered the building!!!

My eye has a pulse, I realize, timing each painful throb with the beat of my heart, and every one of my muscles feels ragged and torn, like I've just run a marathon without proper training beforehand.

Setting the cup on the bedside table, I stretch my arms above my head, wincing as a sharp sensation lances through me, making my body convulse. Dropping them, I reach up and run a hand through my hair, pausing when I meet tough resistance.

"What…" I start, pulling it past my chin to inspect the issue. A clear substance mats the strands together, and I wrinkle my nose, trying to place the scent.

"You don't want to know," Kal grits out, clasping his hands together.

Mouth gaping, I raise my eyebrows. "What *happened?*"

"Some men found you in that bus station," he says, voice low and dangerous as it lashes against my skin. "I don't know who they are or if they're affiliated with something larger, but I suppose it doesn't really matter. The damage is done."

Nausea rocks through me, bubbling up at the back of my throat. Squeezing my eyes shut, I try to recall the events beyond when I slipped into unconsciousness, but everything comes up hazy. A blurred film with no sound, only the sensation of being trapped.

A feeling I've spent my whole life trying to escape, only to continually find myself wrapped in its arms.

"What did they do to me?"

His jaw ticks, a muscle thumping against his skin. "I don't know. I've been waiting for you to wake up so we could find out."

Tears burn my eyes again, and I drop my hair, ready to brush them from my cheeks when they spill over.

But they never do. I can feel them welling, scorching my eyes with their presence, but none fall. Shame rolls through me like an angry tidal wave, making me tremble violently, and I curl my hands into fists, trying to stave off the fear and confusion.

A memory pushes through to the forefront of my brain: me fighting off the bartender Kal asked to look after me, him shoving his elbow into my face and then stabbing me with a needle.

As I relive that moment, everything else comes rushing back.

I remember running.

Voices.

Kal's insistence on me coming back to him.

And then…*nothing*.

"I don't remember anything past our phone call," I tell him, blinking away the other memories.

His glare hardens, eyes darkening until they're pitch-black. Almost evil. "You passed out before we could hang up. The GHB dose Vincent gave you wasn't strong enough for an immediate effect to take, but I could tell it was hitting you the longer we spoke."

"He roofied me?"

"Yes. I suspect he had something to do with the men who attacked you, but I'm still not sure what." Leaning back in the armchair, Kal grips his knees, squeezing tight; it makes the bandage strapped across his fingers pop off, revealing bloody, broken knuckles.

The color almost matches the shade of the stains on his shirt.

I stare at the mangled flesh, warmth flaring in my stomach and catching in my throat. Pushing to his feet, Kal walks over to the bed, perching on the edge of the mattress, and grips my chin with his good hand.

"Did you kill him?" I ask, leaning into his touch, even though it hurts. With him, pain is a given.

"No," he says softly, turning my head slowly, his eyes roving over every inch of me, assessing for damage. I frown, opening my mouth to protest, and he shakes his head, turning me forward so I'm forced to meet his gaze. "Don't you want to watch?"[47]

I knew it.

Kal breaks the lock on the outbuilding with a pair of bolt cutters, pushing open the barn-style door with one hand, gesturing for me to step inside with the other. I don't know why he doesn't just use a key. Maybe to add a little flair to the otherwise uncomfortable state of our situation.

My bare feet meet loose dirt, and a harsh chill in the air has me wrapping my arms around myself despite the thick robe Marcelline gave me when I left the bedroom.

After a quick, slightly invasive exam ensuring I hadn't been *sexually* assaulted, we headed downstairs. Marcelline handed me some painkillers, and we left through the back door. The second we rounded the mansion and the little shack came into view, vindication washed over me.

"You know," I say as we walk inside now, trying to speak over the nerves pounding between my ears, "this place is not at all discreet. I pegged it my first day here."

Kal glances down at me, switching on a light that illuminates a short hallway. "I'm not trying to keep it a secret."

"You're not?"

"From the people on the island? Hardly."

"Because you own half of it?" We reach the end of the hall, pausing outside a closed door.

"I don't own half the island," he says, brushing a piece of lint from

---

47 I say this a lot I feel like, but I love this line. I just love this couple I guess, LOL. Sue me!

my robe. "I'm an investor in a *lot* of their most profitable businesses and inherited several commercial properties from my grandfather. On top of that, I've logged an unholy number of volunteer hours at the only clinic around and am a very consistent donor to their research programs and other things they need funding for."

"So...you own the *people*." Which, I suppose, would explain why no one interfered at the bar earlier. Who wants to get involved with the devil's business?

"You'd be surprised what people are willing to overlook when their needs are met and then some."

With that, he pushes open the door, revealing a large room with cement walls lined with cabinets and Vincent on display in the middle of it, stripped and strapped to a gurney, gagged with a dirty rag.

Unease ripples along my skin in the form of goose bumps as I take in the dime-sized wounds decorating his stomach and the blood-soaked gauze wrapped around his left hand. A little metal cart with wheels sits next to the gurney, a variety of tools sitting on top, next to a tray collecting fingernails.[48]

Not just the clippings either.

Kal walks to a bucket sink across the room, rinsing his hands beneath the spray. He glances at me as he dries off, an unreadable expression on his face.

I swallow the knot in my throat, moving inside, letting the door swing shut behind me.

Vincent moans, eyes widening when he sees me, and begins thrashing on the table. He strains against his bindings, shaking with such force that the gurney rolls back and forth.

"What're you going to do to him?" I ask, watching as Kal approaches the gurney, picking a vial and needle up off the side table.

---

48 I personally have some serious issues when it comes to finger/toenail stuff, so this makes me physically ill. Apparently, I love writing stuff that grosses me out LOL.

He squints, turning the vial over and sticking the needle in the top, extracting the liquid inside. Replacing the glass bottle, he looks up at me, maintaining eye contact as he plunges the needle into Vincent's neck, pushing down on the applicator.

Vincent's screams grow in volume and intensity, as if they're being forcibly removed from deep inside his chest.

My heartbeat kicks up the longer I watch him writhe in agony, wondering how strong of a dose Kal just gave him. If he'll pass out before he gets to the good stuff.

"We don't have long," Kal says, slipping on a pair of latex gloves. He picks up a circular saw from the floor, plugging it into an outlet nearby.

My lips part. "You're using *that*?"

Glancing at the saw, he nods once. "I don't half-ass these things, Elena. Men who cross me don't get mercy."

It's not as quick as I'm expecting, but the second he brings the blade down to Vincent's chest, I'm stuck staring, enraptured by the way skin and bone split open for him, bowing to Kal's precision and force.

Like souls bending for their reaper.

Heat stirs in my core as I watch him work, filling me with unease that has less to do with the gore in front of me and more to do with the fact that I'm apparently not at all disgusted by it.

I keep waiting for the shock to settle in, for numbness to flood my body as my brain tries to block out the trauma, but it never happens. A small fire burns in my chest as Kal opens Vincent's, and I clench my thighs together in an attempt at relief.

Maybe it's because I grew up a Mafia princess; I'm definitely no stranger to death.

Or maybe it's that the violence comes as a tribute to me, being wielded on my behalf in a way no one has ever done for me before.

When you grow up in the world of *la famiglia*, you're taught to take the abuse. Fight back when you can, but on the whole and especially where men are involved, you're expected to put up with it. That's why I was still going to marry Mateo de Luca.

Why I thought I could handle him.

When Kal finishes several minutes later, brushing his forearm over his face and smearing blood over his cheek, I'm met by an intoxicating, complicated wave of arousal.

Cleaning up quickly, he ushers me from the building back into the main house; I don't even protest, too lost to the storm raging inside me, threatening to drown everything in its downpour.

Guiding me into the en suite bathroom through our bedroom, he positions me in front of the glass shower, reaching inside the stall to turn on the faucet. His hands are caked in Vincent's blood, his clothes ruined, but he doesn't seem to give that a second thought when he reaches for me.

The air grows thick from steam and lust, pressing down heavily the longer we stand in silence.

Pushing the robe from my shoulders, he keeps his eyes trained on mine as he proceeds, like he's afraid that looking away might shatter the ethereal moment pulsing between us.

Slipping his fingers beneath the hem of my dress, the same red number I've had on since yesterday, he starts a slow ascent up my thighs, pausing for a breath when he reaches my hips.

His throat bobs at the same time cool air brushes my lace panties, goose bumps popping up on my thighs. Skimming a thumb over the scar on the inside of the left one, he frowns when I wince, biting the tip of my tongue as pain radiates from the site.

My heart thumps erratically, knocking against my ribs like a caged monster desperate to be set free. Self-consciousness rears its ugly head, making me wonder if he can hear it too; how embarrassing it'd be for my husband to know how he affects me.

Kal continues pulling my dress up, exposing my stomach and pausing once again when he gets to my breasts. There's a dangerous heat in his gaze that has my insides melting, molding, *burning* for his touch on my skin.

He shifts, moving up farther still, thumbs grazing my nipples and making them pucker as a blush crawls over my chest. In one swift motion, he rips the clothing over my head, tossing it to the floor, then takes a step back, nodding at the shower.

"Do you need help?" he asks, tearing his eyes from mine, leaving me charred.

Licking my lips, I shake my head and turn away, stepping beneath the hot spray and letting it wash the grime and dirt off me. I take the bar of soap from one of the built-in shelves and lather myself up, scrubbing any evidence of the last twenty-four hours from where it lurks beneath my skin.

Facing the wall as I run my hands over my body, checking for extra damage, I hear the door creak open. See Kal reach past me for the bottle of pomegranate shampoo I brought from home, watch him pour generously into his palm and then wring his hands together.

Seconds later, I feel them embed in my wet hair, working the shampoo into my scalp, massaging and kneading. As I find a cut on the inside of my thigh, my knees buckle and my hand slips from between my legs, brushing my lace-covered clit as I try to catch my balance.

Tension coils in my belly as the sudden touch mingles with the smoothness of his ministrations, and I bite back a moan just before it escapes my lips.

Frissons of heat crackle and sizzle beneath my skin, making my blood boil in a way that leaves me wanting more.

With him, I always want more.

He moves me so my head is directly under the water, rinsing with careful fingers.

"You did good, little one," he murmurs, his voice so soft, I'm not even sure he actually says anything at first.

My hands come up, bracing against the black tile wall. "What?"

"Fending off Vincent and those men. Not everyone in your shoes may have fared so well. You did good."

My throat constricts with the warmth in his words, tightening as they caress their way over my skin like honey. Labored breaths stumble their way from my chest, and it feels like I'm hyperventilating as I chase that sensation, needing it to incinerate the foul memories.

Turning slowly, I deliberately hold my breath, not sure how he'll react to the change in position. He's close, just outside the spray, leaning halfway in to help.

Furrowing his brows as I tilt my chin up, he opens his mouth to say something, but the words seem to catch on his tongue when my hands flatten against the hard planes of his chest, sliding up around the collar of his shirt.

Exhaling long and slow, I shift forward, launching myself into his arms and yanking him down as, for the third time in our short marriage, I kiss him.

CHAPTER 19

KAL

I'VE KISSED LESS THAN A HANDFUL OF WOMEN IN MY LIFE.

I've fucked far more than that, trying to erase the feel of abuse from where it was imparted onto me at a young age. Even when my thoughts and feelings were still confused and complicated, my body knew what it'd been through.

Kissing itself is just not something I've ever been very fond of.

It's too intimate. Vulnerable. When your lips are locked with someone else's, there are too many variables left open for an attack, and I've spent my life on high alert, always anticipating an assault.

But when Elena plasters herself against me, clasping her arms around my neck and dragging my lips to hers, I let her. It's a much more innocent gesture than the scenarios playing out in my mind—thoughts of pinning her against the wall and spearing her on my cock, as if the trauma from the last twenty-four hours wasn't enough.

I shouldn't want to add my own brand to the mix.

I don't know how, but every time our lips meet, she tastes fucking divine, like a holy scripture written to absolve me of my sins, something sweet and succulent and entirely too pure for her own good.[49]

Then again, a completely pure soul probably wouldn't have looked at me the way she did after I killed Vincent. Probably wouldn't kiss me while I'm still covered in his blood and intestines.

Perhaps she's darker than either of us know.

Her breasts press flush against me, nipples searing into my skin, and I step into the shower, into *her*, since I'm getting soaked anyway. Forcing her backward, I move so she's pinned between the wall and me, reaching down and gripping her hips until she whimpers beneath my touch.

My breath is hot as it fans across her face, the action almost requiring conscious effort on my part as I get swept away in the slippery feel of her mouth warring with mine. She's frantic, on a mission to take what she wants from me, and I groan as she nips at my bottom lip, my resolve crumbling with the slight sting, my cock stiffening behind my zipper.

Sliding my hands from her hips, I move around, cupping the firm globes of her ass cheeks, and shove my pelvis forward, lifting. She hops into the movement without breaking our kiss, and both of us cry out as she wraps her legs around my waist, and I slam her back into the tile wall.

"I want you," she mumbles into my mouth, sighing softly when I bring a hand up, tracing that little pomegranate etched into her skin before flicking my thumb over one pebbled nipple.

The water pours down on us, her head just barely out of the spray, and she blinks up at me with those golden eyes, flushed with *need*.

I know she wants me—that's always been part of the problem.

But right now, with her glorious body on display, breasts heavy as

---

49 I never tire of the way he describes her.

they rise and fall with each of her stuttered breaths, her pussy pulsing where it meets my stomach, water stroking down every inch of skin I want to drag my tongue over, I can't remember anything except the fact that she's *mine*.

Regardless of the situation that led us to this point or the lack of love or reality between us, that caveat remains.

"You're sure?" I can't help but ask, needing verbal reassurance even after I examined her earlier.

She nods. "Make me yours."

Tearing myself from our kiss, I dip my head, pushing her ass up until I can take a nipple into my mouth. I lash my tongue out in quick, short bursts, and her entire body shudders.

"Oh, my little Persephone," I say, slowly drawing circles around the dusky pink peak, keeping eye contact as I lap at her. "You already are."

Despite the purple bruising around one eye, she pinches them both shut when I close my lips over her, sucking and roving until she's a panting, squirming disastrous beauty. Her fingers thread through my wet hair and tug, encouraging more, grinding her hips forward as she begs for it.

Pulling back, I release her tit with a wet pop, shifting to repeat my actions on the other; I fit the flat of my tongue on the underside and trail up, replacing droplets of water with my DNA, engulfing her when I reach the nipple.

My fingers dig into the meat of her ass, definitely leaving bruises, but there isn't a single part of me that cares at the moment.

I want her covered in my marks. Purpled from my fingertips, lips red and raw from my own, pussy swollen and dripping my cum.

Flesh broken and bleeding for *me*.

After tonight, I want there to be no mistaking whose bed she lies in. Whose cock she takes, any way I'll give it. Whose blood sings for hers.

My body temperature spikes at the notion, the urge to brand her as quickly as possible taking over my actions. Scraping my teeth gently over her once, I test her reaction; she arches into it, as if silently begging for more. Taking her nipple between my teeth, I bite down, watching her chin snap up and her eyes pop open.

"*Fuck*," she breathes, fingers tightening in my hair.

"You like that?" I murmur, increasing the pressure.

Her throat contracts and she nods.

Grinning, I nip again, setting her down as I slide lower. I shift, pulling my arms around her thighs so I can drape them over my shoulders, dropping to my knees on the shower floor. Her pale pink panties are soaked through, doing nothing to hide the outline of her swollen sex to my hungry gaze.

I lick my lips, glancing up at her as my hands glide over her thighs, and slip a thumb beneath the fabric on her hips. They're lace, so they tear with little effort, and I toss them aside, taking a moment to admire the silken flesh between my wife's legs.

One of her hands comes up to her breast, kneading softly. With each move I make, she watches, eyes blazing. I inch forward, coasting my lips up the expanse of her thigh, and she never removes her gaze.

I pause, seeing the new cut from whoever accosted her at the bus station: a sliver sliced into her skin by an amateur knifeman, hooking on the end of the *K* I put there.

Elena blinks down at me, emotion welling in her irises, like my hesitance is making every bad memory flood back. Gritting my teeth for a second, I move in and score over the wound, reopening it.

Blood beads in the cut immediately, and I cover the area with my mouth, slowly running my tongue over the coppery fluid.

I swirl back and forth, letting her soak my taste buds, reveling in her lack of resistance. In the look of awe that shines in her gaze.

She shivers, scratching at my scalp as I suck at the site, desperate to memorize the taste, but she never breaks her stare. Like I'm the actor in a play put on for her own viewing pleasure, and she can't bear to look away in case she misses something important.

She wants a show, I'll give her fireworks.[50]

Skimming my way past the wound, I drift inward, smearing her blood and loving the way the crimson complements her creamy skin, like a field of red and white poppies.

My gut clenches tight as I reach her glistening pussy, brushing my nose over her lips and inhaling the tang of her arousal. Wrapping my arms around her thighs, securing her in place against the wall, I slowly dive in, parting her with my tongue and flicking at her clit with the tip.

She cries out at the first lap on her sensitive flesh, legs already shaking against my ears, like she's been waiting for this exact moment.

It spurs me on, sending a shock wave down the length of my spine, and I redouble my efforts, fusing my mouth to her sopping core, licking and swirling and teasing until *I'm* groaning into her, high on her sweet taste.

Before the night we shared together, it'd been years since I'd been with anyone else. After a bit of a chaotic phase, I threw myself into work and tried to establish a relationship with my sister, denying myself the basic carnal pleasures in life.

Until last Christmas, I hadn't known that anything was missing.

Didn't realize that I was practically living without one of my limbs, trying to navigate life as though nothing was wrong.

But it wasn't sex itself that I felt like drowning without.

It was sex with *her.*

I'd been frantic, desperate to sink inside of her after wanting her from afar for so long. She'd been just as frenzied, matching my energy

---

50 We love a good callback!

with each thrust, eager to obey my every command, and our time had been short. A spark that ignited quickly and burned out before it could fully expand.

I have no intentions of that being the case now.

"*Kallum…*" she chokes out, jutting her hips, pushing herself tighter against me. "Please."

Her clit throbs beneath my tongue, and I suckle greedily at the bundle of nerves like she's the antidote to a life of misery. Her gyrations send electricity surging through my veins, and I lap faster, harsher, trying to create more friction against her.

"Please what?" I ask without removing myself from her pussy. The words vibrate against her skin, and she trembles violently, on the precipice of release.

Shifting my efforts, I angle my tongue slightly and switch to counterclockwise motions, slowing the speed until she's tossing her head back and riding the movements.

Pausing when I don't hear any words on her part, I raise an eyebrow, pulling back. She grunts, yanking at my hair, trying to get me to go back in.

"Please *what*, Elena?" I repeat, my voice thick.

She frowns, her eyebrows knitting together. "You already know *what*."

"I want to hear you say it."

Releasing the stress on my scalp, her fingers go slack, and she glares down at me. "You're joking, right?"

"I'd never joke about making you come." My cock is rock-hard just thinking about it.

"Then why don't you just *do* it?"

"I will," I promise, accenting the word with a puff of air on her clit. She jolts, fingers repurposing themselves in my roots, her throat working over a swallow. "As soon as you ask me to."

Gritting her teeth, she flares her nostrils, her brain likely having a difficult time even trying to process what exactly I'm telling her to do. In any other situation, she'd probably already have done it, but as she floats in that exotic limbo state, release just out of reach, obedience is the furthest thing from her mind.

Still, after a beat, she whimpers in frustration. "*Please* make me come, Kallum. I'm *begging*."

Before she's even finished the sentence, I'm shoving back in, spreading her open with my tongue before driving back up and feasting on her clit. It swells under my ministrations, pulsing in time with the beat of my heart, and then finally as I draw figure eights over the hood, she breaks.

Mouth parting on a silent scream, her thighs tighten around my ears. She tugs on my hair until pain lances across my scalp, coming so hard that it seems to steal the breath from her lungs.

I slurp at her juices as they mix with the water from the shower, almost blowing a load myself as she soaks my face.

As wave after wave of pleasure rolls through her, like a tsunami after an underwater earthquake, she curls and arches her back, as if trying to prolong the sensations.

Finally, she slumps against the wall, and I pull back, giving her one last lick along her seam before wiping my mouth on the inside of her thigh and gently removing her legs from their vise grip around my neck.

She pants, breathless, as I stagger to my full height, my dick so hard I can barely see straight. Glancing down at it as it strains against my slacks, she smirks, smoothing a shaky hand over the length.

I jerk into her motion, probably only a pump away from busting. Her naked body almost seems to glow as she steps forward, molding herself to me once again, an invitation in her golden eyes.

"Your turn?" she asks, but I shake my head, reaching down to once again pull her into my arms. Her legs lock around me instantly, and I turn so we're propped against the glass shower door, holding her up with my hips as I fumble with my zipper.

"Won't last in your mouth," I grit out, my hands struggling to keep up with the frantic desire racing through me. I pause, raking my gaze down the wet curves of her body, awestruck by the soft planes, the delicate swells, the fingerprints I've already left behind. "Need to come inside this sweet pussy again."[51]

"*Yes*," she hisses, reaching between us to help get me out.

Her breath catches as my cock bobs free, a pearly bead bubbling at the tip, evidence of how much I want her. She bites her lip, looking at me from beneath hooded lashes, and wraps her fingers around my shaft, the tips not quite touching, dragging them up and down slowly.

I moan, dropping my nose into her hair, inhaling deeply. Her motions send sparks spiraling through me, seizing my balls to the point where they ache with the need for release.

"Christ," I rasp, clutching her thighs until I feel the skin break, "I can't, Elena. You feel too good, and I'm not coming in your hand our first time."

"Technically, this is like the fourth time," she says, speeding up her pumps, tightening her grip until my vision blurs. "Come for me, *Kallum*."

Shaking my head again, I shove her hand away, pushing her ass into the glass behind it.

"I'm fucking going to, little one." Taking my cock in my hand, I pump once, positioning myself at her entrance. "And you're going to wish you hadn't opened that door. By the time I'm done with you, I'll have pumped you so full, it'll be seeping out of your pores. You're going to *sweat* me, and no one else is ever going to touch you again."

---

51 My favorite thing about writing sexy scenes is the tension and the desperation. Ugh. It's just so good.

With my free hand, I grip her chin, forcing eye contact, and then I press inside of her, slowly sheathing the entire length in her wet heat.

She cups the back of my head, pulling me into a hot, open-mouthed kiss, and we moan together as our bodies join, legitimizing our marriage and solidifying my obsession once and for all.

CHAPTER 20

ELENA

I FEEL FULL.

It's the only thought flourishing in my brain as Kal impales me on his cock, the tip practically tickling my womb as he pushes in to the hilt. Arousal clogs in my throat, blossoming in my chest like a flower after an arduous night; one by one, each petal unfolds until the bud stretches fully, ready to soak in the sunlight.

He moves slowly, *achingly* so, our mouths tangling in a kiss I feel in my toes. Bracing me with the tops of his thighs, Kal claws at my butt cheeks, using them to pull me up and down, as if trying to ease me into the motion.

Sure, it's been weeks since I last had him inside me, but I don't need a warm-up. Don't *want* one. My pussy convulses with each thrust in, trying to clamp down and keep him in place, my body racing toward another release when he hits that sweet spot.

But then he's retreating, pulling out just to shove back in, and the lack of immediate fulfillment has me digging my fingernails into his neck, trying to get closer.

Extracting his mouth from mine, he huffs out a shaky breath, glancing between us, watching with glazed eyes where he disappears into me.[52]

Droplets from the shower rain down his skin, clinging to the wet strands of his inky hair and soaking his clothes. Though he doesn't seem to mind the latter, focusing instead on the nakedness in front of him.

The lust flushing his face makes my stomach twist deliciously, but it still isn't quite enough.

"*Kallum*," I cry, losing track of the number of times I've said his name at this point. He cants his hips forward, sealing our skin together, and I flutter around him, distraught.

His eyes flash with something sinister as he looks up at me, cocking a brow.

"Something the matter?" he asks, continuing his sensual assault.

There's still a bead of my blood collected at the corner of his mouth, and I lean up, licking it off with the tip of my tongue. I revel in the metallic flavor, my body lighting up like the Fourth of July when I recall the way it felt to have him draw it from me.[53]

The slight of pain, drowned out by the crazed glint in his dark gaze as he sucked and laved, as if it was the juice of a pomegranate and *he* was starved in the Underworld.

Capturing his bottom lip between my teeth, I tug sharply, loving how the gesture causes him to ram harder into me. I gasp, trying to memorize the feeling of having him fully seated inside me, and then he pulls back, *tsk*ing.

"What is it? Is my cock not enough for my slutty little wife?" He punctuates each word with a sharp jab of his hips, his tip stabbing against my G-spot, making me dizzy.

"More," I croak, shifting my hips, trying to guide the movements myself.

---

52 They're just so horny for each other, it makes me happy.

53 Do not try exactly what they're doing at home (unless you research it properly first)!!

He pinches my ass, landing the flat of one palm against one cheek. "I'm trying to go slow."

"I don't *need* slow," I say.

Chuckling darkly, he pulls out until he's just barely inside me, my pussy clenching around air. "I wasn't doing it for you, little one."

Kal pistons his hips, fucking me so hard all of a sudden that the glass door rattles on its hinges. My palms slap against the material, slipping with the force of each brutal thrust. Tension coils tight in my stomach, threatening to unravel at any moment.

"Good little wives need good fuckings," Kal says, pressing his lips to my temple. "And I've been neglecting you, haven't I?"

"God, *yes*," I squeal, my voice low and raspy like it's been raked over coals and burned to a crisp. My head knocks against the door as he fucks me, and I wrap my arms around his neck to keep from falling. "*Yes*, Jesus, *please*. Right there."

"No saviors here," he says, teeth grazing my forehead. "Just me, your husband, dragging you to hell with him."

If this is hell, lock me up and throw away the key.

The tension in my core begins to expand, like a fireball being blown outward, incinerating everything in its path. I pulse around him, clutching the start of an orgasm, trying to pull it over me but unable to make it work.

"I'm…almost there," I whimper, not even caring about how desperate I sound at this point.

I am desperate. Miserable, anguished, and wretched for every second not spent with this man inside of me, filling me with his darkness, not even stopping to ask questions about my own.

"Fuck, me too," he says, increasing the strength of each thrust, like he's trying to break me wide-open. "You feel fucking incredible."

His hand comes up, collaring my throat with his long fingers, and then he's squeezing, stealing the air from my lungs the way he has before.

Only the squeezing doesn't stop where it once did; pressure bears down on the sides of my neck, my pulse skittering as it becomes almost impossible to breathe. My eyes meet his, wide and uncertain, but the satisfaction ripe in his makes my blood sing.

It's a strange sensation, willingly having your oxygen taken away, but the suffocating feeling seems to culminate into something bigger, something *better*, pleasure mixing with fear.

"That's it," he croons, making me quiver with delight. "Take my cock, little one. Just like that." When he pushes his hips flush with mine, a low groan ripping from his throat, my vision darkens at the corners and I come undone, my chest tight as my brain floats on.

I spasm around him, screaming as release floods through me, my inner walls coaxing and milking him dry. A satisfied grunt huffs out as he plasters us against the glass door, his hand falling from my throat to bracket my rib cage.

"Jesus Christ." His breaths are harsh against my wet hair, and with his free hand, he reaches behind him, shutting off the faucet.

For several minutes, neither one of us moves. We don't speak, cocooned in the safety of silence, unwilling to be the first to shatter it.

A chill snakes up my arms, making me shiver, and he smirks, finally pulling out of me. I wince at the sudden loss, trying not to pay much attention to the chasm his absence leaves inside me, wondering how similar this will be to the last time we had sex.

If he'll ditch me before I can even process what happened.

"Are you okay?" he asks, setting me on my feet and taking a step back. His gaze sweeps over me, doctor mode in full effect as he assesses my body for signs of distress. A finger brushes the scar on my thigh, and he frowns, a dark look clouding his features. "I shouldn't have done that."

I blink, glancing down at where he touches me, wiping some of the smeared blood from my skin. "I liked it."

One brow arches, and he swallows. "Yeah?"

It's a single syllable, spoken on the tail end of an exhale and loaded with insecurity. I can *feel* it, the uncertainty, and it catches me off guard for a moment to think a man as deadly and powerful as Kal might ever feel vulnerable.

Nodding, I cover his hand with my own, bringing it up to where I can feel him leaking from between my thighs. "I like anything you do to me," I whisper, trying to level the playing field with my admission, even though it's physically painful for me to indulge.

Still, if Kal Anderson asked me to tear my bleeding heart out of my chest and serve it to him on a silver platter, I'd do it, no questions asked. I'd probably ask him to oversee the operation, to make sure I was doing it correctly.

I just don't think he returns the sentiment.

"You're not on birth control," he deadpans. It's not a question but a statement, and the authority with which he says it gives me pause.

"No," I say, pushing a strand of hair from my shoulder. "Papà never even let me *think* about sex, let alone explore methods of preventing complications from it."

He doesn't say anything for several beats, during which my heart rate kicks up, pounding in my ears. I feel faint, exhausted, and, for some reason, scorned.

"I'll set up an appointment with a friend of mine, and we'll get you on it."

He steps past me, pushing open the door and walking across the room to the sinks, pulling a white towel from a wall-mounted hook. His clothes drip onto the floor as he returns, holding the towel out for me, and I step into it slowly, processing his words.

"Do I get a say in whether I go on it?"

Wrapping the towel around me, he tucks the corner beneath my armpit, turning me to face him. "I'm not so old that I can't recognize bodily autonomy," he says, reaching up to cup my jaw. "It's your body. I just thought it would be easier."

I glance at the dip in his throat, studying it as I mull his words over in my brain. "If I asked you to wear condoms, you would?"

Kal's face screws up. "Of course. I'd be missing out on the *glorious* sight of my cum dripping from your sweet little pussy, but I'm not a monster. As legitimate as this marriage is, I'd be insane to bring children into the mix."

Something pinches in my chest, but I ignore it, nodding instead. "Okay. I'd...be willing to try, I think."

"If it doesn't work, we'll figure something else out." He cradles both my cheeks in his hands, bending down to press a featherlight kiss on my lips; the act is far more gentle than I'd ever have imagined him capable of being, and it stirs something wanton in my belly.

Guiding me over to the sink, we quickly brush our teeth, and I can't keep from staring at him in the mirror, knowing the domesticity I'm being granted is only the result of my attack and nothing more.

It doesn't mean anything, Elena.

Still, when I climb into bed moments later, exhaustion finally settling over me, I pull the blankets to my chin and roll on my side. I watch as he grabs pajamas from his dresser and takes them back into the bathroom, returning minutes later completely changed.

He towel dries his hair, then tosses the terry cloth into a nearby hamper, walking to my side of the bed with a plastic first aid kit in hand. Flipping the top open, he carefully plucks out a packet of anti-bacterial ointment and a wide Band-Aid.

"Ooh," I say, wiggling my eyebrows as my body fights sleep. "Are we going to play doctor?"

Ignoring me, he slips his hand beneath the covers, finding the wound on my thigh and tearing the ointment packet open with his teeth. Squirting a pea-size amount onto his fingertip, he joins the other hand, slathering the cool gel over the cut.

I suck in a breath through my teeth and watch his jaw clench tight.

Silently, he peels the plastic apart, pulling the Band-Aid free, then secures it over the cut, his thumb tracing the outline of the K.

Setting the first aid kit on the nightstand, Kal pushes to his feet and rounds the bed, pulling back the covers so he can clamber beneath them.

My breathing hitches, the intimacy of his proximity making me shiver, heart pounding like a siren in my chest.

He doesn't say anything else though, just picks up a leather-bound copy of Witter Bynner's complete works and settles in.

I roll over again, propping my cheek on my pillow, studying him as he slides on a pair of black-framed glasses and begins to read, eyes scanning the page in a slow, hypnotic fashion.

Absorbing the clean slope of his sharp jaw and the tiny dimple in his cheek that clefts when he's deep in concentration, I do my best to commit it all to memory in case this has been a fluke, and I wake up tomorrow with him ignoring me all over again.

The dread swirling around in my stomach promises it is.

Nothing good can last.

For some reason, that's the fear that keeps me from falling into an immediate slumber. Not the fact that someone is *clearly* coming after me, just like Kal said they would, or that my world back in Boston is probably crumbling to the ground.

But the notion that whatever stone was turned tonight, be it through trauma or the natural progression of surrender, is fleeting.

That I'm stuck in a loveless marriage, a prison, like I always feared I would be.

"How come I haven't seen you naked?" I blurt, trying to erase the anxiety with conversation.

Kal's eyebrows raise above his glasses, and he glances at me. "I can assure you, it's just as big when you see the full picture."

Heat flares in my cheeks as I think about the size of his dick, and I shift my thighs absently, scooting closer without fully meaning to. "No, I just… You've seen me naked. I'm naked now, in fact."

"No complaints here."

One of his hands comes down, sliding over my waist, and when I open my mouth to say more, he yanks me toward him, pulling me flush with his side.

My clit throbs where it touches him, already jonesing for another hit, but it's clear Kal's using the premise of sex to distract me, so I give up asking, trying to find contentment in what I *do* know about him.

Right now, I know he's willing to do anything it takes to protect me, and despite our situation and everything that complicates it, that feels like a major feat.

It takes the sting out of the knowledge that he has more blood on his hands than just my own.

I lie against him for a while, staring at the wall across from me, listening while he occasionally turns a page, the even rhythm of his breathing lulling me into slumber.

"*You were spring, and I the edge of a cliff, and a shining waterfall rushed over me,*" he recites softly, the line barely registering in my brain before sleep welcomes me once again.

CHAPTER 21

KAL

"YOU LOOK ODDLY WELL RESTED."

Taking a bite of my croissant, I look across my desk at Jonas, cocking an eyebrow. "*Oddly?*"

Scrubbing a hand over his beard, he shrugs, shuffling through the papers in front of him. "In all the years I've known you, I've never seen you look like anything less than a zombie. Just a bit interesting, that's all."

"Interesting," I repeat, swallowing the last bite of pastry. "That's a fancy word for boring."

"Ah, deflection. So it *does* have something to do with a certain little lass." He leans back in his chair, folding his hands together. "Did you finally consummate your marriage?"

"I'm not talking about that with you."

"Consider it—what's that American football term? Running interference?" He pulls a packet from the bottom of his stack of papers; it's the contract I signed years ago, just before my grandfather's passing, giving me access to a multimillion-dollar trust fund the old bastard had set up in my name.

He'd already signed over ownership rights to a half dozen

businesses on Aplana as well as stocks and shareholdings in a variety of different companies, but I suppose he never quit trying to atone for only finding out about me when it was too late to save my soul.

One stipulation for the trust was that I had to be at least twenty-five before the funds became available to me. And I had to be *clean*, which meant extracting myself from the life of crime I'd fallen into.

A much more difficult feat than outsiders seem to realize.

Once you're part of the Mafia, that's *it*. They don't let their people go without a fight. Frankly, when I let Rafe know months ago about me wanting to step down, I'd expected more resistance than I got.

I've been waiting for the other shoe to drop with that one.

Another condition was that I had to be *married*, and it *had* to be legitimate.

Of course, having amassed my own wealth over the years, I had no interest in bowing to the terms just for my paternal grandfather's guilt money.

But then I tried reconnecting with my sister. She and our two brothers had been strategically left out of the will, the inheritance, and the trust fund.

In fact, they were never even supposed to see a penny from it, which is why I'd been writing Violet's checks from my own savings, intending to transfer the trust money into an offshore account and leave the personal bank information with her.

But she kept rejecting my checks, and as the expiration date to access the trust funds drew nearer, I knew drastic measures needed to be taken.

I knew Miles, my grandfather's estate attorney, would eventually come by for the proof. I had just put it on the back burner recently, with all the other things going on in my life taking precedence.

"No one would use a football term to describe meddling," I say, brushing crumbs from my desk into a trash can and taking the contract from him. I flip through the neatly printed pages, noting the scribble of my signature and the neat cursive of my grandfather's at the bottom of each page.

"In any case, your expiration date is pretty soon. How are you planning on proving to Miles that you're serious about Elena?"

Tapping my finger on the page above the marriage clause, I exhale. Under normal circumstances, the existence of a wedding at all would prove my loyalty, but in a world where marriages are forged all the time for this exact reason, I suppose I can't begrudge my grandfather for wanting to secure his legacy.

And it's not like my marriage is real where it matters—in our souls.

Our hearts.

Just on paper, and in our bed.[54]

Scrubbing a hand down the side of my face, I sigh. "Well, I'm certainly not giving them bloody virginal bedsheets."

"She wouldn't have them now anyway."

I narrow my eyes at him, and he shifts in his seat, toying with the collar of his leather jacket.

"Birth control," I say finally, remembering the conversation I had with Elena after fucking her silly in the shower.

Jonas cocks an eyebrow. "Please tell me you're using it."

I make a face, sitting forward to pull up a browser on my computer. "I'm making her an appointment with Dr. Martin, and she'll be going on it. I'll pass the prescription along to Miles."

"You think that'll satisfy him? She could technically be going on it for any reason. And doesn't he want an heir? How does that help you?"

"There's no real time constraint on the heir addendum. Birth control suggests that we're sexually active, so when she stops having

---

54 Keep telling yourself that, bud.

the script filled, it'll be evidence that we're trying to get pregnant." Typing in the online scheduler, I add a note of identity to my request, then hit submit. "It'll do."

It has to.

After we've looked over prospective replacements for the three Flaming Chariot employees we lost and set up an intelligence meeting with the Ivers International team, Jonas leaves the office, and my phone nearly vibrates off the desk.

A tabletop pendulum sits on the wooden filing cabinet in the corner of the room, swinging side to side, immediately drawing my negative attention as I pick the phone up.

Irritation floods my being as I scan the screen, hitting accept before I can talk myself out of it.

"Carmen," I say, expecting her shrill voice to fill the speaker, but I'm met with a low timbre instead.

"Anderson." Rafe's voice is clipped, unlike I've ever heard from him before. "Thought I would have to chase you down in order to speak to you, but it appears you're just as eager to chat with my wife as you've ever been."

"Believe me," I say, leaning against my desk, crossing one loafer over the other, "I'm never eager to do anything regarding that she-devil."

He makes a grunting sound. "In any case, I didn't call to talk about Carmen."

Of course he didn't, because any conversation about her inevitably ends in admitting defeat where she's concerned. She's a lost cause, drifting out to sea while everyone chooses to look on.

"How's my daughter?"

A laugh tickles the back of my throat, but I swallow over it, aware that I need to navigate whatever it is he's about to say carefully. "You mean after you deliberately had her attacked? She's as well as can be expected."

It's on the tip of my tongue to mention the tight warmth I've buried myself in twice now since yesterday, but I bite down on the urge, not wanting to fan the flames just yet.

"I have no idea what you're talking about," Rafe replies, and I can imagine him fingering the edge of his massive thumb ring, staring down at the same insignia that was etched into the card left at the bus station. "It's just been a while since she answered her mother's texts, and we were starting to get worried."

"Maybe don't spread lies about the way her marriage started, and she'd be more inclined to speak to you."

"What were the lies exactly, Kal?" He pauses as if waiting for my answer but barrels on before I can say anything. "Did you not murder her fiancé while he dressed for his wedding? Force me to bear witness to the ceremony where you stole my little girl's hand after already stealing her virtue?"

"I *forced* you to do nothing. I presented the situation and gave you the opportunity to make a decision. You chose safety over the contract she had with those media vultures."

He sniffles, and I blink into the empty office. *Is he crying?* "The fact of the matter is, Dr. Anderson, that we want our Elena brought home. I don't care what we have to do to get her back, but please, stop keeping her captive. She's my...*bambina*."

His voice breaks on the last two words, the Italian thrown in dramatically, and a thought snaps into place in my brain, pushing me into a standing position as anger grows sour in my gut.

"What are you *doing*, Rafe?" I ask slowly, glaring at the only framed picture I own; it's one of a sixteen-year-old me, sandwiched between Rafe and Carmen during their anniversary party. Carmen's arm is wrapped tight around my waist, keeping me close to her side where I'd stay for years, like an idiot.

I don't know why I still have the photo.

In it, Rafe stares on, oblivious. The way she needed him to be.

And then one day, he wasn't.

Things were never quite the same.

Which I suspect is why he's being so cagey now—this has all the makings of a setup, and the idea that he's trying to lure me into some kind of trap has my blood boiling.

Especially since he hasn't asked me to do a single job for him since I initiated our little arrangement, and while I'd begun to think that meant he was accepting my retirement, now I'm realizing that maybe his plan all along was to take me out in a more creative fashion.

Beside the picture frame, the pendulum sculpture keeps ticking, making the muscle beneath my eye twitch with each swing.

After a moment, Rafe clears his throat, and when he speaks again, the sadness is completely absent. "I want money. You fucked me over in this Bollente deal, and I had to square off a nice portion of Ricci business just to get out of it."

"I wasn't the one who told you to sell your daughter," I say. "Or who asked her to come to my bed."

"Just like you never asked Carmen, right?" he spits, growing more agitated with every passing second.

I never went to Carmen, I want to say. *It was always her coming to me.*

But I don't.

Sucking in a deep breath, I steel myself against the rage building like water behind a levee, threatening to drown me in its ferocity. I focus on the smooth swing of the pendulum, blocking out everything until all I can hear is the ticking.

Tick.

Tick.

Tick.

An itch crawls deep beneath the surface of my skin, and I round my desk as Rafe drones on, pulling the pistol out from the drawer.

Lining it up, nerves eating at the steadiness in my grip, I unlock the safety and pull the trigger, watching as the bullet sparks across the room.

It passes clean through the picture frame, fracturing the glass in an explosive connection, and lodges in the wall behind it. Shards fly off the frame, the force knocking the pendulum off balance, and I watch as it crashes to the floor, one arm breaking off, finally falling silent.

"Do you hear me, Anderson?" Rafe asks. "You have two choices: money or your sworn fucking loyalty in the form of services. Otherwise, you're dead."

Pulling the phone from my ear, I tuck my gun back inside its drawer and hang up.

I find Elena in the backyard a little later, hauling sacks of soil out of a cardboard box and dragging them over the grass to where she's set up a makeshift workspace against the hedges.

Marcelline stands a few yards over, steeping a tea bag in a blue ceramic mug while she watches.

Brushing a sweaty piece of hair from her face, Elena turns to survey our yard, putting her hands on her hips. The lavender dress she has on perfectly outlines the heavy swell of her ass, and as I approach her, I'm flooded with the memory of grasping it while pulling her onto my cock.

For a moment, I can forget about the other things going on and lose myself in her presence. She's like a cozy spring afternoon, recent blossoms and fresh sea air carried across a breeze, and it wraps around me, blotting out the ugly reality of everything else.

I've never been the kind of man to run from adversity, but as I stand there staring at the woman before me, the one I've dragged into my mess, I find myself wishing I could. Wishing this could be the life someone like Elena deserves.

"Don't be mad," she says before I've even reached her, spinning to face me. There's a look of elation cast over her delicate features, a softness erasing deep-set rigidity. An afterglow I can only explain as a residual effect of mind-blowing sex.

"Why would I be mad?" I ask, reaching out to frame her cheek with my palm. My thumb grazes the underside of the bruise around her eye, noting that the swelling and purpling has gone down significantly since last night.

"I'm about to fuck up your yard," she says, pointing to the bags of soil. "And I have no clue what I'm doing. Marcelline's supposed to be reading the Wikipedia page, but..."

She rolls her eyes around to look at my housekeeper, who shrugs, sipping her tea. "But gardening is not part of my job description."

Elena huffs. "Neither was helping Kal kidnap me, was it?"[55]

My insides churn at her flippant use of the word, and I wonder what all her sisters told her about what the news says back home. If it changes the way she views all of this.

Clearing my throat, I drop my hand and stuff it inside my jacket pocket. "I've got a few meetings keeping me busy the next few days, but I could probably help you this weekend."

"Really?" Her eyebrows raise, and she nods at the rectangle she has marked off with driftwood. "Do you know anything about planting flowers?"

"I assisted on a successful triple bypass during my residency and have stitched up more open wounds than you'll likely ever see in your lifetime. I'm sure I can handle plants."

Leaving the two of them outside, I return to the Asphodel and

---

55 LOL. She has a point.

hunker down in the library, trying to rid myself of the strange feeling curdling in my stomach. It's not quite painful—almost a nauseating wave that crashes against the shore over and over without ever fully receding.

Unscrewing a bottle of fifty-year-old scotch, I pour three fingers into a tumbler, pick up the first book my hand lands on, and flop down in one of the two leather armchairs in front of the dormant fireplace.

Opening the book, I balance it on my knee, my eyes glued to the page without actually reading. My heart beats rapidly, repulsed by the way my stomach burns with awareness, trying to ignore the fact that the Riccis once again played me.

Because that's what all of this boils down to; if not for the friendly guidance and promise of luxury Rafael gave when we met, my entire life would likely be different.

I might have a shot at a relationship with my sister.

Might be married for *love* and not because I needed a queen on my side of the board.[56]

Might still have the medical career my mother wanted for me without ever feeling like I needed to give it up to make up for all the lives I've ended.

Minutes later, the library door creaks open, Elena slipping inside. She shuts us in together, tiptoeing over to stand directly in front of me.

"Are you okay? You seemed…tense outside." She glances at the spine of my book, cringing. "Uh-oh, Dorian Gray? I know you have some mileage on you, but honestly, thirty-two is young nowadays. The oldest man in the world is one hundred and fifteen, you know? You still have time."[57]

---

56 I think this is a super important section that showcases some of Kal's own trauma, which subconsciously drives a lot of his choices and thoughts.

57 This was written in 2021, so I have no clue how old the oldest person in the world is now. But the sentiment remains!

Shutting the book with a snap, I toss it onto the end table and lash out with one hand, grabbing her wrist and pulling her down into the chair with me. She squeals, adjusting so she's straddling me on her knees, pussy sitting pretty on top of my dick.

It hardens beneath her immediately, ready for its next fill.

"Is the oldest man in the world really that old?" I ask, skimming my nose along her jawline.

Shivering, she shrugs, slipping her arms around my neck and grinding down on me. "I have no clue, but it distracted you from your funk, right?"

Pulling back just enough to stare deep into her eyes, I exhale, shaking my head slightly. "*You* distracted me. You seem to have a natural talent for that."

"Oh." Grinning, Elena leans in, running the tip of her tongue over the shell of my ear, then nipping at the lobe. "Well, let me make it up to you."

Her hand retreats from my neck, sliding down my chest before diving into the waistband of my pants; she crooks her elbow, wrapping her fingers as tight around my growing erection as she can, smoothing the pad of her thumb over the glossy tip.

Leaning my head back, I let out a long breath, my stress morphing into impending release as blood rushes south.

"Someone's ready for me," she whispers, stroking my heated flesh. Reaching down, she pops open the fly, scrambling to pull me out, and lifts herself up.

"Always," I grit, pushing her dress to the tops of her thighs, fisting the material so it stays in place. I let out a throaty growl when her pussy bares itself to me, glistening like a dew-soaked rose petal. "Jesus, little one. Do you ever wear panties?"

She grins, taking me in hand and lining us up. "Nope, and now I definitely never will."

Sinking slowly, she takes me inch by inch until her ass rests on the tops of my thighs. Gasping sharply as I bottom out, she swallows, her hand flying up to tangle in my hair.

Rotating her hips, she glides up and down cautiously, like she isn't quite sure what to do, and it hits me in the gut again that she's completely inexperienced, giving me a whole other set of issues to worry about.

But it's so hard to care when she feels like heaven on fucking earth. Like a goddess coming down just to save my wretched soul from damnation.

"I'm sorry," she murmurs, a faint blush creeping over her pretty cheeks.

"Christ, what are you apologizing for?" I can barely edge the words out, her pussy gripping me so tight I see stars. My hands clamp down on her hips, hopping on for the ride.

"I'm... This is all new to me, and I don't want to mess it up."

"You can't," I say, biting my lip as she starts to slam down harder, apparently finding that spot that makes her body sing. "Keep that up, and I'm going to blow in you before I'm ready."

"Oh, shit," she mewls, arching her back, her inner walls fluttering. "You say that...like it's supposed to be a bad thing, but it sounds...really good to me."

"My slutty little wife likes making me lose control, hm?"

Nodding, her hand finds one of mine, bringing it up and locking it around the column of her throat, the counterclockwise swirl of her hips drawing electricity to my balls. They seize up, my orgasm barreling through me, and I squeeze her neck at the same time her pussy spasms, unable to stave off any longer.

Splotches of white flash across my vision as I release as deep inside her as I can get, the pulse of her pussy sucking me dry. She drops her head to my neck, sinking her teeth into the skin on a groan, biting down until she breaks through the barrier.

Lapping her tongue along my neck, she pulls back, sealing her lips to mine in a kiss that brings me to the brink of salvation before stealing it away. I taste copper on the back of her teeth and almost come again without any extra stimulation.

Later, when she falls limp against me, cradling her head on my chest while she waits for the feeling to return to her legs, I feel that familiar sense of foreboding from before, although now it has an entirely new target.

CHAPTER 22

ELENA

"I'M TELLING YOU, THE WOMAN IS LOSING HER MIND."

Rolling my eyes, I scan the tilled soil outside, huffing when, once again, I see no significant growth in the garden I planted last month. Stems are beginning to sprout, peeking up above the soil, but no flowers have flourished. Not even the daylilies, despite supposedly having a short blooming period.

Part of me is starting to wonder if maybe the air of death that surrounds the house is keeping the flowers underground, where they're safe.

If letting Kal help weed and prepare the soil didn't suck the life from the area.[58]

I glare at the window planter above the kitchen sink, where the mint Marcelline started sprawls out of its container, thriving in the sunlight provided.

Through the speaker on my phone, Ariana rambles on about how badly Mamma misses me.

---

58 This was one Elena and Persephone parallel I wanted to include but also subvert a bit. The idea of Elena being this modern Persephone straddling the line between life and death, but she is really bad at growing plants/keeping them alive.

"I mean, she sits on your balcony every single night, staring out like you're dead or something."

Sadness weasels its way into my soul, the idea of being the source of my parents' heartache not something I like to entertain. Even if their own motives aren't necessarily always the most selfless, my lot in life has been to not add to the unhappiness rife in our world.

It's something I plagued myself with, even as a child, going to great lengths to be what my parents wanted. The perfect little Mafia princess, docile and submissive, willing to do anything to make them proud.

Anything for a chance at seeing the glimmer of pride in my father's dark eyes or for my mother not to look at me like a younger, worse version of herself she could live through.

Still, I am where I am, *who* I am, because of them and their choices. The least my mother can do is cut me a little slack, yet she's still trying to make me feel guilty, still trying to control me, when we aren't even sharing the same land.

"In the States, most people who grow up and get married move out of their parents' houses," I tell Ariana, picking at a dead piece of mint, tossing it into the garbage disposal. "In fact, it's a little embarrassing I didn't leave sooner."

"Not that you'd have been allowed to go anywhere," she says, and when I pick up the phone, reloading the video chat, I'm met by her big eyes as she leans into the camera, applying a thin layer of makeup to her water line. "You're lucky Kal got you out when he did."

I raise my eyebrows. "That sounds ominous. What are you not telling me?"

She grins her little lopsided grin, twirling a strand of her chestnut-colored hair around a manicured finger. "Nothing really. Just...things changed a bit when you left."

"Like what?"

"I don't know. Everyone got really tight-lipped. Papà hardly comes out of the study, and when he does, there's this weird look in his eyes, like…"

She trails off, and I grip the edge of the marble counter, waiting for her to continue. "Like *what?*"

"Like he's a dead man walking." Ariana glances at something past the camera, widening her eyes slightly in an annoyed gesture she's done since we were kids. "Anyway…how's married life? Figure out where you're at yet? I know Mamma is still hell-bent on finding you."

Feeling uneasy about the way the last subject cut off so quickly, I decide to ignore it and move on with her; my sisters aren't the kind of people to keep quiet about anything, least of all something that would put them in danger.

At least that's what I tell myself as I head down the hall to the library, ducking inside while Kal's at yet another meeting.

Over the last few weeks, we've certainly gotten a bit closer physically, anyway. The man is a statue made of stone, and each time he fucks me, a little piece of the exterior chisels away. But the fragments are so small, it never feels as if I'm actually making any progress.

He's wound tighter than the crank on an old grandfather clock, and every time we fuck, it's evident he's trying to funnel his frustrations directly into the act.

Not that I'm not enjoying the ride; my body is constantly sore in places I didn't even know existed, my mind swept away each night on a tidal wave of ecstasy. It's just that the ride is more like a roller coaster, and the theme park attendant isn't letting me off.[59]

And the problem is I *want* him to open up to me. Since the night of my attack, I've given up on the quest to keep my attraction a secret and instead embrace it every chance I get.

---

59 God, that would be a nightmare.

Sometimes that's by milling about in his office, perching on the edge of his desk while he goes over real estate contracts and malpractice suits—not his, somehow; instead, he likes to keep up to date on big ones rocking the medical world, *"just in case"*—and slowly parting my legs until he sees what I'm offering and abandons his work to do me instead.

Sometimes it's by prodding him with a million questions, starting with unimportant ones until he's irritated enough to answer what I really want to know.

Like how he never met his father and that it wasn't until after his mother died that he found out he had siblings.

Or how he grew up impoverished, and it was my father's help that dug him out of it.

Whatever the case, I'm working at thawing his icy heart, and each day, my affection for him grows tenfold. Which wouldn't be a problem, except that it's such a stark contrast to how I felt at the start of our union, and it lines up too perfectly with what Mamma said would eventually happen.

"You'll learn to love him," she'd said, and although the context—and husband—were entirely different, I can't help the flare of rebellion that comes at having her be right about this.

I don't tell Ariana any of this, of course. As far as she knows, my relationship with Kal is real and has depth, despite whatever vitriol my parents are trying to spew against us. I assure her they're being dramatic each time she brings up the fact that the entirety of Boston seems to think I was kidnapped, and since she knows how they are about narratives, she usually agrees and moves on.

And technically, I was kidnapped. They're not wrong about that much.

But they don't have the full story either.

"Every time you call, all we do is talk about me," I say now, trying to redirect the conversation so my anxious thoughts cease. "I'm tired of me. What's new with you and Stella?"

"Nothing's ever new with that one," Ari says, snorting. "I have a recital in a few weeks though."

My heart drops to my stomach. "Shit, you do, don't you?"

"Yep." She pops her lips on the last *p*, making me feel like an asshole. "*The Nutcracker*, for our school's Christmas in Spring. Weird time to celebrate Christmas, if you ask me, but I guess it's easier to theme that way."

Guilt pinches in my chest, making me recall all the other recitals I've been to. How I haven't missed one since she got her first leotard. "I'll be there."

Ariana blinks once. Twice. "Don't make promises you can't keep."

I don't know where that attitude is coming from and can't help wondering what's going on back home that I'm not being told about. And even though I make the same vow again, meaning it wholeheartedly, it isn't until later that I realize how difficult coming through might actually be.

Marcelline has a driver take me to the Flaming Chariot a little while after my phone call with Ariana ends, us hanging up as soon as Mamma enters the room and bursts into tears at the sight of my face.

When I climb out of the town car, nodding to the driver that he can leave without me, I stand on the curb of the bar for a moment, holding my purse tight to my side as the memory of the last time I was here resurfaces.

The needle puncturing my skin, the way Vincent looked at me like I was somehow beneath him, the assault that came after.

My throat swells, blocking air as I relive the memories. Goose bumps rise on my arms, sending a shiver grating down my spine.

A normal person would probably have been disturbed by Kal's form of solving the problem, but in truth, I haven't lost even a wink of sleep over it. That could have something to do with the fact that we've been partaking in rigorous activities every day ever since, and maybe I'm too exhausted to really think about it, but still.

I like the finality of how he took care of it.

Until now, I've pushed it to the recesses of my brain, but being back at the bar, staring down the face of my nightmares, I'm overcome with the urge to run.

Soft laughter off to my side draws my attention temporarily from the building, and I turn my head slowly, apprehension threading through each of my muscles, drawing them tight. A girl with black hair split into two French braids stands a few feet away, mimicking my exact stance, arms crossed over her chest as she stares at the bar.

Scrunching my nose, I look away from her, trying to calm the nerves rushing through my veins like a raging rapid.

How long after a traumatic event do you have to wait before you can face your demons?

"Sixteen."

Eyes widening, I glance back over at the girl standing beside me. She tugs on the hem of a sheer black blouse, shaking her head, and I panic for the briefest second, wondering if I've spoken out loud.

Casting me a sidelong look, she drops her hands. "I've come by this place sixteen times in the last couple of weeks, but I can never bring myself to actually go in."

Relief washes over me, and I let out a quick breath, scanning her more thoroughly; she's dressed in all black, her jeans rolled to the ankle, a resin sunflower pendant draped around her neck, providing the only source of color.

Even her eyes, warm but dark and guarded, reflect the morbidity of her outfit choice, and I can practically hear Ariana's judgment of the bland fashion.

"People who wear black all the time are not normal," my sister would

say. *"Either they worship Satan or hate themselves. There are too many colors available on this green earth to sit and choose one that lacks any at all."*

And Mamma always wonders why she can't keep a decent boyfriend.

Pairing the outfit with the girl's pale skin and slender frame, she could easily pass for a vampire. Maybe *that's* why she can't go in.[60]

"Are you afraid of what's inside?" I ask finally, once the silence between us turns awkward.

She purses her lips. "Something like that."

More silence passes between us, and I tuck my hair behind my ears, shrugging. "We could go in together. I know the owner. I don't think he'd let anything happen while he's inside."

Not again anyway.

Kal doesn't strike me as the kind of person to make the same mistake twice.

The girl tilts her head to the side, giving me a once-over. I shuffle my feet together, uncomfortable with her perusal, currently regretting my decision not to wear underwear beneath this navy shift dress. I can feel *everything*, including the weight of her stare.

"You know Kal?"

I hold my left hand up, wiggling the diamond there so it glitters in the sunlight, letting the slight pang of jealousy that she knows his name slice through my chest.

Better I embrace it, I suppose, than suppress it.

Puffing her cheeks, she lets out a low whistle, rocking back on her heels. "Oh, so you *know* him know him. You must be Elena."

Pushing her hand between us, she gives a half smile, waiting. I blink at her palm, taking it tentatively, pumping twice like Papà taught me.

---

60 THE IRONY.

When I don't say anything further, she lets go and presses her lips together. "I'm Violet, by the way."

"Ah," I say, roving my eyes over her features again, trying to figure out if I've met her somehow and forgotten. In truth, I haven't done much exploring of Aplana, except for visiting the farmers market a couple of times with Kal and picking up muffins from a bakery on the north end with Marcelline.

Since my last foray out in public didn't end so well, I've sort of holed up at home, resigning myself to a hermit's life the way I probably would've ended up doing as Mrs. De Luca anyway. At least as Kal's bride, I'm not being forced to attend or host social events; in fact, most of the time, he almost discourages social interaction entirely, content to lock himself in the Asphodel and fuck his time away.

He's not keeping me from making friends, but I almost like that he seems to want to spend all his time wrapped up in me, so I don't do anything to deter that.

"You have no idea who I am, do you?" she says, letting out another little laugh, though this time there's a hint of irritation lacing it.

"I'm sorry," I rush out. "I'm new to the island, and—"

Holding up a palm, she shakes her head, and I notice a green tint spread over her thumb; it's etched into her fingerprints, almost like the color belongs beneath her skin.

"Honestly, it's fine. I don't tell anyone about him. Why should he tell them about me?"

My eyebrows scrunch together in confusion, jealousy burning the back of my throat, even though I'm not exactly sure why. "How do you know him?"

She looks at me silently for several minutes, so long the jealousy drifts elsewhere, lighting my nerve endings on fire, and part of me wants to give in and lash out accordingly. But I tamp down the reaction, channeling the more evolved thoughts of Kal having a past that doesn't involve me.

Much of it happened before anything could've transpired between us anyway, regardless of the longevity of my own feelings. They certainly have never been reciprocated, and now that they're more complicated than ever, I can't tell where he stands on the issues at all.

Probably at the same place on the map that he's always been at, using me just like he said in the very beginning.

But if this is what getting used by Hades feels like, I'll prolong my stay in the Underworld.

Violet licks her lips, playing with the end of one braid as a couple passes by holding hands and talking about visiting the beach. She gets a strange look in those dark eyes, something forlorn and familiar, so I ask my question again, trying to bring her back to the matter at hand.

"How do you know Kal?"

Shifting her eyes toward me, she smiles sadly. "I don't."

CHAPTER 23

KAL

THE DOOR TO JONAS'S OFFICE FLINGS OPEN SUDDENLY, SLAMMING into the wall so hard the knob obliterates the plaster. Elena stands there, fury bleeding so clearly from her that it makes those golden irises glow, brightening them against the backdrop of the bar behind her.

"If you're fucking another girl, I want to know right now."

Leaning back in my chair, I fold my hands over my lap, taking her in. Her hair spills down her back in wind-swept waves, while the little blue dress she has on does absolutely nothing to hide her figure from me.

Curves I've grown addicted to, my drug of choice.

To my right, Jonas pushes back from his desk, scooping the file with the bouncer applications into their folder, though he doesn't make any move to leave the room.

I *should* be surprised to see her here, but I'm not. Aside from the fact that after her attack, I had her phone outfitted so I'd be able to track her location at all times, there are just certain things you can't change about a person.

Once Elena gets a taste of freedom, she won't be recaged without a fight.

Frankly, I'm surprised it's taken this long for her to venture off our property. There are only so many days you can spend staring at a plot of dirt, waiting for spring to arrive.

"Elena," I say, forcing my voice to stay even despite the irritation flowing through me. Not at her but at everything else in my life. "I'm in the middle of something. Can this wait?"

"I don't *know*, Kal, because we never discussed sexually trans-mitted diseases, and I've just had the most interesting conversation with some girl out front who *knows* you." Her lips curl back in a sneer. "You're the only one I've been with, so as far as that goes, *you're* okay, but am I? Who fucking knows, since apparently I really am the cliché virgin archetype, and I just trust that a man with so much more life experience than me—a freaking doctor, even—would know better."

"Jesus." Dragging a hand down the side of my face, I rub at an ache in my jaw. Looking at Jonas, I nod toward the door. "You can see yourself out."

"I wouldn't mind staying for the show."

I pin him with a look, and he huffs but gets to his feet anyway, making his boots thud harder against the floor than normal. When he reaches the door, Elena shifts slightly to the side to grant him passage, never taking her gaze off me.

"Go easy on him, will ya, love?" Jonas says, and I have to grip the plastic armrests on my chair to keep from launching myself at him and tearing his intestines through his asshole for even looking at her, after everything.

She turns, blinking, clearly taken aback, though by his accent or the fact that he's speaking to her at all, I can't quite tell. It's instanta-neous, the way his attention extinguishes her fire, fingers pinching a flame until it no longer exists.

"Who are you?" she asks, narrowing her eyes, taking in the leather jacket stretched across broad shoulders, the unkempt beard, the general sense of danger that follows him like a storm cloud.

Her foot inches backward ever so slightly. Jonas doesn't seem to notice, but I catch it, and the retreat twists my stomach in knots.

"Jonas Wolfe. Pleased to meet you," he says, tipping his chin down in acknowledgment. "Not surprised you didn't know that though. That one over there is bloody terrible at introductions."

He hooks his thumb in my direction, and I feel the barrier between my patience and my lack thereof waning the longer he stands here, defying me openly.

"How about I introduce you to the inside of a casket?" I say, unhooking my gun from where it's strapped at my waist, cocking the hammer and loading a magazine into the chamber.

Pointing it directly at Jonas's kneecap, I let my index finger ghost over the trigger, counting down in my head to see how long it takes him to move.

He ignores me, giving Elena a conspiratorial smile. "Not the most polite fella, is he?"

"Not really," she quietly agrees, shifting her eyes to mine. The heat from before slowly morphs to something duller, something needy.

There's a discomfort hidden in her depths, and it takes me a second to recognize how walking back in here after being attacked might make her feel.

That although it's been weeks, she might still need to ease into it, and by barreling inside to confront me, maybe she's skipped a few important steps of recovery.

Even the strongest glass cracks under enough pressure.[61]

"*Goodbye*, Jonas," I snap, pinching one eye closed to better my

---

61 One of my favorite things about Kal's character is the way he tries to keep from invalidating anyone's feelings. You see this more throughout the series too, but I just adore that quality.

aim. Just as I start to pull back on the trigger, not caring that there are customers outside, he yanks open the door.

"All right," he says, waving the folder in my direction, nodding at Elena. "Again, pleasure to finally meet you, Miss Elena. I'm sure I'll be seeing you soon."

She nods, not breaking my stare, and then he's slipping from the room without another word, pulling the door shut behind him.

"Lock the door, and walk to me slowly," I command, crooking my index finger in a come-hither gesture.

It takes her a moment, hesitation flickering across her features for a breath, but then she turns, obeying with shaky hands. Her throat bobs hard over a swallow as she starts toward me, pressing her palms into her stomach, more demure and submissive than I've ever seen her before.

The contrast is almost startling, the girl who burst into the office just minutes ago not even comparable to the one standing in front of me.

"Now," I say, putting the gun on the desk as I sit up straight and smooth my hands over my thighs. "Have a seat."

Her eyebrows draw inward, and she glances around, noting that the only other chair in the office is the one tucked into Jonas's desk. Slowly, her eyes slide back to me, that sweet, familiar blush creeping up her neck.

"Is that appropriate? Your friend could come back in."

"With the door locked? Doubtful." Patting my lap, I raise my brows expectantly, watching as she wrestles with uncertainty. "You can sit wherever you'd like, little one, if you really aren't comfortable. On the desk, on the floor. You can even remain standing. But regardless, I need you to communicate with me, starting with what you were spewing when you stormed in here."

Curling and uncurling her fists, she struggles, eyes shifting around the room as she seems to search for the words. Finally, she nods again, then closes the distance between us, draping herself over my lap.

The dress she has on hikes high up on her thighs, and I tug it down as she gets situated, desperate to feel her that way again but also aware that she's clearly going through something. And right now, she needs more than a quick, rough fuck.

"So," I prompt, tangling my fingers in the hair at the nape of her neck, tilting her head back slightly. "You met a girl outside."

She swallows, her throat working with the motion. Her eyes are wide in this position, vulnerable as she's forced to stare up at me, and it sets my entire fucking soul on fire.

"And you automatically assumed she was someone I've been intimate with in the past? Or am currently being intimate with, if your earlier accusation stands."

"She said she *knew* you."

Tugging her head back more, I skim my nose over the smooth expanse of her neck, inhaling deeply. My lips part, my top row of teeth gently scraping the scabbed bruise decorating the valley between her throat and shoulder.

I've seen many works of art in my lifetime, all different variants of the term, but I've never seen any as breathtaking as her. The pale canvas of her supple flesh painted with the evidence of our sins.

"I know a lot of people, Elena. I don't sleep with everyone I meet." Biting down, I sink my teeth into the thick muscle running up the side of her throat, pulling her into me as she jerks with the onslaught of pain.

"She knew me too," Elena whispers, fingers fisting in the collar of my shirt. "Seemed pretty surprised that I couldn't return the sentiment. And it just made me realize..."

When she trails off, I pull back until our noses graze each other, waiting for more. "What?"

"I barely know *you*," she says, and though it's delivered with as much softness as she can muster, I don't miss the implication hidden beneath its surface. The accusation still rife in her tone, as if she *wants* to believe in me but can't fully bring herself to.

Sucking in my next breath feels like trying to swallow hot coals, and I release it slowly through my nose, focusing on the steady thump of her pulse beating at the base of her throat.

My tongue is thick when I speak, an obstacle I have to talk around. "What do you want to know?"

Somehow, before she even opens her mouth again, I know her answer's going to be *everything*.

CHAPTER 24

ELENA

SOMEHOW, EVEN BEFORE HE SAYS ANYTHING AT ALL, I KNOW HE'S not actually about to tell me *everything*.

Why reveal all your moves when the game is nowhere near over?

Kal shifts me up his lap, maneuvering me so my ass is cradled by his forearm, partially resting on the chair, and I'm somewhat looking down at him. It feels like a silent acquiescence, like because he knows he can't very well give me all his secrets, he can at least give me some of the power.

He slips his left hand between my thighs, and for a second, I think he's about to try and distract me by gliding up and under my dress, but he doesn't. His fingers squeeze once, then settle on a solid grip, and he looks at me as though waiting for me to proceed.

I wring my hands together and shrug. "To be honest, I don't know where to begin."

"We don't have to go over a lifetime of issues in one afternoon. Why don't you start with what bothers you the most, not knowing?"

He's so logical, so levelheaded, that it almost makes me feel stupid for even coming in here at all. Even though it's obvious that my slight freak-out was an extension of something bigger, at least to me, embarrassment weaves a gnarly tapestry in my chest, impossible to ignore.

I nibble on the inside of my cheek, racking my brain. "*Are* you sleeping with anyone else?"

"Would it trouble you if I was?" he asks, glancing down at where his hand sits. "For reasons...other than risking your health?"

Dropping my gaze to his collarbone, peeking out from where I've pulled down his shirt, I weigh the consequences of admitting the truth. Of breaking myself open for a man I'm already aware can't ever love me and how it might feel to bleed out for once and not have him blot up the mess.

But I always did like the pain.

"Yes," I mutter, my tongue still not completely on board with my heart. "I'd hate that, actually."

His fingers flex, the metal of his wedding band icy as it presses into me. A hard look passes over his face, causing his pupils to dilate, but the rest of him remains perfectly still. "No. I'm not."

Breath whooshes from me, relief draining my lungs, and I start to move on to the next question, my mind firing full speed ahead. The hand on my thigh clamps tight, shooting a sharp spark of pain through the length of my leg.

The area blossoms bright red, and he relaxes his hold right when I move to shove him away, smoothing the pads of his fingers over the site.

"*Ow*," I say, annoyance flaring in the pit of my stomach.

"I think the better question, though, is why you think I'm sleeping with someone else." Now, his hand does inch up, the tip of his middle finger disappearing beneath the hem of my dress, pausing there. "Was I unclear about the fact that our marriage is real?"

I shake my head. "No, it's just—"

"Just what? Insecurity? Jealousy?" Another inch slips past, and my breath hitches as he grazes the scarred K. "I'll admit, your jealousy is fucking delectable, little one. Gets me hard as a goddamn rock just thinking about it."

As if on some sort of cue, I feel his erection stiffen beneath me, straining against the fabric of his suit pants. Moisture collects between my legs, flushing my body with need.

Raising my eyebrows, I tear myself from watching his ascent, goose bumps sprouting along my skin. "Don't most people think jealousy is a turn-off?"

"Less evolved folks than me, perhaps. Or more, depending on how you look at it." I gasp as he brushes the tip of a finger over my core, the sweep brief and featherlight, as if he's just testing the waters. "But what it tells me, with *us*, is that you're as fucking crazy as I am."

I blink, my heart actually stalling out inside my chest. "What?"

"The thought of you even looking at someone else fills me with an indescribable *ache*," he says, punctuating the last word by thrusting a finger into me, making room where there previously was none. "An ache I have no right to feel, no right to indulge, but God, I can't help it sometimes. Anyone glances in your direction, and I'm tempted to rip their fucking heart out. I like knowing you feel it too."

He curls against me, stroking slowly, maddeningly, and my head falls back onto my shoulders, my neck practically snapping in half with the sudden weight.

My chest rises and falls in time with the motion of his finger, and he watches me with parted lips and hooded lids, like he's growing aroused with each stuttered breath expelling from my lungs.

"Do you get it, little one?" he says, plunging two more fingers inside me, spreading them so I'm stretching around him, desperate to be filled. "No one awakens that sensation in me, so how could I ever find myself drawn to another's bed? You make me feel…"[62]

My soft gasp distracts him, my orgasm pooling at the base of my spine, coiling so tight it makes my body bow inward. The squelching sounds coming from where he pushes in and out of me reverberate off the office walls, so loud I wonder if they won't absorb through the plaster and reach the ears of the customers outside.

Somehow, without ever removing his fingers from inside of me, Kal lifts and backs me up so we're plastered against the door, snaking his free hand down the length of my body; he yanks the neckline of my dress beneath my breasts, thrumming one pebbled nipple before dropping to his knees.

"Jesus, do you hear that? How wet my voice and fingers make you? Do you feel how badly your sweet little pussy tries to suck me up?"

Really, I'm having a hard time concentrating on the words coming out of his mouth, much less the obnoxious way my body opens for him.

Shoving my dress to my waist, he glances up at me, the dark look in his eyes cinching the muscles in my chest. "Do *not* let that fall," he says, taking one of my hands and clasping the material to my hip, leaning in so his hot breath skates across my pussy.

"Kal, there are people—"

He smiles, devilish and hungry and *foreign*. I've never, ever seen him *smile*.

Bringing his forearm up, he uses it to pin my hips against the door, bracketing me between his lips and the wood. I swallow, the ferocity in his eyes roping my stomach into one giant knot.

"I *want* them to hear, little one. Want them to know what I do

---

62 Hehe, and this man thinks he isn't in love? Please.

to you, what *only I can*." One lick, splicing right up my seam as he drives his fingers in quicker, and I'm already on the cusp of a fucking revelation. "If you're jealous, I'm a goddamn psychopath."

Latching his mouth to my clit, he fishes a groan from my esophagus, searing my insides as it puffs past my lips. Moving in fast, short flicks, his tongue lashes against me, sending frissons of electricity singing through my nerve endings.

"Look at me, Elena," he says around swirls, his mouth vibrating against my lips, creating a delicious sensation that duels with his ministrations. "Look at your husband when you come for him."

"Oh *God*." My head slams back against the door, eyes fluttering shut.

"I doubt He could get you off like this," Kal says, teeth nipping at my second pulse, pulling me to attention. "Eyes on me."

His command leaves no room for protest, his stare pulling me in and refusing to let go. Sealing his lips around me, he sucks my clit into his mouth, pressing the flat of his tongue to its hood.

"What?" I croak, remembering his unfinished admission, my hips rising to meet the full motion, chasing sweet release. "What do I make you feel?"

Lust flares in his irises, darkening them until they're as black as his hair, and he releases me just enough to free his tongue for a second, leaving me wanton and empty.

"*Alive*," he growls, diving back in to get the meal he dropped to his knees for. "You. Make. Me. Feel. *Alive*." As he works me over, impaling me on his fingers and massaging with his tongue, my pussy quivers, threatening to explode. "You there? Come for me, *wife*. Show me how crazy I make you."

I nod, frantic, barely able to keep eye contact as the euphoric wave rears its head, crashing over me with such force that my vision splits, breaking in half as my body convulses. He laps at me, grunting and groaning like I'm the most satisfying delicacy he's ever tasted, and his sounds spur me on, dragging out shock after shock as my orgasm pounds through me.

My body slowly drifts back to Earth's orbit as he disentangles himself from me, my juices coating his mouth. He wipes his lips and fingers over the scar on my thigh, as if in some kind of post-lunch ritual.

Pushing to his feet, he smooths his hands down over his chest and rights my skirt, leaving my breasts exposed to the air. I note the outline of his cock, barely constrained by his pants, as he pauses to admire the rise and fall of my shoulders.

"Such pretty skin," he says, eyes locking on to the cut he likes to draw from each time we fuck.

"Mark it," I say, my voice barely a whisper.

His eyes snap to mine, blazing with unabashed desire. He swallows thickly, his Adam's apple jumping, and takes a step closer. "Yeah? You'd like that?"

I nod, licking my lips, letting myself look between us again. Even though I've just come, my body soars to life at the evidence of his arousal, my pussy clenching as if starved.

Reaching out, he cups my breasts, squeezing the undersides in his palms, then sweeps his thumbs over the pebbled peaks. "On your knees then."

That's not exactly what I had in mind, I think, dropping to repay the favor anyway. Willing to do whatever it takes to keep this man looking at me like I hung the stars in the sky with my bare hands.

Maybe, for a man so used to the dark of night, that's exactly what I did.[63]

He unbuckles his pants, slowly dragging the zipper down one

---

63 THEY'RE SO CUTE I COULD CRY.

tooth at a time. Shallow breaths spill from my chest as I blink up at him, mouth level with his cock when it bobs free, curving slightly up toward his abdomen.

My mouth waters at the sight of his thick, veiny erection, and immediately I lean in to kiss the purple crown. I haven't given many blow jobs, as he's seemed somewhat reluctant to receive them, but the hiss that escapes each time my mouth connects with him makes me feel like I'm doing something right.

Kal threads his fingers through the hair above my ears, holding me in place with his cockhead against my lips.

"I want to tell you everything about me," he says, moving my head from side to side, coating my flesh in the pearly beads of precum oozing from his tip. "You make me want to spill every secret I've ever had, Elena. That's not something that happens…well, ever. Not for me."

I don't respond verbally, parting my mouth and taking him between my lips instead, showing him how his admission makes me feel. And even though I don't feel like I'm getting answers to anything else today, the promise hidden in his words somehow makes up for that.

I'm okay with not knowing everything yet if there's time to figure it all out.

Pulling him farther into my mouth, I swirl my tongue over his shaft, hollowing my cheeks when I reach as far as I can go. His fingers in my hair are warm, gentle, despite the urgency in his breathing and the distraught tone of his words.

"I'm not surprised my little slut wife has such a dirty fucking mouth," he grunts, hips jerking as I lap at the slit in his tip, then push back onto his length. "You were fucking made for me, weren't you? Made to take my cock. Made to be my little cock whore."

I hum in agreement, his dirty mouth stirring an eagerness in my belly, the need to make this *phenomenal* blotting out everything else in my brain.

My nails claw at his pants, digging into his thighs as I try to scramble closer, bobbing up and down in time with my second pulse.

"Touch yourself," he says darkly, the command sending a shiver down my spine.

I pull off with a pop, my pussy clenching in anticipation.

"I don't want to be sore," I say. "I can't."

"You will," he replies, a challenge lacing his brow. Renewing the force of his grip on my scalp, he yanks me to his slobbery cock, smacking me across the cheek with it once, twice, before pushing back in. "Relax your throat, and play with your pussy. Can you do that for me?"

I hesitate again, my fingers twitching, but eventually nod slightly. He exhales, shoving to the back of my throat. I flatten my tongue at the last second, his command about relaxing barely registering enough for me to go through with it, and try not to retch.

His eyes never leave mine, even when he keeps me flush against him, my nose tickling his pubic bone. When it becomes evident he doesn't plan on letting me up until I touch myself, my fingers drift to the apex of my thighs, swiping through my sopping folds.

As soon as I make contact, I wince, still sensitive from the orgasm he gave me. Heat floods my face and my vision blurs, and Kal drags me off, sputtering and coughing as oxygen invades my nostrils.

Saliva coats my lips, dripping down my chin, a thin layer connecting me to him. I feel that familiar pressure building inside me, taking precedence over the soreness.

I circle two fingers over my clit, working furiously as ecstasy courses through me, and he chuckles, pushing past my lips and repeating the same air-robbing motion.

A wave of something that looks twisted, stuck between pain and pleasure, washes over his face, and as he removes my mouth again, he sighs.

"I'm going to come, little one. Mark you, like you asked. And you're going to wear it out of here, like a good little slut wife." He brushes over my swollen mouth with his thumb, and I rub myself faster, trying to get to where he is. "Okay?"

I nod, sticking my tongue out in acceptance.

Sliding back in, his crown pokes my throat, coasting in and out for several strokes, as if gearing up for a finale. My clit swells to the point where it feels like it might burst, sparks flying where my fingers work, and then he pushes to the hilt, keeping me in place.

All other thought dissipates as I focus on relaxing into his hold, absorbing the salty musk of his arousal and the way his abdomen ripples with his impending climax. My fingers fly, rubbing and kneading, my chest getting light as it becomes more and more difficult to breathe.

I feel it, my consciousness floating past my fingertips, just out of reach, and with it, my release.

"I want to hear it," he says, tapping my nose. "When you come with my cock in your throat, I want to fucking hear it."

It begins before he's even done speaking, erupting like a volcano as the corners of my eyes darken. My clit throbs beneath the pressure of my fingers, and as Kal pulls away just enough to thrust back in, I cry out as shock and elation mix in my gut, powering through every nerve in my body.

"That's it." Kal groans, the sound soft and primal, and I swear I feel him grow still, ropes of hot semen rushing out as he comes.

He withdraws from me while the stream continues spurting, dragging his slit over my lips and then pointing down at my breasts, coating them in his seed.

Collapsing against the door, he gulps in a lungful of air, brushing sweat from where it percolates on his forehead. "Jesus. I think one day you might kill me."

Catching my breath on the ground, I take a minute to collect myself. "Wouldn't that be something?"

"I wouldn't mind, if it was you." His words are harsh, quiet, and uneasy. "It'd be my life's honor, I think. Going out your hand."

My heart feels heavy and at odds with what just happened. "Well, it's a good thing I don't have any plans to murder you then."

"For now."

Confused, I push to my feet on wobbly legs, looking around for a tissue to dry myself with. I walk to the desk and pluck one from its box, but he clicks his tongue in disapproval.

"What are you doing?" He joins me, taking the tissue from my fingers. The somberness from seconds ago is gone, and I feel like I'm getting whiplash. "Did you think I was kidding about you leaving here covered in my cum?"

My cheeks flame. "I just thought it was kind of a heat of the moment thing."

"It's always the heat of the moment with you," he says, that weird fucking smile back in place as he maneuvers my arms into my dress, pulling the neck up over my breasts. His cum is cool against the soft fabric, hidden beneath it, but I can smell it.

I know it's there, like a secret the two of us share, and the notion makes me feel...*alive*.

CHAPTER 25

KAL

I'LL NEVER FORGET THE LOOK IN THE EYES OF THE FIRST MAN I EVER killed.

At sixteen, I'd already been under the Riccis' guidance for three years. I met Rafael during one of my mother's trips to the Dana Farber Cancer Institute for clinical trials of a drug that *could* stop the growth of her cancer cells.

Rafael had been sitting in the lobby, awaiting news on whether his grandmother was in remission. He sat tall, in his crisp navy suit, twirling rosary beads around his fingers like a man who didn't fully believe in their power.

I remember passing him on my way to the cafeteria and the gold metal of his thumb ring shining in the fluorescent lighting.

In my short time on Earth, I'd never seen anything or anyone so inherently *lavish*. The man oozed luxury and authority, and he knew it. Let it collect in the air around him, daring someone to try and assert otherwise.

I didn't officially meet him until our last day in Boston. I'd been standing outside, watching my breath appear and disappear in the chilly November air, trying to mask the disappointment on my face for when the nurse brought my mother out.

Rafael stepped outside, dressed in another dark suit, and pulled a cigar from his breast pocket, lighting up as he leaned against a concrete wall with a NO SMOKING sign hanging on it. He'd glanced at me, nodding as if he understood some unspoken request.

"Just you and your mom, kid?"

I swallowed, nodding, aware that I wasn't supposed to be talking to strangers. But an obviously *rich* stranger, hanging around in a hospital? How bad could he be?[64]

He sucked on the end of his cigar—Cohiba Behike, a brand I would eventually come to know by heart—and dipped his chin. "What's your name?"

My eyes narrowed.

He chuckled at my expression, laughing as if we were sharing an inside joke.

A few moments later, he was joined by a leggy brunette, wrapped in a deep purple fur coat, cradling a baby to her chest. They made their way to a blacked-out Cadillac waiting in the emergency lane, but not before he clipped me on the shoulder, dropping a card to the ground bearing the Ricci Inc. insignia.

It was a simple crest, a lion wearing a crown made of skulls, but nevertheless, it engraved itself on my brain that day, as if it was always meant to be there.

But it was the woman I couldn't stop staring at, and when her dark, captivating gaze met mine just before she climbed inside her vehicle, I was a goner.

Too young and stupid to realize her attention was a bad thing. I just liked that she looked at me.

---

64 Poor, sweet, innocent baby Kal.

After my mother died and my biological father rejected me *again*, I sought out the Riccis, unaware of how their presence would alter the course of my fate forever.

It'd started innocent, with me running tickets for one of the illegal gambling operations Rafe ran from the back of a deli in Roxbury. But when he started training me to fight, to *defend*, I knew things were turning.

And when I carried out my first hit, I did so in the dead of night, in a dirty alleyway while the man who'd been accused of ratting on Rafe's father pissed himself.

When I put the bullet between his teeth, blood spraying across his wife's white blouse, brain matter splattering against my face, all I could see was the horrified look in his eyes. The pure terror, frozen forever in time, as he looked up at me, pleading for mercy.

In the years since, it's that look I've never forgotten, although not because I was disturbed.

Because I felt *nothing*.

When I drag my scalpel down the chest of one of Elena's attackers in the present day, it's that feeling I try to focus on. Pushing what's left of my moral compass to the recesses of my brain, I tap into that chasm that exists within me, using it to stave off the things a normal person would feel.

Guilt. Worry. Nausea as the man's flesh opens. His eyes are wide and teary as he stares, screaming around his gag, probably begging me to stop.

For a moment, I'm tempted to listen to him. To play the part my grandfather wanted me to, the part my sister would be more open to learning about.

But then I see the ring on his right hand, matching the one Rafael wears, and I'm reminded why that isn't something I can do just yet.

Tony had been chilling at the docks a couple of afternoons after I chased Jonas from the bar's office, and Jonas just happened to recognize him from a picture he'd seen a few weeks ago circulating online, where Rafe and Carmen were trying to look like grieving parents.

It couldn't be a coincidence, we figured.

He lured him into a fake coke deal, then bagged him, gagged him, and dropped him on my doorstep.

And even though I'd resigned myself to an early retirement in both medicine and *official* business, I couldn't look the other way when he showed up.

I needed Rafael to get the message about his daughter: that she belongs to me.

My incision isn't deep enough to fully penetrate Tony's skin on the first pass, but it's enough to make him a bloody mess as my blade reaches his belly button.[65]

I reach forward, yanking the gag from his mouth with a gloved hand. Sweat rolls down his forehead, coating his dark buzz cut, and he sucks in a large gulp of air, on the verge of hyperventilating.

"Ready to tell me why the don sent you to rough up my wife?"

He nods, coughing, opening his mouth to speak. But all that comes out is an ear-piercing wail, and I stuff the gag back in, the muscle beneath my eye twitching. I'm tempted to push the cloth back until he's suffocating on it, unable to even breathe, but I close my eyes and try to calm myself with a few inhalations.

"I'm going to take this from your mouth one more time," I say finally, exhaling slowly. "And the only sound I want to hear from you is the answer to my question. Got it?"

Nodding again, he starts groaning, clearly trying to speak. I tug the gag free, leaving one end of it hooked inside his dry lips, just in case.

---

65 I had forgotten how graphic this book gets. LOL.

"Money," he chokes out, voice catching from where he's parched. "The don said he needed money, and you'd be more willing to dish it out if he threatened something you care about."

My stomach churns, irritation growing into a quiet fury. "His own daughter?"

"He's in trouble," Tony grits, pinching his eyes shut and hissing when I press one finger against a broken rib. "*Fuck me*! I'm answering your questions."

"Too well, I'm afraid." I dig my palm into his side, shifting my weight until the bones fracture more, and he screams out. "It sounds rehearsed. Like Rafael knew I'd find you."

Gasping through the pain, Tony thrashes on the table, straining against the straps keeping him down. "Of course he knew! That's why he used Vincent in the first place, to make it easier. Aren't you fucking known for being able to find anyone?"

"I'm known for a lot of things," I say, wrapping my fingers around my scalpel, grazing a red nipple with the sharp edge, not surprised to officially learn Vincent was a pawn. "Particularly performing autopsies on the living."

"Oh, Christ, no. Come on. I'll tell you anything you want to know."

I pause, the tip of the blade resting near the linear wound on his chest. "Why'd he push the kidnapping narrative?"

Tony shakes his head. "Not him, Carmen. She leaked it to the press immediately. Said you'd been fired or something and were retaliating by taking her firstborn."

Scoffing, I roll my eyes internally. *Of course she did. Jealous bitch.* "What else?"

Tony exhales, glancing around the room as he racks his brain. "He wants you dead. Even if you pay, he'll kill you."

Smirking, I try to feign surprise. As if I hadn't known that'd be his plan the second I decided to retire from the Mafia.

You don't really *leave* this world. Either you're in it until the day you die, or you live on the edge of insanity, aware that hits don't expire. Waiting for them to come for you.

"Guess I'll only be *paying* him a visit," I tell Tony, unsure why I feel the need to when he won't be able to relay the message. Dropping the scalpel to the table, I reach down to the floor, retrieve my circular saw, and adjust the scrub cap protecting my hair. "I'll be sure to give him your regards."

Later, after the echo from his screams has ceased its repetitive pounding in my brain and I've cleaned the blood and other debris off the floor, I sever his heart from where it's cocooned in his chest cavity, dropping it into a plastic biohazard bag along with his thumb, with the ring still attached.

After vacuum-sealing the contents, I shove it in a duffel bag and leave it by the outbuilding's door, ready for Jonas to send to Boston.

"This is ridiculous."

For a moment, my heart skips a beat, wondering if Elena's seen the headline fronting Aplana's Sunday paper: SOCIALITE STILL MISSING FROM BOSTON; PARENTS SAY SHE MAY BE IN DANGER.

I'm not entirely surprised to see it printed there. Each time I decline one of Rafe's messages, I can almost feel him growing more and more desperate, and desperate people will do whatever they have to in order to survive.

I can only imagine how much money my marriage to Elena hemorrhaged from his bank account. For a man whose funds were already dwindling, I'm sure he's panicking without my backing.

Or maybe it's the heart and finger I sent him, the message clear: I don't really give a shit if his kingdom burns or not.

In fact, that's exactly what I'm hoping for.

When I glance up, though, Elena's bent over the garden at the back of the yard, hands on her hips, squinting down at the dirt.

"I don't understand how not *one* of these flowers has bloomed. It's almost summer!"

Folding the newspaper, I place it on the glass patio table, kicking my ankle up over my knee. "Maybe you got a bad batch of seeds."

She shakes her head. "That isn't a thing, Kallum." She pauses. "Right? Seeds don't come already ruined. Oh my God, do they?"

My name rolling so easily from her lips makes my chest pinch tight, and I get to my feet, walking over to the pile of dirt. She's not wrong; none of the flowers have even sprouted through, the soil as brown and neat as it was when we laid it.

"It's not a big deal," I say, reaching out to tuck a strand of hair behind her ear. "When you don't succeed in one thing, you don't pitch your towel and stop trying. You move on to the next until you find what you're great at."

She makes a face. "I already know what I'm good at, but thanks for the vote of confidence."

Pulling away, she bends down, sifting her fingers through the dirt as if searching for a single sign of life. I cross my arms over my chest, watching.

"Then why is this garden so important to you?"

Sighing, she glances up over her shoulder, hands clumping in the soil. "I wanted something at the Asphodel that felt like *mine*. My balcony back home was covered in all sorts of plants, and I'd go out and read, surrounded by the fresh flowers, and just feel at peace. I thought…maybe if I tried to recreate that feeling, I wouldn't be so lonely here."

Again, that pinch flares in my chest, like thorns embedding themselves in my muscles and poisoning me. She looks away, wiping beneath her right eye with her index finger, and I'm reminded of my mission here.

That she's a pawn in the grand scheme of things. An unwilling participant in a game much larger than she even understands. Means to an end.

Though that doesn't stop me from telling her to follow me as I glide through the backyard in quick strides, eating up the distance to the padlocked gate bordering the beach. She scrambles to her feet after me, curiosity more powerful than self-pity, sticking close to my side.

I push open the old gate to where a long strip of worn black stone splits the stretch of golden sand in half, leading a path down to the dilapidated dock. Before the sand, right where it meets the grass, bloom the brightest wild beach roses, painting the area in beautiful hues of pink and purple.

"Consider this your…Elysium, my little Persephone."

Elena beams, sweeping her gaze over the flowers, a genuine smile pulling at her lips. "It's beautiful."

My eyes fall to her, appreciating the view. "Indeed," I say, and when she glances up, her smile falters, cheeks morphing to match the flowers.

She looks at the blue water, then grips the hem of her T-shirt between her fingers. "How much of this beach is secluded?"

"There isn't another house for miles." It's the only reason I feel comfortable letting her beyond the property I can see from the house.

Pouting dramatically, Elena whips her shirt up over her head, baring the swell of her naked breasts and that little pomegranate tattoo. Immediately, my cock stirs to attention, my tongue eager to run over the line work I've practically memorized at this point.

"Bummer," she says, hooking her thumbs in the elastic waist of her white cotton shorts, shoving them down over her hips. Untying her hair from the loose bun it's in, she shakes the dark locks free, completely naked as she backs away from me. "Guess we'll have to find another way to make it more interesting."

I swallow, my tongue thick inside my mouth. "Make what more interesting?"

"Skinny-dipping."

Turning on her heels, she bounds out toward the water, completely unabashed in the way the sea air collides with every plane and crevice of her body.

I stand on the shore, watching as she wades in to her knees, spinning to look at me.

"Well?" she calls out. "Aren't you coming?"

She wiggles her eyebrows, and I swallow again, a knot lodging hard in my throat.

No one's ever seen me naked.

I don't even like glimpsing the scarred topography of my body and the vivid reminders of a life that was thrust upon me before I knew what I was agreeing to.

The longer Elena stands in the water, waiting patiently, the more uncomfortable I feel about her perusal. Already, I'm far too concerned with the way she looks at me, and there's a niggling thought catching in the back of my mind that maybe this will be what turns her off from me.

Maybe she'll finally see I'm the monster everyone always warned her about.

"I don't bite," she calls, drifting farther back into the water, cupping her hands over her breasts, deepening her cleavage. "Well, I do, but you like it."

Snorting in spite of myself, I shake my head slightly, my dick straining against the confines of my pants. It throbs, desperate to reconnect with her, and finally I exhale, remembering how she said she's lonely.

How, in the entire time we've been on Aplana, this is the first time I've seen her look something other than miserable, barring sexual activities.

So even though it feels like I'm skinning myself alive as I begin popping open the buttons on my shirt, I do it anyway.[66]

---

66 These are my favorite moments to write in romance. The tiny insecurities and vulnerabilities that one person lets the other they love in on.

CHAPTER 26

ELENA

HE TELLS ME TO CLOSE MY EYES, WHICH I DON'T LOVE, CONSIDER-
ing the fact that I'm just past the point in the ocean where my feet
can touch the bottom. But I do it, because he's starting to look a little
green, and I don't want to make things worse.

I don't know *why*, but the man has some sort of complex about his
body. And while I'm sure it's something I shouldn't pry about, I just
don't know how many more times I can have sex with a fully clothed
man and not feel like a stranger to him.

The water ripples, pulsing against my skin, and I hear when Kal
enters it, hissing as if it's cooler than he was expecting.

"What?" I say, my vision dark from behind closed lids. "God of
the Underworld can't handle a little cold?"

I whoop with surprise as his arms glide around my waist, and my
eyes fly open, hands searching for something to steady the top half
of my body with. My fingers clutch at his shoulders, reveling in the
thick muscle beneath his skin, and then I pause, feeling pockets of
uniquely rough yet soft flesh.

The same spots graze my stomach as I press into him, and my
heart sinks low in my chest, thumping hard between us.

Meeting his gaze as my fingers continue their exploration, I do my best not to look down, sure that whatever I find there will humanize him. That I won't be able to resist the brokenness, and my attraction will let loose and morph into something real.

Something that can hurt me.

Sadness burns the back of my throat as I recognize the puckered skin, counting eight spots on his right shoulder, then five on the left. I slide my palms in, cupping the base of his neck, absorbing the force of his swallow.

His eyes betray nothing—no vulnerability, no awareness, no shame. They stare at me blankly, a practiced ambivalence reflecting back, even though I can tell by the way the tendons in his throat tense up that he doesn't like any of this.

"I'm no god," he says finally, releasing a stilted breath. His fingers dig into my ass, holding me upright, and I feel his cock bob against me, seeking entrance without him even guiding it. "Just an unlucky soul who somehow has managed to cheat death over a hundred times."

Taking a chance, I drop my chin, coasting my gaze over his slick, sun-soaked skin. For the most part, it's smooth and bronzed, the tone apparently natural given his propensity for the indoors.

But the larger planes are marred, decorated by shiny divots that shimmer in the light reflecting off the water. Some are smaller than others, some long and wide, scattered in various places along his entire torso.

There's a particularly lengthy one stretching over his rib cage, and I tentatively drop my hand to the mark, smoothing my thumb over it. It's gnarly, mangled, and a little less pink than the others, bubbling up past the surface of his skin.

He sucks a sharp breath through his teeth, and I freeze, eyes widening. "Oh shit, I'm so sorry. Did that hurt?"

Adjusting his hold on my ass, Kal chuckles, hoisting me up higher on his waist. My pussy pulses where our skin meets, the onslaught of immediate sensation making me dizzy.

"It's not a pleasant feeling," he says, his mouth so close to mine it's distracting. "Not really painful, but scars tend to be a lot more sensitive than normal skin." He shifts, dropping one hand to the crack of my ass while the other winds beneath my thigh, sweeping over the K there. "The nerve endings regenerate, and the keloid scars like that are usually the worst because of all the extra collagen."[67]

Slowly, I drift my hand over the site, watching his face for signs of distress. "What happened?"

He smirks. "Which time? Hit men don't always get away with things, you know."

My fingers touch one close to his collarbone. A zigzag shape. "Here?"

"Bullet grazed me during a warehouse raid while I was looking over shit for your father out of town. I ducked a second too late."

It occurs to me now just how dangerous his life has been under my father's employment. How different would he be if he'd never met Rafael Ricci?

You'd never know.

"What about here?" I poke an oval scar on his shoulder.

"Chihuahua bite. My mother told me not to pull his tail. I didn't listen."

That makes me smile, and I continue my perusal. Holding my breath for a moment, I focus on the biggest scar, trying to imprint the feel of the rough edges into my palm and reconciling them with the stoic figure holding me. "With this one?"

Something cold passes over his face, making me shiver, and he

---

67 Translation: Scars are really fucking cool, y'know?

starts to move deeper in the water. I'm not sure how long before he loses his footing, but it feels like we're edging dangerously close to drowning here.

A metaphor if ever there was one.

"I was betrayed," he says softly, his right hand coming up, twisting in my hair. "And I vowed not to ever let anyone close enough to me to hurt me like that again."

It feels like an admission, though I'm not exactly sure of what. A promise of sorts, the kind whispered against skin and spoken to your soul. It breaches mine, uncertain as it brushes the surface, and I lean in, ghosting my lips over his when I speak.

"You're not unlucky," I whisper, afraid of shattering the bubble that's risen up around us, my heart beating so fast that it's making me sick.

Maybe his words are a warning, but I don't even care.

I bask in them anyway.

Flexing his fingers in my roots, he exhales, the cool mint of his breath rolling down my chin. "I certainly don't feel like I am right now."

Insanity.

That has to be what drives me to return to the Flaming Chariot, as if I haven't had enough issues around there as it is.

But curiosity is a raging bitch where I'm concerned, and I'm on a mission to find the girl from the other day and figure out who she is to Kal.

If she's the one who betrayed him.

The bouncer outside gives me a once-over as I unfold myself from the back seat of Kal's town car, folding his massive arms over his chest.

The bottom half of an anchor tattoo peeks beneath his shirtsleeve, and his eyes are the most crystal clear blue I've ever seen.

I stand there stupidly for a second, getting lost in their translucence.

He clears his throat, waving a palm in front of my face. "Sorry, no minors allowed. Dunkin' is that way."

Confused, I glance behind my shoulder to see if someone's stepped up behind me. A woman in a floral maxi dress passes by, chatting away on her cell phone about some Hollywood scandal, but otherwise, there's no one else on this part of the sidewalk.

I look back at the bouncer, pushing my hair off my shoulder. "Um, no, I'm not looking for Dunkin'. I was hoping I could wait inside at the bar? I'm…trying to find someone, and I'm hoping they'll show up if I stake this place out long enough."

"That's loitering, and it's strictly prohibited."

His clipped, dismissive tone makes me bristle. "It's actually not loitering, because I've just told you my express purpose for wanting to hang around."

The man looks at me and shrugs. "You enter the bar and don't order a drink, that's loitering, according to business policy."

"Okay, then I'll order a drink."

He snorts, but somehow his face remains still. "Sweetheart, if you think I'm about to believe you're over twenty-one, you're a lot dumber than that short little dress you have on makes you look."

I *know* I don't look that young, and he's just being an asshole because I'm clearly out of my element here and don't resemble his typical patronage.

Fire bleeds into my soul as he hurls his insult, and I reach up, tying my hair into a low knot at the back of my head. "Dress stays short so I have free range to do this."

My leg kicks up, my body shooting first, asking questions later, aiming for his crotch. But then someone's gripping my biceps and yanking me away, twisting so I'm facing the street. I lock up when he grabs me, fear shooting so suddenly through my gut that I almost double over from the way it seizes up.

"Whoa, whoa, what in the bloody hell's going on here?" a vaguely familiar British accent asks, the hands leaving my biceps almost as quickly as they appear, like touching me burns him. I peek up, noting the trim, dark beard and the leather jacket, letting out a slight breath of relief when I realize it's the man from the back office the other day.

Wolfe something. Kal's friend or confidante, the part owner of the bar.

Recoiling from his touch, I cross my arms over my chest and lean to the side, shooting daggers at the bouncer. "What's going on is that I'm being insulted by your employee, who refuses to let me go inside because he thinks I'm bad for business."

"We have enough of a problem keeping the riffraff away as it is," the bouncer says to his boss, shrugging. "Just trying to maintain an orderly bar while we're still understaffed."

Kal's friend frowns, flipping his head so the mop of dark brown curls atop it falls from his eyes. "Blue, you have a habit of harassing potential paying customers?"

Jonas Wolfe, that was his name.

"I wasn't harassing her. I was—"

Scrubbing a hand down the side of his face, Jonas sighs, glancing at me. "Maybe you should pay a little bit more attention to who you're keeping out of the bar before you go insulting their intelligence. You know what Dr. Anderson would do if he knew you called his wife stupid and implied she's trouble?"

The bouncer—Blue, apparently—eyes me, raking over my form more fully now. He lingers a little too long on my legs but snaps up to my gaze before I have a chance to feel creeped out by it.

I don't get unsettling vibes from this guy—no part of my girlish intuition is telling me to run or steer clear the way it did with Vincent. Blue just seems like an asshole.

"His wife?" Jonas nods, and Blue puffs his cheeks out, releasing a slow breath. "She's a little young for him, don't you think?"

"Nobody asked what *you* think," I snap, but Jonas holds his hand up as if to silence me.

The gesture infuriates me more.

"I'm going to murder both of you," I say in a low voice, grumbling mostly to myself as I envision a bloody end for the two of them.[68]

The image flashes across my brain before I have time to think it through: violence, crimson painted around a room, their mangled bodies strewn about haphazardly, waiting for someone to come clean them up.

Blinking it away, I press a hand to my stomach, trying to ignore the heat coiling there. I don't even *know* these men, yet here I am, imagining being their executioner?

Jonas laughs, the sound boisterous and startling compared to the quiet, reserved nature of my husband. "You shouldn't threaten assassins, love. They take those very seriously."

Growing more irritated by the second, I put my hands on my hips and cock an eyebrow at the two men. "Well, we've established that I belong here. Can I go in now?"

"Unfortunately no, although it certainly has nothing to do with the way you're dressed." Unlike his employee, Jonas doesn't even look at my outfit, instead focusing on a spot beyond my head, like he's looking for someone. "You've got bad luck written all over you."

"I do not!"

He nods, ignoring me, and grabs my elbow, starting down the

---

68 Elena's subtle violence feels like such a fun juxtaposition to Kal's more obvious brand of it. These two are perfect for each other, I'm just saying.

street away from the bar. "You do. It's this…purity within your presence. Bad shit just flocks to you, doesn't it, love?"

"Stop calling me that."

"You're right. Anderson probably wouldn't like that very much either." His long legs eat up the sidewalk, and even though I'm not *short* by most standards, I'm having to practically sprint just to keep up. "He's rather fond of you, hm? It's like you've finally managed to dislodge the stick up his arse."

My nose wrinkles up, my body rejecting the sentiment. "I haven't done anything."

"Don't suppose you'd have to. The lad's been proper obsessed with you for ages." He glances down at me as we round the corner, a Dunkin' coming into view at the end of the street. "Well, not *ages*. It's a rather recent development, but boy oh boy, did it hit him hard."

Jonas's words make my face heat up, and when we stop just outside the doors of the donut shop, he releases my arm, turning to face me.

"I don't know what you're talking about," I say, shrugging, not wanting to let him know how his claim draws my throat closed. I cross my arms over my chest in case my heart beats so hard he can see it.

"Technically speaking, he could've married anyone," he says. "But he *chose* you."

"He was blackmailed into it. We both were."

A look of dark amusement passes over Jonas's face, and he smiles, revealing two rows of bright, unnaturally white teeth. He reminds me of his namesake, staring down at me like a wolf who's just caught his dinner and never learned not to play with his meals beforehand.

"Right. I forgot about that." Clearing his throat, he shoves his hands into his jacket pockets, pressing his lips together. "Still, Elena. Think about it. Is a man like that ever blackmailed easily?"[69]

---

69 Jonas playing matchmaker, because he's the cutest.

My nerves jumble, blending wildly together and spreading like poison through my gut. "I don't know…"

In truth, it's the same thought I had when he first approached me, demanding my hand. After he'd already taken out Mateo, eliminating my choice in that matter.

Not that I *miss* Mateo.

But it did feel mildly suspicious.

Narrowing my eyes at Kal's British friend, I take a step back, and he laughs again, the sound so rich and infectious, it sends a twinge of homesickness through me.

I haven't heard anyone laugh in weeks.

"I'm not saying he wasn't forced into doing it," Jonas says finally, lifting his shoulders. "I'm just saying…maybe it's not the full picture. Maybe you should see if anyone has the other side of the photograph."

And when he turns, leaving me in front of Dunkin' to head back to the bar, I stand there for several minutes, wondering what to do with the information he's just given me.

I should go ask Kal what he's talking about or complete my mission to find Violet.

Instead, I head inside, order a long john, and settle in at one of the outdoor metal patio tables, pushing all my problems aside until I've finished eating.

CHAPTER 27

KAL

DROPPING MY HEAD INTO MY HANDS, I DIG THE HEELS OF MY palms into my eye sockets, creating kaleidoscopes of color spotting across my vision.

A vein in my temple throbs painfully, maniacally, as I pore over the list of possible IP addresses of the flash drive culprit, growing more agitated with Ivers International's incompetence at finding the person.

Earlier this morning, a third flash drive appeared, that same grainy footage not attributed to my state-of-the-art security but filmed with an outside party's camera.

Marcelline brought it in with the mail, and when I plugged it into my desktop, I was met with the black-and-white evidence of me baring my soul to my wife, both of us stark naked in the ocean.

Somehow, compared to the others, which caught us in the middle of lascivious acts, this one felt more intimate. More exposing.

More purposeful.

I just can't figure out why they're appearing in the first place.

If it was about outing me to the press, for any number of the crimes I've had expunged from my record over the years, most likely they would've been leaked already.

I don't imagine this is Rafael's doing, considering the more violent and less public avenues he's already attempted at extorting me. Even though attacking his daughter and trying to scare her hasn't worked in his favor, I don't believe he'd pivot so drastically.

The narrative being pushed in the media makes his family look like victims. This—photographic evidence of Elena enjoying her time with me—does not. If someone other than me got a hold of these flash drives, his whole story loses credibility.

Leaning back in my desk chair, I stare up at the vaulted ceiling, losing myself in thought for several minutes. The house is silent tonight, Elena having turned in with a new copy of Virginia Woolf's *A Room of One's Own* she bought at the only bookstore on the island.

For the first time in a long time, I reach beneath my desk, my hand smoothing past the pistol secured just above my thigh, and tear off the Polaroid taped to the underside.

Unlike the crumpled, worn one I keep on hand of Violet, this one is so infrequently handled that it's still in mint condition; the edges remain straight, the colors on the picture itself only slightly warped due to the passage of time. Otherwise, it's as if the photo's just popped out of its camera.

My mother sits up in a hospital bed, a pink bandana pulled tight over her head, because she'd just begun losing her hair after restarting chemotherapy treatments. I'm seated in a plastic chair at her side, watching her with the big, terrified gaze of a child who doesn't fully understand that she's quickly fading out of his life.

She's spooning chocolate pudding out of a plastic cup, staring at whoever's behind the camera, but her smile points at me. Even as she sits there, her body devouring itself from the inside out, she's trying to reassure me that everything is okay.

That it will all *be* okay.

"That's the love of a mother," nurses would sometimes say, because

keeping in high spirits while trying to fight off a terminal illness isn't something everyone can do, year after year, day after day. Yet she made it a point to, always trying to get me to see the brighter side of things.[70]

She was strong. Determined. I never once saw her cry, though I would often hear the sniffling when I would use the bathroom or as I fell asleep tucked into her side. But she'd clear the tears before I could see them, as if that would make it hurt less somehow. As if keeping me in good spirits was more important than anything else in her life.

Everything she did was for me, and all I could think about was how unfair it all was that she had to be sick in the first place.

That big, toothy grin of hers stirs an ache within me that I haven't allowed myself to feel in years, and a fresh dose of shame injects itself into my veins, because I can't stop thinking of how disappointed she'd be in the way my life turned out.

"You look like you've seen a ghost."

Elena's voice yanks me from my introspection, and I jolt up, straightening my spine as she enters the office. She makes her way over to me, taking a seat on my lap before I've even managed to ask her to.

Like she knows it's where she belongs.

She looks at the photo, then back at me, as if waiting to see if I'll continue.

"My mother," I offer, smiling softly. "She passed when I was thirteen."

One arm slides up around my neck, slipping around my shoulders, and Elena presses her head into mine. "Cancer?"

"Invasive lobular carcinoma," I say with a slight nod. Pain lances through my heart at the term, sawing the organ in half. "When she was first diagnosed, they just called it an abnormal growth in her left

---

70 Okay, reading this after watching a loved one go through this exact experience and watching them do this exact thing for their child…it's hitting WAY different now. *sobs*

breast. I don't think they wanted to acknowledge it was *that* particular form of cancer, because she was so young."

Like being struck by lightning, a sudden, sharp pang splits my chest, shocking me to the core.

Thirty-two. My mother was thirty-two when she died.

The realization that soon I'll have been on this planet longer than her cuts deep, prodding at a scabbed wound I once believed was healed. Yet the way it throbs and chips away, drawing new, fresh blood, suggests otherwise.

"She's beautiful," Elena says quietly, pulling me gently from the downward spiral of my thoughts without even necessarily meaning to. She stares at the picture with a soft look on her face, unaware of the existential crisis brewing in the back of my mind, content that I'm once again sharing one of the secret facets of my life.

If it were anyone else, I wouldn't dare. Would never have even brought them back to my house to live, much less started spilling my guts.

I'm not usually a gambler. Don't like leaving my life in the hands of fate. But something about this woman makes me want to risk everything.

"She's the reason I got into poetry as a kid. She was always reading Shakespeare and would quote Chaucer like scripture. She would've loved you."

I push some hair from her pale shoulder, leaving my next thought unspoken, hidden in the depths of my soul where it belongs. *Would she have loved me?*

"That's true. I'm very lovable," Elena giggles, and the sound pierces my chest, a dull knife being shoved through flesh and bone and arriving out the other side.

Shifting forward, I reach into my pants pocket for my wallet, retrieving the photo I keep there. It's a small copy I stole from Violet's high school graduation series that I kept over the years as a reminder that someone out there could have a relationship with me, even if her father wasn't interested.

Turns out she doesn't want one either.

Elena's spine stiffens, and she leans in, peering at the picture. "Who's that?"

Her tone is curt, significantly less playful than it was three seconds ago, and I smirk, squeezing her thigh, practically soaking up her jealousy. "My sister."

"Your sister?" Blinking, she frowns. "That's…the girl I met outside the Flaming Chariot."

"You met Violet?"

"She was standing outside on the curb and said she'd tried going in several times but couldn't get herself to do it." Tilting her head to the side, she studies the picture some more, seemingly lost in thought. "I guess now I get why she acted so offended that I had no idea who she was. What kind of wife doesn't recognize her own sister-in-law?"

"The kind who doesn't know what she looks like?"

"Great, Kal. Now she thinks I'm an asshole."

"Join the club."

Pursing her lips, she slumps back against me, removing her arm from my shoulders to drop it into her lap. "Do you have other secret family members I don't know about?"

I hesitate, the word *grandfather* materializing on the tip of my tongue before I swallow it down, not ready to open that can of worms. Besides, she didn't ask about the dead ones.

She notices my pause, narrowing her eyes, and I smirk again, trying to play off the silence as being distracted by her.

Palming her ribs, I glide my hand up, my thumb grazing the underside of her right breast through the pale blue silk pajamas she has on. "Violet has two brothers, but I don't know them."

Her throat works as I touch her, eyes falling to where my fingers continue their ascent, engulfing her entire breast in my hand and squeezing until she gasps.

"I know what you're doing."

"Enjoying my wife?" I say, dropping the photo to the desk and dipping my head to the crook of her neck, baring my teeth against her skin.

She leans into my bite but doesn't close her eyes. "Violet said you don't ever talk about her."

"I don't." Elena tenses in my lap, her spine going rigid, and I sigh, pulling away and letting my hand fall. "The man who helped create me, if you want to call him that, had just brought home his firstborn son when he had an affair with my mom. He was married and had nothing to do with me. I thought when Violet was older, maybe it'd be easier to connect with the rest of the family if I connected with her first. But she doesn't want me around."

Not that it's stopped me from trying.

"Oh, Kal—"

Something in her tone prickles my already red-hot nerves, and I exhale sharply, reaching up to collar her throat in my hands. Her breath catches, getting stuck beneath my palm, and my cock stirs behind my jeans at the heady sensation of having someone's pulse at my mercy.

"No pity, little one. Don't give me that." She shifts, rubbing over my throbbing cock, and even through the layers of clothing, I can feel how hot she is. "You want to give me something, you want to make me feel better, you give me that sweet little pussy."

Elena's gaze turns glassy, but I can't tell if it's sadness or desire pooling there. She blinks the sheen away, tilting her chin down to stare at me through hooded lashes.

"Okay," she says, turning around so she's straddling me, grinding into my growing erection. "Whatever you need, Kallum. Take it from me."

Later, after I've pumped her full, she lies on her back atop my desk, fiddling with the torn strap of her pajama top and staring up at the ceiling.

"What are you thinking?" I ask, drawing my fingers through her sensitive flesh, smearing my cum over her skin. I'm grateful she's on birth control now so I can mark her like this every chance I get.

I'm standing above her, my dick hanging, drained, between my thighs, neither of us particularly eager to move from the quiet of the room.

She looks at me, a thoughtful expression on her face. "I was just thinking about Ariana and Stella. How lucky I am that I grew up close to my siblings."[71]

Even though I'm sure she doesn't mean it that way, her comment slices right through the stitches barely holding me together, severing the sutures and cracking my pain wide-open all over again.

"You miss them," I note, letting my hand fall to my side.

She nods. "Always. Ari has a recital coming up soon, and it kills me that I'll have to miss it." She gives me a sidelong glance as if gauging my reaction. I aim for mild, at best. "Not that I don't enjoy Aplana. Honestly, it's been so refreshing in the weirdest way, even though I live as a captive now."

"You're not—"

Giggling, she curls her legs up, shaking her head. The gesture seems fake. Forced. And it makes me uneasy. "It's okay, I've already grown quite accustomed to my Stockholm syndrome. I just miss my old life a little too."

Gritting my teeth, I stare at the place on an end table where

---

71 LOL. I get what she means, but why is this kind of a burn?

the picture of her parents and I used to be, wondering if I'm really about to say what my brain wants me to. The words formulate on my tongue, ignoring all the red flags, and shoot out of my mouth before I have a chance to stop them.

"Then let's go to Boston."

CHAPTER 28

ELENA

WHEN I BRING UP MY SISTERS, I'M CERTAINLY NOT EXPECTING KAL to offer to take me to them.

I feel like it kind of goes against the rules of kidnapping, bringing the captive around the people who want her home.

Then again, I've never been on the business end of a situation like this, so what do I know?

Marcelline helps me pack, quietly taking clothes from my dresser and placing them into my open suitcase. I glance at her as she moves, toying with the journal in my hands, wondering if I should take it with me.

Before coming to the island, writing was as second nature to me as breathing. It was where I funneled the inspiration gathered from the poems and books I read, jotting down random musings or fictionalized anecdotes about my life.

I haven't touched the journal since my arrival, inspiration few and far between despite the serenity around the house. Technically speaking, the Asphodel is the perfect place for a writer's retreat, though it feels odd creating anything in a place so plagued by death and darkness.

Perhaps that's why I haven't tried.

"What do you think, Marcelline?" Holding up the journal, I turn it so she can see the pink leather cover. "Should I try to pick up an old hobby?"

She purses her lips, twirling the end of a strand of her strawberry-blond hair. Most of our relationship up to this point has been me firing words at random and her dodging every bullet, ignoring my comments and questions unless Kal is around.

"What's the hobby?" she asks, her voice raspy, as if rough from lack of use.

"Um, writing." I perch on the edge of the bed, flipping through the pages, my neat handwriting floating by with each turn.

"Like stories? Poems?"

Heat scorches across my face, flames of embarrassment licking my cheeks. "Both, kind of. I used to do it all the time, much to my parents' dismay. They wanted me focused on etiquette and housework. But to be honest, I kind of forgot about it anyway since coming to Aplana."

She nods, widening her blue eyes. "Yeah, the island has that effect on people. Like you come here, and your previous identity kind of just…evaporates. Some locals call it the New England Bermuda effect. I had an aunt who said Aplana was filled with an ancient, ancestral magic that replaces a person's nature with that of the island's."

"Do *you* think that?"

"No, I just think it's easy to forget everything the second your feet touch sand." Marcelline shrugs, pointing at my journal. "Doubly so when you're busy falling in love."

The heat spreads from my face, scoring a path down my sternum and finally settling in my gut. I lean forward, shoving the journal into the front pocket of my suitcase, and try to steel myself against her comment, even as my pulse beats so loud and fast, I think it might launch out of my throat.

"Definitely the sand," I say quickly over the bile teasing my esophagus.

Marcelline presses her mouth into a thin line, then nods, dropping one last T-shirt into the suitcase. "Yeah," she agrees, clamming up like every other time I've tried to start a conversation. "You're probably right."

I don't see her again before we leave the house, and I dart outside to the backyard before we load into the town car, speaking in low, soothing tones to the garden that *still* has not bloomed.

Staring out at the expanse of soil, I sigh, unsure of what exactly to say. "All the gardening blogs suggest talking to your plants. They swear it makes a difference. Even my sister Stella said it might be beneficial, although there's no actual science to back that data up, and she's super smart. She would know. So here I am. Temporarily. We're about to go to Boston for a bit, but when I come back, I expect a fully flourishing garden, okay?"

If Mamma could see me now. She'd probably accuse me of witch-craft and burn me at the stake.

"I get it," I tell them, hoping the bulbs can hear beneath the dirt. "You're afraid of what waits for you on the other side of the soil. You're warm and comfortable where you are now. Safe, even. It's terrifying, trying to find courage to take a leap of faith, but you can't spend eternity hiding. Eventually, you have to take the opportunities that are thrust upon you and trust that the universe knows what it's doing."

Hope bursts like a backed-up pipe in my chest, but I stuff it back down where it belongs, not wanting to entertain that thought.

"April is the cruelest month," I add, quoting T.S. Eliot's "The Waste Land", like the flowers might appreciate the sentiment.

"Breeding lilacs out of the dead land, mixing memory and desire, stirring dull roots with spring rain. It's time."

When I turn around, I see Kal hovering by the back gate, watching me with an unreadable expression. I approach him slowly, shame heavy in my chest.

"Is your garden a big T. S. Eliot fan?" he asks, his face shifting into one of quiet amusement.

"Don't laugh," I say, glancing up at the sky, noting the thick clouds rolling in over the ocean. "Love is the greatest act of revitalization, and I happen to think poetry is the best way to relay that."

He doesn't say anything as I move around him, leading the way to the front of the house where our car sits, Marcelline already in the front passenger seat.

It's raining when we take off, which doesn't really do much to quash my nerves as soon as we board Kal's jet. Once we're in the air and able to get up and move around, I unbuckle myself from my seat and go to the bedroom, climbing under the luxurious covers, trying not to let Marcelline's words from earlier take root in my soul.

"She doesn't know me," I whisper to myself and the pillow. "She doesn't get to decide if I'm falling in love." I pause, considering. *At what point does an obsession become more?*

Probably when you start to feel it's being returned.

"If you're jealous, I'm a goddamn psychopath."

Scoffing, I push the memory of him saying that to me to the dark recesses of my brain, where I push everything else I don't want to deal with. "Besides, that would be crazy, right?"[72]

A throat clears in the doorway, and my entire body locks up, fear streaming down my spine. I push up on my elbow, looking at Kal as he leans against the doorway, a martini glass filled with a red liquid in hand.

---

72 NO, it would not, Elena. You are correct.

Just the sight of his devilishly handsome face causes my stomach to flutter, and I swallow over the lump that forms, blocking all coherent thought.

"Talking to yourself again?" he asks, entering the room and setting the glass down on the shelf above the bed. For several seconds, he doesn't make a move to get in the bed with me, and apprehension floods my psyche, making me wonder how much he heard.

"I'm great company," I say, lifting one shoulder so it's outside the blankets.

"Can't argue with that." Reaching up, he grabs the drink again, holding it out to me. "I had Marcelline make this. Thought it might help with your apparent fear of planes. Don't ask what's in it, because I have no idea, except I told her to use pomegranate syrup."

Eyeing the drink, I arch an eyebrow. "You keep pomegranate syrup stocked on your jet?"

"I do now." His gaze doesn't waver from mine; it's strong, bold, daring. Everything I've always wanted to believe myself to be, he manifests without even seeming to try.

"You know I'm not twenty-one yet, right?" I joke, tension thick in the air between us.

"Age, I do defy thee," he says, Shakespeare rolling off his tongue as he gestures for me to take the glass. I'm not even sure he realizes he's done it or if he even notices the way it changes the atmosphere and rewrites the coding of my DNA.

Maybe he's just so used to quoting poems to me that it doesn't taste any different falling from his lips now. Maybe he doesn't mean anything by it.

"Your plants will grow," he notes after a moment, dragging a finger along the bottom edge of the glass.

Frowning, I cover my face with my hands. "So you did hear me out there. That's embarrassing."

"It shouldn't be. I like hearing you, no matter the context. Whether it's the light sound of your breathing when you're asleep next to me or you reciting poetry to your garden or those noises you make when you come on my cock." He leans in, brushing his nose against mine. "I want to hear it all."

Heart in my throat, pulsing until I can feel nothing else, I take the drink from his hand and sip. As the sweet liquid glides down, cooling me where his gaze makes me warm, I know.

In the pit of my stomach, in the fabric of my soul, I *know.*

I'm in love with my husband.

When we land in Boston, I'm not expecting every news camera in the city to be waiting at the airport gates, desperate to get an exclusive first look at the girl kidnapped by Doctor Death.

I don't know why—maybe because the people in Aplana didn't seem to care or believe the story—but it certainly never crossed my mind that people would be *salivating* to hear my side of it.

Kal follows me down the plane stairs, sticking close to my side as we're greeted immediately by a security team. The one in front, with a neck as thick as a tree trunk and olive skin, nods at Kal when we approach.

Cameras flash from behind the glass windows, making me a little dizzy even as I keep my gaze trained on my shoes. For the first time since leaving Boston, I'm wearing pink Louboutins, paired with a black Givenchy lace and velvet minidress I'd never have dared wear while under my parents' roof.

Or with Mateo, considering the top is sheer and the skirt barely grazes midthigh. He'd have considered that an invitation.

Half of me had been expecting Kal to balk at the attire or at least try to get beneath it, but when I came out of the jet's bathroom, he'd barely noticed the change at all.

"Best course of action is to just take her straight on through," the security guard is saying. "There's an SUV waiting for you in the parking lot, and it's scheduled to take you right to the Riccis' home front."

I blink up at Kal. "We're going to my parents' first?"

He looks at me quizzically. "Of course. That's the entire reason we flew in."

Butterflies erupt in my stomach, a swarm taking flight all at once. I wrap my arms around it, trying to ignore the sensation.

Kal's features harden, and he asks for a second alone. "Elena. What is it?"

Dread pulses in a harsh stream up and down my spine, my skin burning up with the weight of my parents' judgment. Now that we're back in town, I can already feel my soul clamoring for their approval, even though neither of them fully deserve it.

"It's nothing," I say, giving a little shake of my head.

The creases at the corners of his lips deepen the more his frown curves down, and then he's stepping into me, reaching up and fisting the back of my head, tilting my chin up so I'm forced to keep eye contact. "Don't lie to me, little one. Don't shut me out when I've not done that to you."

Not entirely true, I insist silently, although he has given me more than I'd ever anticipated. Maybe I should learn to be happy with what I've got.

"I just didn't realize I'd be seeing them so soon."

"Do you not want to? As far as I know, your sisters still live there—"

"No, it's okay. Really." I flutter my lashes, eager to move on from the subject. "I think I was just hoping we'd get some alone time before."

"We were alone on the flight."

Rolling my eyes, I glance out my peripheral at the crowd around us; they mill about, paying us no attention, and we're facing away from the windows. "I meant *this* kind of alone time," I say, lowering my voice along with my hand, cupping him through the fabric of his dress pants.

His fingers tighten, pulling at my roots, and he grunts. "Be careful what you ask for, little one. I'm liable to bend you over the stair cart and fuck you in front of the whole city."

The thought sends a delicious tingle racing down my back, warming in my core. "Then why don't you?"[73]

Stepping even closer so my hand is trapped between our pelvises, Kal grins wickedly. Craning his neck, he presses his lips against the shell of my ear, making me shiver. "You want them to watch while I fuck you? Show them how wrong they were about the bad doctor and his little captive? That you're not only a willing participant in all of this but a desperate, needy little cock whore who begs for my cum every night?"

Do I want that? For people to bear witness when he's inside me, claiming me, marking me as his?

"All the men would be so fucking angry with me for getting to be with you." His voice breaks, as if he's losing himself to the fantasy. "And the women too, mad that you've attained what none of them ever could. And all they'd be able to do is watch."

"Fuck," I breathe, the word slipping out before I can stop it, my pulse jumping between my thighs. That one syllable is confirmation, though, and all he apparently needs to know.

Groaning, he retreats, and I'm left cold and unsatisfied, choking on how much I want him. His grin widens, revealing those perfect

---

73 Some characters just like playing with fire.

teeth that spend so much time sinking into my flesh, and he wipes the corner of my mouth where a little drool has leaked.

"We'll put on a show," he promises, squeezing the back of my neck. "Just not yet. First, we have business."

I nod, letting him lead me back to the security team, lost in the thoughts swirling around in my brain, coagulating to solidify just how gone I am for this villain.

CHAPTER 29

KAL

AS BADLY AS I'D LOVE TO HAVE ELENA SPREAD WIDE ON THE BACK seat of this rental SUV, I figure it's maybe not the best idea so close to seeing her parents.

She seems to settle a bit more once we've survived the throng of paparazzi and news broadcasters, each anxious to be the first to sell the story of her return. They mock and call out to her, apparently unaware that it's *me* at her side, her deranged captor, hidden beneath a thick scarf, knit beanie, and Ray-Bans.

Even though we had a brief discussion on the jet about what to say if she happened to catch any of the press questions thrown her way—nothing, preferably, and "no comment" if she absolutely needed to respond—I found myself filled with an inordinate amount of anxiety as we walked out of Logan, waiting for her to snap.

For her to turn to the cameramen and feed into the story, tell them I not only kidnapped her but forced her to marry me and murdered her ex-fiancé.

All true, technically, but still. For some reason, she's the only one who doesn't hold any of that against me.

And it wouldn't matter to the outside world that I murdered an abusive prick who probably would've tried to kill her once their marriage was final, especially after he found out she wasn't a virgin. Nor would it matter that I was trying to protect her and extract myself from this world when I did it.

When presented with the bones of a monster, the general public will believe the story they're told without digging any further.

They're spoon-fed lies, and because they're typically too stupid to think for themselves, no one ever questions why their soup tastes like poison.

"Ariana says Mamma is still hell-bent on having me come home," Elena says after a long stretch of silence, shifting in her seat.

I glance at the bra—pink, matching those heels I'd kill to have wrapped around my waist right now—visible through the lace top of her dress and make an unintelligible sound with my mouth, trying to downplay exactly how much I disdain her mother.

At this point, too much has happened between us for me to ever be able to break that part of my past to her. My history with Carmen Ricci will forever live in the grave she tossed it into, and I'll live on regretting that it ever happened in the first place.

But like all deaths, the death of a relationship is permanent. The ending of all endings. Finality in its purest form.

I can only hope she lets it stay that way.

"Would you ever consider…moving to Boston?"

My eyes find Elena's, wide and curious as she stares at me. Rubbing my thumb over my knee, I cock my head, pretending to consider it. "Full-time?"

"Yeah, you know. Become a Bostonian. *Pak ya ca in Havid Yad,* and all that fun stuff." She smiles, giggling at the exaggeration of her accent, a glimmer of something that looks an awful lot like hope shining in her gaze.

"Do you have a problem with Aplana?"

Her face falls, her smile freezing in place. "Not a *problem*, but...."

"Then I don't want to hear about how badly you'd like to leave," I snap, not processing the words before they're spewing from my lips, landing on the seat between us with a dull thud.

Turning my head forward, I pinch the bridge of my nose, blowing out a breath. My other hand snakes across the leather for hers, but she shrivels back, folding them in her lap. "Jesus, I knew coming back was a bad idea. Look, I'm not—"

"No, no. I heard you, loud and clear. I won't mention moving again."

When I look back over at her, I watch her push her nose higher in the air and pointedly look away.

"Elena," I say, my patience wearing very thin. The SUV rolls to a final stop, parking on the street in front of the Riccis' home, the brownstone dull from years of sunlight exposure. "I didn't mean it like that."

"Really? The great Kallum...*something* Anderson, speaking without thinking? I thought you didn't do that."

I squint, smothering a laugh as she fumes, wishing it didn't make me want to fuck her all the more. "Something?"

Her eyes narrow into slits. "I don't know your middle name. Because really, I still feel like I know nothing about you. Yet you want me to stay with you on your tiny little island and never ask questions, like some kind of slave."

You are the only one who knows anything about me.

"Asher," I say quickly, clenching and unclenching my jaw. Undoing my seat belt, I slide across to her, grabbing the buckle on hers before she has a chance to unlatch it. Trapping her between myself and the door, I lean in, running my hand up her thigh, admiring the sleek feel of her unmarked skin beneath my callouses. "My middle name is Asher."

"Kallum Asher Anderson," she breathes, chest rising and falling rapidly, like she isn't able to consume as much oxygen as she's putting out. She drops her gaze to my mouth, making my dick lengthen slightly.

"My name sounds like a prayer coming from these pretty pink lips," I murmur, grazing my hand along her side, bringing my thumb up and pushing into her mouth. "One I certainly wouldn't mind answering."

The tip of her tongue swirls over the pad of my thumb, eyes blazing with liquid fire. Arousal stirs in my chest, spreading like ivy outward, and I'm powerless against the soft moan that falls from me.[74]

"I can't stay mad at you when you look at me like that," she says, speaking around my thumb, a furious blush creeping up her neck. "It isn't fair."

"When I look at you like what?" I muse, the hand on her thigh traveling until it reaches the soft silken heat at its apex, my knuckles ghosting against her clit. No panties, even in fucking Boston.

Carmen's going to lose her shit.

A shaky gasp escapes her, making her eyelashes flutter as I dip one finger in the moisture collecting on her flesh, dragging it up to draw circles on her clit. She grips my bicep, clawing me to the point of pain, and swallows audibly.

"Like you're sorry."

The sentence sounds like an accusation, something you'd hurl at another during a heated argument as evidence of wrongdoings. But it *feels* like something worse.

Something she's aware of that I'm not ready to admit. Not even to myself.

---

74 I knew going in that their age difference would be a point of contention, so I wanted to make sure it never felt like there was an imbalance of power between them. Kal sees Elena as an equal—maybe even more powerful than him.

Our driver yanks open the back door on my side of the vehicle in the next second, and I spring forward, ensuring she's completely covered, cursing under my breath when I hear the shocked, collective gasp of a crowd.

My head starts to throb before I even hear her voice, violent fury rippling so abruptly through my veins that I tear myself away from Elena, afraid it might glom onto her.

"*Dio mio*! Back for less than a few hours, and you're already publicly corrupting her. Great way to prove your innocence, Kallum."

Elena stiffens at her mother's use of my full name, pulling the hem of her dress down as she shoves open her door. Unbuckling from her seat, she climbs out of the car, rounding the back end. She's met by a round of cheers, whooping and hollering from what appears to be the entirety of Louisburg Square.

Taking a moment to collect myself, I scrub my hands down my face, trying to regulate my shallow breathing. When I turn my head, Elena's been engulfed by the crowd, disappearing from my sight within seconds.

But Carmen stands at the door, watching *me*.

CHAPTER 30

ELENA

"*DIO MIO,* YOU MUST'VE PUT ON TEN POUNDS SINCE YOU'VE been gone."

Mamma's comment slices through the air of our living room, bouncing off the white walls and matching furniture, embedding itself in my skull where her criticism usually makes its home.

Now that the neighbors and childhood friends have filtered out for the evening, having spent every second since my arrival gushing over how happy they were to see me alive, despite my vehement denial that I was ever a captive, we're all sitting around awkwardly.

For the most part, when the shine of my return wore off and they finished asking about the island, everyone disappeared, as interested in my life as they were before I ever left Boston.

It didn't necessarily feel *good* seeing people I'd known for years become visibly bored by the truth behind my disappearance, but at least Kal looks less likely to commit mass murder now that the house is silent.

Or *was* silent.

Mamma sweeps into the room, a long red silk robe dragging on the floor behind her, a glass of white wine in one hand. She stands beside the white stone fireplace, keeping her distance while we wait for Papà to arrive with Ariana and Stella, who'd apparently been otherwise occupied.

"You could've at least *tried* to dress like a Ricci," she notes, curling her lip back as she rakes over my outfit. "Instead of Kallum's cheap flavor of the month."

I don't respond, knowing she'll eventually tire of the insults. Her game always was criticism first, pleasantries second, and it's just a matter of waiting her out.

Sipping slowly, Mamma keeps her dark gaze trained on Kal and me, the heat of her stare almost causing me to get to my feet and move to a different chair.

My fingers twitch in my lap, nerves eating away at any source of comfort created by my husband's proximity. *Pleasantries would be great any time now.*

But Kal seems completely unaffected, leaning back and slinging his arm on top of the sofa. His fingers toy with the ends of my hair, setting me further on edge, my body primed and ready for more.

Always ready for more where this man is concerned.

Nonna staggers into the room a few minutes after we settle in, wearing a royal-blue pantsuit and grumbling about getting cheated at her bridge game. She notices me, her wrinkled face splitting into a smile, and walks over, bending down to scoop my upper half into a bear hug.

"*Nipotina!*" she says, warmer than she's ever been with me. The slight hint of booze I get, mixed with stale perfume, tells me why. "The way your mother's been pouting around here the last couple of months, I'd begun to think you died and I missed the funeral."

I shake out a laugh, but it doesn't sound normal. "No, just got married." As if she wasn't there the day it all happened.

"Kind of the same thing, eh?" she says, slurring the words from one corner of her mouth, then slides her gaze to Kal beside me. "No offense, of course, dear. It's just I know men in my son's world. Hell, my husband started the family business here. I know how taxing it can be on a marriage."

"Maybe don't compare virtual strangers to the shitty men in your life." His eyes leave hers, darting quickly across the room and back—so quick I don't have a chance to see what he looked at. "I can promise you, we're quite different."

Mamma snorts into her wineglass.

Nonna squints at him, hiking her purse farther up her shoulder. "You'd be surprised how often I hear that." Yawning, she pushes white bangs from her face, patting my cheek as she straightens. "I'm going to turn in before your father arrives, but I'm sure I'll see you at the recital."

Nodding, I watch her head down the hall past the stairs, ambling toward the in-law suite at the back of the house.

My skin prickles with awareness of Mamma's continued perusal, and I start to push to my feet, but Kal tangles his fingers in my hair, twisting until they're flush with the nape of my neck. I glare from the corner of my eye, pulling gently so as not to alert Mamma to what he's doing.

"She's trying to get under your skin," he says in a low voice, only loud enough for me to hear. "Don't let her have that power over you."

"She's just *staring*," I hiss back, my voice just as low.

"Jealousy, little one. It's not as attractive on everyone as it is on you."

I let out a tiny, exasperated sound. "I don't even know what she's jealous *of*."

His mouth parts as if to answer, but in the next second, the front door is flying open, Papà and my sisters hustling inside, water dripping off their raincoats onto the dry floor.

"*Grazie a Dio*, Rafael!" Mamma snaps, splashing her wine as she gestures toward the foyer. "You're tracking mud everywhere."

Papà mutters something under his breath in Italian, coming into the living area looking primed for an argument. He stops dead in his tracks when he spots Kal and me on the sofa, eyes nearly popping out of his head.

"Elena," he says, blinking like he doesn't really believe I'm real. "You're here."

I get up when I feel Kal release his grip on my hair, although the way he lets his fingers comb through the strands emphasizes his reluctance to do so. Moving to wrap my arms around Papà, I kiss his stunned, ruddy face on both cheeks, the memories of the last time I saw him disappearing the second I'm engulfed in his warm embrace.

For a moment, I can almost forget that he risked my safety by forcing my hand in a marriage for personal gain. Twice.

I can almost forget the fact that he overlooked years of abuse, just because he so badly wanted to maintain his power in Boston and needed the alliance with Bollente to do so.

I *can* forget all of that.

But…I don't.[75]

As I pull out of his hug, something chilly skates across my skin, a foreboding sensation that makes me a little queasy. Like I'm chasing something that doesn't deserve to be caught.

Kal gets up silently, moving in to stand directly behind me. His large palms clamp down on my shoulders, yanking me back into his front, and then he's holding out a hand to Papà, a mask of stoicism guarding his features.

Ariana and Stella stand under the archway connecting the living

---

75 The growth! I love seeing this return of hers in action.

room to the foyer as if waiting to see what happens next before launching themselves inside.

"Rafe," Kal says, nodding in acknowledgment, even though the gesture feels vaguely passive-aggressive.

Papà doesn't reach out, ignoring Kal's offer entirely, eyes glued to me. They harden the longer the silence stretches, but then my sisters must decide it goes on for too long, because they bound into the living room, giggling and squealing, pulling me away from Kal and into their arms.

As far as I can tell, not much has changed about them in the weeks that I've been gone; Ariana's chestnut hair seems a little lighter than it once was, the freckles on her face more prominent now that it's springtime, and Stella's wearing the same thick-framed glasses, that familiar, bland expression forever etched onto her round face.

"Okay, officially, we've gone *way* too long without seeing you," Ariana says. She pushes back, grabs my biceps, and gives me a once-over. "Although we need to talk about how you're fucking *glowing*, E! You have to be getting a healthy dose of vitamin *D*."

She wiggles her eyebrows, and I roll my eyes, pushing her away. Mamma bristles, moving away from the fireplace to glare at us from a closer vantage point.

"Ariana, honestly." Sip, then glare. "Is that an appropriate way to talk to your sister?"

"What, I can't be happy that she's getting some?"

Papà makes a strangled sound in the back of his throat. "*Che palle*, Ariana. Watch your tongue."

Scoffing under her breath, she turns back to me, playing with the ends of my hair.

"They somehow got even stiffer after you left," Stella whispers, pushing her glasses up the bridge of her nose.

"How else would two emotionless robots accurately play the part of grieving parents?" Ariana says, just barely keeping her voice down.

"Have they really been that bad?" I ask, glancing over Stella's shoulder at Papà, who walks over to a sideboard near the doorway, pulling out a cigar and lighting up. Something I've never seen him do outside his office.

"It's been pretty bad," Ari says, rubbing her palms over her arms. "Papà is rarely home. Stella thinks he has a mistress."

Stella sputters, shaking her head wildly, dislodging some of the light brown hair from her low bun. "I didn't say *that*. I said I'd be surprised if he didn't, which is not the same as an accusation."

"Whatever," Ari says. "I'm sure he does have one. You know Mamma doesn't put out anymore. Not since her affair."

My heart practically falls out of my chest, that single sentence a wrecking ball to my entire worldview. I swing my gaze to hers, then back at my sisters, trying to process what they've just said.

"Sorry," I say, blinking. "Her *what*?"

Ariana and Stella glance at each other uneasily, as if trying to decide what all they should tell me. Stella glances down, noticing the diamond on my left ring finger for the first time, and it completely steals her attention, cutting off whatever they were about to say.

"Jesus, Mary, and Joseph," she says, yanking my hand closer to her face. "That's freaking huge."

"I'll bet it's not the only thing that's huge—"

"*Enough!*" Papà snaps, stalking over and grabbing Ariana's wrist, twisting it backward as he drags her away from me.

My eyes flicker to Kal, who stands back silently, hands shoved deep in his suit pockets. That muscle beneath his eye thumps erratically, the only sign that he's at all bothered by any of this.

Or maybe he's not bothered by how my parents are *acting* so much as the fact that he's here, having to endure the interactions at all.

"I've had enough shame put on this family between the two of you," Papà says, starting from the room, pulling Ariana along with him. "You'll wait on the rooftop for Father Sabino and your mother. Maybe they'll get you to shape up."

His words cause my chest to tighten, anxiety unspooling in my stomach. *What is that supposed to mean?*

"The *rooftop*?" She strains against him as he leads her up the winding staircase. "What are they going to do, push me off?"

"Don't be so fucking dramatic, Ariana. You're lucky I don't put you in a convent after everything you've pulled."

Their shouts echo off the walls, bouncing against the ceiling and bounding back down to us before trailing off and silencing entirely. Stella shifts uncomfortably, glancing over her shoulder at Mamma.

Sighing, Mamma takes a step forward, putting her hand on Stella's shoulder. It's the kind of comforting gesture I might have gotten a few months ago, but that is decidedly absent right now, despite the stories I've heard of how badly Mamma was missing me all this time.

When she steps into Stella, I slide my foot to the side and step into Kal, finding solace in the sturdy feel of his body against mine and that cinnamon and whiskey scent that somehow clings to him.[76]

Mamma catches the movement, narrowing her eyes at me. "Stella, *carina*, why don't you run upstairs and get a head start on some of your finals? I'm sure your world history essay won't write itself."

Of course. Mamma loves hiding Stella away under the guise of academic pursuit, when really, it's because she doesn't think Stella is interesting enough to remain. Ariana gets taken aside because she demands too much attention, and Stella's kept a secret because she doesn't demand enough.

Meanwhile, I seem to have struck the perfect balance over the

---

76 The way she's seeking comfort from him now versus when they first got married and she thought her parents would comfort her. I love this full-circle moment.

years. Purposely, to keep the two of them from the abuse our parents are capable of.

The pit in my stomach says I haven't done as good of a job as I thought.

Stella scoffs. "If only." She hesitates for a moment, looking at me with an uncertain gaze, like she isn't sure if she should leave me.

"Your sister will still be here tomorrow, I'm sure," Mamma offers, pushing Stella toward the stairs. "Run along now."

After giving me a last air-stealing hug, Stella disappears in the same direction Papà and Ari went, the dull thud of her sneakers the only sound for several minutes. Then a door slams shut, and suddenly it's just the three of us, drowning in silence.

KAL

I LET THE SILENCE FILLING THE RICCIS' LIVING ROOM SOAK INTO my skin for a moment, appreciating it while I can, aware that Carmen has a knack for shattering things.

If hearts were made of glass, the remaining pieces of mine would be jagged and splintered, wholly incapable of being glued back together.

Her round eyes swing between Elena and me, like the pendulum I broke weeks ago, trying to decide which of us to rip into first. Tension coils tight inside my stomach, stealing the breath from my lungs as it takes up more space than necessary.

"Why don't you two have a seat," Carmen suggests, motioning toward the couch we *just* got up from.

Her voice is like nails on a chalkboard, making my hand twitch against Elena's side, itching to make the sound stop once and for all.

"No thanks." My mouth parts to say the same thing, but it's Elena's words that fill the room, earning a shocked look from her mother.

"Did Kallum ruin my sweet, innocent daughter's manners?" Carmen says, glaring at me. "Have a *seat, bambina.* Show your mother some respect."

"The way you've respected my marriage by spreading rumors and lying to the tabloids about its nature?"

Frowning, Carmen says nothing for a beat, and I can practically see the cogs churning in her brain, searching for a way for her to turn the tables and make herself out to be the victim.

She's got that fucking glint in her eye, the one that flared to life each time she'd show up at whatever house I was renting after I turned eighteen, sobbing with mascara smeared down her cheeks, begging me to forgive her for being weak when it came to her husband.

It was always *"The children need their papà,"* and *"He'll hunt me down and kill me if I leave."* Never just the truth, which was that she never intended to leave Rafael in the first place.

She had her cake, and she wanted to eat it too.

Meanwhile, I should've never been subjected to her bullshit in the first place.

I had no business fielding the guilt of a much older and more experienced woman. I shouldn't have been cake—I should've been a goddamn kid.

But when that's all you know, when someone manipulates you during your formative years, it's a tough cycle to break away from.

"I'm not sure what your sisters have told you about my reaction to your…*whirlwind* wedding, but I'm sure it's been greatly exaggerated." Carmen settles in an overstuffed armchair, crossing one leg over the other, strategically rolling her ankle to make her leg appear longer through the slit in her robe. "Perhaps if you'd answered even one of my calls or texts, Elena, you'd have known that."[77]

"I have messages *from* you talking about how you want to rescue me," Elena says, pulling her phone from where it's stuffed in the cup

---

77 As weird as it may sound, writing Carmen was actually so interesting. She makes a very, very good irredeemable villain, and she's an expert at making you believe otherwise.

of her bra, opening up a thread of texts. She scrolls through them, reading out loud every plea and promise from Carmen.

"Are you saying I was unwarranted, all things considered? You were uprooted from your life. Mateo was…" She drops her voice, even though no one around is going to say anything. "Dead. I was worried for your safety."

"I was never in *danger*. Papà *signed off* on the freaking marriage certificate."

Carmen's wineglass pauses en route to her red lips, her eyebrows drawing down. "*Scusi?*"

"God, did he not tell you?" Elena asks, and I suddenly feel faint for the first time since my first hit.

Throat working as she swallows, Carmen's eyes dart to mine, hurt reflecting there, *still* trying to call out to me.

"It's true." I shrug, ignoring the pain pooling in her irises. It does nothing for me.

Setting her glass on the coffee table in front of her, she presses her fingers to her lips, her gaze unfocusing as she gets lost in her thoughts. Probably trying to figure out how she can wield this new information against us.

"That isn't possible," she decides finally with a little shake of her head. "Your father wouldn't just *allow* you to marry Kallum."

"Well, Mamma, he did, and when *Kallum* leaves Boston again in a few days, I'm going back with him," Elena snaps, her body straightening like a band that's been stretched far too thin, far too many times.

Carmen blinks. "Like *hell*."

Not letting her say another word, Elena spins on her heel and trudges from the room. Seconds later, the front door bangs closed, echoing off the ceiling.

Gritting her teeth, Carmen glares at me. She pushes to her feet, and I hold up my hand, halting her. "I wouldn't suggest coming any closer."

"What are you going to do? Kill me?" Laughing, she runs a shaky hand through her hair, freeing some of the strands from where they're trapped inside the collar of her robe. "Good luck getting Elena to forgive you."

My hands vibrate, fingers flexing around empty air as I take a step forward. Usually, there isn't much of an *urge* to cause harm; it's always been more of a necessity to me, a way to maintain a certain level of respect among my peers, and, for a long time, the sole source of my income and connections.

Outside of the specific code of conduct requiring made men and their associates to get a boss's permission before carrying out a hit, I don't like to take lives frivolously. It feels like cheating.

I want people to *earn* their demise at my hands. It makes their pleas for mercy much more delicious when they're denied.

And while Carmen's certainly earned her spot in hell, at least in my book, I don't *really* have a reason to snuff her out.

Not one that the others will believe anyway.

No matter how badly my bones ache for the chance.

"She'd learn to," I tell her, my lips curling up at the corners. "A couple rides on my cock, and she'd forget all about her cold, vindictive bitch of a mother."

Carmen just smirks, and the gesture infuriates me. My hair stands on end, heat rolling down my back like fire across a grassy field, while the urge to wrap my fingers around her throat and squeeze until her eyes pop from their sockets becomes a little overwhelming.

I pinch my thigh, trying to steady my blood, reminding myself that she's just doing it all on purpose.

"You haven't told her, have you?" she asks, arching an eyebrow. "I'll give it to you, she's a very pliant girl. *Eager* and willing, the way

Rafael brought her up to be. But I don't think she'd forgive you for sleeping with her mother."

The way she phrases it makes it sound like I was willing. *I didn't fucking know better.* "Tell her, and I'll slit your fucking throat."

Clicking her tongue, Carmen turns away, walking back to the armchair. She picks up her wineglass, taking a big gulp while sitting down and crossing her legs again. "As much as I'm sure you'd love to, we both know you won't. I know that look in your eyes, Kallum. You *care* about Elena. Moreover, you care what she thinks of you, and I think we both know there's no coming back from something like this."

When I don't say anything to refute the matter, knowing she'll just twist my words anyhow, she laughs, throwing her head back like this is all some big fucking joke.

"Well," she says, taking another drink and wiping her mouth on the back of her hand. "Guess you'd better get to her before I do then."

I contemplate the logistics of Carmen Ricci's murder in three different ways before I stalk out of her house, intent on finding Elena. She's tucked in the back seat of the SUV, scrolling aimlessly through her phone and complaining to Marcelline about her mother.

The window is cracked, perhaps to cool the interior now after a brief rain, and I pause before opening the door, listening quietly.

"…and honestly, she acts so prim and proper all the time, and then tonight my sister tells me she had an *affair*? What the hell? My mother doesn't even like when men wear ankle socks because she says it's immodest, but she was screwing around on my father? And wants to judge *me*?"

She blows out a breath, and Marcelline sits in her usual stony silence, punctuating Elena's story with the occasional *mhm*.

Hooking my fingers around the door handle, I yank it open,

revealing my wife with her feet propped against the opposite window, lying on her back as she stares up at her phone. She rolls her eyes toward her forehead, looking at me upside down.

"Is she still breathing?" she asks, the question a stab wound to my chest, proving Carmen right.

Elena probably wouldn't forgive me.

"Your mother is plenty alive," I say, slipping my hands under her back and lifting just enough so I can slide beneath her. She grunts as I do most of the work, her body going limp and molding into mine the second I let her go.

Sighing, Elena drops her hands, pressing her phone into her chest. "That did not go the way I was hoping."

I thread my fingers through her hair, my chest pinching for her. "I know."

"My fault for having expectations, I guess." Her voice catches at the end of her sentence, and she sucks down a gulp of air, rolling so she's facing the back of the seat. "Was your mom normal?"

"Normal's relative, I think."

Elena hums, closing her eyes as her nose brushes the leather seat. "Well, relatively speaking, I think my mother's insane."

Snorting, I take a second before responding, the pinch in my heart expanding into more of a dull pang, something bold that I can't possibly get rid of.

Because I can't stop wondering what Elena must think of me.

Later, there's a knock at the door of the penthouse we're renting during our stay; Elena's sprawled out in the bed, breathing heavily and twitching through some kind of dream, so I slip out quietly, hoping she doesn't hear me leave.

When I open the door, I'm not at all surprised to find Rafe standing on the other side, smoking a cigar even though the hallway has a bold NO SMOKING sign.

I guess some things really don't change.

We stand there for several beats of time, just staring at each other, until finally he breaks first.

He always breaks first.

"Aren't you going to invite me in?"

"No," I reply flatly.

His face screws up, and he takes the cigar from his mouth, huffing a plume of smoke in my direction. "You know, you used to respect the order of things. Used to understand that *I'm* your boss, not the other way around."

"You're not my boss, Rafe. Simple as that. I haven't done a job for you in months, nor have I been gathering intelligence or patching up any of your men. I don't work for you anymore."

"That isn't how this works," he snaps, pointing the butt of the cigar at me. "You don't get to just *leave*. There are protocols in place. Oaths that can't be broken."

I shrug. "Sounds like a family problem. Send them my condolences."[78]

"I put you through medical school. Kept you off the streets. The very least you could do is act like you're grateful."

"I'm grateful you were too stupid and selfish to keep your daughter from me, and now she's mine, forever. But my gratitude runs out about there, I'm afraid."

"You're not as invincible as you seem to think, Anderson. Don't forget I made you."

Smirking, my hand reaches for the door, and I begin to ease it shut, my quota for bullshit capped. "Oh, I won't."

He swears under his breath as the door clicks into place, and I stay there for a moment to see if he's going to knock again. The old

---

78 Kal is such a bastard. I love it.

Rafe would never have let something like this go without a fight, but maybe age is catching up with him.

Or maybe he has something worse planned.

Can't be worse than what I have planned for him though.

I pad back to the bedroom and slip beneath the covers, propping my elbow on my pillow as I stare down at my wife, brushing a strand of sweat-soaked hair from her cheek. A text flashes across my phone screen, Violet once again declining my most recent wire transfer.

"Pride cometh before the fall," I mutter to myself, opening the secure banking app I have set up through Ivers International, canceling every future payment I have scheduled to deposit into her account.

Then I text my grandfather's estate attorney, telling him I'm in Boston and want to set up a meeting to dissolve the trust altogether.

ELENA

I MEET MY SISTERS AND LORENZO, THEIR BODYGUARD, FOR BRUNCH at an upscale harbor diner the next day, and for a while, it almost feels like old times.

They sit across the table from me, Ariana's hair twisted into a bun and the sleeves of her light blue blouse buttoned at her elbows. Stella, meanwhile, tucks her hair into the collar of her button-down, leaning over her plate as Ari details some Hollywood scandal overshadowing the news of my "big return."

"…and I'm just saying, men like that who champion women's rights so vocally are always the first to be accused of sexual harassment. They're too good to be true."

Stella scoffs, bits of egg flying from her mouth. "You don't believe that girl's story, do you? They met one night in New York City, and he just *had* to have her? She's a little nobody from Maine, and he's a rock *god*. Why would he pick her?"

Ari tosses a bagel chip at her. "I'm choosing to believe the victim, asshole."

"In America, it's innocent until proven guilty," Stella says, shaking her head. "And don't act like you weren't singing the latest Aiden James single just *last week*. I can hear you in the shower, you know."

We make it through eggs Benedict, copious amounts of turkey bacon, and endless flutes of sparkling cider before anyone brings Mamma up.

It's me. I bring her up.[79]

"You guys said she was *despondent*," I accuse, pointing at Ariana with my fork. "That she wanted me home."

Ari shrugs, taking a bite of a cheese Danish. "She *was*, I swear it. There were days that she wouldn't even leave her room. I don't know why she acted so gross to you last night."

"Maybe she's jealous," Stella offers, shrugging her bony shoulders.

It's the second time someone has suggested as much in the last twenty-four hours, and I don't like that everyone seems to be catching onto something completely invisible to me. "Of *what*?"

"I don't know." Stella squints at me through her glasses, pursing her lips. "Take your pick, I guess? You know how Mamma is. Now imagine getting stuck in a life because of who your family is and never getting out of it. Once you're stuck, you're *stuck*."

"We're all stuck in this life," I say.

"Are we?" Stella takes her glasses, pushing them up into her hair-line. "Or have you spent the last few months being wined and dined by your incredibly dangerous, disturbingly handsome husband on an island completely removed from any and all *Ricci* drama?"

I poke at the remainder of my eggs, scowling. "It wasn't like I took a vacation. I was…"

Trailing off, I realize my sisters don't technically know the full

---

79 It's me, hi, I'm the problem, it's me!—Elena right now.

details of the reasoning behind my marriage to Kal. And I'm not exactly sure what our parents told them, so I decide to clear the air once and for all, hoping it'll eliminate the massive weight bearing down on my chest.

"Someone recorded Kal and me the first time we slept together."

Ari snickers. "First implies there was a second and third and—"

Stella wraps her arm around Ari's neck, clamping her hand over her mouth. "We already know that. Papà wasted no time in telling everyone how Kal seduced you. Not that you needed sympathy in the public's eye, being kidnapped and all."

Annoyance flickers in my gut, but I ignore it, setting my fork down. "Okay, well. The people who recorded us were blackmailing Papà and Kal, and they wanted me to marry Kal…I guess."

Blinking, I glance down at the gold tablecloth covering the table, realizing my own details on the optics are blurry.

Shaking off the eerie feeling, I continue. "Whatever, I don't know the exact details, but the point is someone forced *both* of us into the marriage. Maybe Kal didn't approach everything in the best way, but we're both *victims*."

"*Are* you?" Ari asks, shoving Stella's hand away. "I mean, that's why you *got* married, but…what's making you stay married?" She reaches for a strawberry off her plate, plopping it in her mouth. "You certainly don't *look* like a victim."

My mouth parts immediately, a reflexive response poised on the tip of my tongue before her words fully process. Snapping my lips shut, I sit back in my seat, my stomach dropping to my knees.

Stella quickly changes the subject, moving on before I've answered Ariana to talk about the physics course she's taking at Harvard over the summer, her fifteen-year-old brain apparently growing bored of the marriage talk. But Ariana watches me throughout the rest of brunch, silent and steady, and I wonder if she sees what I'm trying so desperately to hide.

The truth.

Supper with my family is a big deal.

I'm not sure if it's the Italian heritage or the fact that it was the only meal Papà could ever manage to make it to, but Mamma would always break out the *good* dishes after spending the day using paper plates, and she'd make a spread fit for an army.

The next time we go to my parents' house, the night of Ariana's recital, supper seems more like an intimate affair than the massive feast it once was.

Kal and I walk to the courtyard through the kitchen, noting the twinkling lights strung up, dwarfed in comparison to the city skyline just beyond. The table is set with Mamma's wedding china, as if her company bears great importance, and there are only enough table settings for the seven of us.

I can't remember a single time in family history where we ate with fewer than eight people. If not a group of girls from school—whose parents hadn't yet realized *whose* house they were going to—then any number of the other family members. On occasion, we'd even host certain diplomats, each Ricci daughter putting on her best dress and fakest smile so Papà could pretend everything was fine where business was concerned.

The lack of abundance here makes me uneasy, and I pause just inside the threshold, unsure if I want to continue or if we should just pack up and head home. Keep living in our little bubble.

Since my realization on the jet, my feelings for Kal have shifted to the forefront of my thoughts, blotting out everything else until I'm living and breathing and *bleeding* for this man.

I'm not even sure if it makes sense, so I keep the sentiment to myself, afraid that this secretly broken being before me doesn't really want this marriage to go on.

Afraid of what it means if he *does.*

Kal pauses just ahead of me, seeming to sense that I'm no longer at his side. He turns, furrowing his brows, and moves to stand in front of me.

"Elena?"

Shaking my head, I try to dispel the sudden fog blanketing my brain, like vaporized anxiety finding a home in my body. "I…I don't feel very well."

He doesn't say anything for a moment. Just blinks down at me until my unease is due in part to his study. Finally, he smooths a hand down the front of his black tailored suit, glancing over his shoulder at where my sisters lean into each other, whispering conspiratorially.

"Do you want to leave?"

Chewing on the corner of my lip, I consider it, guilt slamming down on my shoulders. How is it possible that a place and the people I once longed for now feel like the singular bane of my existence?

"Say the word, little one, and I'll have you back in Aplana before you can take your next breath." He inches forward, a husky look falling over his handsome face. "Imagine all the fun we could be having."

I almost fold. It'd be so easy to feign illness and let Kal take me back to where the rest of the world ceases to exist.

To fall into each other and pretend like none of this is doomed.

Too easy though. After the way she acted when I left the first time, there's no way Mamma would let me leave quietly. She'd probably burn Boston to the ground, just to keep me under her wing, a nice little doll she can dress up and manipulate forever.

So instead of accepting Kal's offer, I shake my head again, straightening my spine until it cracks.

"I made you come here. It's only fair I see it through, right?"

His mouth curves down, the muscle below his eye pulsing. "You didn't *make* me do anything. I did it because I—"

"Supper is served!"

One of my parents' private chefs pushes a cart through the French doors, wheeling a covered baking dish over to the table. Nonna and Papà file in after, Papà taking his usual spot at the head of the table. Normally, Mamma would sit at the opposite end, and everyone else would find a seat between, but Kal walks over to the table and plops down in Mamma's chair.

Stella and Ariana freeze, lifting their heads as he sits. I feel the heat of their gazes on me, but I can't tear mine from my husband, stomach tightening until it's forcing bile up, burning the expanse of my chest with the onslaught.

God, this is going to be a long night.

Quietly, Nonna sits on the other side of Stella, patting her elbow and saying the bucatini all'Amatriciana smells amazing. Papà and Kal are locked in a staring contest, although it's beginning to feel like something more.

Something they aren't telling me.

Normally, we wait to eat until all the guests are seated at the table, and since Mamma hasn't yet arrived, the Riccis all sit back in their seats, sipping drinks or buttering rolls.

Kal, though, reaches to the center of the table, removes the cloche from the pasta dish, and makes himself a plate.[80]

Taking the seat to Kal's left, I unfold my napkin and settle it over my lap. My voice is hushed when I speak, barely audible, but Kal

---

80 A bastard, I tell you!

leans in and listens as he shoves a forkful of bucatini into his mouth. "Why are you locked in some sort of dick measuring contest with Papà right now?"

"Mine's bigger. Contest over." He tucks his napkin into the collar of his shirt, clearing his throat without dropping my father's stare.

I make a face. "Ew. What's going on with you two? Aren't you worried about how this might look to the Elders?"

"How what might look?"

I shrug, moving my hands in a circular gesture. "*This.* You, undermining his contract with Bollente Media, marrying the daughter he promised to them, and now the obvious power struggle?"

"There's no power struggle to be had here, little one. Your father has none." Finally, Kal looks at me, his eyes smoldering, causing heat to pool between my thighs. "The only one here with any sort of power, especially over *you*, is me. Your husband."

His words make my throat constrict, even though they sound vaguely threatening in nature. His tone, though, oozes sex, and although my brain is struggling to keep up with every single emotion rolling around in my body, it's that one it latches on to.

Like a familiar friend, arousal shows up and overpowers everything else, making me forget what I was even just complaining about.

Clenching my thighs together, I shift in my seat, reaching for the glass of water in front of me. I take a sip, keeping my eyes locked with Kal, until Papà clears his throat, drawing my attention.

"*Bambina,*" Papà says around his whiskey. "How's school?"

My hand freezes in midair and I choke up, almost dropping my glass. I take another sip, buying a few seconds while I scrape together an answer. "I...dropped out."

Okay, not a good save, but whatever.

His eyes widen, and he sets his tumbler back on the table. "*Perché?*"

I can feel Kal watching me, but I look right at Papà. "I didn't want to do it anymore. Teaching literature doesn't interest me."

"I see." Papà's nostrils flare, and he taps his thumb ring against his glass. "I suppose you didn't think to inform the person on the hook for your student loans that he'd be having to pay for them sooner than he thought?"

Shame scores my face, fiery as it lashes against my skin. Ariana and Stella glare at the table, while Nonna downs the rest of her wine.

"Never mind the fact that I *said* from the beginning that school wasn't your destiny. But you didn't want to believe me. Had to learn the hard way and screw me over in the process."

Kal stiffens beside me, fingers tightening around his fork until his knuckles bloom white. My foot kicks out, pressing against his in a silent plea not to send the utensil through my father's throat.

"I'm sorry, Papà," I say softly, the anger in his gaze revitalizing the nausea from before. It blows up, like a vapor expanding to fill the shape of its container, and I grip the edge of the table, trying to stave off the vomit rising in my esophagus. "I hadn't even thought about that."

"Of course you didn't, because you're still an immature, selfish little girl."

Mamma's voice interrupts the quiet din of the patio atmosphere, and for once, I hear the malice threaded in her words. It's not disguised at all in her tone, and when she rounds the table in a floor-length, bright red evening gown, I *see* it written on her face.

The woman who helped me get ready for my wedding and the woman standing here now are not the same person.

Not even a little bit.

Or maybe the problem is that I'm different.

Kal shoves back from the table, making the dishes clatter with the force. Murder rims his dark eyes, setting them aflame. "*Carmen.*"

She grins, lifting a brow, bringing her wineglass to her lips. "Oh, come on, Kal. I know my daughter. She's quite the chip off the old block, wouldn't you say?"

Sighing, Papà rubs his temple. "Carmen, what are you doing?"

Sitting in the chair at his side, her grin grows, stretching so wide across her face that it looks painful. She swirls the wine in her glass, gesturing toward my sisters. "Girls, why don't you take Nonna to her room for a nap? We don't want her falling asleep at the recital."

Ariana snorts. "I don't want to miss whatever this is."

But Stella elbows her, yanking her up from the table; they flank Nonna on both sides, catching her when she droops forward in her drunken stupor.

"I was *going* to tell you," I say, putting my water down. "It just kind of slipped my mind with everything else."

"Yes," Mamma says, leaning back in her chair, "hard to remember important things like who your family really is when you're too busy spreading your legs for the first man to ever pretend he cared about you."

My face heats up, bile scratching and clawing at the base of my throat, dragging irritation up along with it. "What's wrong with that? He's my *husband* after all."

"Because your father wanted him away from *me.*"

CHAPTER 33

ELENA

MY MOTHER'S ACCUSATION HURTLES THROUGH THE AIR LIKE A slow-motion car crash, slowing time as the world simultaneously implodes around us.

On impact, my ribs are crushed, splintering into a million little pieces and swept away in my bloodstream. My heart feels like an overinflated balloon, popping when stretched to its limits, and I try to swallow down the ache in my throat as my eyes find Kal's, hoping for some kind of hint that she's lying.

That she's just trying to get under my skin and make me feel bad for abandoning her.

Jaw clenched, Kal meets my gaze, eyes guarded but transparent. His shoulders slump just the slightest fraction, and his Adam's apple jumps, and I quickly drop my stare to the table, feeling tears burning behind my lids at his silence.

It's a sign. An admission.

Just not the one I'd been hoping for.

"*Manache*," Papà grumbles, drawing an imaginary cross over his chest. "My decision had nothing to do with you fucking him over ten years ago, Carmen. *Cristo.*"

Mamma tsks, taking a long swig of her wine. Her hand wobbles on its descent, and I can't help wondering if she's mixing, the way the other mob wives seem to, relying on a nice chemical cocktail to get through their miserable lives.

"Oh dear, did I expose some of Kallum's dirty laundry? You two just looked so…*cozy* together, I couldn't fathom that he hadn't told you about our affair yet."

Our affair.

The phrase tastes bitter on my tongue, like biting into a fruit that hasn't quite ripened yet, all because you couldn't stand to be patient. Just another day, a little extra self-control, and you might have bitten into something juicy and delectable.

Instead, you're left with the dull flavor of your mistakes, wondering why the man you've fallen in love with shares *anything* with another.

Much less your *mother.*

My hands itch to wrap around her neck and squeeze for using his full name so flippantly. Like she's at all deserving of it.

Even without knowing the details, I know she isn't.

"Except I *told* you the other night she didn't know." Kal's voice is a hot blade to my skin, laced with rust as it slices through me.

"Did you?" She shrugs one shoulder, humming. "Must've slipped my mind. We talked about *so many things.*"

Looking at the hollow of Kal's throat, the divot I've run my tongue over more times than I can even count at this point, I lick my lips, afraid to go any higher. "When did you speak to my mother?"

He flattens his palms on the table, his wedding band catching in the light. "You knew about this. It was the other night, right after you went outside."

"Ah yes, when you so kindly tossed him into my waiting arms."

"*Carmen,*" Papà snaps, rubbing his hand over his face. "What the fuck are you *doing?*"

"The only way I would be tossed into your arms is if they were torn from your body and set on fire," Kal says, curling his fingers. "And even then, it would be so I could join you in the afterlife and personally drop you on Satan's doorstep."

There's hatred in his voice, venom spewing from the tip of his tongue, but I grew up on the principle of thought that love and hate were just two sides of the same coin. The only difference was circumstance, and as my eyes volley between Kal and my mother, one a rabid beast ready to destroy its prey, the other a hungry predator looking to feast, I realize I can't quite tell where the two lie in regard to that coin.

"You slept with my mother?" I ask, my brain still struggling to process.[81]

"Well, there never was much sleeping involved, if you know what I mean," Mamma mutters, laughing at her own joke, even though everyone else on the patio remains eerily still, one comment away from complete annihilation. "I certainly hope you two are better with contraception than we were, because I'll tell you. That man is *potent*, if you know what I mean." She hiccups, confirming to me that she's at *least* a little high, although that certainly doesn't lessen the sting. "Oops, did I say that twice?"

The implication hangs heavy in the air between the four of us, souring my stomach, threatening to expel the contents. My throat tightens, the weight of this revelation wrapping its claws around me until I'm gasping for my next breath and praying it never comes in the same thought.

I think I'm going to be sick.

"Jesus Christ, you really are a bitch." Kal rips his napkin from his throat, throwing it on the table as he pushes to his feet, turning to look at me. "Elena. Can I please have a moment alone with you?"

---

81 Oh god, the drama. Greek tragedy, anyone?

My heart pounds in my chest, rattling my entire beating. I can barely hear them over it.

"I don't think she'll be going anywhere with you again, Kallum." Mamma sloshes her wine in his direction, glaring. "You stay away from my little girl."

I stare at the centerpiece in the middle of the table, letting my eyes lose focus in the brightness of the dahlias and lilies. Flowers I would've had at my wedding or funeral, their presence now ironic, since I've never been more convinced that I'm dying.

Yet that's what heartbreak feels like; it's having someone reach into your chest and tear the organ from your body, except they don't use any tools or care to make it a clean extraction. They yank and twist until it pops free, leaving all the broken muscle and tissue behind, veins spilling with nowhere else to pump into.

It's visceral, blinding pain that sparks in the wound and creeps outward, testing the waters to see how much you can take.

Betrayal slithers like lava down my spine, obliterating everything in its path. Looking up at Kal, I'm struck by how immediately your entire view of a person can change when presented with new information about them.

When I felt the scars on his body, proving a lifetime of evil deeds, I saw a man trapped in a monster's body.

When I saw the pictures of his mom and sister, my heart ached for a boy with no one, who grew up and filled the cracks in his soul with whatever scraps of attention and affection he could get.

Now, all I see is a liar.

A man I don't even recognize. His shape shifts into a sinister being as I stare at him silently, still hoping beyond hope that he'll refute what my mother's saying. That I wasn't his sloppy seconds, his only option.

His revenge piece.

"You're of no use to me dead, little one."

I suppose this solves that mystery.

Pushing my chair back slowly from the table, I keep my eyes trained on my glass of water, refusing to look at anyone in fear of an instant breakdown.

"If you'll excuse me," I choke out woodenly. "I don't want to be late for Ari's recital."

I feel three pairs of eyes on me, feel the surprise from all of them. "Elena," Papà says, and I hear his chair scrape across the concrete, creaking as he stands. "We should probably talk about this—"

Shaking my head, I press my lips together, afraid of what might slip out if given the slightest opportunity. A sob tickles the back of my throat, and no matter how many times I try to push it down, it refuses, lodging itself there like agony demanding my attention.

Whoever said the stages of grief don't just apply to death was onto something.

Turning on my heel, I sidestep my chair and head back into the house, passing through the kitchen. I swipe my purse and coat from the sofa in the living room, almost making it to the front door before a hand grabs my wrist, yanking me backward.

"Don't you dare leave this house without talking to me," Kal snaps, turning me around so I'm facing him. "*We* don't do that shit."

Trying to twist out of his grip, I snarl, "*We* don't do anything. Don't tell me to open up about how I'm feeling when you've been lying to me the *entire time* I've known you."

"When would have been a good time to bring it up? I couldn't very well be buried in your pussy and casually dredge up the fact that I've seen your mother in a similar state."

The sentence burns as it slaps across my face, worse than if he'd just killed me on the spot. At least the pain would likely be over soon. "Well, lucky for you, she cut out the middleman and did it for you. Solved that dilemma real quick, didn't it?"

My free hand claws at the front door, turning the knob and wrenching it open. Yanking on my arm again, I glare up at him.

"Let *go* of me."

His gaze sears straight through me, skipping my heart altogether and igniting my soul on fire. But not the good kind of fire, that grazes your skin and fills you with warmth. It's the kind that singes and steals, destruction in the form of flames.

"I *can't*," he grits, although his fingers retract at the same time, reaching up to card through his hair. "Jesus, Elena, just give me five minutes. I swear, it's not... it's not how it sounds."

Part of me wants to, *aches* to stay back and hear what he has to say, but the anger pulsing through me takes precedence, wanting him to suffer.

"I can't," I repeat.

Ari floats down the staircase, half her face decorated in sparkly foundation and gold makeup, completely oblivious to everything that's just happened.

I catch her as she starts to slip out the other side of the door, raising an eyebrow. "Are you going to the recital already?"

She nods. "We always rehearse a few of the trickier numbers before the show." Peering up at Kal, she purses her lips, then looks back to me. "Want to come with?"

Nodding, I follow her out to the car sitting idle at the curb, Lorenzo behind the wheel. And when I climb in the back, chancing a single glance over my shoulder, I see Kal still standing in the doorway, frozen in place like a statue.

When we drive away, I let my sobs choke free. Ari scoots closer, letting me cry on her shoulder even though she doesn't seem to know what's going on.

I always wondered what would happen if I bled wide-open and he wasn't there to blot it up with his tongue or fingers or first aid kit.

Guess now I have my answer.

CHAPTER 34

KAL

I HAVE HALF A MIND TO CHASE AFTER HER.

Do for Elena what no other has ever done for me.

But it's all for naught if I don't figure my shit out here first.

So even though it feels like returning to hell when I walk out to the courtyard, I push through the anger bleating against my skull and walk to my end of the table. Palming the back of the padded chair, I stare down for a moment at the uneaten pasta, the glass Elena left behind, smudged with pink lip gloss.

Rafe's disappeared, probably off to light another cigar, leaving just me and his wife. Carmen slurps at her wine, clearly beyond incapacitated, and giggles. "Trouble in paradise, *amore mio?*"

Clenching my jaw, I raise my eyes, zeroing in on the suckling sound, letting it fan the flames inside of me. They stretch beyond belief, until I can feel my skin buzzing with the need for violence.

"Give me one reason why I shouldn't gut you right here, right now," I say in a low voice, careful not to reveal just how angry she's made me. If they know you're bothered, they use it against you.

Which makes all this my fucking fault.

"*Dio mio*, you never were any good at flirting." She sets her glass down, reaching to adjust the strap of her red dress when it slips. Her fingers curl around it, then pause, and she drops her hand as if suddenly thinking better of it.

Bedroom eyes turn up at mine, and she shifts, tilting her bronzed shoulder as if she's trying to entice me.

Gripping the chair until my fingernails start to split from the pressure, I resist the urge to laugh in the bitch's face, knowing that'll only feed her antics.

"One reason, Carmen." Reaching for the waistband of my pants, I slide my hand around, dislodging the gun tucked in the back.[82] Smoothing my fingers over the cool metal barrel, I unlock the safety and cock it, pointing at her with the mouth. "Doesn't even have to be a good one necessarily. But you'd better think real fucking fast before I make the decision for you."

She doesn't even flinch, as if unaware that none of my threats are ever hollow. Fixing her strap with a sharp snap against her skin, she sits up straighter, giving me a bland look.

"You're not going to kill me, Kallum. If you were, you would've done it the second you found me in bed with someone else."

My side throbs spastically, like my flesh is being carved open all over again after finding myself on the other end of an ambush. In my *own* home.

It was a rival family member, someone from Southie; if I'd been expecting either one of them to be in *my* bed, he wouldn't have had the upper hand.

But you don't expect the people you care about to betray you right under your nose.

I remember the searing pain where the knife went in, thinking that would be the end of it. At that point, I hadn't been doing

---

82 I bet we could make a drinking game out of the times my MMCs pull guns from their pants.

lethal hits all that long, and torture certainly wasn't something I even thought of when doing Ricci jobs, so when the knife entered, stayed in, and began to move, I remember the shock absorbing the brunt of the initial torment.

I remember waking up mid-surgery; I'd been flown to a nearby hospital after an anonymous tip alerted the cops to my state. They'd been so concerned with the loss of blood and possible abrasions to my liver and spleen that no one bothered to clean the wound or try to free some of the broken muscle that would eventually produce the mass of scar tissue on my side.

I remember the pain after the surgery; they called it phantom pangs. Said I'd probably feel them the rest of my life, long after everything else healed.

They said I was lucky. That a guardian angel must have been watching over me, because the damage to my spleen had been pretty significant, but they'd managed to repair the rupture.

It was my nineteenth birthday.

I never felt lucky.

Not one time in my life, even with the countless brushes with death, did I feel lucky.

Until Elena.

All Carmen ever made me feel was *sick*.

She never even told me why she did it, though I assumed it was because she could. Because there are few better ways to fuck with someone's head, especially when you sense them pulling away from you, than to make them think you no longer give a shit if they live or die.

It was that, the unknowingness, that kept me on the hook for years. The woman I'd looked up to, sought comfort from, manipulated and turned on me, and I never knew why. She'd used me, preyed on my innocence, and tossed me aside.

Eventually, I decided it didn't matter. I was glad she let me go, even if doing so left claw marks on my skin.

The chair creaks beneath the weight of my grip, the wood hidden beneath the soft fabric bending at my whim. I school my features, gritting my teeth against the fury building like a cyclone in my chest, spiraling out of control.

Raising my arm, I point the pistol right at her forehead. "We can remedy that mistake now. I certainly don't want to make the same one twice."

She swallows, watching me with those glassy eyes. "Elena will never forgive you for killing her mother. She's hurt now, but she knows who's always been there for her. She'll always choose this family over a stranger."

Releasing my hold on the chair, I begin to slowly creep around the table, keeping the gun trained on her. "You took her away from me, so that little fear tactic doesn't really apply anymore, does it? What do I care if she forgives me, if she's not going to be warming my bed and cock at night?"

Carmen scoffs, disgust flooding her features. "As crude and vile as ever, I see."

I move closer, brushing my index finger over the trigger. "You know what's *crude*? The number of times I've told your daughter to get on her knees and watched her choke on me. How I've broken her skin and lapped at her blood so many times, the flavor is practically embedded into my taste buds."

Pausing right beside her, I lift the gun to her forehead, pressing the mouth to her temple. "She gets off on it, you know. The pain. Never looks at me like I'm sick or deranged or some kind of monster. I bet if I got her pregnant right now, she wouldn't eliminate the *problem* or make me feel like I'd done something wrong. *You* were the adult. I didn't fucking know what I was doing."

"Oh please. You were hardly ever really a child, Kallum."

Anger bleeds into my brain, still trying to grapple with the fact that I'm saying any of this out loud. I've only recently been able to subconsciously admit it all to myself. "Do you know why I did it, Carmen? Do you get why I chose her?"

Carmen's tongue swipes quickly across her lips, beads of sweat popping up where the gun is flush with her skin.

"It's because she's as fucked up as me."

"You can't talk about my daughter this way—"

The sound of a dull pop cracks against the air like a whip, and Carmen shrieks loudly, jolting in her seat. Even long after the realization sets in that a blank was fired, she still screams, the ear-piercing noise quickly becoming an irritant to my already frayed nerves.

Her hands come down, clamping around the arms of her chair, and she presses her back as far from me as she can manage.

Which, all things considered, isn't far. But I appreciate the effort.

Makes it feel a little less like a conquest and more like a reckoning.

"I'll talk about *my wife* any way I please. Because you know what was really vile here tonight, Carmen?" I wait, though she still doesn't answer. "What you did was vile, and if I didn't care so much about your fucking daughter and how this might affect her, you'd be drifting to the bottom of the Charles right now for fucking everything up so spectacularly."

"I'm sorry," she sobs, crumbling under the slightest bit of pressure, just like she used to. It's a wonder Elena has any backbone at all. "It wasn't…" She blows out a breath, trying to collect herself. "I was in love with you, Kal. I just didn't know how to…navigate it. You scared me."

Her words float to the recesses of my brain, the secret places dormant in the years since our relationship, if that's what you can even call it. Part of me expects them to ignite the old feelings, the young, confused, and immature sense of accomplishment I used to feel when showered with her affection.

But she made a kid with nothing feel loved before she broke him down into pieces.

Now, all I feel is empty.

And as I let that feeling take root in my heart, spreading outward, I realize something else.

She may have loved me, but I *never* loved her.

Losing her never felt like being dismembered or having the blood drained right from your body, creating a loneliness unlike anything I've ever known.

It never felt like spending your life as a sinner and finally getting a taste of heaven, only to have it ripped right out from beneath your fingertips.

But it takes a woman like Elena to elicit feelings like that. It requires kindness and warmth. Not the kind of fires lit just for the hell of it but the flames that *flourish* with passion and understanding and just a touch of darkness.

It's Elena's innate *goodness* that makes the loss fucking unbearable.[83]

Without her, I feel like one half of a soul, existing aimlessly, waiting for the earth to reclaim me the way I have so many others.

Months ago, when I forced her hand, I hadn't even realized anything in my life was missing. Didn't realize I *wanted* someone there to balance me out, to peel back the curtains and shed a little light, so long as I also got to paint her in shadows.

She's only been gone for minutes, and all I can focus on is her absence.

Anguish claws a path up my spine, leaving behind bloody, gaping

---

83 I've said it before, but the collective love of poetry between Kal and Elena really shines when they talk about each other, and I just adored writing such beautiful thoughts, especially in his mind, compared to how he feels about literally everyone else.

wounds that only deepen with each passing second I spend not chasing after her.

Carmen's still sobbing, fake tears staining her cheeks, and I drop the gun slightly, shaking my head. "It's a nice sentiment, but it's an entire decade too late. And frankly, I don't want your explanation. Or your love. The only one who deserves it is Elena, because she's the one who cares about you."

Flicking my wrist back, I whip it forward, lashing the barrel of the gun against her cheekbone, reveling in that familiar *crack* that resounds at the impact. She screams, her hands flying to her face as she chokes on her saliva.

"Let that be your fucking lesson here," I say, stepping away. "You get to live, because I don't *care* enough to kill you."

As she continues screaming, I drag a hand through my hair and leave her there, heading inside, my chest somehow lighter than ever despite everything else going on.

Rafael leans against the staircase when I pass through the kitchen, smoke billowing up around his head. "You didn't mean to fire a warning shot, did you."

He doesn't *ask*, just states his sentence as though it's the most obvious thing in the world.

I stuff my hands in my pockets, lifting a shoulder. "Sounds like you already know the answer to that."

Grunting, he takes another puff, watching me. "I'll kill the kidnapping story if you pay what you owe me."

Blinking, I almost laugh, tucking my pistol into the back of my pants. "I don't *owe* you anything. I don't even think anyone is interested in your fabricated story anymore."

"That contract you fucked me out of with Bollente cost me a quarter million. I shut down the Montaltos in King's Trace and sold what product we had there, but if the Riccis have any chance at withstanding all this, the blackmail, the debt collectors, the feds snooping when they realize I'm not paying the local police to turn a blind eye anymore…I need *financial* support, Kal. Don't fucking think you're screwing me out of this too."

Smirking, I start toward the front door again, brushing past even as he reaches an arm out, trying to stop me. He's considerably shorter than me, so I just lift my arm, dodging his grip.

"The problem with your appeal, dear Rafael, is that I don't give a fuck if Ricci Inc. burns to the ground. If it doesn't, fine. If it does, good riddance." Yanking open the door, I give him a half salute with my middle finger. "You've taken enough of my life at this point as it is. It's time for me to repay the favor."

CHAPTER 35

KAL

THE THEATER LISTED ON THE TICKET FOR ARIANA'S RECITAL IS A HALF hour drive across town, and I hop in the rental SUV as I walk out of the Riccis' house and head there immediately.

It's an ornate building with massive Greco-Roman columns framing the front and stained-glass skylights obscuring the night. After handing an usher my ticket, I'm sent in the direction of the appropriate auditorium, but I spend a few extra minutes pacing outside, just in case Elena hasn't gone in yet.

Fifteen minutes pass, and she doesn't show up, so I go inside and find my seat.

We're in a private box, apparently, only accessible through a separate set of stairs, guarded by an usher with braces who smiles brightly at me when I flash my barcode.

"Mr. Anderson, seat 11B." She glances around, then hands my ticket back. "Will the rest of your party be joining soon?"

"My party?"

Pulling out a clipboard, she flips through a small stack of papers, nodding as she apparently finds the information she's looking for. "Yes, we have a private box reserved for Mr. and Mrs. Anderson and the adjoining box, number twelve, booked for a Mr. and Mrs. Ricci and two guests."

Shaking my head, I stuff my ticket into my suit pocket, sidestepping her. "I have no clue if they're coming or not. Can you make sure Mrs. Anderson and I aren't disturbed?"

The kid frowns, her blush visible even in the dim lighting. "Sir, I must inform you that explicit relations are strictly prohibited on the premises, resulting in fines of up to one thousand dollars."

Tapping my foot impatiently, I reach into my pants for my wallet, pulling a wad of cash from the flap. "Consider this a down payment."[84]

I don't wait for her to accept it, shoving it into her fist and pushing past, stepping over the velvet rope barring the staircase. Bounding up the flight, I try to calm my racing heart, preparing myself for the possibility that she isn't up here.

Still, when I shove aside the curtain to our box, my heart beats so fast it feels like it might explode. Her silhouette is lit up by the stage below as she leans forward in her chair, slumped over the balcony railing. I step down into the box, quietly approaching, my hand reaching out to grasp her shoulder, when she speaks.

"Don't."

It's one word, long enough to drive through my chest and pierce the organ beating just for her. She doesn't even glance over her shoulder or move a muscle, her body so in tune with mine at this point it seems to just *know* when I'm around.

Or maybe she knew I'd come. Maybe that's what she wanted all along.

My hand falls to my side, that familiar fucking ache pulsing in the pit of my stomach.

---

84 It will always be funny to me that Kal was one of the easiest characters for me to write, because I am not smooth like him at ALL. This is the evidence we need to know I am not writing fictional versions of myself, LOL.

"Elena, I—"

"If you came here to apologize, you can save it."

Her attitude catches me slightly off guard, considering the last time I saw her, she'd looked as miserable as I felt. Crushed, like the revelation of my past bore any consequence on our future.

Devastated, like I'd chosen secrets over her.

Taking the seat next to hers, I stretch my legs out, pushing my feet against the balcony's footboard, and fold my hands in my lap. If she's not giving me the silent treatment, perhaps she's had time to sit and reflect on what she's learned tonight, and she's decided to move on.

"I didn't come to apologize," I say softly, leaning up to whisper in her ear. "Although I *am* sorry. But really, I came to make sure you were all right."

She doesn't say anything for a while, silently staring out as stagehands begin setting up props, rushing from one end of the stage to the other, racing against the clock to be ready in time for the show.

Sighing, Elena shakes her head. "I'm not. Not even a little bit, Kal. And I *really* don't want to talk about any of it with you."

Squeezing the seat rests, I lean back, trying not to let my frustration show. "You're my wife, little one. We *have* to talk about it."

Turning to the side, the wall sconce provides just enough light for me to see her beautiful face cast in shadows. Her golden eyes almost glow, or maybe I'm imagining it, creating passion and fight where I'm afraid there is none.

"How legitimate is our marriage *really*? And don't give me that bullshit line about it being as real as mine with Mateo's would've been. I didn't marry Mateo. I'm not wearing his ring. I married you, and I'm wearing yours, so tell me, *Kallum*…"

Her voice breaks on the last syllable, making the ache in my chest expand until it's ready to destroy me. She quickly straightens her chin, glancing back down at the stage.

Swallowing audibly, despite the soft chatter floating up from the floor seats, she reaches out, wrapping her fingers around the railing, and tries again. "How much of it was real, and how much did you do to get back at my mother?"

The urge to lie braises the tip of my tongue, my defenses slamming down into place the second she accuses me of a revenge plot. "It had nothing to do with her."

"She acted like you were in *love*," Elena hisses, twisting her body to throw the accusation in my face. Like boiling hot water, it washes over me, agonizing welts cropping up along my body and making me jerk in surprise. "God, no wonder she tried to keep me away from you. She already knew what you were like, how all of this would end. I could've saved myself a lot of trouble if I'd just listened."

"You and I are *nothing* like your mother and me." I take her chin between two fingers, keeping her in place while I lean in and force her to look at me. "What I feel for you isn't even in the same fucking universe."

Trying to pull away, she huffs when I refuse to let go. "Then why couldn't you tell me?"

"I don't…I don't *know*, Elena."

Pinching my eyes closed, I let my head fall forward, shame flowing like a river through me. It empties in my blood, making me feel more like a goddamn monster than any crime I've committed ever has.

I was afraid you wouldn't see it the same way as me. I was afraid you'd leave.

The words scrape the tops of my teeth, desperate to be spoken, but my body refuses to let them out.

Off to the side, we hear footsteps as the house lights dim even more, and a voice asks the people in the box next to us if they need any refreshments before the show.

"Ice?" a familiar voice asks. My soul recoils, making me regret not putting a bullet in her at the house.

I hope her face is purple and swollen. A nice little homage to the way I arrived at that hospital all those years ago.

I'm a little surprised they still showed up, and so soon after me. Perhaps they'd been hoping to corner me and instead found themselves escorted to their seats.

Elena jerks her chin from my grip, and I let her go, blood rushing between my ears as my body tries to block out the sudden onslaught of noise. The director trots on stage, asking everyone to be polite and courteous as the show begins.

A sniffle here. The unmistakable crinkling of a chip bag being dug into. Another sniffle. Someone's baby crying slightly farther away, all completely audible through the musical score.

Tensing up, I lean back in my seat, attempting to focus on anything but the noise around me.

The auditorium darkens until our box is almost pitch-black, the stage erupting in flashes of color as the lights crew introduces the first scene. I don't know shit about ballet, so for the first few minutes of the show, I sit watching the dancers as they flit about in time with the music.[85]

But somehow, even as the orchestra crescendos, I still hear the little noises from before. They worm their way into my brain, like little parasites looking for bits of sanity to feast on.

I hear the ticking of my old Rolex watch and that fucking pendulum statue. The slurping sounds Rafael made the day I went to his office and convinced him to give me Elena.

Like floodwaters after a hurricane, every single sound that's ever

---

85 Before COVID, I loved going to shows in the city. I saw a lot of plays, ballets, concerts, and stand-up and pulled heavily from those experiences to create the ambiance of this scene.

seemed to trigger me comes rushing to the forefront, like ghosts haunting me after a brief blip of peace.

My eyes shift to Elena, who's watching me instead of the show; I can just *barely* make out the soft slope of her nose, the shine in her golden eyes, the outline of those plump, pink lips. Slowly lifting my hand, I press my palm into her cheek, and suddenly, the noise stops. Everything just…settles.

My response to the stimuli doesn't, but as the absence of misplaced noise washes over me, eventually the racing of my heart and the tightness in my chest lessen too.

"Are you okay?" she leans in to whisper, splitting my heart right down the middle.

"That's my line," I return, smoothing my thumb over her cheekbone.

She scoffs. "It looked like you checked out there for a second. Sorry for *caring*."

When she moves to pull away, I shake my head, framing her face with both hands. "Don't apologize for that. Not ever."

Her eyes turn glassy, tears shining in the spotlight reflecting on us from below. Dropping her gaze, she sighs. "I can't do this right now."

Gripping my wrists, she pries me off her, shoving my hands back so they're in my lap. The rejection stings, like stepping on a bee in your bare feet, the sensation spreading through my nervous system.[86] We sit quietly for the next several acts, our stony silence worse than any other possible sound I've heard.

An intermission finally takes place, the lights in the auditorium brightening just so the patrons can see their hands in front of their faces.

After jostling in my seat for several minutes, trying to get the

---

86 Fun fact: while writing this book, I stepped on a bee, and it stung me. It was the first time I'd ever been stung by anything, and clearly it made a lasting impression.

anxiety coursing through my veins to dissipate, I exhale, pushing up on my armrests, and get to my feet. Elena turns her head, looking at me, and laughs to herself, although the expression looks completely devoid of humor.

My jaw tenses. "When you're ready to talk, you come find me."

I start to turn around, moving toward the stairs, and she hisses, "Stop trying to make it look like I did something wrong here, Kal. *You* lied, *you* fucked up. Not the other way around. If I don't want to talk about it, then I sure as fuck don't have to."

My mouth opens to refute her words, but I clamp it shut as I realize...

She's right.

Nodding, I acquiesce, holding my palms up in surrender. "You're right. I—"

"And if I *did* want to talk about it, what would I even say?" She shoves to her feet, the theater seat bouncing closed as her weight leaves it. Pulling at the hem of her short, lacy black dress, she walks over to me, gaze red-hot even in the dull lighting.

I don't have to *see* her eyes to know they're *burning*; I can feel them, licking down my chest, setting my soul ablaze. They're dousing me in kerosene as she steps back to admire the flames.

I would happily spend the rest of my life on fire if it meant getting to keep her.

"Would you want me to tell you how it wrecked me, hearing that you had a relationship with my *mother?*" Elena asks, her voice just a *smidge* louder than necessary, and I can't help wondering if it's because she knows who's in the box beside us. If she wants them to hear. "Is that something that would make you happy, Kal? Knowing you *finally* ruined me?"

The last syllable cracks, right as she stops in front of me, her toes pressing against the tips of my black oxfords. Every muscle in my chest constricts, making breathing goddamn impossible while she's standing here, baring her soul, accusing me of being the reason it's bloody and bruised and broken beyond repair.

My hands twitch at my sides as she steps into me, pushing me flush with the wall, jabbing her index finger into the middle of my chest. I want to haul her into my arms, then rain apologies down with my mouth and hope somehow they make up for things.

I try to reach for her, but she juts her chin sharply, hands circling my wrists, pinning them back. I could easily overpower her, but the longer I stare at her, the longer I stand here absorbing the misery rolling off her in waves, the more I realize I don't want to.

This is what I asked for.

"Answer the question," she snaps, moving so her hips brush mine, the hem of her dress shifting slightly up with the motion.

Gritting my teeth, unsure if she's trying to be seductive on purpose or if she just can't fucking help herself, I exhale harshly through my nose. "*No*, Elena, that doesn't make me feel good."

Releasing one of my hands, she scores her fingernails down the front of my pants; I hiss when she drags them across my dick, which stiffens under her touch.

"Careful, little one. I'm starting to get the wrong idea here."

She tilts her face up, the heat from before still glowing in those golden eyes, rage and lust mixing together and warring for dominance. Without saying another word, she cups me through my pants, squeezing hard, and my free hand naturally flies up, fisting in the back of her hair.

Yanking her head back, I curl my body so I'm looming over her, waiting for a grin to grace her pretty features.

It never does, and after a moment, I see this for what it is.

She's not interested in having a conversation; the hurt and anger are still too fresh, flashing on repeat in her mind like an out of control fireworks display, exploding until nothing's left but the charred remains.

Still, her body doesn't seem to be on the same page as her brain, reaching out to me like it just can't help itself.

And if that's how I have to get her to come back to me, so fucking be it.

Backing up until her legs connect with the drink holder on one theater seat, I grip the roots of her hair so tight, it pulls a startled gasp from her lips. Her hand comes up, latching on to my forearm like she's about to try and tear me away, but instead, she clamps down, clawing at me through my suit.

"Are we done talking?" she rasps, reaching behind with her other hand to steady herself on the seat.

"That depends. Are you going to say anything I don't already know?" Her nostrils flare, and I chuckle darkly, bending to skim my nose over hers. "When I said I wanted to talk, I didn't mean I wanted you to goad me into a reaction. But if you're not ready for more, I'll give. Whatever you need from me right now, little one, I'll hand it over."

Her eyes stay on mine, but her breathing scatters, making my dick throb against her stomach. Trailing my other hand slowly up her side, memorizing the gentle curve of her hip, the swell of her breast, I stop at her throat, curling my fingers around it.

"You want me to fuck you until you can't remember how shitty I made you feel? Want me to shove my cock into you, make you come over and over, until you're begging me to stop?" I glance out at the still-packed auditorium, hearing the low chatter from her family's box, and wonder how much of this they can hear.

A wicked grin splices across my face, the malice in it palpable, and I dip down, grazing my mouth over her ear. "Want me to fuck you right here, right now? Where anyone in the city might hear or even see the way you come apart for me?"

Throat bobbing beneath my grip, she licks her lips, her eyes illuminating like a bitch in heat.

It's a single nod that comes next, barely perceptible with me holding her neck in place, but I catch it all the same. My heart pushes past my rib cage, lurching into my esophagus, cutting off my air supply as I imagine what I'm about to do to her.

Raking my gaze down her body, I swallow, my cock *weeping* precum just at the thought of people bearing witness to the reclaiming of my wife.

Letting go of her hair, I snake my hand down the front of her dress, hiking the skirt to her hips in one sharp tug. She gasps as the cool air brushes against her bare pussy, making her shiver.

Ghosting my knuckles over her seam, I peer down at her face, watching carefully for the slightest change in demeanor. Her lips part as my thumb comes up, swiping across her clit. The moan that falls from her mouth is the sweetest fucking sin I've ever experienced.

I catch it with mine, covering her lips in the same second I increase the pressure, matching each stroke of my tongue to the long, languid swirls of my thumb. She pulses beneath me, her body coming alive like an instrument being fine-tuned by its master, and I groan into her, wanting nothing more than to crawl inside her skin and never come back out.

Pushing myself deeper into the kiss, until all I can fucking taste is this one singular moment in time, I release her throat, using that hand to pull the bodice of her dress down over her breasts. One strap rips free, making her hiss into me, but I ignore it, pinching a nipple between my fingers, then rolling it under my thumb.

Her hips swivel the faster I move against her, desperate for the slice of euphoria only I get to give her. Sliding her arms up my chest, she claws at my neck, tiny slivers of pain making me jerk forward in rapture as I almost topple over into the theater chair.

"Fuck," I curse, dragging my mouth from hers.

Taking a step back, I drop to my knees, the state of the dirty floor not even a concern as I become eye level with her glistening pussy. I dive forward, needing to taste her at least once before anything goes further, sucking one lip into my mouth before pulling back.

"Think you can balance yourself on the chair?" I ask. My voice is so husky, so fucking needy, that it's almost unrecognizable. She shifts, resting her elbows behind her and sliding her ass onto the armrest, leaning back to give me a better view. "Spread your legs, little one. I want to see just how fucking angry you are."

Silently, she obeys, tilting her hips up as her knees fall open. My breath hitches, the scent of her arousal drilling itself into my brain, something I never want to forget as long as I live. I lean in, scaling my nose up the inside of her thigh, inhaling as I try to imprint the entire scene into my memory.

"Do you think anyone can see?" she asks softly, and I glance up as my tongue finds her scar—*my scar*—and flicks out over the mangled skin.

Scoring my teeth over her flesh, I revel in the way she convulses, wishing I could bottle her mannerisms and noises and drink them down. Make them a part of me.

"Do you *want* them to see?" I ask, my breath coasting across her pussy, my mouth mere millimeters away.

She stares down her body at me, twisting and untwisting her lips before giving the slightest nod. Goose bumps flourish on her skin like tiny blossoms, a spring bloom just for me, sending all my blood south.

"Of course you do." I inch closer, flicking the tip of my tongue against her silken flesh, savoring the taste. "My wife wants to show everyone what a little cock whore she is, doesn't she?"

"I want *her* to know," she says in a low voice, tangling her fingers in my hair. "I want her to know it's nothing like what you had with her. That she can't make you come like I do."

"*Fuck*," I moan, her jealousy a live wire to my cock, making my vision blur. Bringing my thumbs up to spread her, I lick up and down her seam, sucking and nibbling, avoiding her favorite spot until the very last second. "Horny little bitch. You want to make Mommy jealous?"[87]

I don't want her to be a part of this, but I understand if that's what Elena needs to feel better. I'll do whatever she wants.

"Please," she whimpers, bucking her hips, asking for more.

Sliding my arms beneath her thighs, I lift her slightly, digging my fingers into the meat of her ass before diving in for my feast.

Her head falls back immediately, fingers scraping across my scalp as they twist and pull, trying to edge me even closer. My tongue alternates between light circles and sharp figure eights, flicking and licking and massaging until her thighs are shaking.

They clench, covering my ears so all I can hear is my own blood rushing between them. My heart pounds in my throat, and I redouble my efforts, sealing my mouth over her lips and sucking *hard*.

"Oh, *shit*," her muffled voice moans, so loud that I'm sure everyone around us can hear it.

"Look at me," I command, my mouth vibrating against her skin. I slide my hand down, pushing two fingers into her sopping pussy, curling up until her back bows. "You don't *ever* look anywhere else when you come on my tongue, little one. Eyes on me, and my name on those pretty lips."

She resists, biting her lip as I dive back in, adding a third finger and driving in until she's tensing, her inner walls fluttering around me.

I feel her pulse in my chest, the quiver of her muscles in my bones, but she looks away, and all I can see is the hurt that remains. It's written all over her face, and I know how badly I've fucked up.

---

87 Have I mentioned lately that this was, clearly, inspired by Greek mythology? LOL.

What I don't know is how to fix it.

"*Wait,*" I say, feeling her orgasm sticking as it crests, like she wants to let go but is still having a hard time getting out of her head. Reaching into my suit with my free hand, I quickly pull out my pocketknife.

The same pocketknife I used on her months ago, branding her skin with my first initial, like I knew even then what importance she'd come to hold for me.

I flick it open, watching her for signs of distress or reluctance, but just like last time, when I gently press the blade into her thigh, all it does is renew the fire in her eyes.

Still stroking with my other hand, I point the tip of the knife into her skin, pausing for the briefest second. Waiting.

She clamps down around me tighter, the slightest shift of her hips telling me all I need to know.

Slowly, I nick her, my mouth watering as blood beads beneath the blade. Increasing the pressure just slightly, I drag it up, across, then up again, finishing with a flourish.

She hisses at the pain, white-knuckling my hair as I toss the knife aside and lave my tongue over the wound, lapping at the coppery essence before it can make much of a mess.

Her answering moan almost causes my dick to unload before I've even gotten it out, and then she's tugging, pulling me into a standing position.

My fingers slide from her with a wet pop, and she brings them to her mouth, slipping them between her lips. Cleaning herself off me.

"*Goddamn*, you are a little cum slut, aren't you?"

"Only for you," she breathes, wrapping her hand around my neck and yanking my face to hers.

"You're goddamn right," I say into her mouth. "*Only for me.*

Never for anyone else. I swear I'll end any man who even breathes near you if I think I need to."

Her blood and arousal conjoin on my tongue, the mix sending ripples of pleasure along my spine. "What about me?"

"This cock is yours. Every part of me belongs to my wife. And right now, I need to fill you up," I grunt, plundering her lips with mine, trying to soak up as much of her as I possibly fucking can.

She reaches between us, helping free me from the confines of my pants with frantic fingers. My cock bobs out, red and fucking enraged, and she slips her fingers through the cut on her thigh, using her blood to coat my dick before positioning it at her entrance.

"*Fuck*," I choke out, the sight of her smeared around my shaft reminding me so much of the night I took her virginity. When I gave in to an obsession for the first fucking time, let it consume me, damn any and all consequences.

As one of my hands comes up, cupping her breast roughly, the other guiding me into her wet heat, I'm met with a wave of déjà vu, flashes of white splashing across my vision as I bottom out inside her.

I swear to God, up until this very moment, I've never believed in soulmates. Never thought myself worthy of having one, figuring that whoever would be unlucky enough to get stuck as mine would probably just avoid me altogether.

But as I pick up my pace, the smell of blood and hot, heady sex drifting around us, I can feel the pairs of eyes from across the auditorium glued to our shadowy passion. I see the smile that curves over her lips when we hear "What is that moaning?" from the box to our right, and I swear, she's it.

My soulmate. My fucking queen.

My little Persephone.

Pressing down on her sternum to keep her from flopping around, I piston in and out, letting my grunts and sighs and groans match hers as they collect like smoke, wafting around us. The chair squeaks as we fuck, and I lose myself in the blissful feel of my bare cock inside her.

"So...fucking...tight," I grit, mesmerized by the way her tits bounce with each thrust.

"Harder," she moans, just as the director takes the stage again, announcing the return of our dancers. The lights start to dim once more, and I buck against her with enough force to uproot the seat from where it's bolted in the floor. "Oh God, yes. *Right there.*"

Wrapping my hand around her throat, I pull her up so she's forced to make eye contact with me as I drive into her. "Do you feel that? How *perfectly* we fit together? *That's* real, Elena. I can't fucking fake it, and neither can you."

She nods, frenzied, lifting to press her mouth against mine in a searing, soul-sucking kiss.

The intensity of it makes my stomach flip, and I frown, my rhythm stuttering. Yanking back, I squeeze the sides of her throat. "Don't kiss me like this is goodbye."

Staring into my eyes, she doesn't respond, and that uneasy feeling collapses into something bitter, a chasm of despair I convinced myself wasn't coming.

"Make me come," she says woodenly, such a stark contrast from the writhing, moaning woman from seconds ago that I get whiplash.

My fingers tighten around her, irritation sparking something hot and furious inside me.

"Fine," I say, renewing my thrusts until I can hear the wet slapping of our skin together above the din of the music below.

Even as it crescendos, swelling like the orgasm I can feel building inside of her, that's what I hear. My skin prickles, knowing everyone else can probably hear it too—or at least her family in the box beside us.

"But don't say I ruined you when we know damn well it's the other way around."

She grunts, threading her fingers through mine, increasing the pressure on her neck. "How did *I* ruin *you*?"

"You *consumed* me from the moment you approached me at that cocktail party years ago. I've not even thought about another woman since." I'm close, *so fucking close*, my hips picking up speed as release barrels through me. "Now, be a good little bitch and come for your husband."

I groan, watching her vision slacken, knowing she's drifting out of consciousness. The way she so willingly grants me control over her life, over the very base act of breathing, damn near sends me over the edge as I watch her face redden and eyes go dark.

I release her the second her pussy clamps down around me, tightening almost to the point of pain, and gulp down the strained gasp that falls from her lips.

The dancers take the stage at the same time her nails scrape against my chest, my name catching on her lips. "*Kallum*."

"*Yes*," I hiss, my balls drawing up, threatening to follow her lead as her juices flood my dick. "Ah, fuck, I'm coming. Gonna fill this perfect pussy right up, reward my wife for being such a good little slut."

She squeals, a second wave racking through her, spasming violently around me. Then my vision's blurring, my own release crashing over me in a tidal wave of ecstasy, unloading stream after stream of hot, sticky semen into her until it's dripping out while I'm still inside.

Letting out a low groan as the music around us seems to explode in volume, I slump against her, trying to steady my eyesight.

"Get off me," she snaps, pushing at my shoulders.

I brace my hands on the chair and move to stand on wobbly knees, glancing down at the cum-and-blood-stained beauty before me, admiring the new scar on her thigh and my fingerprints on her neck.

She's my magnum opus. An oil painting I want hanging on my wall for the rest of eternity.

"You're so fucking beautiful," I mutter, not sure if she can hear me.

I reach to help clean her up, but she bats my hands away, righting her dress as much as possible. "I need to go to the bathroom."

Clenching my jaw, I take a step back, nodding, even though that same uneasy feeling flares up again in my stomach. A warning sign if ever there was one. I take my seat, tucking myself back into my pants, and wait while she disappears through the curtain.

Five minutes pass. Then ten.

After a while, the unease morphs into something deeper, something sadder.

Something more permanent.

And when I leave the ballet early, sneaking into every single restroom available to the public, looking beneath every stall, I'm not surprised when all I find is her phone, abandoned on the back of a toilet.

A scrap piece of paper is tucked beneath the device, and my heart lodges deep in my throat, bringing with it a wave of nausea.

> *I loved thee, though I told thee not,*
> *Right earlily and long,*
> *Thou wert my joy in every spot,*
> *My theme in every song.*

I stand in that stall far longer than I should, reading and rereading John Clare's words, unable to shake the irony of how we seem to have come full circle.

I wonder if it felt this crippling for her when I was the one who left.

ELENA

ARIANA STARES AT ME AS SHE BITES INTO HER TUNA SANDWICH, not saying anything.

In fact, neither sister has said anything in forty-five minutes, and it's starting to grate on my nerves.

"Okay, *what*? Why are you two being so fucking quiet?"

Pinching off the crust from her grilled cheese, Stella looks at me. "What should we be talking about?"

"*Anything*," I moan, dropping my head to the table. "Come on, you guys. I so don't want to be alone with my thoughts right now."

They share a look, and Ariana exhales slowly. "Well, there's…a lot to unpack here."

"Yeah," Stella agrees. "For starters, Mamma and Kal? Yikes. Talk about grooming. I kind of hope Papà tells the Elders. Or maybe the police."

My temple throbs, the memories from last night like a scalding hot iron bearing down on my brain. "Not really the direction I was hoping this would go."

I haven't stopped long enough to really think about the reality of everything that happened, and when Kal showed up at the theater last night, I let jealousy and hurt cloud my judgment. Let him fuck me in a public place, where my entire family could hear.

And judging by the blush painting my sisters' cheeks when I arrived at the diner this afternoon, they definitely did hear.[88]

"Hey," Ari says, pointing a crinkle-cut fry at me. "Beggars can't be choosers. Either you drive the conversation, or other people pick the topics. Those are the rules of society."

Stella snorts. "Who made the rules?"

"I did. Just now." Ariana pulls her phone out, scrolling silently for a few moments before turning the screen around to face me. A news article is pulled up, timestamped for this morning.

SOCIALITE RETURNS TO BOSTON AFTER FAKING KIDNAPPING; FATHER'S COMPANY ANNOUNCES PERSONNEL CHANGES, NEW INVESTMENTS.

"Would you rather talk about *that*?"

The headline makes my blood boil, amplifying my simmering anger toward my parents and burrowing it even deeper. I haven't seen them since I left the house yesterday; rather than stay in the penthouse like I had been, I went uptown to Nonna's Millennium Tower apartment, confident in the fact that Kal wouldn't come find me there.

Not that he *couldn't* but that he would choose not to.

And he never did.

Even though it meant he got my message loud and clear, I still couldn't help the little seedling of hope that embedded itself in my psyche, wishing he'd come after me again.

That there would be no limit to the number of times he'd chase me to the ends of the earth, no matter how many times I pushed him away.

Clearly, that's not the case.

---

88 I mean, we saw that coming, right?

I guess it was kind of dumb to assume he would, since I never even gave him a real chance to explain himself.

My parents never reached out either, although after leaving my phone in the theater, I suppose I effectively cut off communication with them. Of course, neither of them know I'm aware of Nonna's apartment, which means they'd never come looking for me here.

I only discovered it after her last New Year's bender, when she refused to take a cab from a hotel bar down the street, noting she had a secret apartment in the luxury building.

Lucky me, I suppose.

"What's there to talk about?" I say, pushing the phone away. "At least the world knows Kal didn't *actually* kidnap me now."

"Yeah, but they think you're a liar." Ari squints, pursing her lips. "Or they *would*, if a certain rock star's picture wasn't pushing you from the spotlight."

I shrug. "They can think what they want. I know the truth."

Stella wipes her mouth with a napkin. "Don't you think it's odd timing, erasing the kidnapping story and revitalizing the company all at the same time?"

"Not really. With me back in town, how were they going to keep the lies afloat?"

Shaking her head, Stella sits back in her chair, sighing. "It just seems fishy."

"That's business, baby," Ari says, exaggerating her voice as she speaks. "Our parents are some shady motherfuckers."

She and Stella erupt into giggles, their carefree spirits trying their best to lift mine, but as I let my gaze slide past them, glancing out over the harbor beyond our dockside restaurant, sadness floods the cracks of my heart, tainting the evidence that anyone else was ever there in the first place.

"So what are you gonna do?" Stella asks me, sipping her water.

"You're not in school, and your marriage is…in limbo. Are you gonna go after him?"

"He slept with our *mom*, Stel." Ariana shoots her a look. "Big ick."

Stella rolls her eyes. "It was, what, over a decade ago? It's not like they continued their relationship, and he left Mom and immediately went to Elena. It sounds like he was a *kid* for most of it, which is… super gross."

My nose wrinkles, although she has a point.

Ariana shifts in her seat, turning so her body is angled slightly away, and stares hard at her phone.

"If you love him," Stella says, adjusting her glasses, "then you love him. Plain and simple. That doesn't just go away, no matter the circumstance."[89]

Sighing, I push my food around on my plate, letting that sentiment soak in, searching for the truth within it.

What do I do with the love in my heart if I can't funnel it into him?

When I go back to Nonna's later, armed with tinfoil-wrapped angel food cake and an old iPad Ariana brought for me to hook up to the Wi-Fi, I strip down and lounge on the bed for a while, trying to find comfort in the silence, like Kal always seemed to.

But all it does is remind me he's not around to help fill it.

The hurt and betrayal I felt from last night come roaring back, searing my insides as they threaten to overturn every emotional development I've had in the last few months.

Rather than try to stuff them down like before, to curl into myself and fold in order to fit other people's expectations, I let it all wash over me. Sobs rack my body as I stare up at the ceiling, aching and grieving for me, for Kal, for my family.

---

89 One of my absolute favorite things to write is and always will be sibling relationships, and these three are no different. The way their dynamic is flawed but they have each others' back is just so dear to me.

It's a strange sensation, grieving for what isn't *lost* but missing or absent. Part of me wants to acknowledge the accessibility of these things, while the other part knows I need time to make sense of everything.

That knowledge doesn't really help though.

So instead of lying there and feeling sorry for myself, I slip from the bed, draw a bubble bath and drop in some of Nonna's essential oils, then dig my journal from my overnight bag and write it all down.

I don't hear from Kal the rest of the time I'm in Boston. A week passes, and then another, and still...nothing.

Every day that goes by, I'm left wondering why he lied to me in the first place. What he gained from making promises and pledges, staining my heart with his darkness, when he didn't even bother sticking around to see what became of it.

Every part of me belongs to my wife.

But is that really true if he can't be honest with me? If he's not *here?*

According to my sisters, Mamma's been staying at her sister's in Roxbury, not having been back to the house since the night of the recital. So on the day I return to pack away some of the more sentimental items in my old bedroom, I'm a little stunned to find her sitting on the four-poster bed, flipping through the worn pages of Edgar Allan Poe's complete works.

I walk inside, and she doesn't glance up. I stand there, frozen, noting the faded yellow bruise dusting her right cheek from where she said she slipped on a patch of ice on her way to the recital.

My heart skips a beat, knowing better but trying not to read too much into that.

"You know, I specifically asked your father when you were born not to teach you Italian." She smooths her fingers over the page, smiling sadly. "I knew from the *moment* I laid eyes on you that you were a force to be reckoned with. There was immediately so much strength and tenacity and fire in your beautiful eyes, present in your lungs every time you cried. I worked overtime to undermine any potential advantage you could have over me."

I don't say anything, knowing she's not looking for a response.

"I was jealous of a *baby*," she says. "*My* baby, because I knew she was going to grow up with opportunities and beauty and grace I was never allowed. Everyone who met you was so captivated by this...*aura* you had. This *brightness* that drew them to you. And you were good at everything you tried: reading, writing, creating. Even gardening, which I never mastered. Sometimes it seemed like you'd just walk into a room, and plants would bloom."

I almost snort at that.

She turns a page, exhaling softly. "It felt like I was living in my daughter's shadow, and your father certainly was never any help. He told you to jump, and you asked how high, desperate to be the perfect little girl in that man's eyes."

My cheeks burn, shame settling on my shoulders, weighing me down like a cement brick.

"When your father met Kal, we could tell he needed...well, a lot. His mother had just died, and he had no other family. So we took him in, made him feel like one of our own." Swallowing, she finally looks up, meeting my gaze across the room. "I remember the first time I felt like maybe he was confused about his feelings toward me, trying to work through them, and I...took advantage of that. Soaked up all the attention he gave me, because your father certainly didn't give me any. It felt good, after I had you and Ariana, to feel wanted again. I *needed* that.

"When I found out he'd decided to marry you, I just...couldn't believe it. Not because you weren't lovable, but here you were, doing exactly what I'd always been afraid you'd do: taking everything that once belonged to me."

"He didn't belong to you," I mutter. When she doesn't reply, I continue, louder. "Is that why you pushed the kidnapping story? To punish me for something that wasn't even my fault?"

She nods. "I thought if the world turned against your union, maybe he'd give you back. Even had your father send men out to rough you up, thinking maybe Kal would realize he was in over his head."

A lead weight drops into my throat at the revelation, and I suck in a deep gulp of air, trying to ignore the initial shock settling in. *Of course Papà orchestrated that. So much for blood loyalty.*

"Did you ever think maybe I didn't *want* to come back? Or that none of what happened between us had anything to do with you?"

"I know it doesn't make sense to you," she says, waving her hand dismissively. "You don't know what lengths people will go to when they're in love."

And there it is. All of the sadness and regret she spewed just seconds ago, erased by a single sentence. Evidence that she doesn't really mean anything she's saying; she's not sorry, and she doesn't feel bad.

She just wants me to think she does. She wants me on her side, because she's still trying to punish Kal.

Nausea bubbles inside my stomach, curdling like spoiled milk. It propels me forward, my interest in hearing what she has to say dwindling completely.

"What do you even know about love?" I ask, crossing the gap between us. "You've certainly never shown it to any of us. All you know how to do is manipulate and hurt people. No wonder the men in your life can't fucking stand you."

As I reach the edge of the bed, I bring my hand up, lashing

through the air with a single pump of my arm; my palm cracks against the yellowed skin of her cheekbone, and she lets out a cry, holding her forearm up to block me.

"That's for trying to wreck my marriage," I say, rearing back to land another slap on the same cheek. My hand vibrates with the impact, tingles shooting up to my fingers as my print quickly blossoms on her skin. "*That* is for ruining my childhood and trying to ruin my adulthood."

She tries to push me away, but I shove her hand back, curl my fingers into a fist, and whip my knuckles at her face, not even wincing from the immediate onslaught of pain that radiates up my arm.

"And *that*," I sneer, shaking my hand out as she chokes on a tooth dislodged by the contact, "is for Kal. You don't *hurt* the people you love. You don't go out of your way to make them suffer."[90]

Walking to my old bookshelf, I put a couple of trinkets from Nonna in my bag, grab the important files—birth certificate, social security card, and other essential items for starting over—tucked away in a secret compartment in the closet, and head for the door, ignoring her tears the way she ignored mine for years, swapping comfort for criticism every chance she ever got.

"You used to call Kal Hades incarnate," I say over my shoulder, pausing with one foot out the door. "I get it now. You wanted him to be the villain in your story, so you dressed him up as one. Painted him as a monster, when really, all he ever wanted was a little bit of unconditional love."

I pull my new phone out, unlocking the screen and opening the draft of an email I worked on before my arrival. After spending the entire first few days after the recital writing down my feelings, I began writing down other things too.

---

90 My favorite Elena moment, both to write and read. I'm so proud of her.

Everything I knew about Ricci Inc.

"I used to want that from you too." I adjust a couple of the finer points, adding in more incriminating evidence, and push send. "But then I realized monsters aren't capable of returning love. And the longer you spend chasing it from someone who cannot ever give it back, the more of a monster you become in turn."

Spinning on my heel, I pass through the door, content in my soul with the way I leave her there, knowing the sun is about to set on the entire Ricci empire.

CHAPTER 37

KAL

THE DAY I RETURN TO APLANA ISLAND, JONAS IS WAITING ON THE Asphodel's porch, drinking something dark from a mason jar. He holds it up in greeting as I approach, nodding his chin.

"The king of our little underworld returns," he says, leaning back in the white rocking chair. "How was Boston?"

"If I never go back, it'll be too fucking soon."

Marcelline opens the door for me, having returned not long after we touched down on the mainland, noting that she didn't feel comfortable being an accomplice to any more of my crimes. I walk past her, trying not to linger in one spot too long, unwilling to let the emptiness of the house get to me.

Moving into the kitchen, I pause in the doorway, spotting Elena's hairbrush on the island. Her pink nail polish on the sink. The copy of Shakespeare's *Macbeth* that I had her read aloud to me one afternoon while I shoved my head between her legs.

Her giggles, her attitude, the way she could easily match my intellect, holding conversations with me without me needing to slow down or catch her up.

Her love.

"Jesus," I mutter, taking a sharp turn and stalking down the hall to my office, pushing the door open with so much force the doorknob knocks into the drywall.

"I couldn't help noticing the lack of a certain lass," Jonas says, looking over his shoulder as if expecting Elena to materialize from thin air. "Am I correct in thinking you've come to your senses about this marriage?"

Pouring two tumblers of scotch, I bring them to my desk and settle in behind it, sliding the opposite one across to him. He sits in the leather armchair in front of me, accepting the glass, his mason jar abandoned.

"You'd be...correct-*adjacent*," I say, taking a drink, allowing the burn of the liquid sliding down my throat to momentarily dull the ache in my chest. Scrubbing my hand down my face, I exhale slowly, circling one finger around the rim of my glass. "I dissolved the trust."

Jonas blinks once. Twice. Three times. He swallows his drink audibly, leaning forward, his leather jacket rustling with the motion. "You what?"

"Violet's not taking my calls, and she's been extremely adamant about not wanting my money or my presence in her life at all, really. What's the point of me letting the trust sit unused if the one person I want to have it won't take it?"

"It's accumulating interest—"

I nod, already aware of any angle he might go over. On the plane ride home, my grandfather's estate attorney explored every potential avenue of funneling the money out, and while I could've donated it to charity or kept it for a rainy day, ultimately I decided to buy myself out of Ricci Inc.

Normally, it wouldn't be so easy, but since Rafael needed the money, my involvement with his family has been all but scrubbed from the face of the planet.

"Wait," Jonas says, holding a finger up. "You bought your way out of your wife's family's company?"

"I wanted to retire anyway. I'm getting too old for this lifestyle."

Jonas rolls his eyes. "Bloody hell, mate, you're *thirty-two*. Are you sure this isn't one of those crazy, impulsive moves you make when you feel backed into a corner?"

He doesn't have to come outright and say it, but the implication is there: like my marriage.

At least how he saw it.

To him, it was something that appeared out of nowhere, sprung suddenly because I was being blackmailed, and it happened to align with the fake trust guidelines.

It was reckless and dangerous, and it resulted in far more than I ever could've imagined.

But it, just like my decision now, had nothing to do with *impulse*.

"Every single decision I've made in my adult life has been carefully coordinated after exhaustive consideration. I don't take risks unless I'm sure of the outcome." My words to Elena all those weeks ago pop up fresh in my mind, proof that even back then, I was trying my best to be honest with her.

I couldn't give her all the details, but I *tried.*

"Nothing impulsive about it," I say, gulping down another mouthful of scotch. "I wanted out of the Mafia world, and I'm taking the steps to ensure that happens."

"You've said yourself you don't ever actually *leave* that world." Setting his drink down, Jonas folds his hands together, raising an eyebrow. "What makes you so special?"

"On paper, I won't exist to these guys. When the feds come for Ricci Inc., at least I'll be left out of it as they'll expunge my name from their records." Pausing, I shrug. "My reputation, the power my name holds, though, that doesn't go away. Notoriety is forever, my friend. I'm just stepping back from the more public aspect of things."

Blowing out a long breath, he shakes his head. "Boston must've done a number on you, eh? Never thought I'd see the day."

I don't reply, leaning back in my chair with a shrug. Something shiny catches in the light beneath my desk, and I bend down, picking a diamond stud earring up from the floor where it must've fallen during one of our many office trysts.

Its presence causes a lump to form in my throat, burning up the length of my esophagus, and I grit my teeth against the sensation, flicking the jewelry into a trash can nearby. Jonas presses his lips together, shifting as if uncomfortable in his seat.

"Right, so where is the little wife again?"

Reaching out to the computer, I shake my head, pulling up the Massachusetts government site and double-checking that I have all my forms together before sending them to the attorney to look over. "Seeing as she won't likely be my wife much longer, I suppose it doesn't matter."

Over the next couple of weeks, I steer clear of town and most every room in my house, taking to sleeping in my office in an attempt to avoid anything that might remind me of Elena.

It's like trying to live without the fucking sun.

The one time I do go to the Flaming Chariot, Blue approaches me at the bar and practically kicks me out, saying that I'm harshing the vibe, and since he's tending for the summer tourist crowd, he's more reliant on tips and can't afford me chasing away customers.

Normally, I'd probably fire him and tell him to get off the island, but instead, I just leave, heading back to the Asphodel to drink my evening away.[91]

When I arrive, I walk around back, not in the mood to see Marcelline just yet or to feel the weight of her judgment over the fact that I haven't shaved in days. The stubble on my jaw is starting to itch, but I can't bring myself to care.

"You're starting to look too much like your jungle rat friend," she's been telling me, referencing Jonas in disdain every chance she gets. "Lord, I hope that girl comes back to you."

Me too, Marcelline, but two weeks and no phone call? My odds aren't looking great.

I must've stood outside her grandmother's penthouse for hours after the recital that night, fist raised and poised to strike, ready to drag her back to Aplana with me.

To hell, where I wanted to keep her.

Still do, if I'm completely honest.

I want her by my side so bad it makes me fucking sick.

But every time I tried to knock, I remembered how little of her life has been left up to choice. Since she was born, everything's been decided *for* her, and I played right into that same notion when I forced her to marry me.

Regardless of the feelings that developed after, I would never be able to exist, in semi-decent conscience, thinking hers were born out of necessity. A way for her to cope with the life thrust upon her rather than the culmination of fate.

So I'm giving her time.

Space—to grow, forgive, and reflect.

The beauty of *opportunity.*

After spending so much of my time obsessing over her, determined

---

91 His depression was quite satisfying to get to, I won't lie.

to ruin her for any other man, and reveling in the warmth her existence inherently gives, the distance is torture.

If she doesn't show before our days are up, *then* I'll go after her.
Track her to the ends of the fucking earth and beg for her to return,
if that's what it takes.

Until then, I wait.

Rounding the corner of my house, I immediately tense up, the
hairs on the back of my neck rising at the feeling of not being alone.
There's a certain thickness in the air, a blockage in the wind that
wouldn't exist without another warm body to absorb the weather.

A flash of dark hair first grabs my attention. Then, as my eyes
sweep the yard, I notice the black clothes draped over the slender
body.

Disappointment flushes my chest, and I sag forward, trying not
to buckle beneath the weight of hope.

I approach her quietly, like a predator sneaking up on its prey,
although she's hardly even that to me at this point.

"Violet." I stop several feet away, getting a whiff of lavender and
vanilla as the wind kicks up, rustling her braided hair. "What... How
did you find me here?"

My sister sizes me up fully before responding. "I know people."

I frown. "Sounds shady."

"Maybe we're a lot more alike than I care to admit." She lifts one
shoulder in a half shrug, her big brown eyes crinkling at the corners.
"I got a call from the bank the other day, saying they were putting a
freeze on my account while they tried to figure out who kept attempting to make deposits on my behalf. Did you know that's a pretty
popular phishing scam?"[92]

"I did."

---

92 It IS a popular phishing scam, and in college, I almost fell for one. LOL.

She blinks, almost as if she wasn't expecting that answer. "Okay. Well…are you aware that they now want to close my account due to suspicious activity because of how many times you tried to deposit money?"

"You could've just accepted the deposits, and not only would you have money, but you'd have free rein over your bank account." I cock my head to the side. "Not that it matters either way now. There won't be any more deposits."

Turning away, I walk over to the patio, taking a seat in one of the metal chairs. Violet stands in place for several beats, seeming to have some sort of internal battle, then finally gives up and joins me, sitting across the table, crossing one leg over the other.

"Bankruptcy?" she asks in a flat voice, as if already convinced of the answer.

My eyebrows furrow. "What? No, I'm not bankrupt. I have enough money in my personal savings to not ever have to work again."

"Brag," she says, laughing softly to herself. "So what happened to the cash you were so desperate to give me? Tired of me not letting you solve all my problems?"

I shrug, picking at a piece of chipped clear coat on the glass table. "Maybe I realized you were right about my control issues and decided to work on them."

She laughs again, this time louder. "Kal, no offense, but you were practically stalking me for the last several years. I don't feel like you're the kind of guy who just…turns over a new leaf when someone points out a flaw."

Her words dig at the empty valley in my chest, razed after a tornado, waiting for something to grow in the place of my love for Elena. I tap my fingers on my knee, humming as the familiar itch to go and bring her home renews itself inside me.

"Some people are worth trying for."

Violet's lips twist, and she slides her gaze away, observing the pile of soil that was supposed to be Elena's garden. "What's with the dirt?"

"My wife—Elena—tried planting a garden, but clearly her green-house abilities are sorely lacking."

"Hm. Yeah, I don't think gardens are supposed to be so...brown in the summer."

I grunt noncommittally, staring out at the sun setting over the beach.

"I met her, you know." She glances back at me, brushing some hair from her eyes. "Your wife. She seemed...interesting. Beautiful, but a strange match for you, I feel. Based on pretty much nothing but your appearance and rumors, of course."

Smirking, I nod once. "You're not wrong about that."

We sit in companionable silence for a few beats before finally, it gets to be too much, even for me. "What are you still doing on the island, Violet?"

Her fingers curl around the sunflower pendant hanging from her neck, and she sighs. "To be honest, I have no clue. I think that's why I came to find you today, because every time I leave, I find myself coming back and standing in front of your stupid bar, wanting to go in and talk to you."

"You fly to Aplana often?"

She blushes. "My friend's parents have a lot of frequent flyer miles, so I've been using them. The kind of people who don't even notice, you know?"

I just look at her, and she nods.

"Right, *you* know." Clearing her throat, she scoots to the end of her seat. "In any case, I wanted to come find you, because I felt bad about how I acted earlier in the spring. You were only trying to help, and I shouldn't have been such a bitch. It's just...money is kind of a touchy subject."

"It usually is."

"And I'm...sorry I'm not in a place right now where we can...get to know each other. Family is just—"

"A touchy subject." I hold my hand up, stopping her before the knife drives right through my chest. "I get it, Violet."

Neither of us says anything else for several beats, and then she's pushing to her feet, tucking her braids behind her ears. "Well. In any case, that's all I wanted to say. I'm a firm believer in apologies, even if they do damage your pride."

She starts to step off the patio, goodbye on her tongue, when another, completely different voice cuts through the air, making her freeze in place.

"What the *fuck* is this?"

ELENA

KAL'S SISTER LOOKS LIKE A DEER CAUGHT IN HEADLIGHTS WHEN my voice cuts across the backyard, and I take momentary satisfaction in the fact that it seems I have the advantage of surprise on my side.

Then I glance at Kal, who sits casually in his chair, not even sparing me a look, as if he's neither impressed nor shocked by my return.

The satisfaction deflates, and anger takes its place, propelling me over the grass until I'm standing just in front of him. Shoving the manila envelope in his face, I put a hand on my hip and ask my question again.

"Kallum. What the fuck is this?"

He looks at the folder, then up at me, those dark eyes strategically devoid of any emotion. "It looks like an envelope, Elena. How the hell should I know what's in it?"

Scoffing, I unlatch the top and reach inside, shoving the papers in his direction. "Are you trying to say you didn't have your lawyer serve me *annulment* papers? Because I'm pretty sure I recognize your signature, given that I saw it the day I signed our marriage license."

Shifting awkwardly, Kal's sister widens her eyes, inching away from the concrete. "I think I'd better go…"

Kal nods, waving her off. And when she disappears, leaving us alone, my body buzzes with unending electric energy, zinging through my veins like a hot current. I brighten under his perusal for the first time in weeks.

Like a fucking flower deprived of the sun overnight, my heart opens up for him, seeking nutrients where maybe there are none.

Maybe it was premature of me to fly back here.

No response is still a response, right? Two weeks without hearing from him, and maybe that was his way of ending things.

Annulment papers are *definitely* a response, but still.

If he wants to end this marriage, the least he can do is tell me to my face.

"You look good," he says after a couple beats, casually roving his gaze over my form. I feel his appreciation in the tips of my fingers, little sparks of pleasure scattering to the surface.

"Don't give me that. I don't want your compliments. Tell me why you're trying to get rid of me."

When the papers showed up at Nonna's apartment, it was a two-for-one sucker punch: proof that Kal did, in fact, know where I was hiding and hadn't bothered to come see me but also the added insult of him giving me an out of our marriage.

One that, months ago, I probably would've jumped at the chance for.

But a lot can change in a few months.

I sat with it for a while, staring at his signature and the final submission date for filing. The documents cited fraud as the reason, stating that Kal manipulated me into the union and that he took full responsibility for the devious nature of how the marriage came to be.

And while all of that's true, it no longer negates what happened after we married.

The comfort, solace, and acceptance I found in the arms of this killer.

My obsession. My ruin.

My husband.

Steepling his fingers together, he leans back in his chair, blowing out a breath. "I thought it would be what you wanted, little one. Freedom. You're young. You deserve the chance to experience what life has to offer."

Slamming the papers down on the glass table, I take a step toward him, jabbing his broad chest with my index finger. "How dare you try to decide that for me. You only present me with one option, after ghosting me completely after the recital, and that's supposed to be my *choice?*"

Heat flares to life in his eyes, the brown depths darkening with rage. Pushing to his feet, he grabs my finger, holding it to him. "You ditched me at the fucking ballet, Elena. Nice touch, by the way, leaving that poem. I got your message loud and clear."

"Oh, the poem where I said I'm *in love with you?*" I snap, the volume of my voice spiking with my frustration. "If that somehow translated to *'please file for an annulment,'* then I think you need to go back to studying poetry again."

"You think so?" As he steps into me, igniting that age-old song and dance our bodies have grown accustomed, I feel my core twist and flip at his proximity. His scent envelops me as he backs me up against the table, leaning down to bracket me in with his forearms.

A strand of his inky hair falls over his forehead, and I resist the urge to push it up out of his face, trying to focus on my anger before it slips away, lost in the sea of his touch.

"Maybe you should refresh my memory," he says, dropping to his knees, his hands immediately skimming up the sides of my thighs.

I suck on my teeth as he begins inching up the hem of my yellow sundress, clutching the annulment papers to my chest. Every single nerve ending in my body is screaming, telling me to put a stop to this until we have an actual conversation, but then his breath skates across my pussy, and I no longer care about talking.

What's one more bad decision in the grand scheme of things?[93]

"Lift your ass," he commands, and I obey without even thinking, moving forward so he can slip the fabric of my dress up over my cheeks. He swears under his breath, shaking his head. "Still no panties, I see. Adding adultery to our list of sins by flashing other men, or were you just hoping to get lucky with me?"

One of his hands comes up, flattening between my breasts, urging me down; I go without complaint, hissing as my bare butt comes into contact with the cool glass surface, followed quickly by my shoulders as he pushes me all the way down.

Teeth scrape across my clit, and I jolt, the sharp bite sending a flash of delight through me. "I was hoping to get lucky," I say, knowing that's what he's waiting for.

"Of course you were. Perfect little cum slut, ready to be fucked any time her husband takes his dick out." A slap lands on the top of my pussy, pulling a yelp of surprise from my throat. "Now, what was your favorite form of poetic delivery? Recitations with the tongue?"

Kal's fingers run slowly over the scars on the inside of my thigh— the *K*, plus the *A* he added the night of the recital. My own personal brand.

Good luck getting rid of me after that, asshole.

I stare up at the patio covering, tracing the cobwebs with my eyes, seeing his head dip between my legs again. His tongue tracks behind his fingers, leaving a trail of cool saliva in his wake, and when they

---

93 This is just par for the course for these two. Fuck first, ask questions later.

graze my clit, I shiver, my body already dangerously close to falling apart, wound tight after weeks of abstaining.

"The key, as we know, to any good poem," Kal breathes, swiping his tongue across me once. Twice. Three times, until I'm tossing the annulment papers aside, gripping the edges of the table to keep from bowing off of it. "Is *passion*."

With that, he buries his mouth in my pussy, forming a tight seal around my lips. He sucks my clit into his mouth and showers it with lashings of his tongue. An arm snakes up my torso, fingers hooking in the top of my sundress and yanking one breast free.

He squeezes as his tongue penetrates me, massaging in and out, then slides up between my folds and swirls over my clit. Repeating the passage, alternating between the sucking and licking, he creates a tempo that has pressure building in my belly, spreading outward like a heat wave.

"Do you know how many nights I dreamed of having you here, just like this?" he asks against me, the vibrations from his lips sending shock waves of ecstasy through me. "How many times I pumped my cock dry to the image of you spread open and whimpering for me?"

I shake my head in answer, even though I'm sure he can't see. He hums against me, speeding up the flickering of his tongue, and this time when I come, he doesn't even have to ask me to look at him; my eyes immediately seek his, locking in as my orgasm rocks my entire body, back arching away from the table, a strangled sound ripping its way from my throat.

"There. I know I'm a little rusty on my spoken word, but judging by the flush on the audience's cheeks and the cum on my taste buds, I'm inclined to believe I still know what I'm doing."

Wiping his mouth on my thigh, Kal straightens into a standing position, reaching up and undoing the buttons on his shirt. He shoves it off his shoulders, the black material falling to the ground, and then works his pants open, pushing them down over his hips and kicking them to the side.

His cock bobs free, a pearly bead of arousal seeping from the tip of his thick crown, and he strokes himself slowly, dragging his gaze over me. "I will *never* get tired of seeing you like this," he says with a little shake of his head, like he can't quite believe I'm here.

Taking a step toward me, he fists his shaft, rubbing roughly between my lips and smearing my juices all over. Each pass over my clit sends a bite of pain through my pussy—the kind that curls on the end, into immeasurable pleasure.

"You want this?" he asks, lifting one eyebrow, and even though I should say no and put myself together, get back to the matter at hand, my body is in disagreement.

One tiny, almost imperceptible nod, and that's it; he lets out a soft groan, shoving in to the hilt with one thrust of his hips, filling me so completely that I'm not sure I'd be able to get him out if I wanted to. After this, they'll be scraping bits of Kal's DNA from my insides for the rest of my life.

Slamming his hands down on either side of my head, he starts slow, dragging his cock against my inner walls, smoothing the tip over every ridge and sensitive muscle. The table creaks beneath our weight, shifting with each thrust, and I wrap my legs around his waist, trying to pull him as close as possible.

"*Fuck,*" he says, closing his eyes and tilting his head back, that one syllable flooding my entire being with warmth and making me light-headed. "I've missed you so goddamn much, little one. Your pussy, your brain, your smart fucking mouth. The Asphodel is not the same without you in it. I am not the same without you."

I grit my teeth, trying not to lash out while he feels so incredible inside of me. My stomach tightens, another orgasm already rolling up my spine, and I reach up, smoothing my thumbs over his cheekbones, my palms over the light beard dusting his jaw.

His eyes snap open, narrowing. "You're doing it again."

"Doing what?"

"Saying goodbye. Don't fucking do that, Elena. Don't touch me like you think it might be the last time."

I gasp as he picks up his pace, driving into me with such force the table starts to move backward, slamming into the wall before it comes to a stop. "I'm not *doing* anything."

"Don't lie to me," he says, reaching up to collar my throat with one hand, flexing his hold on the sides. "Why did you come all the way here if you weren't planning to stay?"

"You served me annulment papers!"

Growling, he increases the pressure on my throat, fucking me harder, like he's actively trying to split me in half. "I was trying to be mature and respectful about our situation."[94]

"You didn't even come *find* me after I left you at the theater," I cry, release pounding through me, dragging all the hurt along with it. My orgasm crests, looking over the hill as my vision scatters, the ability to speak becoming more difficult. "How can you say you *missed* me when you didn't come after me?"

"Oh, *fuck*, Elena." He squeezes harder still, pistoning into me so roughly I can feel the bruises forming. "I came after you. I wanted to barge into your grandmother's apartment and throw you over my shoulder, take you back home with me where you belong. I stood outside for hours, trying to decide how much you'd hate me if I took that choice from you. If I didn't let you come to terms with things on your own."

I start to spasm around him, my climax erupting before he's even

---

94 While this is technically true, it's also not, and that, my friends, is why Kal's is a morally gray character.

finished his sentence. Black spots flood my eyesight, that familiar sense of floating suspending me in time as I fall over the cliff.

"That's it, my sweet wife. You come on your husband's cock. Make him regret not spending the last two weeks buried inside of you."

"God, *Kallum*," I moan, the orgasm still pulsing, sending wave after wave of euphoria. Tears sting my eyes as euphoria surges through me.

"Does my little cock whore need to be filled?"

I nod frantically, clawing and scratching at his marred chest, propping myself up into a sitting position and yanking him down into a kiss. Rocking my hips back and forth, meeting each stroke with a miniature one of my own, I tangle my tongue with his, relishing in the taste of myself on him.

His palm finds my back, his fingers spreading out and holding me flush to his chest as he pushes in one last time, a raspy, desperate whimper tumbling past his lips. Sweat slicks down our bodies, mixing as he collapses on top of me, making the table groan under us.

I poke his side as it buckles. "Maybe we should move elsewhere."

Pulling himself upright, Kal stares down at me for several long beats, the expression in his eyes completely unreadable. "Okay," he says softly, standing up and tugging me with him. "Let's go inside."

He falls eerily silent once we're indoors, taking me to the living room and guiding me to the couch. He wraps a plush blanket around my shoulders, then shimmies back into his dress pants, zipping them up and perching on the coffee table directly across from me.

I swallow thickly, awareness prickling on my skin, realizing he's likely waiting for me to go first. I open my mouth to speak, but he beats me to it.

"I'm in love with *you*, Elena."

Snapping my mouth shut, I sit back against the couch, smothering a smug smile. "Well, as far as apologies go, that's a good place to start."

He sighs, a small laugh falling from his lips, startling me in how…
genuine it sounds. In all the time I've spent with him, I've never heard
an *actual* laugh come from those vocal cords, and the onset of it now
causes butterflies to erupt in my chest.

Dragging a hand through his hair, he looks up at me, those dark
eyes softening to their natural, warm brown, intoxicating in their
soft depths. "I'll admit, it doesn't feel like any amount of apologizing
will ever absolve me from the sins I've committed against you. Not
that that means I'm going to stop trying, but still. I just want you to
be aware that I know everything I say will feel inadequate." Reaching
out, he hooks a finger over the ring he gave me the day we married, a
small smile splaying on his lips.

"I don't deserve you, you know that?"

"Subjective, but go on."

"When I was a kid, I grew up shrinking myself to make space for
my mother and her illness. It needed the attention, needed the focus,
so that's where the majority of everyone's time and energy went. They
came to visit my mother, came to talk to my mother, and I just slunk
to the shadows, trying my best not to begrudge her any more than I
already did."

He pauses, shaking his head.

"Cancer's a funny disease, in that it inspires jealousy in some
people. There my mother was, slowly decaying, and I had the fucking
nerve to *resent* her for leaving me. Like she had a choice in the matter."

My heart aches, breaking with each word he speaks. My hands
itch to comfort, to relieve his pain, but I know I need to hear this too.

You cannot love a person fully without knowing the darkness
etched into their soul.

I want to know his so well that it becomes my darkness too.[95]

---

95 My all-time favorite quote, and SO TRUE.

"Anyway. I met your parents about a year before she passed, and when she finally *did*, I went looking for my biological father, hoping he'd…I don't know, take me in, I guess." He wraps another finger around mine, covering the diamond. "Long story short, he wasn't interested in a fourth kid. So I fell victim to the system and found myself in a foster home in Boston. Sometime after that, your father approached me on the street and offered me a job."

His throat bobs as he swallows, shifting. "I don't need to go into all the details of the beginning of my career, but the point is I was starved for attention when I met your parents. Your dad gave me a life of luxury, and for a kid with quite literally nothing, the hero worship came easily. Your mom, well. She gave me the affection I'd been lacking from my own, and I guess the attraction kind of just spiraled from there.

"I should have told you about my…history with her," he says, dropping his gaze. "But any time I thought about saying the words out loud and reliving that part of me…I don't have any excuse, except that when I was with you, I didn't want to remember any of that. My hatred, my desire for revenge, became background noise, and then it just seemed too late to say anything at all."

He looks up at me, and I see it there—the fear, the shame. All of it dropped onto the shoulders of a man who never deserved it, because the people he trusted were selfish.

Tears burn my eyes at the cavalier way he talks about it, as if he thinks I wouldn't have understood the context. As if I would have blamed him. "She abused you, Kal. They both did. They stole an impressionable boy off the streets and manipulated him to be their little puppet."

He bristles, his mouth twitching. "It wasn't like that—"

"*Kal*," I say, reaching out to cup his cheek. A tear slips out, rolling down my face as I stare into his eyes. "You didn't know any better. They were supposed to teach you, and they taught you wrong."[96]

His eyes burn with unshed emotion, and he seems to look right through me for a long time, processing my words. Maybe I shouldn't have jumped right into an accusation, but I could feel the apology building, feel the weight of him thinking he ruined me crushing his soul, and I couldn't take it.

"I don't want you to apologize to me for the way you coped with what life dealt you," I say softly, "because I see nothing wrong with the way you are. A little rough around the edges and far from perfect, but…"

"Lucky," he breathes, shaking his head again as if dislodging the range of emotions. "I'm so fucking lucky, if you coming back to me is any indication."

He pulls me to the edge of the couch, palming the back of my head and covering my mouth with his; our tongues dance to their familiar tune, frissons of heat and bright light crackling in my core, passion and love sizzling in my soul.

When we part, our breaths tumble heavily from our mouths, and he smooths his thumb over my lips.

"For what it's worth, I *am* sorry I didn't tell you. You deserved to know. I don't want to hide anything from you, and I don't want you to feel like you have to hide anything from me."

I swallow, nodding, even though the memory of my mother's revelation still feels like a slap to the face. Skimming my hand over his side, I frown, something else bothering me. "Did she do this?"

---

96 In the original version of this story, Kal's still fully struggling with the reality of what happened with him and Carmen. Here, he is more aware of it, but it still takes Elena saying the words out loud to really break through to him. When abuse feels like love, only the real thing can prove otherwise.

His eyes follow my fingers as they smooth over the puckered skin, and he nods slightly. "Indirectly, but yes."

My chest pinches, aching for the damage my parents inflicted on him. For not even being their blood, they sure did a number on him.

"I hate knowing she ever touched you," I admit softly, knowing I won't be able to move past it until it's hurled out in the open. "I know it wasn't...I know I shouldn't care, but I just...hate knowing she ever got to see you like this."

"She didn't," he interjects, catching my hand and flattening it on his skin. "No one but you, little one. What can I do to make you believe that?"

I shake my head, declining that he even needs to *prove* it, saying that there are just some things that only time can help work through. But he doesn't accept that, leaning back and shoving his hand into his pocket, pulling out the utility knife he keeps tucked inside.

"Mark me," he says, holding out the blade.

My hand recoils from him completely, falling into my lap. "God, no! I don't want to hurt you."

"Yes, you do." He grabs my hand, pushing the knife into it and curling my fingers around the handle. "Hurt me so I can feel what it was like for you."

I hesitate, the knife heavy in my palm, the metal cool against my skin. Fear seizes my throat, making me tense up as my mind tries to decide if this is a good idea or not.

Best case scenario: if we divorce and he hooks up with someone else down the line, at least they'll see another girl's initials carved into his skin. It'd serve him right.

Worst case: I cut too deep, and he bleeds out and dies.

Still, it's hard for me to pass up such a rare opportunity, and maybe inflicting a little pain will help me fully move on.

Flipping open the blade, I nod, pushing up off the couch. He grins wickedly, leaning back on the coffee table. I get up, letting the blanket fall around me, and straddle his hips, trying to ignore the immediate arousal stiffening beneath my ass.

"You want a shallow, rough stroke," he says, guiding me to his left pectoral muscle, pressing the tip of the knife into his skin. "Something that'll draw a little blood and scar but not, you know, kill me."

I swallow, throat tight, pressing down with a little force as he gently coaches me; the tip pierces a layer of skin, and his praise makes my pussy pulse.

"Now, flick your wrist and finish the letter," he says, clenching his jaw. The cut opens some previously healed scar tissue, nicking the edge of a site on the last line of my first initial, but he doesn't react aside from the clenching.

Blood beads in the shape of an E, and I stare at it for a beat, mesmerized by the bright crimson color. Before he can sit up and stop me, I'm dipping down and pressing the flat of my tongue against it, savoring the metallic tang, something primal responding in kind to the taste.

I don't know what it is exactly that happens when his blood touches my tongue; maybe it's because he's drawn mine so many times that my body is just happy to repay the favor, or maybe it's something deeper than that.

It's not the first time I've tasted him, but there's something different in it now. A chaotic desperation in the action, and the vulnerability in the situation sets my entire soul on fire.

"*Jesus*," Kal chokes, his hand flying to my hair as I push up, sitting back on him, and toss the knife to the floor. "Fuck, I'm so in love with you, Elena Ricci. Do you believe me now?"

"Anderson," I say, correcting him with a grin. "I filed to have it changed legally. Don't want to be a Ricci when the business goes under."

His eyebrows raise, his entire body freezing as he takes in my sly expression. Eyes narrowing, he tugs at the ends of my hair. "What did you do?"

I shrug, feigning innocence. "Maybe Papà should've learned not to spill all his secrets to his family members, since anyone can email the news stations these days."

Kal twists his fingers in my hair, sitting up so our mouths are almost touching. "Did you *rat*?"

I fold my lips together, knowing how people in this world feel about informants. Yet since I'm leaving the world anyway, I couldn't give a fuck less about their opinion.

Though I suppose it could endanger us at some point. But that was a risk I was willing to take.

Still, it's nice when Kal sweeps me in for a passionate kiss again, plundering until I'm a shivering mess and stealing each of my breaths for his own. "You're crazy," he says, pulling back. "Hope you liked being my *captive* before, because you're damn sure not going anywhere now."

"So no annulment?"

"Absolutely fucking not."

CHAPTER 39

KAL

I SLIP OUT OF BED THE MORNING AFTER ELENA COMES BACK TO the island, trying to reacquaint myself with the parts of the house I avoided while she was gone. The beach, where I showed her my physical, visible scars. The library where she spent so much of her time upon her initial arrival curled up, reading books she'd already been through a dozen times, desperate for something to do.

After giving Marcelline the morning off, I toast a bagel, slather it in cream cheese, and split open a pomegranate, arranging the food on a tray and bringing it to bed before Elena's even close to waking up.

Setting it on the nightstand, I perch on the mattress beside her sleeping form, running my hand over her side like I have repeatedly since last night, just reminding myself that she's real.

That *she* came back to *me*.

The beast's beauty.

Hades and Persephone.

She finally stretches awake, blinking those soft golden eyes up at me, giggling when I lean down and cover her mouth with mine. Pushing me away, she lets out a half groan that makes my cock jolt to life.

"Morning breath," she says, rolling away from me.

Grabbing her shoulder, I pull her to her back, pinching her chin between my two fingers. "After every bodily fluid we've shared, that's where you draw the line?"[97]

Sticking her tongue out, she notices the food from the corner of her eyes, squealing excitedly. "You made me breakfast?"

I shrug, picking the tray up and settling it over her waist. "It's nothing special, and it's probably cold by now."

Rolling her eyes, she ignores the bagel and immediately starts in for the pomegranate, chewing thoughtfully as she studies me. "You know," she says, "I didn't really think about how the downfall of Ricci Inc. might affect you when I was sending all that evidence to Channel Ten."

"It won't," I say, waving my hand. "I already took care of my *official* involvement with your father and his business. As long as my security team did what they were supposed to, I won't even exist to the Riccis. Plus, I'm not worried about anyone coming after us. I know all the comings and goings on the island, and most of the men your father is in bed with will retreat underground, unwilling to make an enemy of me. I know far too many people for that to work in their favor. The Elders will sweep it under the rug just to avoid making matters worse and let your father rot."

"Will any of this affect your medical degree?"

My forehead wrinkles, the reserved, almost shy look on her face creating a little wave of unease inside me. "My degree, other than the fact that my work helped fund it, has nothing to do with your father, or anyone else, for that matter. I earned it, and it can't just be taken away."

"But...you don't practice, and you don't really ever even talk about being a doctor."

---

97 You know, the man's got a point.

Sitting back slightly, I consider this, folding my hands in my lap. Stripping myself of one of the last secrets I have from her makes me feel like I'm cracking my heart open and shoving it into her hands, praying she doesn't leave again. But it also feels necessary, like the beginning of *us*.

"I have this...condition. Misophonia. It's a psychological aversion to certain sounds. Have you ever heard of it?"

She shakes her head.

"Most of the time, I keep it in check, but other times...it's a lot. Sometimes, it's downright debilitating, and I can't focus on anything but the sound or the anxiety it gives me. Even after it dissipates, I'm still reeling from the episode, and I just...prefer to work from home, where I can regulate the stimuli I'm encountering. Not because I'm trying to avoid it, but if I can make my life easier, then I'm going to."

Nodding, she shrugs. "That makes sense."

"My decision to retire from medicine was made separate from my decision to retire from Ricci business. I just... Aside from the sound stuff, I don't have the same passion for being a doctor that I once did, and I'd begun to suspect that I was trying to complete the fantasy for a kid who only ever wanted to help his mom get better."

She chews on a pomegranate seed as she listens, pursing her lips. "What would you say if I wanted to go back to school?"

"I'd say that's great—"

"But I want to learn the craft." Her gaze dips to my chest, running over the Band-Aid covering the shallow wound she made last night, then back up. "I don't want to teach writing. I want to *do* it."

My heartbeat speeds up, swelling to the point where it's knocking painfully against my ribs. "Then I say I can't wait to have a library full of your books."

Later, after she's finished eating and I've finished *my* breakfast, I drag myself from between her thighs and slump onto the bed beside her, hooking an arm behind my head as she lays hers on my chest.

"You know what brought me back to you?" she asks after a comfortable silence, raising her chin to look up at me.

"What?"

"It was the pomegranate syrup on the jet." She smirks, shaking her head. "One taste, and I knew…that was the syrup for me. Too good to live the rest of my life without."

And as she leans up on her elbow, capturing my lips with hers and shifting so she's straddling my hips, sliding down my cock before I even have much of a chance to process what's going on, I chuckle to myself at the fucking irony.

Persephone eating the seed, tying her to the Underworld indefinitely.

My version is a little different, a little skewed and bloody and downright agonizing at times, but the result remains the same.

She's here to stay, and the darkness inside me starts to feel a little less heavy.[98]

Ivers International is a company for criminals, by criminals.

Who better to help keep illegal activity hidden than people who do crimes and get away with them?

Based in the seedy shit stain town of King's Trace, Maine, it's not a place I like to frequent. When I can conduct meetings virtually, I do.[99]

Frankly, if they weren't *typically* so damn good at their job, and I

---

98 There are so many little subtleties like this throughout that really cemented this for me as I tried to map out the framework of the myth, but I think this one is my favorite.

99 For the most part, I write in the same universe, so when something is mentioned in detail like this company and town, it's a safe bet there's a story there.

didn't have a personal connection to the owner, I likely wouldn't still be using them based on location alone.

Still, I decide to drop by a few weeks after Elena shows back up on the island, checking in to see if the team's broken any new ground on the identity of my blackmailer yet.

I haven't heard from either of them since before Rafe's arrest and Carmen went AWOL, so I can only imagine what's going on on that front. After squaring away a meeting with Boyd Kelly, the lead cyber-security engineer, I touch down in Portland and make the short drive up to King's Trace, trying not to let its darkness pull me in like usual.

There's a reason I only ever came to town to do a job. An invisible slime practically coats the small streets, an evil presence haunting every person who steps inside the city limits.

I don't stop anywhere on my way in, parking outside Ivers International and heading inside immediately.

The glossy floors in the lobby look as though they've recently been buffed, and a short-haired receptionist greets me at the front desk, giving me an elevator key after I confirm my appointment. Walking across the lobby to where the silver, sliding doors are, I glance around, observing how disturbingly normal the place seems.

I'm not sure what I was expecting from a security firm, but cubicles and cushioned bench seats certainly wasn't it.

Stepping out when the elevator dings on my floor, I immediately tense up at the emptiness of the top level. Executive names are listed on a plaque right above the reception desk, and I can plainly see several doors lining the hallway, chairs to sit and wait in, and yet…there appears to be no sign of life anywhere.

Clearing my throat, I ring the bell sitting on the desk, rocking back on my heels as I wait.

And wait.

And wait some more.

Growing agitated with each passing second, knowing this is keeping me from relaxing at home, I lean forward, squinting at the plaque. Boyd's office number is the second one down, so I push past the glass partition separating the office doors from the upstairs lobby and head right for his slot.

"I don't appreciate having to wait—"

Cutting off abruptly when I open the door, I freeze in my tracks, more than a little stunned by the petite blond sitting behind the large oak desk, her black Converse propped up on the wooden surface.

Surprised, mostly because the last time I saw her, she'd been in a coma, broken and bloody and struggling to find the subconscious will to wake up.

"Riley," I breathe, my knees buckling at the girl in front of me.

The sister of Boyd Kelly, head of Ivers International's security team.

Her honey-colored hair is cropped close around her collarbone, her blue eyes as deep and disturbed as the uncharted parts of the ocean. A scar slashes across the corner of her mouth, the mangled skin on her cheek from a thigh graft healed but still a little more raised and pinker than the rest of her face.

She looks hollow, the dark circles around her eyes more like craters, the sweater she has on about three sizes too big. I shut the door slowly, and she grins when I come over to the desk.

"You sure know how to make a girl wait," she says, gesturing for me to have a seat.

I do, but only because I'm confused.

"What are you doing here?" I ask, glancing around the office to see if anyone's hiding in the corner. "Where's your brother?"

"Boyd's having an extended lunch with his girlfriend. I was the one who asked you to meet."

My eyebrows shoot up. "What?"

"You wanted to know who your blackmailer was," she says,

leaning forward and sliding a familiar flash drive across the desk, tapping it as it reaches me.

I stare at the drive, then look up at her. "*You?*"

A smile widens on her face, but it looks strained. "Kind of crazy how much I've picked up in such a short time, but I guess that's the perk of being around hackers and IT people all the time now. Amazing what you can find out about a person just by doing a little digging. Even someone as private as you, Doctor."

I narrow my eyes. "Is that so?"

She nods, producing another flash drive—this one *slightly* different from the one she just handed me.

It's the same one I gave Rafe the day I convinced him to give me Elena.

My flash drive.

I look up at her, taking it and slipping it into my breast pocket, aware that this makes her the only other person in the world to know my dirtiest secret.

Initially, there was no one blackmailing Ricci Inc. at all.

It was just me.

My mind whirls, trying to process what she's saying. How an eighteen-year-old girl's held me by the fucking balls these last few months, but more importantly, *why?*

She gulps when I ask that, sitting up in her seat. "I could ask my brother, but you specialize in secrecy, right? Well, I did something… bad, and I need to disappear."[100]

---

100   Read the next book!

ELENA

IN MOST VERSIONS OF THE MYTH, HADES IS THE VILLAIN.

The captor, the thief, the vile being cast from Olympus and forced to live in solitude in the Underworld, among the souls of the dead.

It's his cruelty they speak of, his past crimes they hold against him. No one ever talks about how he *saved* Persephone.

Dragged her to hell as his queen, then curated an entire realm just to make her happy.

How he plied her with love and affection and signed his soul over to her the second he laid his eyes on her form, overtaken by her beauty and purity.

They only see him as the bad guy, because they *want* to see him that way. Need someone to place their bad luck on or to blame when shit goes down.

None of them sees the man I do.

Who right now sits with his ass firmly planted in wet sand, waiting for the next wave to slap against the shore. His hands are so large, they wrap completely around our infant daughter's waist, and he bounces her up and down each time the water laps at them, their laughter carrying down the beach to where I'm sitting, working on my query letter.

I didn't end up going back to school. In the months following my return to Aplana, I watched the life I knew in Boston crumble to ashes, my sisters suddenly finding themselves displaced and having to come stay with us for a while. Kal was busy throwing himself into investments, trying not to let the fact that he hadn't heard from Violet since the spring bother him, even though I could tell it did.

Still does.

And even though I was dutiful about taking my birth control, I got pregnant. At first, Kal was hesitant to show excitement because of his past, but he was amazing about holding my hand through the entire pregnancy, relying on his own medical knowledge to reassure any questions or concerns I had.

I was hesitant too, because of the way he'd once said he didn't want to bring children into the world, but when I told him we'd be having a little girl, I learned it wasn't that he didn't *want* kids, it was that he didn't think he deserved them.

He'd been punishing himself for what my parents did to him. My mother especially.

But when Quincy was born, any doubt I had about his ability to love her or abandon violence disappeared the second he looked into those big, brown eyes.

Not that he's given it up completely. I sometimes find him in the old outbuilding late at night, "tying up loose ends" from the life he has never gone back to. When he left Ricci Inc., he left it for real.

Or as much as one can leave the Mafia.

Sometimes, when he nicks my skin while we fuck or he reopens the initials carved on the inside of my thigh, lapping at me like he needs it to survive, I wonder if that's his way of keeping that part of him in check. If he cures his bloodlust by tasting mine.

Not that I'm complaining.

Their laughter draws my attention from my letter again, and I sigh, slipping the page into my notebook and setting it off to the side, wrapping my arms around myself as I start down the beach toward them.

I finished my first book, a fictionalized account of how I fell in love, a few weeks before Quincy was born, and I've been trying to draft queries to agents ever since, but part of me kind of likes just having the book sitting in my office, a collection of my words and imagination where only I can see it.

Sometimes I sit on the back patio and read through, looking out at the flower garden, which *finally* bloomed after my return to Aplana. Like spring had just been waiting for me to get on board all along.

Eventually, I'll write the letter. But right now, this life feels more important.

Kal whistles as I approach, his gaze hooding as he rakes over my form, lingering on my legs.

"Q," he says to our daughter, nuzzling her dark curls, "you have the most beautiful mom on the planet, inside and out. You got really lucky there. I'd be lost without her, and we'd be a mess."

I scoff, splashing water at him with my foot. "Please, you're the glue holding us together most days."

"That's true. For now."

"Yeah, I dread seeing what you're like when she starts dating. Or invites boys over for sleepovers. Will our kids be able to have friends?"

He grins, his handsome face lighting up with the gesture. "I'm more evolved than that, little one. She can have friends. Even guy friends. Who knows? Maybe I'll have to worry about girls breaking her heart instead. Or her breaking theirs."

Threading my fingers through his hair, I look down at the two of them, my heart aching inside my chest, knowing that regardless of who breaks hers in the future, I don't have to worry about it being this man.

"I love you," I say, bending down to snuggle myself into their little cocoon.

I inhale deeply, trying to commit the smell of happiness to my memory: potential and sweetness wrapped in a tender little package, sometimes full of anguish and stains that muddy the journey but that bring you out whole on the other side.

It's springtime in the middle of winter, a sliver of light shining on your soul that somehow makes you feel less alone.

Because that's what happiness is. The people you find along the way who make life a little more bearable.

And once you find them, you don't let them go.[101]

---

101 The growth, the poetic end. Seeing this play out from beginning to end all in one
stretch like this has been incredible. I miss these characters so much, and I hope
you've enjoyed their story even half as much as me. Keep reading for bonus material!

KAL

I KNOW TOO MUCH. THAT'S ALWAYS BEEN MY FUCKING PROBLEM.

Knowledge is what keeps me awake at night, sitting in the bedroom across from where my wife sleeps soundly, sprawled out on our mattress after the thorough fuckings I gave her earlier.

Yes, plural.

It's the only way I can get her to sleep these days.

My preferred method, of course, because absolutely nothing on this planet compares to the feeling of driving into Elena's sweet, warm heat and splattering her so full of my cum that I'm sure her pussy walls resemble a Jackson Pollock.

There's nothing better than the way her golden gaze hoods with liquid lust when she comes on my cock or how she thrashes in ecstasy each time my teeth score her pale skin, opening her flesh just enough for a little taste.

Nothing better than the coppery flavor of her on my tongue, satisfying something evil inside me.

I love being the only man she's ever willingly bled for.

The only one who makes her beg for it, every single time.

The only one who ever *gets* to, ever again.

What can I say? I'm a jealous motherfucker.

Still, while sex lulls her into a temporary coma, the hormones released during her orgasms pulling her into a cocoon of safety, it puts me on edge. Not because I'm unsatisfied but because I simply can't seem to get enough of the little spring goddess; if I could spend every second of every day rutting and filling her until she bursts, I would.

Her very existence triggers a desperation within that almost blinds me to everything else in my life. Makes me feel like I'm neglecting things.

Which is why, every night, I switch off the baby monitor and tiptoe across the hall to our infant daughter's room, plopping down in the rocking chair by her window, and just stare at her until I'm physically incapable of keeping my eyes open any longer.

I come in here to keep an eye on her, making sure she's not coughing or getting stuck in her crib. Horror stories of things I saw in medical school and as a volunteer physician play on a constant loop where my daughter is concerned, keeping my body from being able to sleep even after I've exhausted it physically.

I'm a father.

Sometimes, I still can't fucking believe it.

Staring into her crib, I focus on the rhythmic rise and fall of her chest rather than the electronic whirring of the light machine on her dresser, casting stars across the ceiling. Long, black lashes fan out over ruddy cheeks as she explores dreamland, the sight creating an ache in my chest.

But it's the *good* kind of ache. The kind that says you have something that matters.

Kids weren't on my radar at all. After Elena returned to the island, it'd been my sole intent to spend the next few years wrapped up in each other, allowing her time to explore her passion for writing and not squander her youth the way I had mine. Meanwhile, I was focused on cleaning up the multitude of fires that sprouted not long after Ricci Inc. imploded.

It'd always been my intention to take down Rafael when I was ready to leave his world, but my sweet, not-so-innocent little wife beat me to it.

In the aftermath, all I cared about was Elena's safety and happiness and ensuring her twenties weren't muddled by a lack of opportunity.

At my birthday dinner, an intimate affair on the beach behind the Asphodel, she informed me that she was pregnant and that she was fully prepared to raise our child on her own if I hadn't changed my mind about children.

And the thing is, I *hadn't*. The thought of bringing a child into the world, after the life I've lived and the loss I've endured, didn't appeal to me until she said it was happening.

Coming from my little spring goddess, it felt...*right*. Like I was getting a chance at having the family I'd so long been denied.

Maybe that's part of the reason I spend so much time in Quincy's room after Elena's put her down for the night. Sometimes it feels too good to be true, and I don't want to blink and have missed a single moment.

Most nights, I sit and watch her like a hawk, occasionally reading some of the great poets aloud while she sleeps in hopes of passing our love of literature along.

It's soothing in a way I didn't realize I was missing before her existence, even if I am in here to make sure she's still breathing.

To make sure I'm not dreaming.

The other reason is the girl calling my phone right this second.

She rings the same time every night, checking in with me from across the country. As per our terms of agreement, aside from her brother Boyd and his girlfriend, I'm the only one she's allowed to contact, which is the main reason I entertain the late phone calls.

It's a nice distraction from the fact that Violet doesn't return any of mine.

Scanning my screen, I note that it's a half hour later than usual, and an uneasy feeling ripples through my gut, wreaking havoc on my nerves.

"Riley," I greet softly, leaning away from the white slats of the crib, grateful that my baby girl is such a heavy sleeper. Like everything else good about her, she gets that from her mother. "You're late."

I'm met by a prolonged silence, the kind I'm typically all too happy to sit in. But there's something unsettling about it coming from her end.

"Riley?" I repeat, slightly louder this time. Quincy turns her head away from me, her dark hair moistened by droplets of sweat and sticking to her mattress. "Are you there?"

More silence. My chest tightens, anxiety carving into the cavity; I grip the arm of the chair I'm in, trying to focus on the sliver of calm provided by my daughter's soft snores.

It's why I take the calls in her room.

"I'm here," Riley finally says, her voice scratchy. "I really wasn't expecting you to answer, Doc."

I ignore the nickname, aware that she only seems to use it when she's upset. "Do I ever not answer?"

"I guess not. So far anyway. Does it ever bother your wife that you spend your nights talking to an unhinged stranger?"

In truth, it probably would, but Elena's well aware of Riley's history and interest in me, though it initially took some convincing.

And a *lot* of orgasms.

After secrecy nearly wrecked the foundation of our relationship in the first place, I found it paramount to keep my wife in the know regarding *every* single aspect of my life.

Even the truth about the blackmail.

As delicious as her jealousy may be, I don't ever want there to be a doubt for her to glom on to that would make her question me.

"You're hardly unhinged," I tell Riley instead, redirecting the conversation from my life and focusing the spotlight back on her. It's a tactic I learned during a psych ward rotation back in med school and one I know she abhors, but she didn't call to talk about me. "No one's blood stains your hands, you know."

"Are those the standards we're measuring my sanity by?" she asks. "My body count?"

"A person's propensity for violence says a lot about them and their mental state."

"What's it say about yours?"

"We aren't discussing me."

She scoffs. "We aren't discussing anything."

Tapping my fingers on my knee, I try to focus on Quincy's breathing, irritation flooding my stomach and making it cramp. "What's wrong, Riley?"

A long crackling sound washes over the line, making me tense further, and I hear her sigh. "Nothing's *wrong*. God, why does everyone always ask me that?"

Her words are slow, enunciated too properly, as if they've been carefully rehearsed. I keep my eyes trained on Quincy, grounding myself in her presence as I process this practical stranger's anguish for the millionth time since she reached out to me.

There's too much inside of her; it bleeds through her pores, consumes every aspect of her being, and tarnishes her soul with each passing second she spends wrapped in the arms of her misery. I thought sending her across the country, where she could hide "in plain sight" would be good for her.[102]

---

102   Kal becoming a dad in real life and then becoming a "dad" to the others in his life is so cute to me.

In the months since sending her, I've never been less sure of anything.

"You sound upset is all." I cross my ankles, leaning back. "I'm just trying to make sure everything is okay."

"Everything is *great*," she snaps, sarcasm dripping from each word like venom. When I don't immediately reply, she clears her throat, taking her voice down an octave. "I just…"

She trails off, and I find myself staring up at the starry ceiling, tracing the points of each shape as I wait for her to continue. I'm sure I shouldn't be indulging these phone calls, since I'm not a therapist, but the first time she broke the silence in Quincy's room, I couldn't find it in me to turn her away.

All she wanted was someone to talk to, even if she never actually says anything.

For a moment, I think she might finally tell me why she contacted me in the first place. Other than getting tangled up in some Hollywood scandal on a school trip, I don't know *what* she's done or why she felt she needed to run.

"I've just had a rough day, and I should probably go. Sorry to keep bothering you like this."

Something pinches inside my chest. "You're not a bother, Riley."

A soft, noncommittal sound comes over the line, cracking open the ache inside me until it's a ghastly, festering wound demanding my attention.

"Send me a pic of Q?" she asks, voice tight.

Even though I know she can't see me, I nod anyway. "Sure."

When she clicks off, I can't shake the feeling of melancholy away. I grab a quick photo of a sleeping Quincy and send it, staring at the screen longer than necessary after it delivers. My fingers move of their own accord, opening up a thread that's been dead for months, sending the picture along to Violet as well.

I don't know that it'll change anything. It's probably more than a little manipulative, but oh well.

I'm not so evolved that I won't exact drastic measures when necessary to get what I want.

If a simple marriage won't do the trick, maybe a child will.

Smoothing my hand down over Quincy's back, reveling in her soft, pudgy baby skin, I let out an exhale, slumping over the crib as the air shifts around me, the sweet and familiar scent of pomegranate shampoo wafting in around me.

"I don't think there's anything more attractive than seeing you with her."

Elena's voice, raspy from sleep, sends a jolt of arousal slinking down my spine, and I straighten up, turning to face her. She stands in the open doorway, the silhouette of her perfect body backlit by a wall sconce in the hall, arms crossed over her chest.

Just the sight of her stirs me, warmth spreading through my chest like a wood-burning fire, and I take a step in her direction. Never able to keep away.

I'm not at all surprised my efforts didn't keep her asleep this time around; she's supposed to hear back from a literary agent in the morning, and I know that even though she tries to act like it isn't a big deal that she's trying to get published, it's still eating away at her.

No matter how many times I tell her she has nothing to worry about. When her head isn't buried in a book and her hands aren't digging in the garden, she's worrying.

"Have a thing for dads, little one?" I murmur, approaching her slowly, like a hunter locking in on his target.

Moving against her, I back us out of the room and into ours, twisting my fingers in the silky pink fabric of her pajamas and yanking so she's flush with me. My eyes find the spot in the curve of her neck and rake over the raised, broken flesh, my cock jerking at the memory of tearing her open just hours ago.

She rolls those golden eyes when she notices where my attention has been diverted, sliding her hands up my chest. The pads of her fingers are soft against the scars lining my torso, her touch almost ghostlike even all this time later.

Like she's afraid of making them worse.

"I have a thing for *you*," she says in a low voice, wiggling her eyebrows. Wrenching one of my hands from her top, she brings it down lower, sliding my fingers beneath her bottoms, guiding me immediately to her slick core.

Groaning, I take my hand out and move until the backs of her knees hit the edge of the bed, then shove her onto the mattress. Her dark hair fans out in a halo around her head, and in that moment, I've never been more convinced that she's Persephone personified.

Innocence and depravity locked in the same soul, like a cocktail whipped up specifically for me. Shoving my knee between hers, I grab the waistband of her shorts and shove them down over her hips, my dick leaking at the evidence of me marring her complexion.

My initials on her thigh, the first time I marked her as my own, joined by faint strips of white decorating her hips and lower belly from where she carried our child. Scars she wears with pride, that I worship each time I'm given the chance, because it's proof that she belongs to me and that we made something together.

Proof that she likes my particular brand of pain.

"Are you just going to stand up there all day, or are you going to fuck me?" she asks after a moment, raising up just enough to pull off her top before flopping back down. Her breasts jiggle with the impact, and I reach down and palm one gently, still not fucking used to her being mine.

Even *with* the evidence, it's hard to believe she came back to me. I'm still not sure I deserved it.

"Demanding tonight, aren't we?" I chuckle, reaching to swipe my fingers through her silken folds, grinning when her hips buck into the movement.

She snorts, but the sound falls off on a sharp gasp when I thumb her clit. "I'm always demanding. You just don't usually take so long to give me what I want."

"Am I depriving you?" I raise an eyebrow, swirling my digit in a slow, staccato rhythm. With my free hand, I untie my sweatpants and push them down, baring my cock to her hungry gaze; her tongue darts out, wetting her bottom lip as I palm the shaft, pumping until I'm so full it hurts. "If my wife needs something from me, she's always free to *ask* for it."

"*Kallum*," she groans, tossing her head back to stare up at the ceiling.

"What is it? What do you need?" Circling faster, each sweep in time with the pulse between her legs, I drop my cock and get on my knees, wrapping one arm around her thigh. "Spread wide, little one. If you won't ask, I'll make your sweet little pussy beg for it."

Her lips are already glistening with arousal, and I lean in and lick upward once, making her shudder. The breath stumbles haphazardly from her chest, tiny puffs of air that sound like they're being torn from her lungs, and I lick again, swallowing down a moan at her taste.

Tangling her fingers in the bedspread, she tries to shift, as if aiming for more friction. I decide to be nice and give it to her, slipping my index finger into her entrance.

"*Fuck*," she hisses, even though it's just the tip, and she's about to be so full of me in a moment she won't be able to speak at all.

"Such a slutty pussy my wife has. You feel how you're trying to suck me in, how you can't seem to get enough of my fingers?" I push in deeper, curling against her inner walls and trying not to blow my load when they convulse around me.

"Already knew that," she manages, knuckles blooming white.

"All you have to do is ask." I add another finger, increasing the pressure on her clit with my thumb, bending down to scrape my teeth over her thigh. My dick leaks a bead of precum onto the floor, and I bite down at the same time she finally cries out.

"*Fuck me*, Kallum, *please*. I can't stand being empty another fucking second. *Fill me* with your cum."

I choke a little on my saliva, surprised that she's already giving in. But I'm not about to argue. Ripping myself away, I push to my feet and withdraw from her. Sweeping my fingers, sticky with her juices, over the blood coating her thigh, I stroke up my dick, on the verge of coming just from the mixture alone.

I don't know what it is exactly, but the sight of her blood splashed across my skin, the tang of it on my tongue, does something *sinister* to me. Like it's stripping me down to my base instincts, my primal need for flesh, and satiating a monster.

Since I don't practice either of my former specialties regularly anymore, I suppose this *is* how I fix that craving.

"*Good*," I say, landing the flat of my palm against the inside of one thigh. "Because there's no way I can stand not being inside you any longer."

Lining the thick head of my dick up with her, I shove into the hilt, sucking in a sharp breath when my balls connect with her ass.

"God*damn*, little one. You get better every fucking time. How is that possible?"

She shakes her head violently, catching her bottom lip between her teeth as she tries to stay quiet so she doesn't alert the baby. Her pussy clamps down around me, vibrating with an impending climax, so tight I'm seeing the stars in Q's room again as they splay across my vision.

"Better not wake her before I've pumped you full." I lean down to whisper against her ear, slowing my thrusts as my hand snakes up her body to wrap around her throat. "Wouldn't want my little cum slut left unsatisfied, would we?"

"No, *please*. I need it," she whimpers, locking her legs around me for an even tighter fit.

Sweat slicks down my body in waves, dripping onto her breasts from my forehead as I fuck her into the mattress, like I'm trying to break her in half.

"Greedy slut," I grunt, my orgasm barreling through me like a bolt of electricity the second she starts spasming around me, fisting my hair at its roots as she tries to refrain from making a sound. I squeeze harder on her throat, each pound of my hips turning brutal, just the fucking way she likes it. "*I'm* greedy too, little one. Look at me and let me hear you *right now*."

"*Kallum*," she squeals, exploding on me the second her vision starts to lose focus, teetering on the edge of consciousness.

"*Fucking* hell," I moan, gritting my teeth as she floods me, my balls seizing up until I'm seeing white. "*Coming*. Gonna fill this sweet little pussy until you're begging me to breed you again."[103]

"Oh God. *Yes*." She pinches her eyes shut, another wave of convulsions racking her body as I finally unload in her.

Collapsing on top of her, I try to regain control of my heavy breathing, and she pops her eyes open, peering down at where my head rests on her chest with a curious expression on her face.

"What?" I breathe, turning to press my open mouth against her collarbone.

"You *want* to breed me, don't you?"

Clearing my throat, I drag myself off her, flipping onto my side

---

103 Somehow, these two developing a breeding kink after their daughter is born felt very on brand.

on the mattress. I prop my head on my elbow and lazily draw my fingers through her cum-stained pussy lips, watching her body flutter back to life already.

"I was caught up in the heat of the moment," I say, discomfort edging its way into my soul, making me feel oddly vulnerable. *What if she doesn't want that?*

She scoffs. "Liar."

Lashing out, I tug her down against my front, fitting her leg over my hip and tracing my hand over hers. "I just…want Q to have siblings she can grow up with. I don't want her growing up alone, especially if we die. I've *been* the orphan kid, you know? It sucks."

Elena chews on her bottom lip, staring at my nose. "Is that why you try so hard with Riley?"

"You mean, do I see her as a chance to reconcile my lack of relationship with the siblings I do have?" I let out a breath, shrugging. "Maybe. I haven't given up hope on Violet yet though."

"She'll come around."

"Yeah." I turn, cupping her cheek with my palm, my heart beating so hard against my ribs that I'm sure she can feel it.

She shifts closer, grinding her pussy against my dick, making it twitch as blood slowly travels back to it. "Well?" she says, cocking an eyebrow and scoring her nails down my chest. "You gonna knock me up again or what?"

I bite down on the inside of my cheek, moving my hand to her throat again. "Does my little cum slut want me to dump more of my seed in her?"

"Babies don't make themselves," she mutters, reaching between us to help move the process along. "Why not fill our little underworld with them? Or at least practice until Q's a little older. Whichever happens first."

"I love you," I say as she crashes her lips to mine, melting into me.

"I love you back."

Soon I'm sheathed in her heat again, bucking until I've drained myself completely, and then we crawl beneath the covers as I switch the baby monitor on, pulling my phone from my pajama pants and setting it on the nightstand. I settle back against the pillows as she curls into my side, my chest feeling like a field in the middle of a spring bloom.

Happiness bursts like sunshine through the clouds inside me, and if I didn't know any better, I'd think my soul had returned to my body after years of evil holding it hostage.

But the truth is I'm not any less evil. My soul just lives outside of me, in the form of my little Persephone.

Just as I'm drifting off to sleep, wondering how the fuck a bastard like me got so lucky, my phone lights up. A text back from Violet illuminates the screen, filling me with more hope yet.

SWEET SIN

A COMPANION NOVELLA

A LETTER TO YOU

Dear Reader,

I know what you're probably thinking.

Why in God's name didn't she put this in the front of the book or just merge it with the entirety of *Promises and Pomegranates*?

The answer, my friend, is pretty simple: it didn't fucking fit.

I swear to you, I tried. I lamented for *months* over how to push these two sort of separate narratives together in a way that made sense and could only come up short. "Sweet Sin" was written independently of *Promises and Pomegranates*, despite it involving the same characters and an overall plot, and without the myth of Hades and Persephone specifically in mind.

Thus, it's a companion novella. It doesn't make sense, story-structure-wise, to put it anywhere but right here, for you to enjoy the glimpse into that fateful night when Kal finally gave in to Elena and his darkest desires. It enhances their story, but it does not hinge on it, or vice versa.

That being said, I do recommend reading it. As always, please see my website for a full list of content warnings, but if you've made it this far, my assumption is that you're pretty comfortable with the content (though again, if not, please check and read responsibly!).

I hope you enjoy this blast into Kal and Elena's past as much as I did.

Love,

Sav xoxo

SWEET SIN
PLAYLIST

"DARK ALLIES" — LIGHT ASYLUM

"HEAVY" — JEREMY ZUCKER

"ANOTHER WAY OUT" — HOLLYWOOD UNDEAD

"WATCH ME BURN" — MICHELE MORRONE

"JOKE'S ON YOU" — CHARLOTTE LAWRENCE

"KILLER" — VALERIE BROUSSARD

"BLOODY VALENTINE" — MACHINE GUN KELLY

CHAPTER 1

KAL

I'M A WOLF IN SHEEP'S CLOTHING.

A predator living amongst his prey, acting as if someone's out to get me too.

Hoping that the blood between my teeth can be forgotten, the stains of the lives lost at my claws erased. Fighting back against the rigid rules of a society that's only ever sought my submission.

Crime and violence pump through my veins, the single defining purpose of my life for nearly two decades—hell, maybe even longer than that. It's hard to believe my villainy began only when I started being paid to do it.

No, the wolf lives inside me, hiding out during the day and pretending the townspeople don't know the truth. Pretending they can't see the ghost of Death himself in my shadow, following me around like a curse I'm powerless against.

In fact, it's not a curse. Not in my line of work.

It's a blessing.

The beast doesn't wither under pressure, doesn't give in when faced with adversity. His bloodlust is insatiable, his appetite for agony unhinged and unconquerable.

No matter how many times I try to run away, try to deny myself the release that comes from life escaping this earth, it lies there waiting for me to return. To welcome the perverse darkness that calls my body home.

Even now, as I wrench my fingers between the lips of a man who's done my employer wrong, reveling in the way his jaw pops as it yields to me and shoving the green silicone dildo from his bedside table down his throat, I can feel a piece of my mind trying to reel me in.

But the evil is stronger, its hold deeper.

It's magnetic.

Still, as the man writhes on his mattress, naked and bound at the hands and feet, bleeding from where I've removed all twenty nails, I realize this isn't the sickest part of me.

Sure, there's a deep satisfaction that washes over me as I slap a strip of packing tape down over the attorney general's mouth. A brutal punishment, but the Mafia hates thieves, and as a fixer, I get to dole out the justice.[104]

A guttural gurgling begins in the back of his throat, and he brings his bound hands to his mouth in an attempt to free himself, but it's no use.

Hopping up on the bed beside him, I pull out my phone and open up my security footage app in one hand, pushing down on the sex toy with the other, trapping his fists between my palm and his mouth.

He put up more of a struggle than I'd anticipated, the smug bastard. Most people who steal from or borrow and don't return payments to Ricci Inc. are at least somewhat remorseful.

They typically have the decency to apologize and plead for their lives, even if it never works.

---

104   This is a characterization I pulled straight from Hades himself. They said he was a just and impartial god, and I wanted that quality in Kal, because I feel like it's easily misunderstood.

I don't give a fuck about being merciful to men as vile as me. Denying them makes my job taste sweeter.

As the man at my side goes limp, eyes wide-open but unstaring at the popcorn ceiling of the motel room, I watch the girl on my screen as she peels off her bloody clothes, secure in the comfort of her expansive bathroom.

Certain that no one is watching.

I remind myself that this was the last task I had before I go and see her in person, and my irritation dissipates slightly.

This infatuation I have with her isn't the stuff you find in happily ever afters; it's nightmare fuel. Horror with a vengeance. The kind of filth you find on the dark web where people go to satiate their most shameful, depraved desires.

My girl puts on a show, shimmying her hips out of the tight jeans she has on, and my cock stiffens at the sight of her pale thighs.

I can't stop myself from imagining how it'd feel to bury my head between them or from wondering if the little whimpers she makes when she tosses in her sleep sound anything like the moans she'd make soaking my chin with her pleasure.

She's as untouched and pure as fallen snow—at least that's what she needs people to believe to keep her father happy. But I see the black and blue splotches coloring her skin and the gash at her ribs that drips with her fresh blood.

I *know* her, and as she pulls the sports bra over her head, baring the heavy swell of her breasts and that tiny pomegranate tattoo that no one else knows she has, I can almost feel the arousal course through her veins.

The second she steps into the shower, I see it; hot water scalds her skin, washing over sore muscles and cuts hidden to me. A normal person might wince against the pain, maybe grit their teeth, but not her.

Not my little Persephone.

Her jaw slackens a fraction as she turns toward the plexiglass shower door, smoothing her hands down over her curves, and then falls open on a sharp gasp. There's no audio with my footage, but I know what she sounds like.

I know everything about her.

When her hand drifts over her stomach, nimble fingers traveling lower to mix the pressure of pain and euphoria, I click out of the app, unwilling to allow my voyeuristic tendencies to cross that line.

The first time I watch her come undone, I want to *be* there, not watching from behind some fucking screen. I want to be the reason she comes, want my name to be the one she purrs as her pussy spasms and her nerve endings explode.

Pocketing my phone, I move off the bed and begin cleanup; my boss, the don of Boston's once most notorious crime family, might like evidence, but I've never been one to give it to him.

Once I've cleared the body from the room and bagged his remains to toss in my basement wood-burning stove later, I get to work cleaning the aftermath.

The routine starts by exchanging the stiff motel linens for fresh ones I picked up on my way in, removing the plastic mattress cover—which I slip on before I've begun my interrogation—and getting to work removing any gore that's splattered elsewhere.

After I've scrubbed the brown shag carpet of its biological traces, I deodorize and disinfect, the weight of my medical background refusing to let me leave until things are up to hospital code.

Using an ultraviolet light, I scan the area for any remnants of the dead man, heave my bags over my shoulder, and slip out the back exit.

Tossing the bags into my trunk, I slide behind the wheel of the black Buick I rented when I got into town and reach into the glove compartment for the book of poetry I keep there.

I know she memorized the pages torn from it at an early age. I know she pours over every book of poems she can find from the public library, trying to recreate the same feeling my copied words elicited in her as a child, though they were never meant for her.

She soaked them up anyway, so I also know she won't find that feeling elsewhere, because it's not in the words, it's in the gesture.

Poetry gifted, not poetry borrowed.

Words that made her feel less alone. Especially when she had to hide her love for literature from cruel parents.

That was long before her father asked me to keep an eye on her after she turned eighteen.

Long before my thoughts turned depraved and hungry.

CHAPTER 2

ELENA

"YOU DROPPED THIS."

My heart kick-starts, shifting into overdrive as I lift my gaze from the worn wooden pew in front of me. Familiar, rich brown eyes stare back at me, heavy and menacing in their unwavering perusal, as if trying to peer into my very soul.

The sharp, angular curve of his jaw gives me pause; I've never seen him without at least a hint of stubble, and that he's likely shaved specifically for this occasion causes the cracks in my heart to double in size.

Frissons of unease ripple inside the organ, partly at having this dangerous man's undivided attention and partly because being inside St. Leonard's so soon after my return home feels like a conflict of interest.

A tendril of jet-black hair swoops down over his smooth forehead, and my fingers twitch where they're pinned beneath my thighs, itching to push it away.

Always looking, never able to touch.

He holds out a slip of paper, crumpled between two long, muscular fingers. Everything about this man screams *fit*, and I can't stop my eyes from raking over his dark form hungrily, despite the context of the situation.

Impossibly tall, probably six-foot-four, maybe even six-foot-five, my father's hit man towers over the congregation, looking more out of place than if the devil himself had stepped inside the aged building.

His all-black, custom-tailored suit clings to his muscles, shoulders straining against the expensive fabric, and something quick and punishing tears through my gut, resonating between my thighs.

It makes my bones ache.

From the corner of my eye, I can see my family making their way from the altar, giving their last stoic regards to the golden casket parked there. My *nonnino*, the retired Don Ricci, murdered in cold blood before he had much of a chance to enjoy civilian life.

That's the problem with the Mafia though. Once you're in, there's no getting out. The reach of Ricci *famiglia* business stretches and refuses release, tightening its grip on its members until they eat, sleep, and *breathe* omertà.

Papà stops and shakes the hands of every passerby, doing his political duty to remain professional and reserved, even in times of duress.

When we were kids, he'd tell my sisters and me not to let emotional attachments surface in our everyday lives, because once something you love can be located, it can be used against you.

Which is likely how my grandfather ended up hanging from the rafters in his old barn earlier this week while his favorite horse ran loose through downtown Grafton.

Reaching out, I tentatively take the piece of paper from the man at my side; a chill runs up my arm as our fingers brush. His skin is as icy as the December Boston air, and a soft gasp falls from my mouth before I'm able to stifle it.

I don't miss the way one corner of his dark pink lips tugs up, though the rest of his expression remains unchanged. The impossible, unflappable Doctor Kal Anderson, regarding me in the flesh for the first time in two years.

Of course, I've been working on my English teaching degree online, with clinic hours at my alma mater, and he's been...*distant*.

Stuffing the scrap of paper into my coat pocket, I force my gaze ahead and try to calm my racing heart. I don't need to unwrap the paper to know it's got his chicken scratch handwriting on it or to remember one of the dozens of lines of poetry that have been etched into my heart over the years.

Mateo de Luca seems to appear out of thin air, dragging crooked fingers through his light brown, cropped hair as he searches the church for me.

My betrothed since birth, Mateo is Papà's attempt at securing an impenetrable alliance between Ricci Inc. and Bollente Media. And though I go along with it for Papà's sake, I'd kill to be out from beneath the scope of that man's dirty little thumb.

There's an evil presence inside Mateo unlike what I usually see in my father's men. It's cruel, wicked, and seeking a vessel to mold, possess, and pour itself into.

The kind of monster that develops out of boredom and a false sense of superiority, not because he truly enjoys the darkness.

"Elena, my darling," he exclaims, his voice bouncing off the columns and murals inside as if we're not at a wake. Bending once he reaches me, he scoops me roughly into his arms, nearly pulling me into his lap in front of the entire church. "I've been looking all over for you. Your mother said you got in last night. I was surprised that you didn't call."

Kal averts his eyes, but I don't miss the way his jaw clenches, nor do I miss the way my body heats at his reaction.

But I try not to read into it, because that's what he wants.

Gripping the hem of my black cashmere dress to keep from

flashing my father's employee, I clear my throat and try to wrench away from Mateo. "Holiday traffic was kind of a drag, so I went to bed as soon as I got home."

Mateo pinches one of my cheeks, and I wince as the pressure hits a sore inside my mouth. I'm still healing from a fight last week—at a diner a few miles from the Fontbonne Academy while I waited for our family driver to pick me up for winter break.

The bruises on my knees and ribs and the cut on the inside of my left thigh are why I'm wearing a sweater dress and thigh-high leather boots, despite the fact that St. Leonard's is notoriously warm inside.

"Want me to give you a ride to the reception?" Mateo asks, finally releasing me. "We could stop for some of that pomegranate frozen yogurt you like."

I *do* like the frozen yogurt, but the idea of being stuck alone in a car with this man for any length of time makes me nauseous. "Sorry, but I think Papà wants me home to help set up for tomorrow."

He pouts, his tan skin shimmering in the bright, fluorescent lighting. "Come on, E. I haven't seen you in months. Spend some fucking time with me."

Beside us, a throat clears, and then a large hand is wrapping around my bicep and yanking me from my seat into a standing position.

"I've been asked to make sure she gets home in one piece." Kal drags me into his side, my body on fire everywhere we connect.

"Oh, come on," Mateo scoffs, pushing to his feet. "Like they trust you with her more than me. You're liable to murder her and dump her body in the Charles."

"Sure that's the hill you want to die on, Mateo? You may be too stupid to be afraid of me, but that doesn't change what I'm capable of."

"Is that a threat?"

"Speak to her like that again, and I'll make it a fucking promise."

Kal squeezes my arm, and I whimper, shuffling closer to try and get him to let up. The scent of whiskey and cinnamon assaults me, and I feel a little lightheaded as I inhale deeply, my nose brushing against the fabric of his suit.

Mateo's eyes narrow, then he smirks and pulls me from Kal's grasp, wrapping his arms around me in a tight, suffocating embrace.

"Be good, my darling," he says, glaring over my head as he presses a chaste, pointed kiss to my hair, although I'm not really sure why.

He's not affectionate unless he's trying to cop a feel, and he's definitely misdirecting annoyance to the one person in this room who could make it seem like he never existed in the first place.

Not that my reluctant savior's interference means anything. Kal's just protective because he's my father's employee. Not because he cares about me.

He's made that abundantly clear.

Frankly, I'm not convinced the man has a caring bone in his entire body.

Yet the poems he leaves on my balcony suggest otherwise.

CHAPTER 3

KAL

MY GOLDEN GODDESS DOESN'T SAY A WORD AS I PEEL OUT OF the St. Leonard's parking lot, fingers flexing over the leather steering wheel as I attempt to control my rage.

The visceral reaction I had to Mateo grabbing her, claiming her, was wholly inappropriate, but like all storm surges, I was powerless against it.

What I really wanted to do was put a bullet through de Luca's brain, bend his fiancée over the church pew, and shatter her innocence as he bled out beneath us.

But I didn't.

Couldn't.

Even if not for the audience, taking that step with Elena isn't something I can afford.

No matter how badly I want to.

There's just too much at stake.

"You had no right to drag me out of there," she says after we drive about a mile in silence, staring out the window as downtown whips past, Christmas trees and Santas on every corner blurring as I weave through traffic. "That was my *nonnino's* wake, and you just plucked me from it like his death didn't matter."

Gritting my teeth, I steal a glance at her. She wraps a strand of warm, dark brown hair around her index finger, holding it there until the tip turns purple before finally letting go.

It's how she distracts herself from me, the onslaught of pain from loss of circulation pulling her mind from thoughts she shouldn't have.

My sweet little masochist.

"Would you have rather I left you to fight off your *beloved* in the confines of his car?"

Imagining his hands on her soft skin, smoothing along her curves, or wrapped in her dark tresses makes me see red. My skin prickles, blood boiling just beneath the surface, and I shift in my seat to try to tamp down the fire spreading through me.

"He's not my beloved," she mutters, crossing her arms. The gaudy ring on her left hand catches in the overcast sunlight, sending a hot spark of fury uncurling in my chest. "He's nothing but a thorn in my side."

Pulling up in front of the Riccis' luxurious Louisburg Square home, I park at the curb and switch off the engine. "Yet you're marrying him?"

Lifting her chin, she meets my eyes, and I feel lost in the golden swirl of her gaze; it's warm and inviting, soft like wintertime and the edges she hides from the rest of the world.

"Is that a question, *Kallum*?" She breathes my name, her ruby-red lips curving around each syllable the way I wish they'd curve around my dick, and I swallow over the knot that forms in my throat. "I'm afraid you already know the answer."

Irritation bubbles up inside me—at her compliance to this world she has no business being a part of and at how much I want her and cannot have her.

Fuck, who I wouldn't murder just to sink inside that virgin pussy for one goddamn night.

What cities I wouldn't burn to be able to pretend, for a brief moment in time, that she could be mine.

"*Why* are you marrying him?" The question slips out before I have a chance to stop it, deafening in the space of the vehicle.

"What else would you have me do? Defy my father and risk excommunication, or…worse? Jesus, even I have to draw the line of rebellion somewhere."

Pursing my lips, I lean back in my seat and tap my index finger on the wheel. Unlatching the child safety feature, I unlock the doors and stare out the windshield as snow begins to float from the sky. "Maybe you're not who I thought you were."

Her face falls, her jaw clenching as if to keep from bursting into tears.

She moves, unbuckling her seat belt, and her rosy pomegranate perfume wafts my way, causing something in my chest to quake with longing.

"Maybe I just know how to pick my battles."

CHAPTER 4

ELENA

I SEE THE MOMENT KAL'S PATIENCE WITH ME WANES; SITTING HERE in his car, I'm stunned too stupid to move as I watch the calm, collected soul I've admired exhale from his body.

His eyes darken to a black I've never seen, homing in on me with a determination I don't quite understand.

Pressing my back into the car door, I try to put as much space between us as I can, not wanting to be in the direct line of fire of this feral man.

Sweat breaks out along my hairline, my dress suddenly too hot and too tight for my body, my tongue swelling three sizes too large inside my mouth.

"Get out." His voice is a harsh growl, cutting me to the bone. But fuck if I don't like the way it slices against my skin.

"Excuse me?"

"You fucking heard me, Elena. I won't ask again."

"What the hell? You forced me to leave the church before I was ready, and now you're kicking me out of the car?"

He reaches across me, pulling on the door handle and forcing it open. My breath catches as his arm grazes my chest, but then he's resituating himself in his seat and turning the car back on.

One hand scrubs at his clean-shaven jaw, so rough against his skin that it bleeds red beneath his touch.

Violence practically clings to him, itching to be set free from where he tries to bury it in his soul.

And even though it's stupid and dangerous and he's convinced himself he doesn't want anything to do with me, I want to be the one who sees him break. Want it to be me he takes his rage out on.[105]

"Make me."

Eyes bugging out, his chin whips in my direction. "What?"

I shrug, pulling the door shut and shifting so my dress hikes up my thighs as I spread them slightly.

Throat bobbing over a swallow, his gaze locks on my fingers as I glide them up my legs, slipping just below my hemline.

His breathing grows shallow as I continue the ascent, letting out a soft whimper when I reach the lace of my panties.

"*Stop*," he grunts, still watching me. Waiting to see what I'll do next.

Smirking, I slip my index finger beneath the elastic of my underwear, swiping lazily at my seam, dipping between my soft folds.

Kal's nostrils flare, his fists curling so tight around the steering wheel that it wheezes under the pressure, and I can't stop the moan that falls from my lips as I swirl around my clit.

It throbs, desperate for him to see me come undone and for him to know that every time I've ever touched myself, it's been to the image of him.

As my fingers move faster, my breaths come in rapid spurts, my mouth hanging open as my eyes stay on his. Anguish colors the

---

105   It's mentioned in *P&P*, but this moment makes it the most clear how Elena pursued Kal first, and I love that for them.

harsh planes of his face, sending shivers of delight and misery echoing through my body in white-hot waves.

Delight because it's obvious he wants me, even if he won't admit it out loud.

Misery because he denies me.

But if that's how my handsome Hades wants to play, I'm not above manipulating the confession from him.

Even if I have to ride my own hand to kingdom *come*.

"Do you remember what I asked you for on my eighteenth birthday?"

For him to kiss me. Fuck me.

He'd refused.

Kal freezes. "I haven't changed my mind."

"Really?" Pulling my hand out from under my skirt, I lave over my finger with my tongue, slurping up the arousal collected on the tip.

His jaw locks.

My pussy weeps in protest, but I ignore it, lifting my knee and hoisting myself over the center console.

"Jesus Christ, Elena, what the hell are you doing?"

I launch myself onto his lap before he has a chance to push me away, planting my knees on either side of his hips.

My dress bunches up just beneath the curve of my ass, but as I settle onto the tops of his thighs and grind into his pelvis, I don't even care.

Gripping my hips, he starts to shove me off him, but I slide my hands behind his neck and lock them there, my hold ironclad.

Papà put Ari, Stella, and me in self-defense classes at a young age, and one of the first things they taught was how to get too close for a perpetrator to be able to attack.

Kal digs his fingers into me, and I writhe on top of him, the pain causing euphoria to build in my lower belly.

"Goddamnit, little one, you're asking for trouble."

Ignoring the jab, I move my hips faster, leaning slightly to create friction on my clit. My panties are soaked, cold where they're pressed against his slacks, but I'm far too sucked into a web of pleasure to give a shit.

"Give in, *Kallum*. Take from me before Mateo does."

He groans, the sound ricocheting off the windows, using his hold on me to increase my speed and pressure. I feel him harden beneath me, my brain locking in on the sensation of his thick cock between my pussy lips.

"I'm not like the boys from your little private schools. I'll ruin you and not think twice about it."

Pressure coils tight inside my stomach, electricity zinging through my veins. "So *ruin me*."

It takes a moment. He sweeps his gaze around, inspecting the street for onlookers, but the windows have fogged up so much at this point that it's impossible to see in or out without some effort.

Goose bumps pop up on my skin the second some kind of switch flips in him, desperation bleeding from his movements.

Tearing the neckline of my dress, Kal's mouth latches on to the space where my throat meets my shoulder, sucking so hard and fast that I cry out from the intensity.

His hands snake up my thighs, heavy and deliberate, and I'm still riding his pants-clad cock when his fingers find my dripping core.

"Merry fucking Christmas to me," he growls against me, biting the space he's just kissed until I'm sure he breaks the skin.

My eyes roll back, my body bucking as he seems to drink from me, a vampire feasting on its willing victim.

Long fingers probe through my sensitive flesh, the lewd sounds of my arousal making my cheeks heat, and then he pulls away to reach into the glove compartment. "Put your hands behind your back."

I obey, disengaging from his neck while he drags a black satin ribbon out and shuts the door.

There's a red stain on the corner of his mouth, and for a moment, he looks positively unhinged.

Fear surges through me, mixed with a strange sense of excitement, and I lean forward to lick the blood from his lips.

It's metallic and sweet, my essence mixed with cinnamon lip balm, and my pussy seems to ignite at the taste.

But he doesn't give me what I really want.

CHAPTER 5

KAL

I'M THREE SECONDS FROM SHOOTING MY LOAD INSIDE MY SLACKS and not finishing what I started here when Elena starts lapping at my mouth, licking her own blood from my skin like a goddamn siren in heat.

My dick is enraged, gorged beyond belief as she dry fucks me, the scent of her intoxicating pussy making my vision blur.

I have to end this before I do something I regret. Something I can't fucking take back.

Pulling the ribbon through my fingers, I take her wrists in my hands and knot the fabric around her joints, pinning them together in a way that won't cause nerve damage if I pull too tight.

Her chest rises and falls against mine, the lace of her bra where I tore the outfit scraping against my suit jacket.

Ensuring the knot is fastened, I lean forward, dragging my tongue along the bloody bite mark and relishing in how she shudders *into* me and not away.

As if she too has sick, violent desires.

Of course, I already know she does. The bruises and cuts on her glorious skin hint at it, and the way she rode my lap while I tore into her proves it.

Still, that doesn't change the facts. Doesn't change the reality that I cannot have her, and certainly not like this.

Trailing my lips up to her ear, nipping the lobe so hard she squeals, I flick my tongue against her tragus. "Get the fuck off me."

I haul her up and dump her into the seat next to me before she has a chance to protest, reveling in the gasp that tears from her chest. She maneuvers around, hands still bound behind her back, and glares at me. "You're an asshole."

Shrugging, I shift the car into drive and reach past her to once again open her door. "I tried to warn you."

Sputtering, she shakes her head. "Aren't you gonna untie me?"

"You're a tough girl, remember?" I wink, keeping my foot on the brake pedal as I shove her onto the sidewalk. She spills like a drunkard outside her home, drawing attention from people as they pass by to look at the Christmas decorations. "Figure it out yourself."

A knock on my front door draws me from my security feed. Very few people are aware that I own a house on Linden Street, the rest content to believe that a man dubbed Doctor Death by the rumor mill in every town he's ever lived isn't a resident within their city limits.

On the monitor, Elena assists her two younger sisters with decorating the large, flocked Christmas tree in their foyer while their grandmother sits on the couch drinking a glass of chardonnay.

Grieving, I suppose, though I've never quite understood the concept. What's the point in crying over a man who chose to live the life of a criminal? How can you delude yourself into believing there's any other possible outcome for a made man?

Elena alternates between feeding lights around the tree to the middle child, Ariana, and nibbling on peanut butter fudge from a tray in the kitchen.

She's barefoot on their hardwood floors, wearing skinny jeans and a T-shirt of some obscure band from long before she was even born, constantly checking over her shoulder as if she expects trouble to appear out of thin air.

Her naivete makes me chuckle.

Like she'd ever know I was there in the first place.

I can still smell her on my fingers, even though I've washed my hands until they bled. Can still feel her grinding on my cock, her wetness coating me, seeping into my flesh as she chased her release.

It should've been enough to sate my hunger for her, yet it feels as though it's done nothing but fan the flames.

Pushing away from my desk, I get to my feet and slip from the office as the knocking grows incessant, hoping carolers haven't decided to stop by again this year.

Keying in the code for the room, ensuring no one can accidentally see my workspace, I move down the hall, taking the stairs two at a time, and throw open the front door.

Elena's mother stands on my doorstep, a red parka buttoned up to her chin. Dark eyes peer into mine as she presses her pink lips together, familiarity floating in the depths of her irises that makes me nauseous.

Something sharp flares in my chest, an abscess that's gone untreated for far too long and is now infected, more sinister and malignant than ever before.

Reaching for the doorframe, I grip it in my palm and keep myself from swaying beneath her penetrating gaze. "Carmen. To what do I owe this immense displeasure?"

Her foot taps on the concrete, a look of annoyance flickering over her face. "It's rude not to invite people in when it's snowing."

Glancing over her shoulder as flurries drift from the gray sky, I slide my gaze back to her and do my best to ignore the irritation spiking in my gut. *Things were just going too well for me.* "It's rude to show up to people's homes uninvited."

"Ah, but that never stopped you, did it?"

A tic forms in my jaw, thrumming through the muscle there and pulling it tight.

Stepping out on the porch, I yank the front door closed and pounce on her, wrapping my hand around her neck and pressing her into one of the porch columns.

I don't squeeze hard enough to fully rob her of air or leave a mark, my fingers placed just so she's aware of who she's dealing with.

I'm not anything like the idiot boy she once claimed to love. The *child* so desperate for attention and affection that he debased himself at her feet to get it.

I know better now. The abuse, the lies, the manipulation. That's all it ever was.

Something that looks a lot like disappointment flashes over her face as her skull connects with the pillar. "It's nice to see some things never change, Kal."[106]

"You've got three seconds to explain what you're doing here before I take you down to my basement and send you home so disfigured, even the man who's been buried in your dried-up pussy the last twenty years won't recognize you."

"Mature." She rolls her eyes, then narrows them when I don't move. "I might be more willing to confess if you took your hands off me."

"You're a part of my world, doll. Don't pretend to be ignorant of why I am the way I am."

---

106 Carmen is truly the worst.

Still, I release her, if only because it burns my palms to have my hands on her skin so soon after caressing the smooth curves of her daughter. My obsession, my ruin. *My Persephone.* The one woman I'd kill to have rule at my side.

Yet the woman in front of me is the main reason I know I can never have her.

CHAPTER 6

KAL

NORMALLY, I WELCOME SILENCE.

Crave it even.

After a decade of either relishing or squirming in the agony of others, the deafening quiet became the only solace available. The only place I could go where not even my darkest sins could try to kill me.

I try not to think about how it morphed into a psychological *need*.

Tonight, the silence only furthers my own personal torture, twisting the white-hot metaphorical knife of betrayal and admonition in my gut until it feels like I might pass out from the pain.

My fingers grasp at my cotton bedsheets. I thrash from one side to the other, replaying Carmen's words in my mind like a broken record.

How could she ever think that showing up and begging me to leave her daughter alone would do the trick?

That it wouldn't create an even greater impossibility between us, make me salivate for the young, untouched flesh even more?

"Please, Kal. If you care about her or me at all, you'll leave her alone. Each time you even so much as look at her, it puts her in danger. You know what the Elders would do if they thought she'd been impure before her wedding night, and that's not even including what Rafe would do."

The thing is, though, I don't.

Care, I mean. At least about anything other than making Carmen suffer for what she did to me and defiling Elena Ricci. Claiming her for myself and ruining her soul beyond repair.

Something tells me she'd enjoy the fucking ride too.

And as much as I want to resist the twenty-year-old goddess, as much as I don't want sinful thoughts of her delicious ass running rampant through my mind, I can't stop myself.

Can't wrench out of the depraved fantasies playing on repeat behind my eyelids, amplified by the silence cloaking my bedroom.

Her mother may have ruined my childhood with her abuse, but my interest in Elena has nothing to do with Carmen, outside of the fact that it pisses her off.

In truth, I just *want* Elena.

I wasn't going to allow myself to have her on principle, because it could make things messy. But now…

Throwing off my comforter, I yank on a pair of discarded black slacks and head for my office, tossing the deli owner passed out in the corner a disgusted look.

For a moment, I consider resuming my work on him. Lustful depravity aside, my main focus is supposed to be the job Rafe brought me to town for: figuring out who leaked word of the Riccis' business being used as a front for a sports betting ring.

I don't know that Tony Pesognelli has the exact answers, but I'm willing to bet a greaseball like him isn't innocent.

Still, even as I prod his knee with a branding iron, waking the balding man from his fitful slumber, my heart isn't in it.

Sighing as he sobs into his ball gag, something I had left over from the last time I entertained a lady companion years ago, I stalk to the other side of the room and flop behind my desk.

Propping my feet up on the wooden surface, I exhale and pull a manila envelope into my lap, opening one side and studying the pictures in it.

My computer monitor comes to life, indicating movement on the security feed, but I don't look immediately.

Instead, I peer into the deep, warm brown gaze that haunted my memory long before Elena ever did.

Black hair twisted into an elegant braid that hangs off one pale, freckled shoulder, a smile that beams for another as she stares off beyond the camera.

There's a softness here I don't see often; she's absent of the sharpness I feel in my veins and the tar in my heart. Everything that makes me *me* and evil by default.

A monster.

It's amazing we're related at all.

Part of me wonders which girl I'll destroy first.

Carmen's words echo through me again as I shut the envelope and tap my keyboard, bringing the camera feed up once more with the push of one button.

Elena stands in front of the floor-length mirror in her en suite bathroom with her sister Ariana checking her makeup. Preparing for the Christmas-slash-birthday shindig the Riccis throw every year.

I normally make it a point not to attend. Crowds and I don't exactly mesh.

But as I zoom in, my gaze roving over my little Persephone's curves, exaggerated in the skintight, blush-colored gown she has on, I notice the slightest hint of a fresh bruise on her right shoulder blade.

The average onlooker might not see the hand-shaped shadow, might not see the wince as she turns to apply mascara to her sister's eyes, but I do.

And as I watch her, my obsession expands, like a balloon stretching to accommodate as much air as it can before it pops.

My girl likes to fight—that's a common fact around Boston. But there's something about this particular mark that makes my insides shrivel.

It looks too familiar to be random.

And as I stalk back to my bedroom, pull on a dress shirt and my trench coat, I know exactly how to quell the typhoon of noise wreaking havoc on my mind.

CHAPTER 7

ELENA

"ARE YOU OKAY?" ARIANA'S FACE TWISTS, CONTORTING INTO A mask of concern. She tucks her light brown hair behind her ears, rubbing her thumbs over each lobe twice before her hands drop to her sides.

It's a calming gesture Nonna taught us when we were kids, insisting the ears are the gateway to healing the rest of our bodies.

She'd say the things we allowed ourselves to hear had the potential to poison our minds and that once the mind was poisoned, it was a slippery slope before the rest of our body wilted as well.

Evidently, she didn't know there were plenty of other ways for that to happen.

Like allowing lust to cloud your judgment and dry humping a man almost twice your age.

A man not only employed by my father and feared by everyone but who's also made it clear he wants very little to do with me.

My hand goes to the hickey he left on my neck yesterday, the flesh tender as I slather foundation over it. The makeup barely hides the purple constellation, and his teeth indentation feels permanent.

It makes my core throb, little sparks of desire igniting low in my abdomen, but I ignore it as a wave of nausea nearly knocks me into the sink.

I've already covered as much of my black eye as I could with several layers of thick concealer after sitting with a bag of frozen peas on it half the night.

Ariana hasn't mentioned anything about it, which tells me I've done a decent job of erasing the evidence of Mateo's temper.

He'd been angry that I left yesterday, and frankly, it was stupid of me not to think there'd be consequences.

Mateo's been proving our whole lives that he'll stop at nothing to have me and that he'll obliterate anyone who tries to stand in his way.

And while I know I don't deserve the treatment, don't deserve him putting his hands on me, there's very little I can do besides fight back.

Papà's on edge all the time, and he needs this wedding to work to try to bridge the gap between all of Boston and Ricci Inc.'s reputation.

Unfortunately, in this world we live in, our loyalty lies in our blood bonds, and I refuse to be responsible for my father's downfall or be killed in the face of my defiance.

Besides, it's not like Mateo left our brunch date without a limp. A black eye in exchange for making the asshole potentially impotent is about as fair as it can get, I think.

"E?" Ariana frowns, poking my stomach with one manicured finger. "Hello? Are you even listening to me?"

Blinking myself from my runaway train of thought, I offer her a soft smile and close the tube of foundation, inspecting my shoulder to make sure the mark's hidden well enough. "Yes, and I'm fine. Just…a little distracted, with everything going on."

She tilts her head, watching me with doe eyes. "You don't seem like yourself. You haven't mentioned the fact that it's your birthday even once."

"Honestly, the novelty starts to wear off once you've had two decades of birthdays."

Her face screws up, and she smacks her pink, glossy lips. "Uh, if you say so. I'm gonna bask in them 'til my body can't physically take it anymore."

I laugh softly, shoving her with my shoulder. She pulls away from the white marble countertop in my bathroom, adjusting her cleavage in the light blue, crushed velvet dress she has on. "You know everyone coming tonight is either related to us or off-limits, right?"

"What's your point?"

Cocking an eyebrow, I wave my hand in her direction. "Isn't all *this* overkill?"

"I'm not gonna dress homely just to make our family comfortable. You know what Nonna always says."

"Dress for the job you want, not the job you have." I roll my eyes at the snippet of stolen—and, frankly, coming from a woman who's never worked a day in her life, tone-deaf—wisdom and point at her stiletto heels. "So when did you decide you wanted to be a hooker?"

"What, you think I won't pull out all the stops to get Kal Anderson's attention?"

My stomach drops, my heart lurching into my throat as she smooths her hands over her stomach, checking out her ass in the mirror.

Gripping the edge of the sink until my knuckles turn white, I try to steady my voice. "Kal won't be here. He never comes to these parties."

She shrugs, unaware of my sudden change in breathing. "A girl can hope, can't she?"

She shouldn't, my heart screams, wanting to lash out and hurt her. Hurt *someone*, rid myself of the fingerprints the bad doctor left on my soul.

Not wanting me is one thing.

Humiliation is another, and when he left me tied up outside our house just yesterday, I'd resigned myself to a fate of not knowing Dr. Anderson beyond the persona he wields in public like a weapon.

A dull ache flares in my temple, but I ignore it as I give my sister a phony smile. "Well, good luck with that endeavor. You couldn't *pay* me to try to impress that vile man."[107]

Ari smirks, flitting to the doorway, leaving a trail of floral perfume and sunshine I can't begin to understand in her wake. "Luckily, you're not the hooker."

The door swings shut as she pushes past it, and I buckle, my elbows landing on the counter with a harsh thud as another wave rolls through me.

But this time, there's no pain accompanying it. Instead, the nausea ripples from the cracks in my bleeding heart and the knowledge that Mafia women don't ever get what they want.

Pinching my eyes shut, I suck in several deep breaths, trying to steel myself against the emotions warring on my insides.

The air around me seems to shift, dropping significantly enough to cause goose bumps to crop up along my skin, and a dark, inky presence settles in, gluing to my body like a second skin.

I swallow over the dryness in my throat, slowly lifting my head and peeling my eyelids back, meeting the harsh, hungry gaze of the man my mother calls Hades incarnate.

"Good thing my admiration of you comes free of charge, little one."

---

107   I swear, it is so much fun to go back in time by reading this after *P&P,* because you can sit and laugh when you know the future.

CHAPTER 8

KAL

ELENA'S WARM BODY TRIES TO ESCAPE MINE, BUT I MOVE IN closer, trapping her against the bathroom sink.

Her heat calls out to me, flames I want to burn my skin. I can't force myself away, even as logic screams at me to stop and take stock of our situation.

But reason has given way to obsession; this girl bleeds into even the recesses of my brain, blotting out everything I know to be fact.

Years of medicine, murder, the quest to regain a family that never wanted me in the first place and leave the one I chose long ago—Elena Ricci blots all of it out, like a black hole absorbing my entire universe until all that's left to see and *feel* is her.

"What are you doing here?" she snaps, her golden-hazel eyes glaring at me through her reflection, making my cock twitch against the curve of her ass.

Pushing her dark hair over her shoulder, I glide my palms over the crisscrossed back of her dress, reveling in the way the fabric paints a checkerboard on her creamy skin.

I freeze, fisting the material where her back ends and using it to pull her more fully into me. "What do you *think* I'm doing here?"

"If you think I'm letting you anywhere near me after yesterday—"

Gripping her throat in one hand and her shoulder in the other, I step back just enough to spin her around, shoving her into the counter once again, this time forcing a harsh breath of air from deep in her lungs.

It rips through her chest, our bodies vibrating where they connect, and something inside of me shifts. A tectonic plate loosening, gearing up for an earth-shattering quake.

"It's your birthday. I owe you a gift, don't I?"

Her pulse jumps beneath my hand, and a bead of sweat pops up along my hairline as I rake my gaze over her form, practically fucking drooling at the perfection.

Her tits press obscenely against my chest, threatening to spill out of the tight dress she's in, and the bite mark I left on her almost preens in the soft lighting, glistening beneath the makeup she tried to hide it with.

Bending down, I run the flat of my tongue over the mangled flesh, ignoring the powdery taste and reveling in the shiver that skates along her spine.

"Do you suddenly not want me, little one? Is that where that sentence was going?" Sucking the spot between my lips, I feast on her until she bows into me, a low whimper escaping her perfect mouth.

She trembles as I release her with a loud pop, shifting to my full height and running my thumb along the slick, dark oval marring her.

Scowling, she tries to push me away, but I grab on to the bowl of the sink and force her to spread her legs so I can wedge myself even closer.

The dress she has on doesn't allow much flexibility, so I reach down and haul her up onto the counter, then rip the skirt right up the middle.

"*Jesus!*" Elena squeals, moving to hold the fabric together as I fit myself between her legs. "What the hell is wrong with you? You rejected me *yesterday*."

"I changed my mind."

"You changed your mind," she deadpans. "Are you seriously *that* fickle?"

"Not fickle." My fingers find her bodice, and the thin fabric rips with the slightest tug, revealing a lacy, nude bra and matching panties.

The taut lines of her flat stomach rescind and reappear with each breath she takes, and I push the straps off her shoulders, letting the dress pool underneath her. "Completely and utterly deranged, my little Persephone."

Instead of wilting like a dead flower under the heat of my gaze, Elena straightens her shoulders, pushing her tits into my chest.

My dick leaks behind my slacks, desperate to strip her now and ask questions later.

But something catches in the light; her left eye shines, the hint of a shadow decorating the lid, highlighting broken blood vessels.

Fury swims in my veins, diving deep and refusing to let go, reigniting my main purpose for showing up here.

"Elena," I say on an exhale, barely able to see past the red blurring my vision. "Where's your fiancé tonight?"

She swallows, eyes widening slightly. *She knows I know. Knows I see what others can't.*

Licking her lips, she releases her hold on her dress, baring her glorious body to me as she slips off the counter.

"Why are we talking about him? I thought you came here to give me something." She tilts her head, sliding a hand up my chest, wrapping it around my neck. "I was hoping it'd be a bit more personable this year."

"Are you saying what I brought last year wasn't good enough?"

"Poetry of others is *fine*, but I want something crafted by you, *Kallum*."

Unsure of why she's protecting that son of a bitch but momentarily placated by the feel of her hands on me, I narrow my eyes. "I don't write poetry."

Scoffing, she takes a step back, resuming her place on the sink. She spreads her legs and uses an index finger to pull the scrap of lace between them aside, revealing her pretty, pink pussy.

Liquid fire spills down my spine, coating every single nerve ending and thought in third-degree burns.

"No one *writes* poetry. You *live* it. *Breathe* it. *Embody* it." She grins devilishly, licking one finger and bringing it down to circle her clit.

Sitting there, stroking her dripping pussy, Elena looks like the predator here. Like a wild cat who's finally ensnared her prey and intends to torture it before she brings it the swift release of death.

"They teach you that at school?"

"*You* taught me that. All those poems you left showed me that art, especially the written kind, exists inside us. Either you *are* poetry, or you aren't. You can't fake it. Can't fake the things you feel in the very thread of your soul."

The thread of your soul.

Her breaths grow fast and shallow, her strokes longer and more languid as her hips move in soft thrusts on the counter. My cock is rock-hard and angry as hell, ready to sink into her, but my mind is having trouble keeping up.

I want to punish everyone in her life, and the best way I know how is to take what she's always been willing to give me. To shatter the last shred of innocence she has, take the sacrificial lamb like she begged me to two years ago.

Fuck her mother, her father, the limp-dicked fucker I'm finding as soon as I leave here. Fuck the rules, my past, and this messed-up world we live in. Fuck the fact that she's young and has the entire world at her fingertips.

Undoing my belt with frantic, shaking fingers, I unzip my slacks and let them fall to my knees, moving closer. Her eyes lock on to mine as I grab her wrist, pulling her hand up and sucking her finger into my mouth.

Dizzying, tangy flavors explode on my tongue, and I have to stop myself from moaning out loud.

Fuck, this is wrong. She's engaged, I'm a murderer, and my intentions here are nowhere near as pure as I'm making them out to be.

I'm going to ruin her, and the consequences will never even faze me.

But I don't stop.

Can't stop.

None of my other sins ever tasted so sweet.

She pulls my dick out with her free hand, and I release her with a moan when she grips me, pumping slowly. "I thought you wanted a poem."

Shaking her head, she guides me to her pussy, gliding the tip through her juices, and I close my eyes for a moment as I try to maintain my grip on reality.

Everything is shifting so quickly, the object of my obsession fast becoming the vixen of my absolute greatest pleasure, and I'm having a hard time separating arousal from restraint and reason.

"I want you to recite poetry on my pussy. Make me *feel* it with your cock."

I curse under my breath, once again gripping her throat, bending to the other side of her neck and biting until the skin breaks there too. I lap at the blood that beads in the cut, knowing in the back of my brain that this is unsafe, but still unable to stop.

She groans, pushing the head of my dick between her lips, and I

suck harder. Furiously. As if draining her of her blood might cure me
of my obsession.

When I pull back, she smiles, delirious. "You're gonna have to try
a lot harder if you want to hurt me, *Kallum.*"

"Do you *want* me to hurt you?"

"I've come a million times to the idea of you marking me, spank-
ing me, making me bruise and bleed." Heat flares in her gaze as I
tighten my hold on her neck. "I want you to scar me."

With my free hand, I fist my cock, slapping her clit with it until
she writhes on the counter. "This won't be pleasant."

"Stop talking and fucking show me."

Growling at her insolence, I shift, sliding my hand up to grip her
chin and force her head back against the mirror.

Downstairs, a Christmas party full of drunk Italians and made
men rages on, and I know her fiancé is around here somewhere.

But none of that registers as she raises her hips in a challenge. Not
giving her a chance to spew regrets or irritate me further, I snap my
pelvis forward, shoving my cock so deep that the thin barrier of her
innocence gives without resistance.

CHAPTER 9

ELENA

"THIS WON'T BE PLEASANT."

Well, no one can call Kallum Anderson a liar, that much is certain.[108]

My lungs sit on the brink of complete collapse, straining beneath the grip of his fingers on my throat and the fire raging where his dick is seated inside me.

Hips flush with me, Kal leans so I'm bent back over the sink, grinding my skull into the vanity mirror.

"*Christ.*" The one syllable is a hiss, a single gust of air pushed between clenched teeth. "You have to fucking relax, Elena, or you're going to break my cock with how tight you're squeezing me."

I manage to choke out a snort. "I thought pussies were supposed to be tight."

"They are—fuck, yours *is.*" His dark eyes find mine, stirring something warm in my belly. "But if this isn't comfortable for you, it's sure as hell not going to be for me."

"Don't pretend like you care about my *comfort*. You were just talking about ruining me."

"You *begged* me to, you dirty little slut."

If possible, my inner muscles draw even tighter with the derogatory term he hurls, and his nostrils flare. Pulling his hips back slightly, he shifts, sliding his cock out halfway.

I tense, my ankles instinctively digging into his ass in an attempt to keep him lodged in me. It hurts, but he's right.

This is exactly what I asked for.

His pain, his passion, his punishment.

A choice to be ruined.

My choice.

Still, I whimper. "It hurts."

A cruel laugh works its way past his lips, and with a snap of his pelvis, he's once again buried to the hilt. "I warned you it would."

The tip of him feels like it's in my stomach, and I let out a breathy squeak. My body recoils of its own volition, trying to escape the agony he's wringing out of me even as dopamine rushes through my veins.

Every pain receptor in my body responds to the intrusion of this dangerous man, but my brain drives in the opposite direction, welcoming brutality with open arms.

Kal's hands keep me in place as he begins a slow assault, his grip on my neck slipping as sweat percolates under his palm.

I pinch my eyes closed and tighten my legs around him, trying to reconcile the conflicting sensations erupting in my core.

On the push in, it feels like I'm being split in half.

Literally. I think he could saw me in two with his fat cock, and he sputters when I tell him so, glaring down at me as he pulls back out, leaving just the head in.

"Fat cock," he spits, voice laced with venom. "Where the hell did you learn to speak like that?"

"None of your business."

His expression darkens, and without another word, he thrusts up, shunting himself as deep inside of me as he can go. Long fingers flexing, he drags me away from the mirror by my neck, bending me like a soft pretzel.

My breathing scatters, my tendons straining beneath his hold.

But I'm so warm, my blood humming like birds greeting the morning sun, that I barely notice my body breaking for him.

Don't notice how dangerous he is or how this connection is already proving volatile.

All I know is it feels *incredible*. Pleasure mixing with pain, sparking into this colossal fire that neither of us have intentions of putting out any time soon.

"If I learn you've let another man touch you," Kal says, but it's so hard to focus as he starts fucking me again, each cant of his hips more forceful than the last, "I'll *kill* him. Cut out his heart and let you watch him choke on it."

A flutter shimmies through my veins, contracting my muscles. Maybe it's because I grew up with the violence, or maybe I'm just fucked in the head, but the image he paints doesn't deter me the way I'm sure he wants it to.

I want to tell him about Mateo. To confide about the abuse I've put up with for years, because that's what was expected.

But I don't, not wanting to sully the moment.

Instead, I meet those nearly black eyes and squeeze around him until his grip on my throat turns menacing. It steals my air, creating a burn that glides down my esophagus, exploding somewhere in my chest.

"Awfully possessive for a man who didn't want anything to do with me twenty-four hours ago," I manage, and then he's shifting, hitting that sweet spot that I wasn't aware of until this moment.

His cock drags against it, and he tightens his fingers until my vision slackens, spots forming around the edges.

Sudden pressure on my clit has me bucking up, eyes widening; I glance down and find his thumb circling me, drawing figure eights over my sensitive flesh.

A moan grates through me, and an inferno rages in my belly, heating where his touch leaves me cold.

"Two years ago, you begged me to take your virginity," he says, keeping his voice low. Dangerously low—it rumbles inside my chest, like he's somehow managed to seep into my pores and now has a residence in my bloodstream. "I refused. Tried to do the *good thing* and stay away from you."

My mouth falls open as he shoves my head back, and my skull smacks against the mirror. Pain splices across the bone, echoing down my spine, and my pussy flutters as my body wars with itself.

He saws in and out, and my thigh muscles scream from being spread open around him.

His gaze remains trained between our bodies, watching as he disappears inside me.

Maybe it's the endorphins pumping through me, but his hands are somehow everywhere at once, sweeping and squeezing and plucking.

He rolls my nipple beneath one thumb and then drags that same print over the mark on my shoulder. I hiss at the contact, but I don't resist when he pinches the skin and finally lifts his head.

I feel a droplet of blood bead in the bite wound.

"But?" I prompt when he doesn't continue. Because there's *always* one.

A muscle thumps beneath his eye. "*But*…I can't get you out of my goddamn mind, Elena. And I'm not a good guy, so for tonight, you're all fucking mine. You'll do whatever I say, when I say it, and how I say it."

My heart ricochets inside my chest as his pelvis drills into me, relentless in its assault. I've seen enough porn at this point to know what comes next; his facial features tighten and twist, and I swear I feel him swell as he drags his length against my inner walls.

He brushes over the cut in my flesh, liquid crimson staining his skin.

Without faltering in his movements, his hand slides up, squeezing gently at the sides of my neck, keeping me in place even as it feels like my body drifts out to sea. Then he touches his thumb to his lips, darting his tongue out to swipe slowly over the digit.

Shock spirals through my stomach, rippling through my ribs, and pressure mounts in my core. Heat shoots through me, something wild unfurling in my bones as he bends, lining our mouths up but refusing to kiss me.

I don't know why, but the denial makes me feel crazier. Warmer. I'm unmoored, floating in a cloud of pleasure as I chase the tail end of my release.

"And maybe when I've stuffed you full of my cum like the little dumpster you are," he breathes, and I smell the whiskey on his teeth, the cool mint, and the *blood*, "you'll understand what I meant when I said I'd *ruin* you. It's never going to be like this for you again, my little Persephone, because no one else fucking owns you the way I do."

I shake my head, too focused on the white noise rushing between my ears to grasp the gravity of his words. Or to recognize that they're what I've always wanted to hear from him.

My body responds though. His head dips to my neck, lips sealing around the wound. He drinks from me like a fucking demon who hasn't tasted humanity in centuries.

"So fucking wet," he growls, and I don't know if he means my pussy or the flesh he's sucking, but it makes me lightheaded regardless. "Can't believe I stayed away as long as I did, knowing this sweet little pussy was waiting for me. God, she's fucking hungry, isn't she? Needs to be filled, don't you think?"

I don't respond, my mouth slackening as he pounds me into the sink, and he grunts in disapproval.

"*Tell me*, Elena. Tell me how badly you want to drip with my cum." A nip at my skin has my back arching, and my pussy pulses around him. "Beg for it, my little slut."

"Oh *God*, please. Please, Kallum."

It should be beneath me to beg this man, but I'm so far fucking gone that I can't bring myself to care.

Besides, the animalistic sound that tears from within his chest makes me feel as though the begging isn't even for me. It's almost as if he needs permission, still.

Needs to know I'm right there with him.

He bites again, and the flare of pain is my undoing. I clamp down around him as he pushes all the way in and freezes, his sweaty pelvis pressing against my ass, my thighs glued to his hips.

A choked moan falls from my lips as I come, and I squeeze my eyes shut, tremors racking the length of my body.

Stars burst and fires extinguish behind my eyelids, my muscles tangling with euphoria until all I can see and smell and feel and *think* is Kallum.

He looms like a depraved god over me, wringing the darkest desires from my bones and playing them like a xylophone.

When he pulls back, red paints his mouth. There's something so erotically fulfilling, completely hedonistic, about my blood coating his flesh that it pushes another orgasm through me just as his floods him.

His groan, throaty and soft, makes my heart seize; it echoes on as he spills inside me, hot cum coating my pussy. Marking me in the most primal, most dangerous way.

"*Christ.*" Kal coughs, as if his release has physically drained him.

An obscene squelching sound splatters in the air as he slowly withdraws from me. I clench nothing and feel the loss in my fucking soul.

They say you feel fundamentally different after losing your virginity—or at least that's what my family's always preached. And I do, but it's not because my innocence was suddenly eviscerated; it's because I didn't realize how right it would feel having Kallum Anderson inside me until he no longer is.

Maybe I should feel bad about that, knowing what I do—that this is a one-time thing, and soon I'll be walking down the aisle with another man at my side.

But I don't.

Not even a little bit.

And that realization is as terrifying as it is freeing.

Kal's sharp brows knit together as he fists his dick, and I glance down for the first time, getting a good look at it; veins bulge against the thick shaft, tracking up to the bulbous head, and a shudder works its way over me.

He strokes, rubbing life into his partially flaccid length, and raises his chin to meet my gaze.

"You've made quite the fucking mess," he says, and a chill races down my spine as I note the blood-and-cum mixture splashed across his skin. "Now, get on your knees and clean me up."

CHAPTER 10

KAL

ELENA RICCI ON HER KNEES IS A SIGHT TO BEHOLD.

A work of art that should be auctioned off to the gods, as they're the only entities worthy of her fierce beauty.

As she situates herself on the tile floor, she reaches for the straps of her dress, pushing them off her shoulders. Since I tore it down the middle, the fabric parts with little effort, slipping away and pooling around her.

The breath evaporates from my lungs as her tight, perfect body comes into full view; watching her on security cameras these last few months is nothing compared to the masterpiece that is the real thing. She's smooth and soft, everything a woman should be.

A balm for my sharp, harsh edges.

Practically a goddess in her own right.

Gritting my teeth against the thought, I suck in a heap of air and try not to focus too much on how goddamn right all of this feels.

How I came to ruin her, but the destruction here tonight has only been my own.

Her breasts rise and fall with each second of immobility that passes between us, and when she shifts, I get a glimpse of the pomegranate tattooed beneath one. Its red ink is a stain I might mind under normal circumstances, but I know the reason she got it.

That she marked herself for *me*.

If she's wondering why I don't join her in her nakedness, she at least knows better than to question it. Lithe hands slide up over my slacks, pausing where they're caught above my knees, and then she scoots closer, eyeing my cock with an awestruck expression.

One part reverence, one part curiosity, and the rest an all-consuming hunger.

"Are you sure this is safe?" she asks quietly, no doubt apprehensive about the virginity smeared along my length.

My brow arches. "Are you questioning my medical expertise?"

"More like your sanity."

She has a point there. I'm questioning it myself.

"If you truly think I'd put you in that sort of danger, I'm not sure we should continue."

Her golden eyes flicker to mine. Panic swirls in them, and I don't like the way it makes my chest tighten. How her fear robs me of air.

"If you want to stop, we'll stop," I mutter, half hoping she does. The other half of me screams in protest, desperate to be inside of her again.

"I don't want to do that," she whispers, reaching up to wrap her hand around the base, giving a short pump as she tries to get her fingers to touch. They don't, and she swallows, sinking her teeth into her bottom lip.

Smirking, I nod my chin. "Clean me up then, *slut*."[109]

Stroking slowly, she watches me carefully, seeming to gauge my reaction so she can adjust accordingly. Her inexperience sends a spiral of dirty pleasure through me; the twenty-year-old Mafia princess may

---

109 We (and by we, I mean me) LOVE a filthy first time.

have talked a good game before, but the innocent aura wafting around her now tells the truth.

I don't know if she's refrained from others because she always wanted me to be her first, but I'm sure as fuck not going to question it now.

Nothing else before this moment matters.

Discomfort wedges behind my ribs at the thought, warring inexplicably with the warmth she provides. As if on a reflex, my teeth grind together, and impatience courses through my veins.

My hand moves, tangling in the roots of her dark hair. "Your mouth," I rasp, unable to keep the desire from my voice even as it hardens. "I said *clean* me, not spread it around. Put my filthy cock in your mouth, and suck it into your pretty little throat until you can't breathe."

"I'm not—"

Without waiting for her to finish that sentence, I shove her hand away and fit my crown against her. I don't force my way in, letting her know silently that there is still a choice here.

We stare at each other.

My heart skips a beat.

Her eyelids flutter.

Then slowly, so fucking slowly, she parts her lips. Flicks her tongue against my slit. A deep blush darkens her cheeks as she tastes me for the first time, and then she pitches forward, impaling her skull on my dick.

She maintains eye contact as she drags herself off, just enough to drizzle saliva over my tip. Then she moves back in, bobbing slowly.

A hiss escapes me as she massages the flat of her tongue against the vein on the underside of my shaft. Exploring, tasting. Attempting to please me.

My grip on her hair intensifies as my hips jerk into the movement, pushing as deep into her mouth as possible.

Retching around me, Elena tries to wiggle free, scraping her nails over my thighs as I start to cut off her oxygen supply.

"*Fuck*. Such a perfect little slut, choking me down like this. I should flood your stomach with my cum, make sure you're not able to eat for days because of how full I'll leave you."

She hums, and I groan, pinching my eyes closed as her throat struggles around me. Flashes of euphoria color my vision, and I snap back to attention just as release threatens in the base of my spine.

When I look down at her again, I see her hand drifting between her thighs, toying absently as she chases her own orgasm. I swell slightly, the sight of her getting off on my depravity so fucking alluring that I almost can't find it in me to resist.

But I have to. At least for right now.

Our night is far from over.

A mixture of sticky fluid connects her mouth to my dick as she sits back, gasping for breath. Sweat glistens across her forehead, and I swipe the string from her, severing us as I yank her to her feet.

"Have you ever done that before?"

She shakes her head, and I can't stop the grin that stretches my face.

"A night of many firsts then."

Before she says anything else, I haul her into my arms and move to the shower. I don't step in, unable to move much more before I absolutely have to be inside her again, and when I have her against the glass stall door, my movements are slow and calculated.

I take my time learning the tempo her body craves, relishing when she clenches around me and moans my name as she buries her face in my neck.

When she comes again, I damn near pass out from the sensation, and I can tell she thinks we're done now as she sags against me.

I pull out and set her on her feet. She frowns, pressing her palms into the glass as she gathers her bearings. "You didn't…"

"Don't fucking worry, little one. I'm *going* to. When you get to that bedroom, I'm gonna push you down on that plush mattress and fuck you so hard you forget your own name. Then I'm gonna come while I'm deep inside you, paint you like my own little porcelain doll." I grip her chin, leaning down to lick her bottom lip, reveling in the taste of us on her. "I like waiting. Making you work for it. When I come for you—*in* you—it'll be because you earned it."

She shudders and skitters from the bathroom without another thought.

I suck in a deep breath, willing my cock to get ahold of itself, before I follow her. The Boston skyline peeks through the curtains on her balcony door, and the glow of a bedside lamp and the faux white Douglas fir Christmas tree in the corner are the only light we're provided right now.

There's something poetic about it as she stretches out on the mattress, parts her thighs for me, a gift all its own, as if aware that all *I* wanted this year was her.

The Ricci family Christmas party rages on downstairs, and I can't help wondering why no one has come after their precious heir.

Why no one has thought to check on their princess, to save her from the evil she's so hot for.

A little thrill races through me as I think about Mateo waltzing in when I'm buried balls-deep in her. How red his face would get hearing her call my name, coming on my tongue, moaning for me the way she never will for him.

God, I'm sick.

Fucked in the head.

Even that isn't enough to keep me away.

If I'm honest with myself, I don't want to keep away. Never really did. In a perfect world, she'd be marrying *me*.

"Flip over and look at the wall. Don't move," I tell her as I walk to the tree, considering for a split second that maybe this isn't the best idea.

I could tuck tail and run before I've done any real damage. Sure, she's less pure now than she was an hour ago, but purity is merely a social construct anyway.

Taking Elena Ricci's virginity isn't quite enough to blacken her soul. To shred hers to pieces the way mine was years ago.

It doesn't eliminate the inherent goodness inside her.

Doesn't really make her mine.

Yet my feet are rooted in place as I stare at the LED lights twinkling in the plastic branches. My stomach cramps at the idea of leaving her half-satisfied and me without having taken full advantage of the guise of privacy here in her bedroom.

Once I leave here, the illusion stops. The notion that she belongs to me, that she's the Persephone to the portrait of Hades that everyone depicts me as…all of that's over.

And I'm not ready or willing to give it up.

Not yet.

So instead, my hand whips out, yanking the strand of lights from the tree; it topples over as they unravel, crashing to the floor. I don't bother fixing it as I pull the plug from the wall and turn back toward the bed.

My dick leaks as I take in the sight of her rounded backside, the puffy, abused flesh winking from between her legs. My palm itches to turn more of her creamy skin crimson, for the color to expand beyond where it's smeared across her pussy and inner thighs, but I want her to beg for it first.

"Kallum," she whimpers, and I can see her arousal dripping from her.

"You may be the birthday girl," I start, inching toward her with the lights wrapped around my fist. "But I refuse to rush the celebration, little one. You asked me to do this, remember?"

Ever the obedient little slut, she keeps her gaze trained on the white upholstered headboard. Her body stays in place, even as her fingers clutch at the goose feather comforter, as if bracing herself for me.

She huffs, shivering slightly when I drag the tip of a bulb across the arch of her foot.

I ignore her, reaching for her ankle. Looping one end of the lights around my index finger, I pull the strand over so it constricts around the digit, knotting gently.

If I tug on the length anymore, it'll tighten, refusing to release me, so I'm careful as I remove it and lift her foot, slipping the loop around her.

Fastening another knot on the adjacent wooden bedpost, I move to the other side of the footboard, dragging the lights along with me.

With just the one string to work with, securing her to the bed is a bit awkward at first; she shifts as I work the second loop around her other ankle, spreading her legs to accommodate the strain of the binding.

"What are you doing?" Her voice is a whisper, and she starts moving her head, trying to get a look at what I've done to her.

"Being festive."[110] For the first time I can remember, the sight of Christmas lights doesn't fully irritate me. Even though they're not lit up, I can't deny how good it looks having her bound and at my mercy.

I can smell her—smell us—as I kneel on the edge of the bed, brushing her hair off one shoulder.

"What do you think Mateo would say if he could see you now?"

She glances at me from the corner of her eye, shaking her head. "He wouldn't care."

---

110   Kal's jokes are seriously underrated.

"No?"

Nibbling on her bottom lip, she shifts, adjusting her grip on the bed. "He'd just expect a turn after, I'm sure."

Fury rages inside my chest, hot and blistering as it tries to seize control of my brain. The primal, animalistic part of me wants to march downstairs and find the limp-dicked fucker in the crowd, drag him by his balls upstairs, and force his eyes open with hooks so he'd have to watch me make a mess of his fiancée.

That part of me thirsts for his blood—and not in the way I crave Elena's.

My gaze falls to the slightly purpled skin on her cheek, hidden beneath concealer. The bruising on her shoulder, older than the mark I left moments ago.

The yellowed patch below her ribs that I'm just noticing—too large to be the result of a hand or even a fist.

Blood boiling, I push to a standing position and glance at the door. All logical thought flees as I think of him putting his hands on her—*hurting* her, and not in the name of making her feel good.

Mateo de Luca wouldn't know what makes Elena Ricci feel good if it reached out and stabbed him in the fucking heart.

She may be his in name, on paper, but he hasn't spent the last two years infatuated by her every waking move. Hasn't spent that time exchanging poetry with her, erasing the bad memories associated with the act with her light and innocence.

He doesn't know her. Doesn't know she belongs to me, if only by extension of a centuries-old myth and my own delusion.

Her soul calls to mine, and her pleasure is mine to create.

"Don't," she mutters, as if sensing the direction my mind has veered. "He's not worth it."

"He may not be." I pause, my heart kicking against my chest. "But you are, little one."

Still, as I start toward the door downstairs, a furious pounding comes from the other side.

We freeze, eyes darting to each other and locking in place.

Like maybe if they don't hear us inside, they'll go away.

"Open the fuck up, *carina*." Mateo's voice drifts through the wood, punctuated by what I imagine to be the side of his fist. Even with the barrier between us and the calculated wording, I can tell he's wasted. "Ariana said you were hiding out in your room. You're always hiding out, like you don't want to be seen with me. What's the fucking problem? Come celebrate your birthday with your man."

Gritting my teeth, I turn back toward Elena.

She drops to her elbows, defeat pouring through her limbs. "Untie me."

My eyebrows shoot up. "No."

Her head whips around, eyes narrowing. "I wasn't asking."

"And I wasn't done with you." Maneuvering beneath the lights between the two bedposts, I situate myself between her spread thighs, reaching up to grip her ass in my palms. "You wanted poetry, yes? Can you think of anything more profound than my tongue on this sweet little pussy while the man you've been promised to listens outside?"

"But I'm…I need to clean myself before you do that."

"You will do no such thing."

"*Kallum.*" The way she exhales my name feels like a prayer. An admission. And I realize how badly I want to hear it over and over, as if her voice has the power to save my wretched soul.

Even as I bend, touching my lips to the crescent shape of her stained flesh, I know that isn't possible.

I'm not damned to suffer in hell.

I'm the ruler of it. The king of its fiery, sinful domain.

Elena Ricci, my little Persephone, is simply collateral.

Nonetheless, for tonight, I'm willing to pretend otherwise.

A tiny moan vibrates up her spine as I dive in, giving several long, languid strokes along her seam. The bitter tang of copper explodes in my mouth, soaking into my taste buds as I erase her innocence for good.

From this angle, she's completely bared to me, and there's an edge of wickedness at the vulnerability in her position.

Dipping down, I use one hand to anchor her hips, bringing the pads of my fingers up to her clit just as my tongue makes contact. She bucks, grinding into the movement as I suckle at the bundle of nerves, my dick kicking behind my slacks at the feel of her pulse.

My face is buried in her from this position, and it's absolute heaven.

Her thighs flex, trying to close as an orgasm tears through her, but I shove my shoulders between them to keep her open.

Another knock on the door temporarily draws me from my ministrations, although it seems to have the opposite effect on Elena; she mewls, arching her back as Mateo calls out her name.

"That's right, little one," I coax, pushing two fingers inside as I lap at her slit, massaging her inner walls with renewed fervor. "Let him hear you come for me."

As if waiting for my command, she convulses, crying out wordlessly. My tongue spears into her, slurping her juices as she trembles violently. Her clit throbs so hard that I'm damn near close to blowing in my pants, and I pinch it to prolong her release.

Dropping to her elbows and pressing her forehead into the mattress, she juts her ass higher into the air, wiggling as if trying to escape me.

After gulping several deep breaths, her ironclad grip on the comforter loosens. "Holy shit."

Mateo's knocking begins again, this time harder and more persistent. "What the hell are you doing in there, Elena?" he calls, and I'm reminded once again that she's technically supposed to be his.

That after tonight, I'll leave town and she'll marry him. Fulfill her duty to her father and family and be the good little wife she's been brought up to be.

And it's fine. I knew going in what this was, that it could only ever be one night.

But still, the idea of him having her in any capacity makes me ill, and I reach into my pocket for the utility knife I carry there. Desperate to claim her before he can permanently.

I push up on my knees and heave a breath. "Do you trust me?"

Her head turns, hair falling back over her shoulder. Silence passes between us, leaden in the air, and she purses her lips. "Unfortunately."

Swallowing, I flip open the blade and drag the dull side over the curve of her ass, wishing I could bottle the way her breath hitches and wear it on my skin forever.

"*Elena!* Open the goddamn door!"

She doesn't make a sound when my hand dips, pressing the tip of the knife into the soft, inflamed skin of her inner thigh.

There's no coming back from this, my mind screams, begging me not to claim her this way. So fucking decidedly, when I know I shouldn't have her at all.

Can't have her.

Elena Ricci isn't supposed to be mine—but she *is*.

Her lack of protest spurs me on, and I press inward, salivating when her flesh gives and breaks open for me.

"Oh fuck," she hisses, curling her toes and straining against her bindings. "What are you *doing?*"

"*Owning* you." A few quick flicks of my wrist and the blade slices nicely, neatly, through her. Blood trickles from the wound, something just deep enough to scar, and a disturbing sense of exhilaration washes through me.

I reach down, untying her ankles as Mateo seems to thrash against the door now, and flip her onto her back.

She's completely flushed, staring up at me with rounded eyes, and I wait a beat for her to pull away. To stop giving me everything I want, the worst things I crave, as if she gets off on pleasing me.

That notion is fucking dangerous.

When she spreads her legs wider, glancing down at the *K* I've etched into her, she smiles.

It's delirious, something she'll regret tomorrow I'm sure, but I'll take it.

Bending down, I swipe two fingers over the wound, coating my fingerprints before laving my tongue over the sight. The fingers come down on her clit, smearing the blood there with a few circular motions, and my mouth follows the path, trailing up to her throat.

When I settle over her, she hooks her calves over my hips, and I work my dick free from my pants. Bloody kisses pepper her skin— around her navel, around both nipples, dotting her collarbone. She's a fucking work of art, and I'm a greedy collector who doesn't ever want this night to end.

"I didn't know you were a vampire," she whispers, the pounding on the door having ceased for now. Reaching between us, she takes my cock in her hand, shifting her hips so she can drag the crown through her cut.

Fisting the bedspread on either side of her head, I try to stave off the release teasing my spine. "I'm so much worse, little one. You should think about that the next time you make a deal with the man they call Death."

Positioning me at her entrance, she gives me a tiny shake of her head. "You're not as bad as you want everyone to think."

You don't even know the half of it.

"Maybe you're not as good as they say," I challenge, pushing her hand away and shoving myself inside her tight, wet heat. Bottoming out, I take a deep breath, willing control into my veins even as she spasms around me. "Maybe we were made for each other."

Her eyes glisten as I rock my hips, beginning a slow fuck that has both of us grunting and groaning, as if we have all the time in the world.

"But you can't keep me," she says, hands coming up to clutch at my biceps through my jacket.

"Doesn't matter," I tell her, my thrusts growing brutal, my pelvis crashing into hers as I chase our collective release. "You're mine, my little Persephone. If not in this life, then at least right here and right now."

"I'm not—"

"Don't you dare deny me, you little slut."

My hand snakes up, groping her breast and wrapping around her throat. I squeeze lightly, nostrils flaring as her gaze sparkles, and the sounds of our skin slapping together reach an obscene volume.

Sweat drips from my forehead onto her chest, slipping down to mix with the blood there, and I feel myself unraveling.

White-hot ecstasy pools in my gut, and I redouble my efforts, pressing my cock against that spot that steals the words from her lips.

"Come with me," I command, fucking her so hard that the mattress squeals in protest. My fingers tighten, but somehow it feels as though I'm the one being strangled. "Soak my cock so I can dump my fucking cum in your sweet pussy."

And Jesus *Christ*, she does. She clamps down around me, and it feels like she's trying to sever my dick from my body. I see stars as my orgasm barrels through me, shooting up my spine as she digs her nails into my arms.

We're a panting, disgusting mess of sweaty limbs when we've come down, and I collapse on top of her for a moment.

My brain seems to short-circuit, and it isn't until I feel myself leak out of her that I roll away, withdrawing.

We don't speak. We just stare at the ceiling in silence as the Christmas music from downstairs drifts beneath her locked door.

Mateo must have given up.

After a few moments, I rake a hand through my hair and get to my feet, walking to the bathroom to clean myself up.

When I return, she's fast asleep, her hair fanning out in a halo shape, her abused body on display for me to catalog and memorize.

I perch on the edge of the bed, dragging a warm washcloth between her thighs and then up over her stomach, erasing the evidence of our night together.

Applying a bit of salve to the letter on her thigh, I smooth a small bandage over the cut and reach for the notebook on her nightstand.

I don't know what the fuck I'm doing when I jot down the poem. Don't know why I feel like I owe her more than I promised, yet even when the ink hits the page, it still doesn't feel like enough.

Something niggles in the back of my mind as I slip from the room and out a back entrance of the Ricci home, escaping detection as people gather in the courtyard for a toast.

And as I stand out on the curb, blinking up at the balcony where Elena rests inside, a sick feeling takes root in my gut, and then I know.

This won't be the last I see of my little Persephone.

I'll be back for her.

CHAPTER 11

ELENA

HE CALLS MY NAME FROM THE OPPOSITE END OF THE FIELD, HIS warm voice carrying through the February air, caressing my skin like the lightest of kisses.

Since that fateful night all those weeks ago, something's changed in him.

Softened him toward me, made him a different person when it comes to my safety and well-being. He speaks to me as if I'm fragile and at risk of shattering at any given moment, always tiptoeing around and holding his tongue.

It's given rage a home in my bones. Makes me want to lash out and hurt him for changing. For amplifying my guilt and shame.

No one knows what happened on Christmas. They don't know that I was given the greatest gift on my twentieth birthday—a choice. Or at least the illusion of one.

For once in my life, my father's rigid rules and the burden of being a Mafia *princess* had no hold on my being.

I was free, for that one night. And when Kal Anderson buried himself inside my pussy and soul, I knew there was nothing more I ever could have asked for.

Nothing as perfect as how it felt for our bodies to mold to each other, how it felt for him to just *take* the only thing that's ever really belonged to me.

It was everything I imagined it would be. More, even, because there's no way to adequately gauge the raw beast that Kal becomes when he lets himself indulge.

When sin takes precedence, and the innate wrongness of a situation ceases to matter to him.

I've been unable to think about anything else since.

It wasn't just poetry that night; it was goddamn magic.

But he was gone when the sun came up, leaving me a hollow husk of a brand-new woman, a black rose, and a scrap of paper that read:

> *Touch has a memory.*
> *O say, love, say,*
> *What can I do to kill it and be free?* [111]
> —*John Keats*

And I hated him for leaving me with nothing but the words of another.

I hate him still, as I sit in this field of dead grass and flowers readying for the spring bloom, wondering how it is they find it in themselves to grow in spite of opposition. How they can continue on, even after they've died for the season.

What makes them want to press forward?

What's so great about the earth that they return?

Smoothing my fingers over the piece of paper, I tuck it safely in the pocket of my jeans as his footsteps approach, his now-familiar scent of cocoa and cedar catching on the breeze.

---

111 Keats was the first poet I ever fell in love with and, because of that, felt very fitting here.

The newly formed scar above his right eyebrow shimmers in the moonlight; I don't know where he got it, but the gash appeared at Christmas and is only just now healing. Whatever the case, he's unwilling to discuss it with me.

Which is just fine, all things considered. I don't want to talk about the scars on my neck or the one on the inside of my thigh that looks like a *K* if you angle your head *just* right.

I don't know what I'll do when he sees it.

"Everything okay?" Mateo asks, stuffing his hands in his pants pockets.

I nod. "Yeah, I've just been writing."

I'm always writing. Since Kal left, the words just bleed from me.

Mateo rocks on his feet, bobbing his head. "Right. Find any inspiration tonight?"

Sighing, I close my notebook and shrug. "No, I'm still stuck. Something just isn't clicking."

"Well," he says, "don't stay out here too long. Your dinner will get cold."

As he walks away, I let out a soft sigh of relief. Who'd have thought the unpredictable heir to Bollente Media could be such a concerned fiancé when he's not beating me.

Getting to my feet, I dust off the front of my dress, ignoring the pang that tears through my stomach at the movement. It always flares when I sit there for too long.

Taking a deep breath, I close my eyes and pull the black rose from my pocket, sending my greatest wish to the universe on a silent prayer.

I don't hear anyone else approach. Don't feel the cloth wrap around my mouth and nose until it's too late, and everything fades to black.

And then, like every other time before, I wake up.

ACKNOWLEDGMENTS

I was beginning to think I'd never be able to write these words. Five months of struggling against massive imposter syndrome and procrastination, and I *finally* finished. I want to say I've learned my lesson, but let's be honest: this is just who I am. I like the rush.

That being said, the first mention here goes to my best friend, Emily McIntire. The person who reads everything I write (even when it's rewritten and scrapped ten times), who reminds me that I belong here, who deals with all my nervous energy, and who inspires me every day. I genuinely don't even know what I'd do without you. Thank you for existing.

To my betas Ariel, Michelle, and Zoe: Thank you for your willingness to work with my crazy-ass schedule and for helping me fine-tune each book. You are the absolute best.

To my editors and proofreaders: I'm so grateful for how pretty and polished you make my books.

To the team at Sourcebooks Casablanca: Thank you for your championship and belief in this book. You've made my dreams come true.

To my cover designer, Cat, with TRC Designs: For bringing my vision to life and making this cover more beautiful than I ever could have imagined.

To my ARC team: You all are an invaluable part of this entire process. Thank you for loving my work enough to want to keep reading and share your love with the world.

To my family: Thank you for always supporting my dreams, even when you don't necessarily like the content.

To Lord Byron, Poe, and Arrow: You can't read, but thanks for the companionship on the late nights and stressful days.

And last but not least, thank *you*. The reader, whom there is no point in any of this without.

ABOUT THE AUTHOR

Sav R. Miller is a *USA Today* bestselling author of adult romance with varying levels of darkness and steam.

In 2018, Sav put her lifelong love of reading and writing to use and graduated with a BA in creative writing and a minor in cultural anthropology. Nowadays, she spends her time giving morally gray characters their happily ever afters.

Currently, Sav lives in Kentucky with her dogs Lord Byron, Poe, and Arrow. She loves sitcoms, silence, and sardonic humor.

Website: savrmiller.com
Facebook: srmauthor

VIPERS AND VIRTUOSOS

He'll go to hell and back for her.

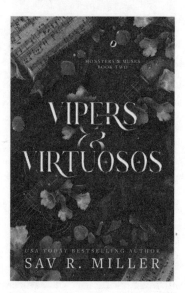

Riley Kelly didn't come to New York City with the hope of changing her life. After a vicious assault left her scarred and deeply traumatized, all she really craves is normalcy. Enter rock star Aiden James, the complete opposite of normal. When he's not playing sold-out arenas, he's working on the next hit album and dodging the paparazzi. His happiness, however, has always taken a back seat. The one shred of secrecy left in his life is his dark, tragic past, and his infamous family prefers to keep it that way.

Only, when Riley catches his eye at a fundraiser in the city, he can't stop himself as obsession takes root. Her blue eyes and peppermint scent are all he can think about, even after their one encounter takes an unfortunate turn. Suddenly, his dream girl is a malicious ghost.

Now, Aiden's on a mission to track her down and make her pay for ruining his career. Even if it means abandoning his life to make hers completely miserable. Even if it means breaking every rule to make her his…

From *USA Today* bestselling author Sav R. Miller comes a dark rock-star romance inspired by the myth of Orpheus and Eurydice.

For more info about Sourcebooks's books and authors, visit:
sourcebooks.com

OATHS AND OMISSIONS

Some women are worth waging wars over.

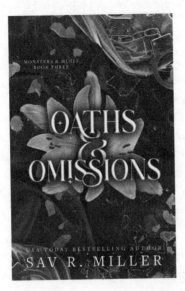

Lenny Primrose has lived her entire life as her rich father's puppet. Now, at twenty-three, she's no longer interested in playing his games. Unfortunately, the only way to avoid being married off to one of her father's business partners is to involve the man he fears most: the British assassin who almost killed him.

Jonas Wolfe would be content to never be in the same room as a Primrose ever again. His days are filled with contracted murder and running his pub—anything to keep from sitting around thinking about his one failed mission. But when Lenny commits a rash crime, Jonas steps in to help, and extracting himself from her family becomes impossible. Especially when she bats her pretty green eyes, proposing a fake relationship that she vows will benefit them both.

Interested in improving his public image, Jonas agrees, and it isn't long before lingering looks become scorching hot kisses. But even as the two grow closer and bond over their common enemy and undeniable chemistry, Lenny still remains distant and closed-off. Turns out she's keeping a horrible secret... one that threatens to tear everything they've built together apart.

From *USA Today* bestselling author Sav R. Miller comes a dark fake-dating romance inspired by the Helen of Troy and Trojan War myths.

THE BLACK ROSE AUCTION

Welcome to the Black Rose Auction,
where every sin can be yours for a price.

Volume One

In **WICKED PURSUIT by Katee Robert**, a Little Red Riding Hood remix, a mob princess with a taste for doing things she shouldn't acquires a stalker who will kill anyone who touches what's his...

In **DIVINE INTERVENTION by R.M. Virtues**, a Goldilocks remix, a witch must work with her ex's father (who she betrayed) and an angel to steal a magical chalice from the auction floor. But things get scorchingly complicated when all three agree that revenge is best served in the bedroom...

Volume Two

In **STOLEN VOWS by Sav R. Miller**, a Rapunzel remix, a virgin is forced to marry a mafia heir determined to kill anyone who touches her—only to flee from him the day after their wedding. But he's done waiting and has the perfect trap in mind to lure her back...

In **IRRESISTIBLE DEVIL by Jenny Nordbak**, a Rumpelstiltskin remix, a society darling is willing to make any bargain to benefit her family, but each deal draws her deeper into a dark and decadent world ruled by the dangerous man who's been pulling her strings from the start...

Volume Three

In **SHATTERED INNOCENCE by Sara Cate**, a Cinderella remix, a woman is being auctioned off to marry the highest bidder, even though the only person she wants is her stepsister. Desperate, the two hatch a plan to have an old flame bid on her behalf...only for him to decide he's playing for keeps and wants them both.

In **ROYAL HEART by Nana Malone**, a Beauty and the Beast remix, a woman must work with the thief she blames for her father's death to steal back a priceless royal necklace. But the dark depths of the auction is no place for unwary hearts, and soon she may be the one stolen after all...

For more info about Sourcebooks's books and authors, visit:
sourcebooks.com